THE
Wrong
GAME

KANDI STEINER

Published by Kandi Steiner
Edited by Elaine York/Allusion Graphics, LLC/ Publishing & Book Formatting, www.allusiongraphics.com
Cover Photography by Perrywinkle Photography
Cover Design by Kandi Steiner
Formatting by Elaine York/Allusion Graphics, LLC/ Publishing & Book Formatting, www.allusiongraphics.com

THE Wrong GAME

"BEFORE YOU CAN WIN, YOU HAVE
TO BELIEVE THAT YOU ARE WORTHY."

— *Mike Ditka, Chicago Bears Head Coach 1982-92*

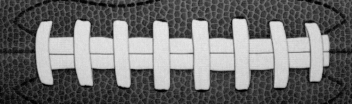

Prologue

GEMMA

This is not the conversation we were supposed to have. On the drive home, I saw every word that would form. I saw how they would be born, first in my mind and then in my mouth, each one standing strong and brave as it slipped from my lips and landed on his ears.

I knew what I'd say. I knew what he'd say. I had a *plan*.

My particular brand of anxiety was having an ungodly amount of stress over that which I could not control. It'd been this way since I was a young girl, and it'd only worsened with age. I made lists, and plans, and deadlines. I gave myself goals, and when I met them, I celebrated only long enough for me to decide what I would tackle next on the list.

It was all about being in control.

So, unlike a normal woman discovering her husband's infidelity, I did not cry or scream or throw objects across the room when I learned the truth. No, instead, when I found the first sign of his indiscretions, I made a check list. And I checked items off that list with a mixture of both dread and satisfaction.

Perfume that wasn't mine staining his shirt? Check.

Text messages from an unknown number, slipping through the cracks of my husband's technology-ignorant fingers onto our shared computer, but missing from his phone? Check.

Hotel rooms booked on a card I shouldn't have known about, one I only discovered by receiving the statement in our teal mailbox? Check.

We painted that mailbox together, by the way. It was one of the first things on the list I'd made when we bought our house. We'd both been covered in that teal paint — the color I loved so much in the store, but actually rather hated once it was splashed on our mailbox.

But it didn't matter the day we painted that mailbox.

On that day, my husband kissed my paint-splattered lips and told me I was the only woman he would ever love.

And I believed him.

My husband was the kind of man who looked at me so adoringly, who said the sweetest things, that I was *certain* I could have tossed him into a pit of gorgeous super models and he wouldn't have so much as even looked at them, let alone touch them. In fact, he'd be searching for me, calling out my name, seeking me out.

My entire relationship with him, I'd believed every word he'd said — perhaps blindly, it would seem. I believed him when he cried the day he asked me to marry him, and when he told me over breakfast one morning that no one in this world made me happier than him. There was never any reason to suspect him. There was never any reason to not feel safe.

And yet...

The last little box on the list I made when I first suspected my husband was cheating on me was visual proof. I had the clues, the emails and texts, and late nights with no alibi. But it wasn't until I followed him, until I saw with my own eyes that his hands could hold another woman the way he held me, that his mouth could kiss hers, that his smile could beam for someone other than me.

And when that box was checked, I still didn't cry. Or scream. Or throw anything, though I did debate shoving my heel down on the gas pedal of my car and leaving it there as I drove toward where they stood, kissing and laughing, pulling luggage out of my husband's car.

No, instead of letting emotion rule me, I did what I do best. Just like with the rest of my life, I made a plan.

I focused on what I could control.

I could control me, what I would say, what I would do. I could control who I told, how our families would find out, how we would go about the divorce. I could control who got what, how assets were split, and where we each would stay as the signatures were scrawled against cold, lifeless pieces of paper that would end our young marriage.

I could control how I would tell him that I knew, and could temper my emotions as I told him.

Perhaps all of this was why, sitting across the table from my husband, my heart was beating rapidly, loud and thunderous in my ears as it threatened to bang right out of my ribcage. It could have been why my breath was shallow, my eyes dry from not blinking, my mouth clamped shut without a single word to offer, though I had so many planned in my head.

I had a plan. I knew how this conversation would go. I had everything in control.

I know about her. I know what you've done. I'm leaving. We're done.

But my uncanny sense of control and my ability to make a checklist didn't matter once I actually sat down at our kitchen table across from the man who'd lied to me for years.

Because he spoke first.

And everything changed.

"Gem," he rasped, his voice broken under the weight of his words. "Gemma, did you hear me?"

"I heard you," I managed.

My own voice mirrored his, broken and raspy, laced with dread. Of course, he assumed it was because of the blow he'd delivered. My sad-eyed, exhausted husband thought he'd broken my heart with his news. But the truth was my dread was born of a different source. It was simply me mourning the absolute conviction with which I'd believed in my plan and its certain success.

Now, I had no plan.

Now, my cheating husband and his secret lover were not the center of this conversation.

Now, my cheating husband had cancer.

The kind that couldn't be fought.

The kind that would end his life.

Soon.

It's okay, I tried to assure myself, pressing a hand to my chest so I could feel how fast my heart was beating beneath my ribcage. *Just make a new plan.*

But, as it went with my special brand of anxiety, my plans not working out the way I envisioned them often left me grappling. Suddenly, everything I thought I had on a leash was running wild, and no matter how I tried to talk myself down, I couldn't. Every time that happened — every time my plan went wrong — my emotions would win, all logic gone, all sense of what should be done lost like a whisper on a breeze.

"Please," he whispered, grabbing the legs of my chair and pulling me toward him. The wood made a terrible noise as it rubbed against our kitchen floor, sparking a wave of chills from my ankles to the top of my spine. "Don't cry, my sweet gem. It will be okay. We'll be okay."

He wrapped his arm around me, one hand cradling my head into his chest as the other caressed my back. Those hands had touched another woman, and they were now touching me, and I wanted to pull away just as much as I wanted to stay there forever.

He was going to leave me. He was going to leave this world.

My tears felt like they belonged to someone else as they soaked his sweater, and I tried to decipher where they came from. It didn't take long for me to realize they weren't born from one, singular source, but rather from all of them — like a waterfall made of glaciers melting all at once in the first warm wave of spring.

My husband was cheating on me.

He loved another woman — one who did not bear my name.

I would be alone, because I would lose him.

Only now, it wouldn't be because of his infidelity. The choice to be alone would not be made by me standing tall, demanding more, not accepting his affair.

Instead, he would fade from the Earth and I would remain, mourning him along with his other lover.

Maybe I cried because, though I had a plan, I secretly prayed he would thwart it. Perhaps I half-envisioned me leaving him, chin held high as I walked away, and half-envisioned him begging me to stay, promising to relinquish his love affair, for our marriage meant more to him than she ever could.

Regardless, it didn't matter now.

Now, I had a cheating husband who would never learn my knowledge of his infidelity.

Because now, I would never tell him I knew.

What would be the objective? With a blow as hard as terminal cancer, was there really any point to leaving him now, to letting him fight the final weeks of his life alone? Was there any point to telling him I knew about the other woman he touched, other than satisfying *my* need to feel in control, to shove my proof in his face and say *Ha! I know what you did!*?

Death has a funny way of putting life into perspective for us. And what had once been so important to me — that need for vindication I held so tightly on my drive home — didn't seem to matter now. There was really only *one* thing that did.

I loved him.

That emotion was easy to pin down.

And because it was the only thing I could truly grasp, I held onto it tightly, knuckles white and aching. Carlo Mancini was my husband, and I, his wife. He was my everything — and that was still true, regardless of who else he'd shared a bed with.

So, I pulled back from his embrace, and kissed his lips — lips I always thought would be *only* mine to kiss — and I told him I loved him. I told him I was there. I held his hand and told him that, come what may, he had me by his side.

And by his side I stayed, until the very day he died.

Somewhere in that warped, whirling span of time, I think a part of me died, too.

I watched cancer wither my strong, commanding husband into nothing but skin and bones. I watched his eyes grow hollow, his lips ashen, his hands weaken where I held them in mine. Every day that I looked in the mirror, I watched my own eyes change, a hardness settling in.

I watched a twenty-nine-year-old girl become an old woman in just weeks — weeks that felt like years, but flew by like days.

And on the day of his funeral, I watched a girl younger and prettier than me mourn him from the back row of our church.

She cried the same tears that I did, though I swore her heart was in more pain than mine. Because she had the satisfaction of being the other woman, of being the one he couldn't live without — so much so that he was willing to risk his marriage, his reputation, his life that he had built. She knew without a doubt that she had been his world, that she had been the last face in his mind before the light was extinguished and he faded off into nothing.

I didn't have that same comfort.

I had casseroles from neighbors and life insurance policies from lawyers and a house full of things that smelled like him. I had a down payment on a condo downtown that I'd secured, thinking I would be walking away from him, away from his infidelity. I had an empty hole in my chest where a young heart used to beat, where love used to grow like flowers, now turned to weeds.

I had a secret to keep, one that would eat me alive every second it dwelled in the dark, unspoken depths of my mind.

And I had a plan.

To preserve control over my future, over my heart, my soul, my well-being, over the life I would lead *after* my husband — I had to eliminate the factors that were uncontrollable. It was just that simple.

And right there, in that first-row pew, with my dead, cheating husband's mother's hand in mine, I made one simple plan, with one simple rule.

Never fall in love again.

It was more than just a plan, more than just a goal. It was a promise.

And it was one I vowed to keep.

Chapter 1

GEMMA

eight months later

"**N**o."

I only had one word for my best friend-slash-boss as we flowed with the crowd spilling out of Soldier Field, the warm, early-September air sweeping over us. Despite the fact that Belle and I had sweat through most of the Chicago Bears preseason game until the sun finally went down, I still smiled, reveling in the last few weeks of summer.

Soon, the heat would fade, and the Illinois winter would hit with all the subtlety of a Mack truck.

I was in no rush to be greeted with the kind of cold that hurts your face. Still, while I would miss summer, it was fall that was my favorite season. It had always held a special place in my heart for many reasons — my birthday, Halloween, pumpkin-spiced everything, and, most of all, football.

"Shut up. You don't get to say no to me," Belle snapped. She swept her long, strawberry-blonde hair off her shoulder before looping her arm through mine. "In our friendship, I'm always right. And trust me when I say I'm right about this."

"I'm not ready to date, Belle. Drop it."

"I didn't say you had to *date*," she stated, matter-of-factly, as she held up one black-lacquered fingernail. "I said you need to get laid. And this, my friend, is literally every man's fantasy." She gestured to the stadium we had just walked out of. "Free tickets to a football game *and* a hot chick to bang at the end of the night — with no strings attached?" She shook her head. "Honestly, I wish I had thought of this first. It's genius."

"I didn't think of anything," I reminded her. "I bought season tickets for my husband to give to him on his thirty-fifth birthday."

"Your *cheating* husband," she reminded me, steering us left toward the street lined with sports bars. And though my face didn't show a single sign of weakness at those words, my stomach tightened into a knot.

Belle was literally the only person who would ever know that Carlo was unfaithful, other than the woman he cheated on me *with* — and not even she knew that I knew. I'd only told Belle after Carlo had passed away, mainly because I knew she'd speed up the process of his death before the good Lord could take him if she found out about his infidelity.

Belle was the kind of best friend who loved fiercely. She was honest with me always — bluntly so — and she never let me get too comfortable in my little land of control. Just when she saw me slipping into any kind of complacency, she would challenge me.

I hated her as much as I loved her for that.

Still, while I knew I'd need *someone* to talk to about Carlo's infidelity, someone who knew the whole story, sometimes I regretted telling her. Where I was all about suppressing, boxing difficult emotions away and focusing on tasks I could complete, Belle was a processor.

She was not the kind of girl to let something go.

Especially *this* kind of something.

"And I say this with the utmost respect for you and him and all of God's creatures," she continued, drawing a cross over her shoulders with her free hand. "But he's not here anymore, Gemma. May he rest in peace." She paused. "And also, be castrated in the name of Jesus, amen."

"Belle."

"I'm kidding." She paused again. "Sort of."

I was ashamed of the small smile climbing on my lips in that moment. If he was still here, if my original plan had actually come to fruition, these types of jokes would be fine to make. After all, what woman didn't support her best friend after she was cheated on? Comments of castration and ill-bidding were welcome, and most certainly expected.

But when he was no longer breathing, when cancer had taken *his* life before I could take *my* life back from him, it wasn't the same. It was cruel, and heartless, and it produced a type of guilt that sat low and unsettling in your stomach.

This was my entire existence, it seemed, for the past several months.

"While I appreciate the attempt to make me laugh, I'm not ready to make jokes about Carlo like that," I said softly. "I probably won't ever be."

"I'm sorry," Belle said on a sigh, squeezing my arm as we flowed with the crowd. "Really, I am. That was too far. You know me, I can't help but make jokes, even when it's wildly inappropriate. Remember when my cousin had a funeral for his cat?"

"And you made a cake that looked like a litter box with little pebbles of poop, and wrote *Sorry your cat hit the shitter, at least you don't have to change any more litter* on it with hot pink frosting?"

Belle pointed at me. "Exactly. I'm awful at death, it makes me feel itchy and so I resort to humor. Apparently, very poorly placed humor. But," she continued, taking that finger she had pointed at my face and re-directing it to point at my lady bits. "Let's bring this back to the real subject at hand, which is that *that region* is about as dry as the Sahara Desert."

I rolled my eyes, pulling my arm from where it was wrapped around hers to fish in my purse. I rummaged around for my lipstick as we made our way toward the South Loop bars.

Play the humor card, Gemma. You're good. Everything's okay.

"*This region* is just fine, thank you," I told her, gesturing to my crotch as I finally found my lipstick. I rolled the burgundy tube up, pointing it directly at my best friend. "It gets plenty of action."

Belle scoffed. "Oh, right. Forgive me for thinking a twenty-nine-year-old woman might want something more than a dildo with three vibration speeds."

"Four," I corrected, smoothing the deep burgundy cream over my top lip and blotting it together with the bottom. "And this twenty-nine year old woman is perfectly content."

Belle huffed, and for the rest of our walk to the strip of bars we frequented after games, she continued, on and on about the importance of my libido not going stale and my vagina getting action.

This was part of what infuriated me about Belle, and part of what I loved — she could argue a fish into buying an oxygen tank. In Belle's mind, she always knew what was right and what was wrong, and she had all the right words to convince you, too.

It was one of the things that made her a successful entrepreneur.

Belle started her own interior design firm as soon as she graduated college. In fact, she already had clients lined up, thanks to outshining the full-time employees at her internships. And, luckily for me, she needed an assistant — AKA someone to run her life. Where she was great with the people, with the design, *I* was great with the numbers, with the organization, and together? We made the best team in Chicago.

She never crossed over — she hung her boss hat up in the office and wore her best friend hat, instead. But, regardless of if we were on the clock or not, Belle was just a boss kind of lady.

And she was adamant about this particular job.

By the time we finally hit the strip of bars we were aiming for, I was in desperate need of a drink, and for my best friend to drop the subject.

But she wasn't done yet.

"Ugh, you haven't said anything in like ten minutes," she said, pulling me to a dead stop outside a bar packed with Chicagoans celebrating the Bears' win. It was the last preseason game, and the entire city was alive with the hope of a promising season — especially in the south side by the stadium. While most Bears fans went back to their tailgating spots or made the commute back into the heart of the city after the games, I was beginning to prefer the rowdiness of the sports bars in the South Loop.

Honestly, I preferred almost anything other than going back to my empty condo.

When Carlo was alive, we would usually watch the games at home with a group of our neighbors. I would cook, he would entertain, and it was everything I'd ever dreamed of having when I was a young girl.

When I bought him the season tickets, I envisioned more for us — tailgating, building a community in the seats around us, starting traditions...

Belle sighed, and I blinked away Carlo's memory.

"Look, I know I joke a lot," Belle said, taking my shoulders in her hands. She lowered her gaze to mine, ensuring I was listening before she continued. "But I'm serious when I say that I love you and I know you've been through a lot in the past eight months."

Her eyes softened, and I forced a swallow, warding off any emotions that might try to sneak in with her looking at me like that.

"I'm not saying you should date. Hell, if anyone is against love as much as you, it's me. Hello," she said, sweeping the back of her hand over her lean body. "Single for life and loving it, okay? But, just because I don't *date* doesn't mean I don't go out, have fun, *meet people*." She eyed me. "And get some."

I just stared at her, still not convinced.

"You have these tickets, right?" she continued. "And you *love* the Bears."

"*Da* Bears."

"I'm not saying it like that."

"Say it, or I'm not listening to the rest of this."

Belle rolled her eyes. "*Da* Bears."

I smiled. "Better."

"I hate you." She readjusted her grip on my shoulders. "*Anyway*, you're like an enigma to dudes. A girl who actually enjoys football? It's gold, Gemma. So, instead of forcing your fun-loving best friend who absolutely *loathes* sports of all kinds, to suffer through every home game with you, take a chance and meet some new people. Have fun with a few guys who have the same interest as you, and, who knows," she said, smirking. "Maybe a big wang to rock your world with at the end of every game. Now *that's* the definition of a win-win."

I couldn't help but smile at that. "I think you're the horniest woman to ever exist."

"Guilty as charged. Now," she said, holding out her hand. "Give me your phone, let me download this app, and just... trust me. For once. This doesn't go against any of your *plans*, right? There's no roses-and-chocolate dating, no Facebook-official relationship status updates, no love, no marriage or babies, or any of that."

Chewing the inside of my cheek, I debated her reasoning. In a way, she *did* have a fair point — I maybe did need a little affection. I was dead set on never trusting anyone again, never falling for those stupid puppy-dog eyes as they stared into mine and told me they loved me and only me. I was done with that.

But football, beer, and a little romp in the sack?

I wasn't *not* into that...

And, if I could be like anyone, it would be Belle. At thirty, she was happily single, successful in her career, and traveling like it was her only job. She'd never needed a man, never even given a guy more than a week to *try* to nail her down. She was my inspiration, my hope that there was a life to live after Carlo.

My heart sank when I thought of him again, because there was a time when all I wanted was everything that Belle just listed. The very things that now made me want to crawl into a ball and hide or start kicking the first man to approach me used to be the only things I desired. I wanted a husband, and a family, and a suburban life. I wanted a partner in life to grow old with, to laugh with, to lean on when life got hard.

Now, I only wanted to lean on myself, because I was the only one I could depend on to not let me fall.

So, instead of letting my emotions take over, I reverted to rule number one of my plan — the one I'd made on how to survive after he passed.

Don't mourn the man you thought you knew. Remember the man he really was.

"Fine," I conceded, shaking Carlo from my thoughts.

Belle did a little hop for joy, but I held up one finger to stop her celebration.

"But, it has to be in a way I can control. If I want to stop, if I never want to see the guy again or I feel icky at any point, I get to pull out. Deal?"

"Deal," she agreed, still doing grabby-hands for my phone. "And make sure he *pulls out*, too. AYOOO!"

I rolled my eyes.

Belle was still smiling at her brilliance, fingers wiggling and waiting for my phone. "It's perfect. Just only talk to them through the app, that way if you hate them after your date — er, after the *game*," she corrected. "You can just delete them. Then, they can't talk to you anymore. And, honestly, I think you should just take a new guy every time."

I handed her my phone, making my way inside the bar as she followed behind, still bouncing like a little girl who was just given twenty bucks to go wild in the toy store with.

"Oh, a new guy every game," I echoed. "Okay, now *that* I could get down with. Then it's more of like a... hangout. A game with a friend."

"A friend who could, potentially, rail you into next year with his hammer cock."

The bartender's brows shot up at Belle's comment as we slid into two blessedly empty stools at the corner end of the bar. I laughed, shaking my head to signal that he shouldn't even ask.

"Titos and water with lime," I told him. "Two, please." Then, I turned back to my best friend, who was feverishly typing away on my phone. "I'm serious, Belle. If at any point I decide I hate this, I get to pull the plug. And," I said, pointing at her. "If that happens, then you're suckered into going to every remaining game with me. And you can't complain. Even if it's below fifty outside."

"Yeah, fine, whatever," she said, waving me off quickly before clicking through my phone more.

The bartender slid our drinks in front of us, and I smiled his way, handing him my card. When he smiled back, I faltered, eyes lingering on him a little longer than they should have. He turned so quickly, I didn't have time to stare the way I wanted to, but that brief smile alone had me clenching my thighs together under the bar.

Belle grabbed her drink and immediately started sipping from the straw, fingers still flying over my phone, but I just stared at the man with my card in his hand as he crossed to the other side of the bar to help the next person. His shoulders were broad and rounded, his waist narrow, t-shirt sitting on the belt of his jeans in a way that made my next swallow harder to accomplish. And when my eyes fell to his ass, perfectly rounded in a pair of dark denim jeans that fell in just the right way off his hips, well...

Let's just say I wanted a better look at the front. And the side. And all angles.

Maybe I am ready to get laid.

"There!" Belle exclaimed proudly, holding my phone out a few inches as if to study her masterpiece. "Your bio is all set. I picked the best pictures, although we *do* need to get some updated ones where you're actually smiling," she said pointedly, her eyes flicking up to mine before landing on the phone again. "Wanna hear what I put?"

"Do I have a choice?"

Belle ignored me. "*Hot Italian chick who loves checking off to-do lists almost as much as watching football. Go Bears!*"

I laughed. "Oh, my God, Belle."

Again, she ignored me.

"*Season ticket holder looking for a cool, DTF guy to use my other ticket at a home game,*" she continued. "*If you love football, beer, and good conversation, I'm your girl. Send me a message, and maybe, if you're lucky, you'll be sitting next to me at kick-off.*"

"That's actually only fifty-percent cheesy and awful," I said, knowing there was little point in arguing any edits. I glanced at the photos she'd picked for me, staring at my phone over her shoulder. The default was a selfie I'd snapped just two weeks ago at the first home preseason game. I had my burnt-orange Bears jersey on, my long, dark brown hair pulled over one shoulder, and a sideways grin. My eyes looked even more intensely green than normal in the lighting I'd caught in my condo that afternoon, the sunlight streaming in through the floor-to-ceiling windows.

Reading over the bio she'd written for me again, I frowned. "What does *DTF* mean?"

Belle sucked a large drink through her straw. "Oh, it means... dark, tall, and fun. Kind of like tall, dark, and handsome. All the kids are saying it, kind of like how we used A/S/L back in the good ol' days of AOL messaging."

"Oh..." I thought over her words, wondering when I'd missed that little piece of lingo. I was approaching thirty, but it wasn't like I was ancient. I still kept up with social media, after all.

"Gotta pee!" Belle said quickly, hopping down off her barstool. She popped my phone into my hand. "Here, start swiping. Right means you think they're hot, left means they don't have a chance in hell."

I laughed. "This is absurd."

She just shrugged. "Welcome to dating in the twenty-first century. Be right back."

Once Belle was gone, I crinkled my nose at my phone, placing it on the bar with the app still up on the screen. I turned my attention to the television behind the bar, instead, watching the game that had just started in California. The San Francisco 49ers were up on the Denver Broncos by three, and I watched the next play, tossing my hands up with a dramatic groan when offsides was called on Denver's offense.

"Oh, come on, ref." I sighed, sipping my vodka. "Idiots."

"They've been calling shit this whole quarter," an older guy huffed at me from down the bar. "You a Broncos fan, too?"

"Bears girl," I answered, eyes still on the screen. "But that was just a terrible call, no matter which team you're rooting for."

"Let's hope our refs just let the boys play this year," the man's friend chimed in, and I noted he was wearing a Bears shirt.

"I'm more concerned about our O line. If we can't keep the quarterback safe, it won't matter what the refs call."

They both grumbled and raised their beers to me at that, and I cheersed their direction, taking another sip before my eyes flashed over my phone.

I sighed, finally picking it up.

For a solid minute, I just stared at the first face on my screen. It was a blond guy with glasses, his face a little round, eyes soft. The photo he'd chosen for his default was him sitting in a lawn chair at what appeared to be a barbecue, a dog in his lap, beer in one hand. He looked fun, like a friend I could watch football with.

But I didn't want to have sex with him.

I swiped left.

Once that first decision was made, I filtered through the next ones a bit quicker. In all honesty, it felt like a game — like some sort of soft-core porn site that no one had to know I enjoyed browsing. The more I swiped, the more I smiled.

Hot lawyer with a cat? Swipe right.

Boating captain with a gaggle of girls in every single photo of his? No, thanks. Swipe left.

Self-proclaimed "rich stud" with a photo of him holding a stack of cash? *Hard left.*

Cute freelance writer with a love for all things Chicago, including the Bears? Yes, please.

This is fun, I thought.

Until the first message popped up.

Hey there, Gemma. How 'bout them Bears?

I stared at the message, thumbs hovering over the keyboard on my phone.

What do I say back? Do I wait to respond? What if he thinks I'm stupid? What if he sees me in person and makes up some lame excuse to leave, and then I'm just sitting at the game alone?

Actually, that might not be so bad.

"Down To Fuck?"

I balked, blinking with my eyes still on the unanswered message on my phone before I peered up at the man the voice belonged to.

The bartender.

"*Excuse me?*" I asked, sure I didn't hear him correctly. But he made no move to correct himself. Instead, he just stood there, staring at me, a little smirk on his full lips as he glanced down at my phone and back up at me.

"Down. To. Fuck," he repeated. "That's what DTF means."

My mouth popped open, eyes skirting to where Belle had disappeared into the bathroom. "No... she wouldn't."

The bartender chuckled, fishing a beer out of the cooler behind him and sliding it over to a group of guys down to my left. "I mean, from the first words I heard her say when you two walked in here?" He smirked again. "I think she would."

My cheeks flushed with heat, fingers flying over my phone as I quickly exited the message and tried to find my profile. "Oh, my God. How do I edit this thing? How do I delete that? Ah!" I threw my phone on the bar when another message came in. "Jesus Christ."

The bartender laughed, picking up my phone from where I'd tossed it like a detonating bomb. He thumbed through a few screens, typed something, and handed it back to me.

"There. I edited it." He leaned over the bar. "But, from the sounds of it, you should have left it. I mean, you *are* looking for someone who's down to fuck, right?"

I closed the app, shoving my phone inside my purse with heat still creeping over my neck. "Nosy, much?"

"Hard not to overhear two gorgeous women talking about getting *railed into next year by a hammer cock.*"

I laughed at that, taking a sip of my vodka as my eyes met his. I finally got my wish, a chance to stare at him a little longer, and *boy*, was he fun to stare at.

His square jaw was lined with a faint shadow of stubble, his dark eyes hooded in a mixture of lust and playfulness. The way his jet-black hair sat in a styled wave reminded me of a Calvin Klein model, and I knew without a second thought that I wouldn't mind seeing his tan skin sporting nothing but a pair of white briefs on a giant billboard — *especially* after that brief glimpse I got of his ass.

Ha! Take that, Belle. My libido is far from broken.

He was the definition of what Belle had *said* DTF stood for — Dark, Tall, and Fun.

"So, which one are you taking first?" he asked, pushing back from where he'd leaned over the bar. He nodded to a woman at the opposite end, letting her know he saw her request for a refill. And as he made her margarita, I pulled my phone back from my purse, sighing.

"Truthfully? I have no idea. I have two messages already, but I have no idea what to say to them."

"Maybe you should start with *hi*."

"You know what I mean," I shot back, rolling my eyes. I opened up the app, staring at the first unanswered message again. "I haven't talked to another man like this since..." My voice faded, heart slinking into my stomach with a mixture of guilt and loss. "Well, in a very long time."

"You're nervous," he stated plainly, walking the new drink down to the woman at the end of the bar before returning to me. "Why don't you ease into it, have a practice run before the real thing?"

I cocked a brow. "And how would I do that?"

He shrugged, those wicked lips cranking into a smirk yet again. "Take me."

"You." I deadpanned.

He nodded. "Yeah. Take me to the first game. I mean, look," he gestured between us. "Obviously, we have chemistry. We could have a good time. I'll buy the pizza and beer."

"Sounds like you're just looking for a free ticket to the first home game," I said, leaning over the bar.

His eyes flashed down to my cleavage that I'd not-so-subtly pushed up with that movement, and when they flicked back to me, they were heated — darker, dusted with a lust-filled promise I somehow knew he could keep.

"Maybe." He shrugged again. "Or maybe I want to be the first one to have the privilege of fulfilling your friend's promise."

"Her promise?" I asked, just as Belle slid into the bar seat next to me.

"What did I miss?"

The bartender tore his gaze from mine, smiling at Belle, instead. And that's when I realized what her *promise* had been.

Getting me railed into next year.

I swallowed.

"Your friend here is nervous talking to guys she doesn't know on the app," the bartender said to Belle as I fought another blush. "So, she's taking me to the first game, as a sort of practice run."

"Oh!" Belle's eyes lit up as she assessed me first, and then dragged her eyes over the bartender. A tinge of possessiveness touched my chest when she clearly liked what she saw. She chewed her thumbnail, nodding. "Oh, yes. I like this idea."

"I didn't agree yet," I reminded him.

"Okay," he challenged. "Then go ahead and respond to..." he peered over my phone screen. "Brad, there."

He and Belle both watched me, Belle fighting a smile as one eyebrow rose on her perfectly symmetrical face. The bartender watched me with a satisfied smirk when my fingers didn't move for the keys, and my jaw popped open, a laugh slipping through.

"Wow. You two just met and you're already ganging up on me."

"I like him," Belle said easily. "And I like this plan."

"You don't even know him. Actually," I said. "*I* don't even know his name yet."

"Zach Bowen," he said, extending his hand for mine. "Pleasure to meet you."

I let him take my hand in his, trying to ignore the warm, buzzing energy that transferred when our skin touched.

"She's Gemma," Belle answered for me, since apparently my sticky tongue was glued to the roof of my mouth. "Gemma Mancini."

"So, Gemma Mancini," he said, his hand still wrapped around mine, eyes hooded and sure. "What do you say? Let me be your practice round."

"*Say yes, stupid,*" Belle whispered.

I nudged her with my elbow.

Zach held my gaze confidently, his dark eyes watching me like I really had no other choice. And in that moment, I couldn't think of a reason not to say yes. He seemed fun. He was hot.

And it would save me from this stupid app for at least one more week.

"Fine," I conceded, and Zach's smirk turned into a full-blown smile, one that had a slight dimple popping under that delicious stubble.

He reached for my phone, the screen still on the unanswered message from Brad. He clicked out of it, typing his phone number into a new text message, instead, and sending himself an emoji.

"There. My number. And I have yours. See you for the game next weekend?"

"Looks like it."

His eyes roamed over me once more, the corner of his mouth pulling up just slightly. "Can't wait."

Belle nudged me under the bar with her knee, her eyes wide in an *oh my God* fashion.

"For now, I should get back to work. I'll check on you ladies in a bit."

"Thank you, Zach," Belle said, waving her fingers daintily as he made his way over to the other side of the bar.

She didn't stop staring once he was gone, though.

"Damn," she breathed, resting her chin on the hand she'd just used to wave him farewell. "Now I *really* hope you get railed into next year."

I laughed, trying not to panic at the thought of another man touching me.

A man who wasn't Carlo.

Shaking my head, I pulled the app back up on my phone, showing Belle the messages that had come through and letting her swipe through the pictures of guys for a while. As we talked, I reminded myself of the one thing I always needed to hear.

I am in control.

It's just a football game. It's just a night of sports and beer and hot dogs. If I want to have sex with him, I can. If I don't, I can just go home alone. No harm, no foul. These are *my* tickets, and this is my plan, even if it was Belle's idea.

There are eight home games this season. That's eight different guys, eight new friends to make, and — *only* if I want — eight potential orgasms that don't come from my trusty vibrator.

I am in control.

Maybe this will actually be fun, I thought, laughing as Belle swiped a hard left on a guy who stated in his bio that he was a "sex machine." She seemed to be having more fun than I was going through the app, so I let her swipe away, content to just sip on my vodka and listen to her commentary.

Every now and then, I'd feel Zach watching me from wherever he was working behind the bar. And when our eyes met, my chest would squeeze, along with my thighs. There was something about his eyes, about the kind of heat that swept over me with that gaze. The way he looked at me, it was as if he already had me in his bed, between his sheets, one hand on my hip and the other hiking my leg up as he settled between my thighs.

He'd only just learned my name, but the way he looked at me? It was as if he knew everything — maybe even more than I knew, myself.

A practice round...

Yeah. This could be fun.

Chapter 2

ZACH

"So," Doc said, eyes mischievous as he passed my mother the mashed potatoes. "Zach has a date tomorrow."

I half laughed, half groaned as the entire table erupted at Doc's announcement.

"What? A date? With who?" My mom said excitedly, her eyes lit up like the giant bulbs donning our Christmas tree each year.

This was at the same time my little brother said, "Yeah, right. Zach can't land a date."

And my dad simply smirked, his smile the same one I had, and nudged me. "Atta boy."

I took a roll from under the warm cloth napkin in the basket, passing it to Doc with a pointed glare. "Thanks for that, Doc."

"Hey, just starting some friendly dinner conversation."

"I see that."

I pretended to be annoyed, but the truth was I never could be — not with Doc. He was a member of my family just as much as the blood relatives sitting at the same table, and every Saturday evening, without fail, we all sat together and ragged on each other in equal measure.

It was just my turn first, tonight.

"Is she a sweet girl? What's her name?" Mom asked.

"Is she hot?" Micah chimed in, waggling his brows.

Mom thumped him with her still-rolled napkin.

"It's not a date," I said, earning me a somewhat-saddened look from Mom. Then, I smirked at my little brother, leaning over the table to whisper, though I knew everyone else would be able to hear, too. "And she's *smokin'*."

Micah high-fived me as Mom rolled her eyes, splaying her napkin on her lap.

"Sure sounded like a date when you told me about it," Doc argued, piling his fork up with a stack of green beans. "And you haven't asked for a night off in... well, ever."

"You think every interaction I have with a girl at the bar is a date," I volleyed. "Including anytime old Mrs. Rudder asks me for a refill on her merlot just so she can watch me bend down to retrieve the bottle from the bottom shelf."

"That old woman would marry you in a heartbeat."

"She'd do the same with you, if you'd ever actually do more than grump at her."

Doc humphed at that, the same way he humphed at pretty much anything that anyone said at the bar. He was the owner — had been since the doors opened back in 1976 — and though he loved the new clientele my ideas had brought in over the years, he still didn't know how to handle a bar that was actually *busy* and not just sprinkled with his regulars.

Almost twelve years now I'd worked in his bar — all because he took a chance on a kid who needed him.

"You know my heart is taken," he said.

"Right. By the little honey down in St. Croix, right?" I shook my head. "I'm still not convinced she's a real person and not a figment of your imagination."

"You don't have to be convinced of anything. *I* know. And that's all that matters."

Doc's smile was more genuine when he took his next bite, eyes all lost in wonder as he thought about the woman he'd been pen pals with for almost ten years now. I never understood that — essentially dating with so much distance between them. They'd only seen each other a handful of times, every time Doc would let me force him to take a little vacation to go down there.

He'd never shown me a photo of her, though.

"Also," I said, addressing his comment about me being a workaholic. "I *do* take days off — every Saturday, same as you."

"Only because I make you," Doc said. "I swear you'd sleep at that bar if I put a cot in the back."

I grinned. "A couch would do."

"You got a pic of her?" Micah asked, pulling the subject back to my *not* date.

"Oh," Doc chimed in at that. His brows rose all the way into his hairline. "I didn't even think to ask about that."

"No, you perv, I don't have a picture." I tossed a bread roll at Micah. "And even if I did, I wouldn't show you. We all know your spank bank is plenty full."

"I do not need to hear about my sixteen-year-old son's *spank bank*," Mom said, holding up her hands with a disgusted face. "New topic. Now."

Micah and I laughed.

My mom and Micah looked exactly alike, other than Mom's hair being longer. Micah had the same soft features as she did, whereas mine were darker, edgier — favoring my father's strong bone structure. Still, just one look at the four of us together and anyone could see we were a family.

"Sorry, Mom. I swear, I'm still your little baby boy. Zach doesn't know what he's talking about. I'm an angel."

Micah circled the crown of his head like a halo, clasping both hands in front of himself in mock prayer.

Mom rolled her eyes. "Right."

Dad took over the conversation then, telling us about his fishing trip with Rod, his best friend from college, that morning. Mom teased him about lying about the size of the fish he caught that somehow "escaped" his hook before anyone could get a picture, and I just smiled, watching the genuine love in both their eyes as they went tit for tat.

My parents were the definition of an all-American love story.

They met when they were in middle school, but it took my dad all the way up until their junior year of high school to get up the courage to ask Mom out. When he finally did, he took her to the homecoming dance, and the rest is history. They were each other's first everything — and I knew without a doubt they'd be each other's last, too.

Growing up in a household full of love taught me a few things — like how to treat a woman, how to apologize like a man, and how to communicate when things got tough. My parents never let me bunker down and hide my emotions when I had them. Whether it was a bad day for me out on the football field or just a simple fight with a high school girlfriend, they forced me to talk about it. And through that, I learned how to recognize my feelings, how to dissect them, and how to move forward.

My friends in college always gave me shit, saying I was a chick, but I didn't see anything wrong with knowing how I felt and talking about it. I'm human, and I learned from one of the strongest men I know — my father — that crying, or hurting, or feeling heartbroken didn't make you any less of a man. I learned from my mother that crying wasn't feminine, it was human, and that even if it *was* feminine — that didn't mean it was less than anything masculine.

That's right, I was a born and bred feminist and proud of it.

I learned a lot from my parents — and one of the strongest things I learned was that I wanted what my parents had — a lifetime partner — more than anything.

Of course, dating for me had somewhere down the line shifted more into the realm of one-night stands and the occasional two-to-three month flings. Maybe it was because I worked so much, or because I still hadn't found a woman to spark the same fire in me that my mom did in my dad.

Or maybe it was because I lost myself when I gave up my dream, and I was still trying to find me before I found *her*.

Regardless, I was reminded every Saturday evening of what the future could hold, if I ever found the right girl to share my life with. And because of how I was raised, I was a bit of a softie — a romantic, if you will.

Micah loved to tease me over it.

"So, you going to bring this girl some flowers and take her dancing under the stars on this first date, Romeo?" he said after Mom cleared the table and brought dessert over.

"Don't tease your brother," Mom hushed him, but she grinned my way. "And if you *did* do those things, I bet you she would think it's sweet."

"Totally," Micah agreed, serving himself a piece of pie. "Or, she'd shove you right into the friend zone box where you usually end up."

Dad laughed, and Mom thumped Micah again.

"No, no, it's okay. Rag all you want, little bro. I love when you show how salty you are that I have a girl to take out tomorrow and you'll be in your room playing video games with one hand in your underwear."

"More action than you'll get, I bet."

I laughed.

"This girl seems like she's the one calling the shots, from what he told me," Doc said. "In fact, isn't it *her* that's taking *you* to the football game?"

"It is, indeed."

"Wait! Football game?!" Micah asked.

"Yep. She's a season ticket holder for the Bears. We're going to tomorrow's game together."

He pouted then, dropping his fork to his plate. "That's not even fair. Tell her if she really wants to have a good time, she should take me."

"I can promise you, little brother — I will absolutely not do that."

"Oh, that's right," he chimed. "You'll be too busy looking into her eyes and telling her how beautiful she is." He clasped his hands together on a sigh, batting his lashes at me.

I rolled up my napkin and tossed it over the table at him.

"And what exactly would *you* do if you were taking a girl on a first date, mister?" Dad asked Micah, pointing his fork. "Because I know we raised you better than to not treat a girl with respect."

"Oh, I'd respect her, alright." Micah waggled his brows. "I'd respect her all night long."

Mom pulled his plate from in front of him as the rest of us laughed. "That's it, no dessert for you."

Micah apologized through his laughter, using his classic puppy-dog eyes. Those earned him an eye-roll and kiss on the forehead from Mom before she gave him his pie back. And, thankfully, the conversation turned from me permanently when Micah started talking about his first few weeks as a junior.

I didn't miss the look on my dad's face as he listened to his youngest son talk about art class and the cute girl who keeps staring at him in the lunch room.

Because Dad never thought Micah would make it to sixteen.

None of us did.

My brother was diagnosed with juvenile myelomonocytic leukemia when he was just four years old.

I was eighteen at the time, in my first semester of college, and football was my life. I had a scholarship and, though I was young and just starting out in my college career, my coach said he saw a promising path to playing pro for me. But when Micah got sick, everything in my life changed.

First and foremost, my priorities.

At first, his survival rate expectancy was dismal. Even with treatment, we were told we'd be lucky to have even three more years with him. Playing football and going to college didn't feel as important with numbers like that staring me in my face.

Sure, I knew I could talk to coach, maybe get redshirted for my first year and come back. I knew that, with my skills and reputation, I could come back any time I wanted to. But right then, at eighteen years old with my baby brother in and out of the hospital like it was a playground, none of that mattered. My parents were doing everything they could to have someone stay home with him, or taking him to and from the hospital, or sitting up with him on the nights he couldn't sleep when he had to stay overnight.

I couldn't do much, but I could help with that.

What was more important was being there for Micah, *with* Micah, and supporting my parents. I knew I could have put in the four years at college, maybe gone pro, given my family the money they really needed and my brother the fighting chance he deserved.

But the problem was, Micah wasn't promised four years.

He wasn't even promised one.

But now, twelve years later, Micah was considered cancer-free and healthy. He still had frequent visits to the doctor for check-ups, and Mom worried any time he had so much as a cold, but his quality of life was better than we ever could have expected.

The fact that he was living *at all* was better than we expected.

I could have gone back to college. I could have tried out for a pro team. But, as it often does, time just kept on ticking, and every year we celebrated Micah's birthday, all I could think about was that he was alive, my family was healthy, I made enough money to help them and support myself, and that we were all happy. That was what mattered.

Life was good.

And I would go back and give up football time and time again for the same result.

"You know, I really would like you to watch your mouth more," Mom told Micah. "I know you're sixteen now, but you're still my baby boy. And I don't want to hear about any of the things you talked about tonight."

"Come on, you know me, Mom," he said, rubbing her back. "It's just video game talk."

"Video game talk?"

He shrugged. "Yeah. You talk trash to look all big and bad. I'm still your sweet little boy. Promise."

He grinned at her and she rolled her eyes, but she seemed content for the moment. I knew in her mind, she could blink and travel back to when her "sweet little boy" had more tubes running in and out of him than the back of an old 90s computer.

We all could.

And *that's* why I would make my same choices time and time again.

After dinner, Micah helped Mom clean up in the kitchen while Dad asked me and Doc to join him for a cigar on the back porch. It was Saturday night tradition, and tonight, Doc supplied the cigars — three dark Robustos with a bourbon kick and warm vanilla aftertaste.

Doc launched into a story from that week at the bar, one I'd already heard but was new to Dad. And as the smoke danced with the warm September wind on the porch, I finally let myself think about the woman everyone had asked me about all night.

Gemma Mancini.

Damn, did she come out of nowhere and knock me on my ass.

If I hadn't already done a double-take at her long, dark, thick curtain of hair falling over her shoulders when she walked in the bar, if her almost neon-green eyes hadn't been enough to make me want to know her name, if the way the Chicago Bears jersey she wore didn't stretch across her curves like a dream — I still would have wanted to know more after the words her friend spoke.

"A friend who could, potentially, rail you into next year with his hammer cock."

Um, I volunteer as tribute.

She'd simply laughed at me when she realized I'd overheard, placing her drink order with me like I was nothing special. And I guess to her, I probably wasn't. After all, I was just the bartender. I was just some guy taking her order as she listened to her friend go on and on about her need to get laid.

Again, if she's looking for a volunteer...

But I'd given her space, filled her drink order without much more than a smile and a nod as her friend set her up on a dating app. I noted her dark, exotic features from a distance, wondering if she laid out every day in the sun to get that tan or if it was just her natural hue. I wondered who, if anyone, got to kiss those plump, burgundy lips of hers. And more than anything, I wondered what the hell I could say to her to get her to see me — *really* see me — before she walked out of that bar.

It wasn't until her friend walked away, until I saw Gemma sitting there all alone, staring at her phone like it might explode in the next second that I knew I had to talk to her.

She was talking football with the other guys at the bar, and call me cliché, but any chick who loves a sport enough to talk the way she was is a turn on. And since it was the sport I had loved my whole life, the one I grew up on, the one that left me more heartbroken than any woman ever had? Well, I was a sucker for it.

But, it was more than just the sport talk.

There was something about her eyes, the vulnerability behind them, the mixture of excitement and absolute fear laced within her irises as she stepped out of her comfort zone. I didn't know her story, but it was easy to see she hadn't done this before — the whole dating app thing. And since I hated it as much as the next person in this generation, I wanted to save her from the misery.

So, I told her to date me, instead.

I smiled as a new cloud of smoke escaped my lips, running over our playful conversation. I'd always been quick on my feet when it came to getting a girl in the sack with me, but most girls didn't fight back. Most girls don't call me on my shit.

Gemma Mancini had no problem doing just that.

I'd had to try for her, and I had no doubt that if I wanted more than one date with her, I'd have to try even harder tomorrow night.

From what I'd gathered, she was determined to take a new guy to every home game this season. Why, I had no idea. Maybe she didn't want to date. Maybe, like her friend insinuated, she really did just want to get laid and had no interest in banging the same guy twice.

But I saw it, what her friend didn't.

Gemma didn't want some random guy touching her.

She wanted *the* guy touching her — the guy who turns her on, the guy who makes her feel safe, and comfortable.

Her red-headed friend might be the type that can fuck with no strings, that is perfectly content having a guy inside her one night and then never speaking to him again.

But Gemma isn't that girl.

And I intended to prove it.

It sounded crazy, I realized, as I took another pull of my cigar, that I already felt like I knew her. In fact, if I said any of this out loud to anyone, I was sure I'd hear how much of a cocky asshole I was being.

But I'd never had a problem being cocky.

Especially when I knew I was right.

"Hey, think you could swing by a little early on Thursday?" Doc asked me when our cigars were spent, pulling me to the side after Dad had gone back in the house. "I know you work the late shift for the game, but I wanted to talk to you about something."

I smiled, but something in Doc's eyes made my stomach sink. He was watching me like whatever it was that he wanted to talk to me about wasn't good news, and suddenly, I felt my heart beating in my throat.

God, please don't say you have to let me go.

The bar had been busier than ever, but I knew the strip we sat on down in the South Loop was growing in popularity. Maybe rent was going up. Maybe Doc couldn't afford to pay me anymore.

Then again, he couldn't afford to pay me when he first hired me, either.

But he did it anyway.

"Sure, Doc," I said after a moment, swallowing. "I'll come in early. Everything okay?"

"Everything's fine," he said quickly, forcing a worn smile. He clapped me on the back. "We'll talk more then. For now, you just focus on that girl of yours."

"She's not my girl. We just met. We talked for like ten minutes."

"Mm-hmm," Doc said, cocking a brow as he pulled the sliding glass door open. "A girl who loves football almost as much as you do. Try not to come in your pants before you make it to the seats, okay?"

A laugh shot out of me, and Doc disappeared inside, both of us knowing I wouldn't make a promise I wasn't sure I could keep.

Chapter 3

GEMMA

It's just a practice round.

I played that thought on repeat like a Britney Spears song circa 1999 as I got ready for the game Sunday afternoon.

Whenever my anxiety flared, whenever my nerves were rattled, all I had to do to calm myself was suppress those thoughts and focus on *doing* something.

So, I did my nails, and my hair, and my makeup. I shaved my legs and my arm pits and, just in case, my lady bits. I lotioned up and sprayed myself with my best perfume. And by the time I walked out the door and climbed into a cab, I was the best-smelling, smoothest, calmest version of me I could manage.

"Heading to the game, I presume?" the cabbie asked me, his kind eyes offering a smile in the rearview mirror.

"You got it."

"Should be a good one. You going alone?"

"Meeting a..." I paused. "...*friend* there."

"Lucky friend."

I smirked at him, and he smiled in return, turning up the volume on the pre-game show as we made our way to the stadium. Cabbies in any other city in America would have asked me what music I wanted to listen to, but on game day in the windy city? There *was* no other option — it was game day, and that was all that mattered.

Excitement fluttered through me as we cruised across town toward the stadium, traffic getting thicker as we approached the south side.

It had been a long year.

I didn't like to reflect on the past much. My grandfather had taught me when I was younger that there was no sense focusing on the past because you couldn't change it, no matter how much you thought about it. All you could do was ask yourself what you regretted, what you loved, and what you learned. Then, you moved forward.

It was because of my grandpa that I adopted the "make a plan, keep it moving" mindset. My parents traveled a lot when I was younger, thanks to their careers as motivational speakers, and so I spent more time with my grandfather than I did with either of them. Funny enough, though they were the ones motivating people all over the country, I was more driven by my grandfather. He was a veteran, a simple country man, and he didn't take any shit from anyone.

He tried to teach me to do the same.

Still, though I knew he would have hated it, I couldn't help but think of him as the cab carried me across town. He was a huge Bears fan, and I wouldn't have even had a date tonight if he'd been alive. He would have been there in the seat next to me, and he would have helped me get over Carlo and move on with my life. He always knew the right things to say.

But he wasn't here, anymore. Just like Carlo wasn't.

It seemed everyone I loved in my life was destined to leave in some way.

Yes, it had been a long year. A *sad* year. And the closer we got to the stadium, the more I realized how ready I was for football, for the first regular season home game with a crowd all singing "Bear Down" together.

And when we pulled up to Soldier Field, it felt like I was coming home.

"This is fine, I can walk from here." I handed the driver a twenty, popping the door open and smiling at the sound of the crowd filtering in. "Keep the change."

"Have fun. Go Bears!"

"Go Bears!"

Once the door was shut and my navy blue Keds touched the concrete in front of the stadium, my stomach fell down to meet them.

I'm about to go on a date.

My palms sparked with heat, heart picking up the pace at my realization. I couldn't date. I hadn't *had* to date since Carlo, and even then, we'd met so young that dating wasn't *really* dating. We'd met my first year of college, when he was working as a graduate assistant. Our version of dating was him walking me across campus to class or studying together in the library.

But before the nerves could take over, I closed my eyes and reminded myself.

It's not a date. It's a football game.

I am in control.

I pulled out my phone to text Zach, but before my fingers could touch down on the keys, Belle's face lit up my screen. I slid the button at the bottom to answer her call, smiling.

"How's your pussy?"

"Oh, my God, Belle."

"Still empty? What time does the game end again?"

"It hasn't even started. I just got here."

"Oh, how does he look? What's he wearing? Oh, my God, are you freaking out?"

I blew out a breath. "I wasn't, until you called."

"Is he with you?"

"I'm trying to find him now. Which means I have to go."

"Just text him while you're on the phone with me."

"GOODBYE, BELLE."

I hung up before she could protest, smiling and shaking my head. Then, I shot out a text to Zach to meet me in front of the Big Beaver Totem Pole at the north entrance.

As I made my way through the tailgating tents, I felt that excitement buzzing to life again. I'd been to so many Bears games, I couldn't count them all — but this was my first year having season tickets. My grandfather had season tickets when he was younger, and he would bring me every now and then, letting me hang with him and his war buddies as they tailgated before the game. I wanted to tailgate, too. I wanted to start traditions, to build memories tied around football season.

I was supposed to do just that, with Carlo.

I bought the tickets before I found out about his affair, before I found out about his illness. In my mind, I pictured us buying a tent and chairs, a long table to play games on, a portable grill. I saw our friends tailgating with us, imagined us high-fiving the other season ticket holders around us every time we scored — just the way my grandfather had.

It was supposed to be ours — this day, these tickets, these memories. He'd been all I could think about when I envisioned the Bears season, and I thought I was all he could think about, too.

Now, I knew he wasn't even thinking of me at all.

He was too busy thinking about *her*.

When I reached the totem, I briefly debated leaving. I hadn't even walked inside the stadium and already, I couldn't stop thinking about Carlo.

I wasn't ready for this.

But I didn't have the chance to change my mind.

"Wow."

A whistle rang out, and when I turned around, it was Zach. His brows were all the way up in his hairline as he took in my tiny, ripped-up jean shorts and Chicago Bears tank top. I felt his gaze like it was a fire thrower, warming my skin from my ankles all the way back up to my cheeks.

"I hope our seats aren't too close, because there's no way those players are going to be able to focus on the ball if you're in viewing range."

"That usually works for you, doesn't it?" I volleyed, stepping closer. The breeze picked up his cologne, and it mixed with the smell of grilling and turf, wafting up the most intoxicating scent.

He chuckled, hands slipping into the pockets of his shorts. His dark hair was styled with a bit of gel, not quite as unruly as it had been at the bar. I couldn't decide which look I liked more.

"Usually, yes. How did it do for you?"

I shrugged. "I think you can do better. Here," I said, handing him his ticket. "Should we get inside? I don't want to miss kick-off."

"You're the boss."

His eyes flashed to my chest again when he swiped the ticket from my hands, and I laughed, shaking my head and leading the way through the crowd toward the entrance. I was thankful for the warm weather for the first regular season game, especially since I knew I'd be bundled up soon enough.

Zach didn't seem to mind the outfit, either.

My hands shook a little as we went through security and had our tickets scanned, and once we were flowing with the crowd toward our seats, I noticed how silent we'd been the entire walk in. I glanced at Zach, but as soon as his eyes found mine, I pulled my gaze away, scanning the food stands as we passed, instead.

I didn't realize I was wringing my hands together until Zach's palm covered them where they were wrapped together in front of me.

"Hey," he said, his eyes finding mine. "It's just a game. Remember?"

I swallowed.

"You love football. So do I. Let's drink a few beers and have some fun, yeah?"

At that, a slow, long breath escaped my lips, and I smiled. "Yeah."

He grinned back at me. "Cool. I'll grab two beers then. You hungry yet?"

"Not yet."

"Okay. Go get settled in, watch the pre-game festivities. I'll meet you at our seats."

"No, no," I said, forcing a steadier breath. "I'll wait."

His hand brushed the small of my back, that same smirk on his lips as he turned toward one of the stands. "Okay, then. Wait here. I'll be right back."

I watched him go, chest still a little tight, eyes fixed on the way the muscles in his back flexed under his Bears t-shirt.

Relax, Gemma. This will be fun.

I repeated that mantra the entire time he ordered our beers, and it got louder and louder in my head as we made our way to the seats. I couldn't help but cast glances at Zach's face as we got lower and lower, the field only seven short rows away from our row.

"Gemma, these seats are incredible," he said when we wiggled past the others in our row and took our seats. He set his beer in the holder, eyes scanning the field. "I've never sat this close before."

"I wanted to be by the end zone," I said, nodding to where our guys were warming up. "I know we're not close enough for it, but I've always loved when the guys score and get so hyped that they jump into the crowd."

"Well, like I said, if they see you?" Zach shook his head. "They might break records with how high they jump."

I blushed, biting back a smile.

"So, can I ask... why did you buy two tickets? I mean, from what your friend was saying at the bar, she's not a huge sports fan. And I know your *new* plan but... it wasn't the original one, right?"

My throat constricted, and I reached for my beer to swallow down the cotton ball lodged in my esophagus before it could grow.

"I bought them for someone else... originally," I explained. "But, I don't really want to talk about it. If that's okay."

Zach watched me, his eyes so intense that I had to tear mine away. I watched the field instead, hoping he wouldn't push.

"Alright," he said after a moment. "Hey, look at me."
I didn't.
"Gemma," he said with a chuckle. "I'm not going to see all your secrets if you look at me for a second."

I smiled a little at that, but when my eyes met his again, I wasn't so sure.

"I'm here for a good time, just like you. Okay? You hold the reins. Whatever you want to talk about, we talk about. Whatever you *don't?*" He shrugged. "Well, then, we don't. You're in control here."

A heavy, relieved sigh left my chest. He had no idea what those words meant to me, how they triggered me in all the right ways.

And yet, somehow, maybe he did.

I am in control, I repeated, and then, I smiled.

Because with those words? All the nerves were gone.

And the game had just begun.

"ARE YOU KIDDING?! OPEN YOUR FUCKING EYES, REF!"

Zach's brows shot up at my outburst, and I swiped my beer from where it was resting in the cup holder, taking a big swig and slamming it back down again.

"Ridiculous, this guy is blind." I turned to Zach for confirmation of my obviously correct assessment, and he just laughed, tossing a kernel of popcorn in his mouth.

"This is amazing to watch," he said.

"The game?"

"You. *Watching* the game."

I flushed, fighting back a smile as I brought my attention to the field for the next play. We were down by three, and less than two minutes away from half time.

And still, even with us being down and the refs being blind, I was having fun.

Maybe it was the beer helping my nerves, or maybe it was Zach. From the moment we sat down, we'd talked, and laughed, and cheered, and — when the occasion was right — boo'd together in solidarity. We were high-fiving all the fans around us when we scored, singing the lyrics to "Bear Down" at the top of our lungs, and talking smack about the other team to anyone not wearing a Bears jersey.

Zach Bowen was the perfect football buddy.

But as comfortable as he'd somehow made me, he still couldn't make our team win. They had to do that on their own. With less than two minutes to go before halftime, we needed to score, and the ref calling holding on us wasn't helping.

Steepling my fingers together over my lips, I focused on the play, heart thundering.

"This part always makes me so nervous," the woman next to me said, mirroring my stance. She was at least twenty years older than me, judging by the touch of gray in her hair and the life lines etched into her face. We'd shared a few high-fives throughout the game, and now, we were sharing our mini-heart attacks.

"Me, too. I think it's even worse being here at the game instead of on my couch or at a bar."

She laughed at that. "Roy and I have been season ticket holders for twenty-two years now, and I'll tell you this — the excitement never fades, but neither does the anxiety."

Zach leaned over me then, smiling at the woman. "Twenty-two years? That's incredible."

"What can I say, we're diehard fans."

"Even in 2016," her husband chimed in, just as the ball was snapped. He was a little shorter than her, and a little pudgier, too. Still, they shared a secretive smile, one that said spoke more than words could. It was a smile only years of love could breed.

Zach and I chuckled a bit at her husband's joke, but then all eyes were on the field. We ran the ball, breaking through the Bills' defensive line enough to move the chains.

First down.

Our section cheered as the guys lined up for another play, but before the ball could be snapped again, the Bills called a time-out.

"I'm Janet, by the way," the woman said as the big screens filled with updates on the other games going on around the country.

I shook her hand first before she reached for Zach, and Roy waved over at us from his seat, still frowning as he watched the screen. It reminded me a little of how my grandpa used to watch football when I was younger — with a permanent scowl.

"Nice to meet you guys," I said.

"Is this your first year as ticket holders?"

I nodded. "It is, indeed. I've been to a lot of games before, though. Just never had the season tickets."

"Well, welcome. And you picked a great section. We haven't changed seats since 2002, after we upgraded to these. We actually have two extra seats," she continued, pointing behind us about ten rows up and to the right. "Those right there. We sold them for this game, but sometimes we invite friends."

"We've been trying to get your seats for years," Roy added, still scowling, though not at us.

"Roy!"

He shrugged. "What? It's true. Wish we could have snagged them up before you, but hey, I'll take what I can get at this point." He looked at us then. "They were taken by the worst people the past few years. At least it's not them sitting next to us this season."

Janet laughed at that, brows raised like he had a point. "He's not wrong. Two guys who painted themselves every game. The one who always sat next to me smelled like old deli meat forgotten in the fridge for months."

"Well, I promise, we don't smell. Well, at least, *I* don't," Zach said. Then, he leaned over, sniffing my neck. "Might have to watch out for her."

I smacked his arm.

"You two are adorable. Newlyweds?" Janet asked, searching our hands for rings.

"Oh, no," I answered quickly, shaking my head. "We're just friends."

Janet eyed me curiously, and when she looked behind me at Zach, she laughed. By the time I turned toward him, he was just holding his hands up innocently.

"Ah, well, we look forward to sharing the season with you," she said, winking at Zach before we all turned back to the field for the next play.

I glared at that too-handsome-for-his-own-good bartender next to me, suspicion creeping in. "What did you do behind my back?"

"Nothing," he said, holding up his hands again. "I swear."

"Uh-huh."

He just grinned, and I smirked back. For the longest second, his eyes held mine, and warmth crept up my neck at the way he looked at me. It was as if those eyes knew me, like we were playing a game and he was three moves ahead.

I wanted to know more about him.

I wanted to know everything.

But the ball was snapped, and we both ripped our attention back to the field.

"Come on, come on," I whispered, watching the clock as our quarterback looked for an opening. But he couldn't find anyone, and we all watched with a cringe as he was sacked to the ground.

"Shit," Zach murmured.

There was no time to spare, and with no additional timeouts, all our guys could do was get back on the line. This time, our quarterback handed it off to our most agile running back, and he found a gap in the line, sprinting through it.

"Yes!" I threw my hands up, watching his speedy legs work him across the field. "Go, go, go, go!"

He made it all the way to our thirty-yard-line, securing the first down, and the entire stadium erupted in cheers.

Zach smacked my ass in celebration, and my mouth popped open. He was still carrying on and celebrating as I gaped at him, hand rubbing the spot that he'd slapped. When he looked at me again, he smiled and shrugged.

"What?" he asked. "That's how we celebrate in football."

"Oh, is it now?"

He nodded. "It is. But hey, I'm all about being fair." He turned, offering his ass to me. "Your turn."

I laughed, crossing my arms and shaking my head. "I mean, I don't know if I'd classify this as fair. Sounds more like a win-win for you."

"Don't act like you don't want to touch my ass," he tossed over his shoulder. "I saw you staring at it the night we met."

My mouth gaped wider.

"I definitely did *not* stare at your ass."

"Sure," he said, nodding. "And I definitely did *not* stare at your rack."

I smacked his ass at that, and he threw his fists in the air at the win.

"See? Don't you feel better?"

I rolled my eyes. "More like violated. Can't a woman go to a bar and not have her tits ogled?"

"A girl built like you?" he asked, eyes flashing down to my chest before they met mine again. "Probably not."

I just laughed, turning back to the field for the next play. Still, I couldn't stop smiling — not with Zach standing next to me. He'd been like that all game — making jokes, laughing, cheering. In a way, I was kind of sad he'd offered to be a practice round, because I knew after tonight, I'd never talk to him again.

We could have been great friends.

Our guys didn't make first down in the next three plays, so with just seconds to go on the clock, we kicked for three points, and just like that, the game was tied.

Halftime.

"I love games like this!" Janet screamed as the crowd grew louder, everyone filing up to the food stands and bathrooms. "Looks like our boys showed up ready to play this year."

"Hell yeah, they did!" I bounced, smile splitting my face.

When Janet and Roy left for the bathrooms, it was just me and Zach, and we sat down in our seats for the first time all game.

"Do you want a sausage or anything? I can run up," he offered, but I shook my head.

"Nah, I'm good with beer for now. I had a big lunch. Besides, if I got *anything*, it would be a hot dog — not an Italian sausage." I grimaced. "Yuck."

"You're kidding, right?" Zach pressed a hand to his chest. "I think... I mean, I'm personally offended right now."

"You and every other Chicagoan. I've just always been a hot dog girl." I shrugged. "Sue me."

"I might."

I smiled. "You can go get food, though, if you want. I can wait here by myself. I'm a big girl, you know?"

"Oh, I don't doubt you could handle yourself. But, I'm good for now." He was still watching me curiously. "Wait, didn't it say in your profile that you're Italian?"

"I am, indeed."

"But you don't like Italian sausages."

I chuckled. "We're not going to move on from the street meat subject, are we?"

"Not until you tell me what you have against Italian sausage."

I sighed, turning in my seat to face him. "Okay, long story short, my dad is German, mom is Italian. They made it together against the odds of our families pretty much hating each other. It was so bad, in fact, that I've never met my mom's side of the family. And, honestly, my mom and dad traveled so much when I was a kid, I never really got *any* of the Italian heritage you would expect. Other than my love for red wine and pasta. Because, duh."

Zach smirked.

"I spent most of my time with my dad's dad, and he was a hot dog guy. He did try to get me into brats," I said, scrunching my nose. "But I wasn't a fan of those either."

Zach nodded, mouth turning down like he was digesting what I'd just told him. "Alright then. Hot dog girl. Note taken." He smiled. "Are you having fun?"

"I am," I said, brushing a strand of hair behind my ear. "Thank you, for coming here with me. I think this *practice round* was exactly what I needed."

The corner of Zach's mouth pulled up in a grin, revealing that dimple on his cheek. "Hey, it's *me* who's honored here."

"Although, I do feel a little gipped in this deal."

He cocked a brow. "How so?"

"Well, we haven't really done much *practicing,* if you know what I mean. Like... we've just been watching the game."

"Isn't that what you invited me here to do?"

"No. I mean, *technically* yes, but you said it was a practice round for this whole..." I waved my hand. "This whole *thing* Belle has schemed up. And, if we're being honest, you've watched *me* more than the field."

"Can you blame me?"

I flushed, shaking my head with a smile. "Are you going to help me, or did I waste my first ticket here?"

He laughed then, propping his arms up on the backs of the chairs. One of them was around me with that movement, and my pulse picked up speed with his bicep so close. "What are your concerns?"

"I don't know," I confessed, looking at my hands in my lap. "I mean, I don't even know what you do on a date now. Like, do we hold hands? That seems weird for a football game."

"If it seems weird, don't do it."

"Do we kiss?"

"If you want to."

Zach's eyes sparked at that, and my cheeks tinged more.

"I just, I don't know. I need to have a plan, but I don't even know where to start. Like, do I make a list of things he should do or say, and if he meets the qualifications, then I kiss him after the game and ask him back to my place?" My brain seemed to like that, because I was already nodding before Zach even answered. "Oh, yes. I feel like there should be a list. Like, *must drink beer and know the lyrics to 'Bear Down.'* Oh, and *must like hot dogs.*"

I winked at him with that last line, and Zach laughed.

"Why do you have to have a list, and a plan?" he asked, taking a swig of his beer. He held up his hand to one of the guys passing by with fresh ones, pulling out twenty bucks to grab us two more before he turned back to me. "I mean, why not just enjoy the game together, have fun, and see how you're feeling? Just go with the flow. You know what I mean?"

"Go with the flow," I deadpanned. "God, if you knew me, you'd realize how ridiculous that proposition is."

"Well, I *don't* know you. Not yet. And neither will these other guys. And, isn't that the fun part?" Zach shrugged, handing me a fresh beer. "You can be whoever you want, especially if it's only a one-night thing. Just have fun with it."

"Are you suggesting I lie?"

"No," he answered quickly, bringing the aluminum bottle to his lips. Then, he shrugged. "But, I'm not saying you *can't* lie. If it's fun. If it's what you want to do."

Carlo's eyes flashed in my mind like a car wreck, those blue eyes I'd thought could never stare into mine while his lips told me anything other than the truth.

But he'd lied to me so easily, for so long, without me having a single clue.

I wondered if he did it just because he wanted to.

Just because it was fun.

"I don't want to lie," I said a little harsher than I intended. "Liars are on the top of two of my lists." I held up one finger. "Things I Never Want to Be," I said, then I popped up the second finger. "And People I Never Want in My Life."

"Okay," he said, watching me curiously with hands up in surrender. "No lying. Got it. But still, I think you should just relax and try to have fun. No lists. No plans. Just... live."

I blinked at him.

"You're looking at me like I just spoke to you in Chinese."

"You might as well have."

"Do you really have these lists? I mean, is this really a thing for you?"

I pulled out my phone, opening the notes app and showing it to him. Note after note, line after line, there were lists. The ones I'd viewed or edited most recently filtered in at the top. And there were lists for everything from what I needed to grab at the grocery store tomorrow to what I needed to accomplish before I turned thirty. The most recent one was everything I needed to do before I walked out the door for today's game.

He tapped that one, pulling it open before I could stop him.

"Shave the goods," he read, and one brow climbed as he smirked at me. "Okay, maybe I can get down with your lists."

I closed the app quickly, shoving my phone in my clutch as he laughed.

"This may be funny to you," I said, smiling despite the tiny tinge of hurt I felt inside. He wasn't the first to make fun of me for how I handled my feelings and anxieties, and he wouldn't be the last. "But, this works for me, okay?"

Zach's expression softened, and he leaned forward, one elbow on his knee as his other hand grabbed mine. "I'm sorry. I'm not laughing *at* you."

"You're laughing *with* me?" I mocked.

"No. I'm just laughing because I'm having fun, and because you're the most interesting, unique, and adorable woman I've ever met."

My heart stopped with those words, kicking back to life a few moments later when Janet and Roy sat back down next to us. Zach just smiled, his eyes still on mine as Janet went on about how bad the lines were, and how it was a rookie move to get up during halftime.

I barely registered a word.

All I could do was stare at the man who still had his hand on my knee, wondering where he came from, and what he saw that I didn't.

Then, I mentally started a brand-new list.

Things I Like About Zach Bowen.

Chapter 4

ZACH

My dad once told me that he knew the very first time he met my mom that he would marry her one day.

He said they were in sixth grade, walking in a single-file line in opposite directions — she was going back to class, his class was heading to the music room. From across the hall, my mom smiled at him.

And right then and there, he knew.

I always thought it was crazy. Even the romantic in me found that a little far-fetched. When *I* was in sixth grade, about the only thing that could hold my attention longer than ten seconds was the Crash Bandicoot video game on my PlayStation.

But here I was, less than three hours into my first night with Gemma Mancini, and suddenly, I got it.

Not that I wanted to marry the girl — I wasn't *that* crazy. At least, not admittedly so. But there was just... *something* about her. I couldn't take my eyes off her, the way she laughed before taking a long sip of her beer, or the way her little nose scrunched up when she disagreed with a call the referee made. I laughed at her stupid jokes, and her stupid rules and lists for her life. I smiled at the respectful way she spoke to the older couple sitting on the other side of her, and at the way her eyes grew wide, cheeks flushing, any time I touched her.

Her hair.

Her hand.

Her leg.

No, I didn't want to go out and buy a ring, but one thing was certain.

I wanted *more*.

Halfway through the fourth quarter, the Bears were down by seven points, and Gemma was not happy about it. She stood with her hands laced over her head, eyes on the field like she could somehow control the ball with her gaze. I just watched her, trying to focus on how much fun she was instead of how much fun football *used* to be. It was easy to think about her, but to let myself remember football, to let myself fall into that deep hole of memories... it would hurt.

Still, I couldn't escape the truth — not when I was this close to the sport that used to be my entire life.

I missed it.

Walking into the stadium, I'd been overwhelmed by how fast everything came rushing back to me — the smell of the turf, the sound of pads crashing together on the field, the roar of the crowd. The last time I'd been this close to a football field was almost twelve years ago now.

I hadn't touched a football since.

Suddenly, my fingers itched to feel the leather again, to trace that white stitching before tucking the ball into my side and running the field for a touchdown. But I couldn't do that to myself, not when I knew what the end result would be. It didn't matter how honorable my intentions were when I gave up my dream, or how it was worth it every day that my little brother woke up and got to live another twenty-four hours.

It was still a wound.

A gaping, sticky, still-tender gash.

And I knew without question that if I opened that cut, even an inch, it'd never heal again.

It was barely being held together by gum and paper clips, as it was.

A loud, exaggerated huff from a few rows behind us brought me back to the moment, to the present game, and I shook off my memories, focusing on the next play.

"Hey!" a gruff voice called out behind us.

I glanced at Gemma, who was still staring at the field. Our guys were way down at the other end zone, the quarterback searching for an open receiver to make the connection.

"Hey!" the voice said again, and this time I turned, finding a red-faced Bears fan glaring down at me from three rows up.

I cocked a brow, and he pointed at Gemma with one stumpy finger.

"You two enjoying the game?"

Gemma turned then, confusion written on her face. Neither one of us knew how to answer. It was a simple enough question, but the way the man asked it, I felt like we were walking right into a trap.

"I hope you are, because the rest of us can't see it back here!" He pointed to our seats, sweat dripping from his curly black mop down to the bit of chest hair poking out of his Bears jersey. "Sit down, there's nothing even going on."

The crowd around us was suddenly more interested in our transgression than on the play taking place on the other side of the field, and I clenched my jaw tight, adrenaline spiking in my veins. I'd had to jump into more than my fair share of fights at the bar, and I knew all the signs of a drunk, angry asshole.

But before I could say a word, Gemma turned all the way around and hung both hands on her hips.

"*Excuse me?*"

Her little mouth gaped open, that plump, pink bottom lip almost pouty as she stared at the man and let her weight shift to one side.

"You're kidding me, right?" she said, incredulous. "We're at a football game."

"Yeah, but you don't have to stand up the whole fucking time."

Again, I opened my mouth, but Gemma held up a finger and pointed it directly at the red-faced man.

"I'll do whatever the hell I want. I'm a season ticket holder, buddy, and if you wanna sit on your ass and watch the game, you should go to a bar or stay at home on your couch."

The crowd around us broke out in a mixture of laughs and *ooooh's.*

"You're literally the only ones standing right now," he pointed out.

Gemma glanced around, seeing the truth in his statement, and though her cheeks flushed a bit, she stood even taller. Her chin held high, she crossed one arm over the other. "And you're the only one complaining about it."

Our opponent puffed his chest, eyes landing hard on me next.

"Control your woman, douche bag. Should have left her at home, anyway."

This time, I clenched my jaw so hard it ached.

My hands were balling into fists of their own accord, muscles straining from the fight or flight kicking in. And with me? It was always fight.

But I was at the game with Gemma, and the last thing I wanted was to get us kicked out. So, I steeled a breath, cracking my neck to alleviate some tension.

"We're just here to watch the game," I told him, as calmly as I could with the anger roaring through me. "And we're rooting for the same team. Let's just take it down a notch."

"I can't root for *any* team, balls for brains, because I can't *see*." He gestured his chubby little hand toward the field.

"How is this tiny little thing blocking your view?" I asked, pointing at Gemma. "Girl is like a size two, if even, and at least two feet shorter than you. And you're three rows up!"

"Tell your bitch to sit down!" he ground out, a vein popping in his neck when that last word rolled off his tongue.

Heads snapped in his direction at that, a few other guys calling out that his comment had gone too far while the women gasped in shock.

Gemma's fists balled together at her sides, and she launched forward, hands catching the back of her chair like she was ready to hike herself over it.

I almost laughed — not because the fact that I was likely about to get my ass in a fight over this girl was funny, but because she was somehow even more adorable when she was pissed.

Before she could plant one foot on her seat to climb over, I caught her by the waist, wrapping both arms around her flailing frame.

"I'm only going to ask you this once," I said through clenched teeth, still holding onto a panting Gemma as she glared at the man. "Apologize."

"Fuck you," he spat.

Tossing Gemma behind me, I climbed over my seat, side-stepping a family of Bills fans until I was in the guy's face. He wound up, ready to hit me first, and I licked my lips with an evil smirk.

Oh please, hit me, motherfucker.

But before he could, security broke through the commotion, pressing one hand hard on my chest to push me back.

"Alright, guys, that's enough. Both of you calm down or I'll throw you both out."

The security guard was smaller than both me and the asshole still glaring down at me, and for a second, I debated the risk versus the reward. The security guard likely wouldn't be able to break us up very quickly — not without backup, anyway. And while getting kicked out of the game would suck, I'd have at least a few unblocked shots. And knocking a few of this man's teeth loose... would that be worth it?

Hmmm...

"Zach," Gemma said, tugging on my arm. Her emerald eyes blended with the green turf behind her, and just as I glanced at that field, our quarterback threw an incomplete pass.

Shit.

Gemma invited me to watch the game, not get her thrown out of it.

I stepped back, hands in the air as the security guard cocked a brow at me before turning to the man above me.

"What's the problem here?"

"These two burban moochers won't sit down so we can see the game."

That earned a haughty laugh from one of the teenagers

I had to sidestep when I climbed over my seat. He was wearing a Bills jersey, and I realized he was recording the whole thing on his phone.

"What the fuck are you laughing at?" the man said to the kid.

"I just find it hilarious that you've got your panties in a knot when *I'm* the one sitting right behind them, and I can see just fine."

The crowd laughed at that, and a few people called out smart remarks about how embarrassing it was for this guy to have a Bills fan put him in his place. Even the security guard had to fight a smile, but it turned to a grimace when he faced me again.

"Unfortunately, the rule is that the majority wins. If most of the fans around you are sitting, you should sit, too."

"What?!" Gemma cried out, throwing her hand toward the guard. "We're at a *football game*, for Christ's sake!"

Again, *adorable.*

The guy who caused the drama gloated, crossing his thick arms over his chest with a satisfied smirk. I wanted to wipe it off with my fist, but suddenly, Janet and Roy stood up in a unified motion.

Janet glared at the man, putting one arm around Gemma and holding her shoulders high. "It's the fourth quarter and we need to rally and win this thing." She looked at the crowd around us. "What do you say we cheer these boys to the finish?" And then, she glared pointedly at the man again. "*On our feet.*"

The security guard's eyebrows shot into his hairline at Janet's spunk, and like a slow, misshapen wave, everyone in that angry, pudgy man's row started to stand.

And then the row with the Bills family.

And then our row.

Until the entire section that could overhear what was happening was on their feet.

"Welp," the Bills kid said, still holding up his phone to record. "Looks like majority rules."

Everyone clapped and cheered, and though I didn't think it was possible, the man's face reddened even more. He swiped his beer out of the holder and stormed past the security guard and up the stairs, dodging popcorn and napkins being tossed at him on his way up.

The Bills kid high-fived me, tucking his phone away as I climbed back over my seat. A timeout was called on the field as Gemma looked up at me, her lips pulled to one side as her eyes sparkled under the stadium lights.

"What?" I asked, reaching for my beer.

"You were going to fight that guy for me."

"You think so, huh?" I took a drink. "Maybe I was just going to sit back and watch you fight your own battle."

She shook her head, little nose scrunching up again. "You were going to lay him out and get thrown out of the home opener game just to defend my honor."

"You upset about it?"

Gemma paused, eyes bouncing between mine like she was trying to find answers to some question she hadn't even asked yet. "No," she finally said. "I'm a little surprised by it, though."

"What, I don't look like the type who will stick up for his girl?"

She bit her lip, teeth rolling over the pink-stained skin as she fought a grin. "I guess chivalry isn't completely dead."

"Not tonight, it isn't, princess."

The way she was looking at me, I wanted her to watch me all night long. I wanted those eyes on me when the final whistle blew, when the door to her house closed behind us, when that tight, burnt-orange tank top was on her floor and those long, tan legs were hooked over my shoulders.

But those emerald pools ripped away at the sound of the ball being snapped, and as if nothing had even happened, all eyes were back on the field.

The game ended less than twenty minutes later to the tune of the Bears pulling a touchdown out of their ass and sealing their first regular season victory with a two-point conversion.

Gemma jumped into my arms as the entire stadium went nuts, and a roar far too deep and, if I was being honest, a tad bit terrifying, ripped from that little lady's throat like she was a linebacker on the team and not a five-foot-two fan in section 124. But I couldn't find it in me to do anything other than laugh.

At least, until we both realized she was in my arms.

One of her hands hooked around my neck while the other fist pumped into the air and high-fived every fan around her she could reach. Her legs were wrapped around me from where she'd jumped on me like a banshee, and when she finally turned to face me, chest heaving and smile splitting her face, we both stopped.

Time morphed, the roaring crowd around us dulled to something more of a distant whisper. The announcer went on, the celebration continued, but in that moment, all we could do was stand still.

And I felt it again.

I didn't know what it was, what to call it, how to name it and classify it and file it away.

I only knew it was something. Something different. Something *more*.

Gemma ran that free hand back through her hair, smile falling as her eyes landed on my lips, both of us breathing.

Both of us staring.

Her hand pressed into my chest, and she unhooked her ankles from where they were clasped behind my back, sliding down the front of me until her toes hit the ground again.

"Sorry," she murmured, pulling her hair over one shoulder as she peered up at me with pink cheeks. "I just... I was so excited when we won."

"Hey, it's all good," I said, tapping her nose. "Practice round, remember?"

She laughed nervously at that, eyes skirting down to her Keds before they climbed back up slowly to meet mine. And when they did, all that sass, that confidence, that fun? It was all gone.

Her eyes were wide, scared, fingers twirling in her hair as she chewed her bottom lip. I watched her swallow, the motion straining her delicate neck, and then she said something.

"What?" I asked, leaning down. The crowd was still loud and boisterous, an off-key chorus of the "Bear Down" fight song ringing out.

Gemma spoke again, but I still couldn't hear her.

"What was that?" I asked again, putting my ear right by her lips.

And of course, as soon as there was a lull in the noise, she screamed what she'd been saying all along.

"You wanna come back to my place?!"

A few people snapped their heads in our direction, smirks and laughs greeting us from all sides as Gemma flushed a deep red and folded in on herself. I chuckled, shaking my head as I watched her retreat.

"It really should be illegal for one woman to be this cute."

Her shoulders drooped, a smile breaking through as she shook her head, embarrassed.

"I agree," Janet said from behind her, squeezing Gemma's shoulder. "Alright, you two. Have fun tonight. The old folks are going to fight through this crowd and head home."

"It was so nice meeting you," Gemma said, wrapping Janet in a hug. "I can't wait to cheer on our boys all season with you."

"Just don't start showing up in body paint," Roy grumbled.

We all laughed at that.

Chapter 5

ZACH

My mind was reeling as we pushed through the crowd back out into the night, Gemma's hands tucked into the back pockets of her shorts. I could still feel the adrenaline of the game rushing through me, and now, that blood was pumping straight to another region in anticipation of what was about to happen next.

It'd been a while since I'd taken a girl home, or gone back to her place. Somewhere around twenty-eight, I got tired of the one-night stands. It wasn't that I hadn't had any since then, just that they were fewer and more far between.

And the thought of breaking that dry spell with Gemma was more than enough to get me hard before we'd even left the field.

I adjusted myself in my shorts, walking behind Gemma to the cab line, but when we climbed inside the cab to head back to her place, Gemma fell completely silent, her wide eyes watching the cars pass out her window.

I watched her twist her hands together in her lap, ignoring every text that lit up her phone. I couldn't help but notice most of them were from Belle.

And I also couldn't help but notice that Gemma was nervous.

She was *can't breathe, can't speak, can't look at me* nervous.

We pulled up to one of the sky-rise condominium buildings downtown less than half an hour after leaving our seats, even with the traffic, and Gemma hadn't spoken a single word to me in that time. Silence enveloped us still us we rode in the elevator up to the twenty-second floor.

With my upbringing, all I wanted to do was get inside that head of hers. I wanted to ask her what she was thinking, what she was feeling, what was making her palms sweat right now. She mentioned it'd been a while for *her*, too, since she'd been with someone — but I didn't know *why*.

Still, I didn't press her. From what she'd told me earlier in the night, she was a woman of control. So, I let her think, let her make her lists and her plans.

She didn't have to know that all that would go out the window the second I had her naked.

"This is me," she said finally, her voice a little raspy as she unlocked door 2206. She stepped inside, holding the door open for me, and once I stepped in after her, I let out a long whistle.

"Wow," I said, surveying the space. Chicago's downtown lights filled the condominium, even as Gemma walked around turning on lamp after lamp. That soft glow only seemed to highlight the space's modern appeal more.

I crossed the hardwood floor, passing her living area until I was standing at one of the floor-to-ceiling windows that overlooked the skyline. The river was also within view, the water reflecting the city lights, small boats still cruising under the bridges.

"Damn, girl," I said, scanning the view. "This is some pad."

She shrugged, still standing by the last lamp she'd turned on next to her couch. Her keys were clutched in one hand, the other rubbing the back of her neck. "Thanks. It's, uh..." She rolled her lips together. "I'm still getting used to it."

"Haven't lived here long?"

She shook her head, eyes falling to the floor. "I used to live in the suburbs... so it's a bit of a change."

"The 'burbs, huh? Guess that guy wasn't *completely* off with his name-calling earlier, then."

"Ugh, that guy sucked."

"He did," I agreed with a chuckle, tucking my hands in my pockets. I leaned against the window, and suddenly, a heated wave of energy fell over us like a blanket.

I let my eyes crawl up Gemma's legs, roaming over the tight fabric of her tank top before meeting her gaze. And as soon as my eyes locked on hers, she dropped her keys.

"Shit," she whisper-yelled, bending over to retrieve them quickly. She dropped them on the table, purposefully this time, running her hands back through her hair with an embarrassed smile before tucking her hands in her back pockets. "Uh, do you want something to drink?"

I didn't answer, but she crossed to the kitchen, anyway.

"I have... well," she said, propping her weight on one hip as she surveyed the contents of her fridge. "I don't have a whole lot, honestly."

The way her apartment was set up, the kitchen and living room were open and connected, making it easy for me to smile and watch her from across the room. I could see the panic settling in on her face as she scanned her fridge.

"I, uh, I have protein shakes, and water, and orange juice. I have some wine, I think," she said, letting the fridge close as she quickly pulled open a cabinet. There was one bottle of red wine inside, and she let out a relieved sigh. "Yes! I have wine."

She pulled the bottle down, holding it toward me.

"See? It's not beer, but hey, it's Italian." She laughed. It was a nervous, flittering sort of laugh.

I just smiled wider.

She swallowed hard, her eyes flicking from mine down to the hem of my jeans before she whipped around, reaching for her wine bottle opener.

"Thanks for coming over," she said, lining up the screw with the cork. Then, she cringed, turning to me. "Was that weird? Should I not do that?"

"Did it feel weird?"

"Kind of."

I raised both eyebrows in answer. "Well, what did I say earlier?"

"Don't do it if it feels weird." She sighed, leaning against the cabinet. "What if everything feels weird?"

"It won't," I assured her, pushing off the window. The poor girl was going to have a panic attack if I didn't help steer the energy here. "This place really is impressive, Gemma. What made you move here?"

Her eyes softened at that, which was strange, because it was almost as if she slipped on a mask in that moment. She turned to the bottle again, working the screw into the cork. "Belle lives a few floors up. I figured it'd be nice to know someone in a new place. Plus, she's my boss, and we work just around the corner. It's convenient."

"Your boss?"

She nodded. "She owns her own interior design firm. And I'm her assistant. Although, if you asked her, she'd tell you I'm more like a partner." Gemma smiled a bit at that. "She likes to do the design, the people stuff, and I take care of everything else. It's nice — fulfills all of my OCD needs."

I grinned, nodding. Taking in the cleanliness of her apartment, I was sure she wasn't joking about the OCD thing. And seeing as how her phone was literally full of lists, goals, plans, and rules? Yeah. It made sense.

"And you just moved in?" I asked after a moment, surveying her modern, all-white couch, and sleek television. The accents in her place were minimal — lots of silvers, grays, whites, beiges. There was a fuzzy gray rug under the sleek, geometric table in front of the couch, and just one, large canvas print hanging on the wall opposite the TV.

It looked like a model home, not one she lived in.

"I bought it about eight months ago."

"That explains the lack of photographs or any other indication that a human being lives here," I teased.

Gemma just continued working the bottle.

"What made you want to leave the 'burbs?"

The cork popped out of the bottle, and she dropped the opener with the cork still in it to the counter. "It's a long story, and I'm too sober to tell it. Can we change the subject?"

"We can," I said easily as I made my way over to the kitchen. I propped my elbows on the counter bar, watching her pour two glasses full of red wine. "What do you want to talk about?"

She handed me my glass, tilting hers up with a smile before she chugged half of it in one gulp.

"Cheers to you, too." I lifted my glass with a smirk, taking a sip.

"Music!" she said loudly, snapping her fingers. Her dark hair swung over her shoulders as she pranced over to a large speaker in the corner of the room. "I should put on music. What do you like to listen to? Here, I can just put on... this."

She tapped something on her phone, and a slow, sexy beat filled the room. When the first verse started, I couldn't help but chuckle.

Let's Get It On by Marvin Gaye.

Her eyes went wide, and she glanced at me over one shoulder. "Oh God, this is too much, isn't it? It's too cliché."

She clicked through her phone as I took another sip of my wine, watching her with a smile.

"I should have made a playlist. God, *why* did I not think of making a playlist?"

She was still talking to herself when I set my wine on the counter, crossing the room to where she stood. I traced the lines of her slender neck, her back, the hair she pulled over one shoulder as she shook her head.

"Probably because I have no *idea* what to put on a playlist for this sort of thing," she murmured to herself, still playing on her phone.

"What sort of thing?" I whispered into the back of her neck.

She jumped a little as my hands slipped around her hips from the back, pulling her flush against me. Every muscle in her body was stiff, her breath caught between an inhale and an exhale.

"Uh... this... um..." she swallowed, still holding her phone, still stiff as a board in my arms. "Oh, God."

"Such a religious woman," I teased.

"*Oh, God.*"

I laughed, spinning her in my arms until she was facing me. I took her phone from her hands, set it on top of the speaker, and slipped my hands into the back pockets of her jean shorts. Then, I settled my gaze on hers.

"Hey," I said, searching those endless green eyes of hers.

The way the low light of her lamps were reflected in them, I could see just the faintest hint of blue swirled around the pupils. But she couldn't hold my gaze, looking at my chest or the floor, instead.

"Look at me."

She shook her head.

"Gemma," I laughed her name, tilting her chin up with my knuckle. "Look at me."

When she finally did, it was the way a little girl looks at a closet door opening on its own in the dark. It was like I was every monster, every deep-rooted fear she'd ever known standing in front of her for the first time.

"Take a breath," I said, and I started with a deep inhale, hers mirroring my own. "Now, let it out."

She blew out a breath, and her shoulders slumped with it, her head hitting my shoulder. She let out a soft groan, shaking her head before lifting it to meet my gaze again.

"I'm sorry," she said on a sigh. "I just... I've never done this before. In theory, it seems so easy, but now that we're here..."

"It's scary."

She smiled. "So, *so* scary."

"If it helps, I'm a little scared, too."

Her eyes doubled at that. "*You?*" She laughed. "You don't seem scared at all."

"I am," I said, and I pulled one hand from her back pocket and held it between us. "See? I'm even shaking a little."

She eyed my trembling hand, then swatted it away, pushing my chest. "You're faking it."

I smirked. "Okay, maybe I'm not shaking," I said, wrapping her in my arms and pulling her flush against me again. Her breath caught, eyes flicking to my lips. "But I am nervous."

"Why?"

I chuckled. "Have you *seen* you?" Her eyes met mine then. "You're beautiful, Gemma. You may be nervous because it's been a while for you, but even if you'd just done this yesterday, you'd still feel what you're feeling right now. And you know what?" I shrugged. "It's kind of the best part."

"Feeling like I need to throw up is the best part of tonight?" She scrunched her nose. "You're not really selling it here."

I fought a smile, lifting her chin again, until our lips were just inches apart. "No, feeling *excited*." I swallowed, searching her eyes before my gaze landed on those full lips of hers I'd been dying to taste. "You're shaking because you want to touch me, because you want me to touch *you*. It's that rush of having someone's hands on your body, someone new, someone who makes your heart race and your breath shallow."

As if on cue, she let out a soft, shallow breath. "I don't know how to do this," she confessed, voice just above a whisper.

"Let me show you."

I slipped one hand over her neck, fingers crawling up until her hair was locked in my grip. I pulled — just a little, tilting her lips up toward mine — and then, when she was balanced on her toes, her sweet breath meeting my lips, I kissed her.

Her warm lips trembled under the pressure of mine, chills racing down her arms, but then she sighed, leaning into me as her body collapsed into mine. She fisted her hands in my t-shirt, and I tightened my grip in her hair. When she opened that little mouth of hers and let me slide my tongue inside, we both moaned, and all the blood in my body rushed to where I ached most.

With my hands holding her steady, I walked Gemma back until her ass hit the arm of her couch. As soon as it did, she lifted her legs, wrapping them around me and pulling my neck down so she could kiss me harder. Her mouth devoured mine, and when I sucked that bottom lip of hers between my teeth and let it go with a pop, I shook my head on a smirk.

"I thought you said you didn't know how to do this."

"I'm remembering."

The words were more of a pant, and then her hands were in my hair, pulling me back down to kiss her. I smirked, running my hands down her back to cup her ass and roll her against my hard on. We both groaned at that, and as much as I wanted to bury myself so deep inside her I'd need a map to find my way out, I knew I couldn't.

Not yet. Not tonight.

Gemma was nervous. She was feeling her way through dating for the first time in who knew how long. I didn't know if she'd been wrapped up in work, if someone had broken her heart, if she'd been in a long-term relationship or never had a boyfriend in her life.

All I did know was she was one of the most beautiful, most unique women I'd ever met in my life.

And I wanted to make her feel good.

I should have moved her to the bed. I should have taken my time, slowed down, stripped every piece of clothing off her with patience and reverence. But after a night of sitting next to her in those tiny little shorts, of watching her perfect breasts bounce in that tank top every time she jumped up and down, cheering for the team — I was past waiting.

"Lean back," I demanded, propping a pillow up on the couch.

When she slid back, she tried to move off the arm of the couch, but I clamped my hand down on her thigh.

"No," I said, taking her mouth in mine as I leaned her back. "That perfect ass stays here."

I pulled back with a wicked grin, Gemma watching me with a mixture of curiosity, want, and apprehension. With her ass still propped on the arm of the couch, she was inverted now, hips higher than where her head rested on the pillow.

I traced the arch in her back on my way back up, slipping my fingers in the band of her shorts and tugging her hips up a little more. She was so small, yet every inch of her was supple and curvy — it was a body unlike any I'd ever seen before.

Bending to kiss her exposed navel, I flipped the button on her jean shorts, tugging on her zipper and slipping the denim down off her hips. The way her thighs touched under the navy blue lace of her panties made me growl with want, and I lifted her leg, hooking it over my shoulder so I could kiss the inside of that thigh.

Gemma leaned up, watching me kiss her from under hooded lids, her lips parted. I tried to take my time, sucking and biting the tender, soft skin between her legs as I climbed toward the promise land. But the higher I kissed, the harder she breathed, her chest heaving and eyes widening as she watched me.

I paused, planting a feather-light kiss over the lace fabric that made her shutter before I let her leg drop and slid between her thighs. I leaned over, bending to meet her lips with mine.

"Just relax," I whispered, kissing her gently. "We're going to take it slow, okay? No sex tonight."

"I can do this," she said quickly.

"Oh, trust me, I know," I growled, biting her lower lip. "But tonight, I just want you to relax. I want you to remember what it's like to feel good." Then, I smirked. "Be a little selfish."

She blew out a breath on a laugh. "I don't know if I can just relax."

"Close your eyes," I said, pushing back to stand again. I ran my hands over the curves still hidden by her tank top, hooking my thumbs in the thin straps of her panties before tugging on them.

Gemma lifted her lips, letting me strip the lace off, and when she was fully exposed, I swallowed at the sight of her perfect pink pussy staring back at me.

She was still watching me, her breaths racking through her chest.

"Close your eyes," I said again, bending until my face was between her legs. I propped one leg on each of my shoulders, hands holding her hips in place.

She swallowed, still breathing hard as she finally did as I asked. She closed her eyes, leaning her head back against the pillow, her legs shaking where they hung over my shoulders. Slowly, with my hands massaging her hips, I pressed my lips to the tender skin just above her clit.

She shivered, letting out a long sigh, hands fisting in the fabric of the couch. I smiled, remembering how she'd had it on her list to shave for tonight. I would have buried my face between her legs regardless, but I swept my tongue over her freshly smooth skin with appreciation.

"Oh..." she moaned, hips bucking. "*Yes.*"

The way I had her bent over the couch, her hips still balanced on the arm while her head and shoulders rested on the cushions, I had the perfect view of her arched body. Even under the tank top, her breasts strained against her bra, heaving with every heated breath she drew.

Swirling my tongue over her clit, I let my hands climb from her hips up under her shirt. I traced the wire of her bra, slipping my fingers beneath it and grazing each hard nipple. She arched into my touch with a moan, and I took the cue, sucking her clit between my teeth and flicking her nipples at the same time.

A sharp cry left her lips, and she hissed, bucking her hips and writhing under my grasp.

My hard on ached for relief under my shorts, but I bit down the urge to say *fuck it* and give Gemma a *real* practice round. I'd take a cold shower later, or get my release when I was alone in my bed the next morning.

Tonight was about her.

With one hand still massaging her breast, I slipped the other hand under my mouth, brushing her entrance with just the tip of my pointer finger before I slipped it inside.

"Oh, God," she cried, hands flying into my hair. She rolled her hips, grinding her clit against my tongue, and I let her take the lead, let her use me the way she wanted to. "More."

I granted her wish, withdrawing my finger and sliding it back inside along with one more. She gasped, arching, hands fisting in my hair. The more I curled those fingers, the more she ground her hips. Around and around — my tongue on her clit, her hips on the couch, my fingers inside her — a hurricane symphony of movement until her entire body tensed.

"Yes, yes, don't stop, oh... *fuck*." She gasped the last word, pussy clenching around my fingers as I tensed my tongue and put as much pressure as I could on her sensitive clit. With that, she tightened around my fingers even more before everything let go at once.

She shook, crying out, hands flying out of my hair and into her own as she rode out her orgasm. I lifted her hips more, digging my fingers even deeper to make it last as long as it could, and when she was spent, when her legs fell lax on either side of my face, I withdrew. Slowly, carefully, one finger at a time as I kissed the insides of her thighs and climbed back up to stand.

Gemma just laid there, hair and hands sprawled out, legs flopped over the arm.

She sighed, eyes fluttering open, and when she saw me standing over her with a satisfied smirk, she laughed.

"Wow."

"How was that?"

"Um, fucking incredible," she said, leaning up on her elbows. She squeezed her knees together, suddenly aware of how spread eagle she'd been. "Can you help me up?"

She reached a hand forward, and I grabbed it in mine, tugging until she was standing. Her legs gave out under the weight, but I caught her, holding her against my chest as we both laughed.

"I'm a little weak," she said. Then, her hand brushed over where my cock was still straining against my shorts. "Oh," she breathed, eyes locking onto mine. "And you're a little hard."

"Just a little."

"Do you wanna..."

"Yes," I said quickly. "*God,* yes. But, not tonight. Tonight was about making you feel good, about getting you back into the swing of things." I spanked her still-bare ass. "How do you feel?"

"Tired," she answered with a sated smile. Her eyes flicked between mine. "I had so much fun tonight, Zach. I haven't had fun like this in... well, I don't even remember."

"I had fun, too," I told her, returning her smile.

Ask her on a date.

The thought hit me out of nowhere, and as soon as it popped in my mind, I couldn't think of anything else. I wanted to see her again. I wanted more than just a practice round.

I didn't want her to take another guy to the next game.

I wanted her to take me again.

Gemma watched me, like she was debating the same thoughts I was. Or maybe like she couldn't believe I was standing in her living room, that she was half-naked in my arms.

"Gemma..." I started, but when she yawned, all I could do was laugh. "Wow, that tired, huh?"

"You wore me out."

"You seem so upset about it."

"Furious, really."

She gave me a sleepy smile, pecking my lips before she bent to retrieve her panties and shorts. She pulled them both on as I leaned back against the wall and watched, trying to think of what to say next.

"So," she said, tucking her hair behind her ear when she was dressed again. Her hands slipped right back into her back pockets, her eyes searching mine. "I guess this is the end of the practice round, huh?"

"I guess so."

She walked toward the door, and I followed — though my feet dragged like they were made of lead. When Gemma opened her front door and held it open with one hip, her cheeks still flushed, the absolute last thing I wanted to do was leave.

"Thank you," she said, watching me. "This was fun. It was... well, it was exactly what I needed."

"Glad I could help."

I leaned down, pressing my lips to hers and holding that kiss for as long as she'd let me. I wasn't ready to leave. I wasn't ready to let her go.

I knew she had a plan. I knew what I signed up for. But now that I'd spent a night with her, now that I'd had a taste, I couldn't just walk away.

I couldn't just let some other guy touch her after the next game, the way I'd touched her tonight.

Our kiss was casual at first, but the longer I held my lips to hers, the more she softened. When I slid my hand through her hair, cradling the back of her head, she melted into the touch. A soft sigh left her lips when I pulled back from the kiss, eyes searching hers — and that sigh was just enough encouragement to make me open my big, stupid mouth.

"Take me to the next game."

Gemma blinked, her sated smile slipping. "What?"

"Don't get on that stupid app again," I said. "Take me."

She swallowed, eyes doubling in size as she pulled them from my gaze and down to the floor. There was a touch of something there... something she'd been hiding all night. It was in the bend of her brows, in the slump of her shoulders, in the pull of her mouth to one side.

She'd been hurt.

God, how I wanted to kill whoever hurt her.

Gemma shook it off — whatever *it* was — and when she looked back at me, it was with a seemingly confident smile. "Hey, this was the *practice* round, remember?"

"Bullshit."

"Look, you knew the deal when you asked me for this," she pointed out, still smiling. "Don't go changing the rules on me now."

"You and your rules."

"I'm doing this, okay?" she said, resolved. "I have a plan, and I'm sticking to it. Besides..." Her voice faded, hand playing with her hair over her shoulder. "I can't do more than one night right now. With anyone."

"Why?"

Gemma smiled then, as if whatever had passed over her was gone now. "So many questions all of a sudden."

"I know. You should take me to the next game so you can answer them all."

Gemma laughed, pressing one hand on my chest, and I let that hand walk me backward until I was in the hallway and she was standing in her doorway.

"You're serious, aren't you?" I asked. I couldn't even hide my jaw on the floor.

"Look, it may not make sense to you, but I'm not trying to date. I'm not trying to *fall in love* or whatever. I'm just trying to watch football."

"And get laid."

Her cheeks flushed. "Yes."

"Well, we didn't get all the way there tonight," I pointed out. "Maybe you need another practice round. Just in case."

She gave me a pointed look.

"What?" I threw my hands up. "I'm looking out for you here. Really, you should be thanking me."

She shook her head. "Okay, and on *that* note, I think it's time to call it."

"Gemma."

"Tonight was amazing," she said, cutting me off. "I had so much fun. Be safe getting home, okay?"

And even though my ego was bruised and beat to shit, I couldn't help but smile as this gorgeous woman kicked me out of her place less than five minutes after I'd brought her to climax with my face between her legs.

I stopped her door from shutting all the way with one hand, shaking my head as I lowered my gaze to hers. "You are absolutely maddening, Gemma Mancini."

She cocked a brow. "Aren't you glad the practice round is over, then?" A slow smile spread across her lips, and she bit that bottom one like she knew it was the one thing that drove me absolutely insane. "Goodnight, Zach."

With that, she twiddled her fingers, and I stepped back enough to let her close the door.

Well, shit.

For a moment, I just stood there, staring at the four black numbers that hung underneath the peephole on her door. I wondered if she was still on the other side, watching me, waiting for what I'd do next.

Just in case, I smiled.

Scrubbing a hand over my head, I took a few steps back, pointing my finger at the peephole. "This isn't over," I said, turning on my heel toward the elevator. "You and I both know it isn't."

I heard a giggle on the other side of the door, but she didn't respond. She didn't have to. Gemma might have thought our *practice round* was over, that tonight was just one date to kickstart the long line of ones she'd have all season long.

But I'd never met anyone like her, and I'd had more fun in the few hours we'd spent together than I'd had in the past twelve years.

If she thought I was letting go that easy, she was in for a rude awakening.

The elevator dinged, doors sliding open, and as I stepped inside, I readjusted my still-hard cock under my shorts. I could still taste Gemma on my tongue, feel her writhing under my touch, and there was no way that after that first taste I was just going to walk away from her.

There was another home game next Sunday — just one week away — and I *would* be there beside her. One way or another, I'd be there.

That was a promise I could keep.

Chapter 6

GEMMA

"I think you should see a therapist."

Belle was dead serious as she judged me over the cup of coffee I'd just poured her on Monday morning. I laughed, shaking my head and filling my own cup before rummaging in the fridge for creamer. She came over before work every morning, but she'd come *extra* early today — punishment for me ignoring all her texts last night.

She wanted the dirt, and I wasn't escaping until I gave it to her.

"Why do I need to see a therapist?" I asked. "Because I stuck to the plan *you* set in place for me?"

"No, because you kicked a tall, sexy, pussy-rocking god out of your apartment right after he ate you out like he hadn't eaten in weeks and you were a steak dinner."

"That's what I was supposed to do!"

"No," Belle said, holding up one manicured finger in protest. "What you were *supposed* to do is have fun, watch football with a new friend, and get an orgasm that wasn't battery-operated. Where in that plan was there any fine print that said you had to boot the poor guy out before his lips were even dry from eating you out? Or that you weren't allowed to see him again?"

"If I saw him again, it would be more than just a game with a friend. It would be *dating*. Which, as we discussed, is off the table."

"Why is getting banged more than once by the same guy dating?" Belle argued. "I see it more as insurance. I mean, you *know* he's fun, you know he's going to stand up for you if shit goes down at the game, and you also know he's going to rail you until the headboard breaks, if you give him the chance."

I laughed. "God, he really would."

"I KNOW. So, let the guy, for the love of Christ."

"I can't," I said, folding my hands over the steaming mug of coffee as I took the barstool next to Belle.

"Why not," Belle whined, kicking her little feet.

I laughed. "Because, okay?" My smile slipped, heart squeezing like the ghosts of my past had just wrapped it in a tight fist. I traced the handle of my mug with my pointer finger, swallowing. "I'm just not ready to take it past a one-night thing right now, okay? Last night was fun, but it was also really hard for me." I looked at my best friend then, pleading for understanding. "Maybe I'm being stupid, or crazy, but I'm trying. And right now, this is what I've got to give. We agreed — a different guy every game. *That's* the plan I made, that's what I agreed to, and that's what my heart and my head have been able to wrap themselves around. I can't see past that right now."

Belle watched me, eyes softening under bent brows as she reached over and squeezed my knee. "For the record, I *do* think you're crazy for not seeing him again," she said with a sigh. "But, I also have no idea what it's like to go through what you have. And even if I don't get it, I support you. Always."

I covered her hand on my knee and squeezed. "Thank you."

"So, does this mean it's time to pick the next guy?" Belle bounced in her chair, waggling her brows.

"I can see you're still really heartbroken over my decision," I mocked, sliding my phone across the counter toward her. "Here, why don't you see if shopping for the next one makes you feel better."

"Retail therapy?" Belle pressed a hand to her heart, pretending to be touched. "My favorite. You *do* love me."

"Shut up and swipe."

She lit up as soon as the screen on my phone did, pulling up the dating app as I rolled my eyes and took the first sip of my coffee. As the hot liquid settled in, warming my bones, Belle swiped and remarked on the messages I'd gotten over the week.

But all my thoughts drifted to Zach.

Last night had been everything I thought it *wouldn't* be. It was fun. It was easy. It was comfortable. I'd laughed more than I had in months, and I'd had Zach's face buried between my legs until I came in what I was almost positive was the best orgasm I'd ever had.

Literally, ever.

We steered clear of the heavy stuff. I didn't have to tell him about Carlo, and he didn't ask. He didn't divulge his entire life story, and I didn't feel the need to fill the silence by asking *him* anything.

We watched the game. We drank a few beers. He came back to my place. We hooked up. He left.

Perfect.

I took a sip of coffee, nodding when Belle asked me about a guy who'd messaged. She took the reins as I let myself be happy about a night well spent. My eyes flashed to my couch, and I smiled, heat creeping up my neck.

I could still feel his hands on my hips, my breasts, his tongue sweeping over my inner thighs. I could feel his fingers inside me, curling, pumping, his mouth sucking me hard in sync with his hand.

I was so nervous, and he knew exactly what he needed to do to kill my anxiety.

He took the lead.

He blew my *mind*.

And then, he stopped me when I tried to do the same.

I felt a little bad for that, for Zach leaving before he let me repay the favor he'd so graciously gifted me. He said he wanted last night to be for me, that I should be selfish — and I listened.

Because when was the last time anyone had told me that that was okay?

When was the last time — or hell, the *first* time — I'd ever thought of me? Of *only* me?

It was like without asking a single question, without hearing a single story about my life, Zach understood me. All he had to do was look at me, and he got it.

I'd never known that level of understanding.

And *that*, right there, was the danger in what I was doing.

My coffee grew bitter when the realization hit me, how close I'd been to going against the number-one rule I'd set after Carlo passed away.

Zach made me feel good. He made me laugh, made me happy — and I wanted more. I wanted to see him again, to go on a real date, to take him to the next game, to ask him about his past and his future and see if we could maybe fit together. When he'd asked to see me again last night, I almost said yes — without hesitation. He said he wanted to see me again and I knew without a doubt that I felt the same.

Which, again, was why I needed rules.

He was the first guy I'd taken to a game, my *practice* round, and already, I felt myself slipping into those forbidden feelings.

It was easy to fall in love. It was harder to climb out of it.

And I didn't want to have to dig my way out of that hole again.

So, as much as I wanted to see him again, I said no when he asked. I held onto that first, hard and fast rule.

Last night was it for us. It was fun, it was surface-level, and it was feelings-free.

Like I said before — perfect.

Still, there was a flutter in my chest as that last thought passed through, almost as if my heart was laughing at me. Because even though we hadn't talked about Carlo, Zach had seen right threw me. He'd known *without* words that I was nervous, and he'd taken control. He'd given me what I needed.

I was already in too far, after just one night.

That's how stupid my heart was.

"Alright, I think this guy is in," Belle said. She handed me my phone, tapping the screen to show me the guy's profile again. "He's checking his schedule now to see if he has to volunteer, because of course he's perfect and gives his free time to the kids down at the Boys & Girls Club."

I laughed as Belle visibly swooned.

"I bet he'll want you to call him Daddy when he's banging you."

"Gross," I said, half-laughing, half-wincing. "What do I do if he really wants that?"

Belle blinked. "You call him Daddy. Obviously."

"I absolutely will not do that."

"Hey, you say that now," she said, picking up her coffee and taking a tiny sip with a smirk. "But when your wrists are cuffed to the headboard and you've got vibrating clamps on your nipples, you'd be surprised what words come out of your mouth."

"I think it's *you* who needs a therapist."

"Just see what he said." Belle waved me off, pointing to the new notification that had just come through on the app. When I opened it, I smiled.

"He's in."

"BOOM!" Belle high-fived me. "Looks like you've got your first *real* round. Hope you got enough practice last night."

I swiped back to the guy's profile, smiling as I read through his bio. He'd only lived in Chicago for a couple of years, was an accountant by day, and a self-proclaimed movie buff by night. He had sandy-blond hair, bright blue eyes, and a chin that gave Clark Kent a run for his money.

He was hot.

But somewhere in the pit of my stomach, I was a little disappointed.

Because he wasn't Zach.

As if I'd summoned the object of my affection with my stupid, private slip of the mind, a text message from Zach popped up over the top of the app.

- I should be making you breakfast right now. -

I smiled, tapping on his text to open it full screen. Belle frowned, leaning over my shoulder and lighting up when she saw who it was.

"Oh my God! He's already texting you?!" She checked the time on her own phone. "It's not even seven in the morning yet. Oh, *girl*, what did you *do* to him last night?"

I laughed, typing out my text back to him. "I didn't do anything. Other than tell him no. And we all know guys hate that."

"And love it, all at once."

"Exactly," I said, sending my text. "He'll be over me as soon as another girl rejects him."

- I don't do breakfast. And I can make my coffee just fine on my own. -

- Stop acting like you didn't have the best time of your life last night and take me to the game this week. -

- I did have fun. But preseason is over, my friend. It's time for the real thing now. -

I smirked, clicking back over to the app and taking a screen shot of my next date's profile — Benjamin.

Then, I sent that screenshot to Zach.

- Meet Ben, real round number one. -

The little bubbles popped up like Zach was typing, but then they disappeared, and no text came through.

"You're ruthless," Belle said, shaking her head with a bit of a smile as she sipped down the last of her coffee. "Okay. My ass needs to shower before work. Meet you downstairs in a half hour?"

"I'll have the to-go cups."

"Bless you."

When Belle was gone, I curled my hair and put on my makeup, all while eyeing my phone. When it did buzz again, it was Benjamin telling me he couldn't wait for Sunday. He finished his message with a *Have a great week, beautiful. See you Sunday.*

Nothing else came through from Zach.

I should have felt satisfied at that, that I'd gotten the point through with my last text to him. I should have been smiling as Belle and I walked the few blocks to the office, should have still been on a high from the night before.

But instead, my stomach felt heavy and tight, almost like it was being dragged along behind me on the sidewalk.

I'd gotten what I wanted. Zach was gone, practice round achieved, and now — it was game time. *For real.*

Ready, or not.

And I was *definitely* not.

ZACH

"Oh, boy."

Doc crossed one arm over his chest, balancing the elbow of the other on top as he scrubbed the five o'clock shadow coming through on his chin. His eyes were fixed on the tickets I was proudly holding up in my hand.

Season tickets.

For the Chicago Bears.

In the seats right next to Gemma's.

"Am I brilliant, or am I fucking brilliant?" I asked, slapping the tickets against my palm before holding them up again.

"You're something, alright."

It was Thursday afternoon, a full four days since I'd had my lips on Gemma's in her apartment. Doc had asked me to come in a little earlier than usual, to get the bar ready for Thursday night football, but before we could even start, I had to tell him my master plan.

"Does she know?" Doc asked, sliding up behind the counter to start making the mixer juices for the night.

I scoffed, tucking the tickets in my pocket. "Of course not. That's part of what makes it so genius. I'm just going to show up on Sunday."

"She wouldn't *give* you a second date, so you're taking it."

"Precisely."

Doc smirked, mixing up our sweet and sour juice. "Were you born stupid, or did you just get this way with time?"

"It sounds crazy," I admitted.

"Because it is."

"*But.*" I continued with a smile. "Sometimes crazy is necessary — especially when it comes to a girl like Gemma. She's not impressed by the easy, by the normal. And though she hasn't told me what happened in her past, I can tell she's been hurt before. Whoever had her last, he messed her up." I cracked my neck. "I can't fix that, but I can show her that I want my own chance to prove I can be more than he was."

Doc lined up the mixers and juices, working through unlocking the taps on the beers and wine next. There was a sideways grin on his face as he shook his head. "Well, you are persistent. I'll give you that."

"Thank you."

"But, this girl isn't a potential employer," he said. "She's a woman. And from what you told me about her, she's the kind of woman who makes lists, and plans, and then sticks to them." Doc leaned a hip against the bar, crossing his arms. "You may think you're going to woo her with this move, show you want her. But, you're messing with her master plan," he reminded me. "Which might just piss her off."

I scratched my head, letting out a heavy sigh. I knew Doc was right. Hell, I knew it when I was doing my research online, trying to track down that couple who sat next to us at the game. When I told them what I was trying to do, they were eager to help — well, Janet was, at least. Roy seemed perturbed, but also like he would do anything to see Janet happy and smiling.

I liked that about him.

And *she* was all about helping me out — especially since, as she had reminded me, she and Roy had a second pair of season tickets just a few rows up from the ones they sold me.

Janet said what I was doing was romantic.

Roy said I was an idiot.

Neither of them were wrong.

I knew it was stupid. I knew it had the potential to blow up in my face. But none of that mattered, because the one thing I knew more than anything was that I wasn't ready to let Gemma go.

"You're probably right," I conceded. But then, I smiled, cutting open a box of Blue Moon with my cutter. "But she *is* super fucking adorable when she's angry, so maybe this is a win-win for me."

Doc laughed.

We fell into our routine then, stocking the coolers, pulling out the bar mats, setting up the old bar games, getting the televisions situated on the right channels. The entire time, Doc hummed along to Bob Dylan, and I thought of Gemma.

I'd never had a woman infuriate me so much within the first week of knowing her.

She kicked me out with a smile on her face, after a night where I knew for a fact that she'd had just as much fun as I had. Still, I kind of loved it.

Gemma was challenging.

She had a plan, and she proved to me the next morning that she was serious about sticking with it. When she sent me the screenshot of the guy she'd *already* lined up for the next game — less than twelve hours after I'd left her place — it took everything in me not to crush my phone in the death grip I had.

I didn't respond, but that didn't mean I gave up.

Now *I* had a plan, too.

There was a fat chance in hell that I'd let *Benjamin* get my girl. Yeah, I'd only had one night with her but I felt that kind of possessiveness, anyway. I wasn't done with Gemma. I was far from it.

And maybe she didn't want to admit it, but she was far from done with me, too.

"Oh, hey, Doc," I said once the citrus wedges were cut. "Didn't you want to talk to me about something?"

He wiped his brow with a rag, chest heaving a little from pulling all the barstools down. "What?"

"At dinner," I reminded him. "You said you wanted to talk to me about something."

Doc blinked, wiping the rag down his face this time. "Oh, it's nothing that can't wait. I'll talk to you about it next week."

"You sure?" I asked, watching him. "I mean, I'm here now. Doors don't open for another half hour."

"I'm sure. I've got some paperwork to handle in the back. Can you finish up out here?"

He wouldn't look at me, and my stomach dropped to the floor at what that might mean. Doc was an honorable man. He looked you in the eyes when he talked to you — always.

I had a feeling that what he had to tell me wasn't good.

I had a feeling it had something to do with my paycheck.

If he did have to let me go, it would be harder on Doc than it would be on me. Maybe he couldn't bring himself to do it yet.

"Alright," I conceded with a nod. "Yeah, I can take care of this. Go ahead."

Doc waved his rag in thanks, tossing it over his shoulder before he headed to the back office.

I wanted to know what he had to say, but there was no rushing Doc. He was like my dad in that respect, and I knew that when he was ready, he'd have the conversation with me — no matter how tough.

So, I filed those thoughts away, focusing instead on balancing the till in my drawer for the night. And as the pre-game show came on for the Thursday night game, the Kansas City Chiefs versus the Cleveland Browns, I couldn't help but smile thinking about a different game that would come on Sunday.

Oh, Gemma.

I hope you're ready to play.

Chapter 7

GEMMA

"I think I'm going to throw up," I told Belle, bouncing a little as I waited at the same totem I'd met Zach under a week before. My new date, Ben, would be here any moment.

And my body was rebelling.

"I love how last week you hung up on *me* in this same scenario. Now, you're interrupting my TV time."

"I don't think I'm ready for this," I said, ignoring her jokes. I couldn't find it in me to joke right now.

Belle sighed. "Hey, talk to me. What's different this week? What has you feeling weird?"

I swallowed down the sticky knot in my throat, eyes bouncing over the crowd as I scanned the faces for Ben's. I wanted to tell Gemma why it felt different, why I suddenly felt like my plan was impossible to stick to. But the truth was, I didn't really know myself.

"Zach just… it didn't feel like a date. It felt like hanging out with this smart-ass guy who I met at the bar."

"Do you think it's the online dating thing that's bugging you?"

I thought about it, digesting her suggestion. Ben had texted me throughout the week, and we'd even talked on the phone last night for over an hour. He seemed like a nice guy. He was funny, sweet, easy to talk to.

"No, I don't think so."

"Is it because you like Zach and wish it was him there instead?"

"No," I answered quickly, rolling my eyes. "He was fun, and he served his purpose. Practice round, remember?"

"Uh-huh," Belle mused, clearly not convinced.

Zach hadn't texted me since I sent him the picture of Ben. And though I'd had a *very* vivid dream about him on my couch the other night, I hadn't texted him, either. It didn't matter that I wanted to. What mattered was that I was staying true to my original goal when I agreed to all of this.

New guy every game. Make a few friends, watch football, drink beers, engage in some touching. I'd had so much fun that night with Zach. I *knew* I could have just as much fun with Ben tonight.

So why was I freaking out?

I tapped my finger against my bottom lip, stomach tilting. It didn't make sense. I'd made my pre-game check list and ticked everything off. I was following the plan I'd made. My anxiety should be in check.

"Gemma," Belle said, her voice softer. "Do you think... I know I was joking with you about seeing someone, a therapist or something along those lines, but... do you think maybe you really do need to?"

"Why would I need to see someone?"

She cleared her throat. "I'm just saying, what happened with Carlo... it was—"

"Fine," I finished for her, stomach twisting into an even tighter knot at the sound of his name. His eyes flashed in my mind — bright at first, like the night we met, and then dull and hollow, like the night he died. "It was fine, okay? People die. It's part of life."

"Yeah, but he was thirty-five. It's not like he was eighty and this was expected." She paused. "And he hurt you, Gemma. He cheated on you."

My nose flared. "Thanks. I almost forgot how that all went down, so glad you could remind me."

"You know I didn't mean it like that."

"I know, I just..." I sighed, pinching the bridge of my nose. This was what happened when I felt out of control. I tilted toward anger, toward being irrational, and I said and did things I would come to regret. "I'm sorry. I didn't mean to snap."

I paused, taking a deep breath.

"I'll be okay. I'm just nervous, I guess."

"You know I'd go with you," Belle whispered. "If you ever changed your mind and wanted to go talk to someone. Just say the word."

"Thank you," I whispered back, and for a moment, I considered it. Belle was the only one who knew about Carlo's infidelity. Not even my parents knew. Of course, they wouldn't be at the top of my list of people to tell. Mom would probably blame me, and Dad would just try to use a quote from one of their books or speeches to motivate me to move on with my life. He'd try to convince me that his infidelity was just a hurdle in life, one of many that people were confronted with and it was how you overcame adversity that determined a person's strength of character. Blah, blah, fucking blah.

I'd heard every line from *Making It: How Our Relationship Survived Against All Odds* in one way or another in my life.

Talking to them seemed impossible. Talking to my grandpa was, too, since he was gone. But could I talk to *someone* about it? To a stranger?

And what good would it do, anyway? I'd been fine. My life had carried on without him. I was excelling at work. I'd lost weight and toned up. I'd started eating better. I was sleeping fine.

I'm fine.

"Oh, shit," I murmured, spotting Ben in the crowd. He was still searching for me. "He's here."

"You can bail, if you want to," Belle said. "I'll be your way out. Say I have explosive diarrhea and can't even get to the store to get Gatorade to hydrate myself. Say you're my emergency contact in this situation."

I paused. "Okay, first, that's disgusting." I chuckled then, picturing the scene. "But thank you." Ben spotted me, tossing up his hand in a wave. "Besides, he's already seen me."

"You going to be okay?"

I sighed, forcing a smile and waving back at Ben. "Yeah. I think so."

"Go get that pussy licked, Tiger."

"I hate you."

Belle just laughed and ended the call, leaving me to face my first real date since I was seventeen. And it didn't matter that I'd convinced myself in my head that this little *plan* was "not dating." Yes, keeping it to one night meant I wasn't engaging in any kind of relationship. But still, I was meeting a guy, for an event, with the intention of sleeping with him. It was a date.

And it was the first *official* one in my adult life.

Unless you count Zach...

I shook my head, because *no* — he definitely did not count. That was hanging out with a friend. That was watching the game.

That was having the best orgasm of my life...

My cheeks flushed, heat still crawling down my neck when Ben finally reached me, a wide grin on his perfect, Ken Doll face.

"Look at you," he said, eyes washing over my outfit.

It was a little cooler tonight than it had been last week, so I wore jeans instead of shorts. But they were ripped up and down my thighs, and I'd worn burnt-orange fishnets underneath them that showed through the holes. Paired with my Bears jersey, tied in a knot at the front, I had a cute, casual look.

"And..." My face fell as I took in his attire. "Look at *you*."

He was wearing a Detroit Lions t-shirt.

As in, *not* a Chicago Bears t-shirt.

"Ah, yeah," Ben said, rubbing the back of his neck with an apologetic shrug. "Did I forget to mention I'm not a Bears fan?"

I blinked. "Why would you message me to *come* to a Bears game if you're not a fan."

"You said you needed someone to sit with you at the next home game," he pointed out. "Which just happened to be against my hometown. I did tell you I moved here from Detroit just a couple of years ago, right?"

I blinked again. "You did."

Ben cocked a brow, smiling like he didn't just show up to a Bears game wearing the away team's logo. And I just stood there, staring at him, wondering if I could still take Belle up on her offer.

Calm down, Gemma. It's not that big of a deal. He's still the same guy you've been talking to.

I forced a breath, and a smile, looping my arm through Ben's when he offered it. As we walked toward the stadium, I reminded myself why I was doing this in the first place.

I didn't want to fall in love. I didn't *need* a man to survive. But, I missed that human connection. I missed flirting, and talking, and having someone to watch the game with who actually cared about football. I missed the feel of a man's hands on my body, of his lips on my skin.

The memory of Zach's mouth hot on my center flashed in my mind like the brightest lights, and just like that, in a split second, it was gone.

But my blush was not.

"Hey, I hope I didn't upset you with this," Ben said once we were inside the gates and climbing toward our seats. He gestured to his shirt. "I'll take it off, if you want. Hell, I'll go buy a Bears jersey right now."

I smiled, squeezing his arms. "While I wouldn't mind seeing you take this off," I said tugging on the fabric. "It's okay. It might be kind of fun to have a little friendly competition."

"Should we place a bet on it?"

"Hmmm... what would you wager?"

He pulled us over to a beer stand, fishing his wallet out. "Bud Light okay?"

I nodded, and he paid the vendor, handing me the aluminum can as we started walking again.

"How about this. If the Lions win, you owe me a strip tease."

I laughed, spitting out a little of my beer. "A strip tease, huh?" I asked, surveying him. "Real original."

"You scared you'll have to pay up?"

I narrowed my eyes then. "My Bears won't lose to the *Lions*. You've got a deal. And *when* we win, it's *you* who owes me a strip tease."

"You really can't wait to get this shirt off me, can you?"

I laughed, leading the way to our seats with relief washing over me. Ben was funny. He was charming. And he definitely wasn't hard on the eyes.

I glanced back at him as we shimmied through the row to our seats, and I smiled.

See? Everything according to plan.

But when I turned back around, my heart skipped, and the universe laughed in my face as I blinked, again and again, to make sure what I was seeing was real.

"There you are," Zach said, a stupid grin on his face as he stood to let Ben and me pass. He was wearing a white Bears jersey, the sleeves tight against his tan, bulging biceps. His hair was mussed, the stubble on his chin thicker than the last time I'd seen him.

He was all sex — the way his hair fell, the way he stood, the way his eyes hung under hooded lids, the way he licked his bottom lip as he watched me. My stomach did a little flip for joy when his eyes slid down to my waist and back up again, but I stamped that feeling down with a hard, heavy shoe.

He was *not* supposed to be here.

"It's almost kick-off," Zach said when I didn't acknowledge his first greeting.

Ben ran into the back of me, because I'd stopped dead in front of the empty seat next to the one Zach was standing in front of. It was the seat Roy should have been in. And the one Zach was occupying belonged to Janet.

He grinned wider at my dumbfounded expression.

"Hey, man," Zach said, extending his hand past me to where Ben stood, waiting. "I'm Zach."

"Ben," he responded, confusion in his voice. He looked at me, but I couldn't stop shooting lasers via eyeball beams at the man I was never supposed to see again.

Everyone stood for the national anthem, jolting me out of my daze, and I wiggled past Zach as he continued to gloat. I took the seat next to him, letting Ben have the same seat Zach had last game. We recited the anthem — the words morphed in my ears, since my heartbeat was currently taking up all the available space — and at the end, the entire stadium cheered.

I didn't.

I poked Zach hard in the ribs.

"Ouch!" he said, rubbing the spot where I'd assaulted him. But then, he laughed. "What was that for?"

"Don't play dumb. What are you *doing* here?" I whisper-yelled.

Ben was focused on the field, and when he looked over at me, I smiled, leaning into him.

"You ready for your Lions to lose?" I sang.

He laughed. "We'll see."

Once his attention was back on the field, I glared at Zach again, waiting for an answer.

"I'm doing the same thing you are," he said casually. "Watching the game."

"Why are you watching the game *here*?"

He shrugged. "I told you, same as you."

"No, not same as me," I argued. "I have season tickets."

Zach smiled big enough to show his stupid dimple then, raising one brow like he was waiting for me to catch on. When I didn't say anything, he leaned down, his breath hot on my ear. "So do I."

"What?!"

I tried to whisper again, but I'd apparently failed. Ben cast a curious glance toward me first, before eyeing where Zach stood behind me. He put his arm around me possessively, tucking me into his side.

"Everything okay?"

His eyes were still on Zach's, who was just grinning like a stupid, smug, son-of-a-bitch.

"Everything's fine," I clipped, focusing on the next play so Ben would do the same. We watched it together, me cheering and teasing him when we sacked the Lions' quarterback. When the play was over, I leaned back toward Zach.

"How can you possibly have season tickets?" I asked, gesturing to his seats. "*Those* season tickets."

"Bought them from some friends," Zach answered easily.

My jaw dropped then, and I turned to face him fully. "You bought their tickets from them?! Zach!" I smacked his arm. "How could you do that? They've had those seats for *sixteen years,* and season tickets for twenty-two. How could you take that away from them? They could miss the playoffs, if we make it. All because of you!"

Zach was obviously not fazed by my outrage, because he just watched me like I was an adorable puppy. And when my rant was over, my chest still heaving, he tapped my nose with his pointer finger before aiming it up a few rows behind us.

I looked up where he was pointing, and there were Janet and Roy staring back at the two of us, Janet waving excitedly with a knowing smile as Roy sipped from his soda with a visible scowl.

"They have those seats, too. Remember?" Zach said, and when I was facing him again, he shrugged. "And they wanted to help."

"Help *what* exactly?"

"Help me get the girl. Obviously."

I rolled my eyes with the loudest, most annoyed huff I could manage, crossing my arms and turning to face the field again. Ben eyed me, and I reached over to squeeze his hand. Everyone was starting to sit, now that the energy from kick-off had settled, and we followed suit.

For three full plays, I didn't look at Zach. I didn't acknowledge him. I tried to pretend he didn't exist. But all my stupid brain could do was toss his words over and over in my head like some loud, wet sneakers in a clothes dryer.

"You're wasting your time," I finally whispered to him, snatching my beer from the holder.

"We'll see," Zach mused, and he tapped the neck of his bottle to mine without asking, lifting his own bottle to his lips.

Before I could respond, our wide receiver made a catch, and my eyes snapped to the field. "Go!" I yelled. "Go, go, go!"

Everyone in our section was on their feet, cheering the receiver on as he ran toward the end zone our seats were at. He was taken down at our twenty, running the ball for a full thirty-two yards.

"Yes!" I was screaming, throwing high-fives around to everyone wearing a Bears shirt.

This. This was what I loved about being at the game, instead of watching from a bar or my couch. Everyone cheered together, and we were all invested.

"Hell yeah!" I screamed, bumping fists with a young kid behind me. When I turned to Zach, I high-fived him before I realized I'd done so, immediately yanking my hand away and glaring at him.

"Now I see why Janet and Roy said these were the best seats in the house."

Warmth trickled down, like his words were rain and they'd fallen from a cloud above my head. I hated the way my stomach tilted, the way my throat tightened, all because of the way he looked at me.

The way he'd looked at me since the day we met.

I didn't respond, leaning in to Ben again, instead.

"Hope you're practicing those stripper moves," I teased, sticking my tongue out at Ben.

He laughed. "Hey, don't go making assumptions now. The game's just getting started."

I squeezed his arm, the high from the play still running through me as I picked up my beer again. And as I took the next sip, my eyes skirted to Zach, and I couldn't help but think of how right Ben was.

The game *was* just getting started.

But I already knew how it would end.

Zach thought he was *so* smart, showing up at the game unannounced, buying the tickets next to mine. He thought he'd have my full attention, but that's where he was wrong.

Two could play this game.

In addition to helping me focus on what I could control, my grandfather also taught me the value in being both patient and competitive. I'd always thrived on competition — with myself, with others. So, add Zach's attempt to thwart my plan to my innate desire to prove to him — along with everyone else — that I could do anything I set my mind to, and I guess you could say he had absolutely zero chance.

I made it my mission to make him feel as invisible as possible, ignoring his flirty and sarcastic comments and focusing solely on Ben. I'd lean into him, touch his arm, laugh at his jokes — and any time he left to go get us beers, I went with him, not giving Zach the chance to have me alone.

At first, Zach seemed to take it as a challenge. He made a few smart-ass comments about Ben's job and hobbies, all while saying it should have been illegal for me to bring a Lions fan into a Bears game with my season tickets.

I didn't disagree with him on that one.

But by the third quarter, Zach had grown quiet, sipping his beer with a permanent scowl as he watched me from the corner of his eye. Every time Ben would touch me, his jaw would clench, fist tightening around his aluminum bottle.

Ha! Serves you right.

Still, the Bears were down, and that was part of the game I was *not* enjoying. It was early in the season, and I knew we had plenty of games coming up. But I wanted to win them all.

I *especially* wanted to win this one, since I had a bet riding on it.

"You know," Ben teased after the Lions cleared a field goal, growing their lead from seven to ten. "Maybe we should discuss the details of this strip tease you're going to give me. Like, do I get to pick the music?"

I stuck my tongue out at him, earning me a deep laugh.

"We never did decide exactly how *much* of a strip tease this was," I pointed out.

"Is there a measurement on stripping? Like, levels or something?"

"Of course," I answered easily, pulling up my sneaker and propping it on the seat back in front of us. "I mean, maybe I'm only going to strip my shoes and socks off."

"Sexy."

I pulled the shoe lace, untying the knot and slipping my heel out. "Mmm..." I said, biting my lip as I turned back to him. "Just a little tease for you, big boy."

Ben laughed, tossing his head back before he watched me again with a curious gaze. "You really are something else."

I smiled in return, but Zach slamming his empty beer bottle down on the other side of me jerked my attention his way. He kicked back in his seat, arms folded over his chest with his eyes on the field.

"You okay over there?" I asked, and I couldn't hide my satisfied smirk.

"I'm great," he clipped. Nodding his chin toward Ben, who was now watching the Bears set up for the next play, Zach lowered his voice. "You can't really be serious with this guy."

"What? He's funny. And charming."

"And about as interesting as a tumbleweed."

I fought back a laugh, because as much as I hated to admit it — Zach wasn't wrong. Ben was sweet, and he was able to joke back and forth with me. But during halftime when he'd talked for twenty minutes about his seashell collection from around the world — complete with photos of every single one — I'd had to actively try not to yawn.

He was a little weird, but hey — he was hot. And, he was exactly what my plan called for.

"Sounds like someone is a little *jealous*," I said, draining the rest of my beer.

"Sounds like *someone* is trying to make me that way."

"I'm not doing anything," I argued. "Other than exactly what I told you I'd be doing at every home game this season. It's not my fault you decided to buy tickets to watch."

Zach smirked, his eyes still not meeting mine. "Whatever you say. I'm sure you're genuinely having *so* much fun with a Lions fan, who's only joke he can keep going with you is about this stupid strip tease."

I coughed. "Jealous." I coughed again.

Zach looked at me then, leaning over until his mouth was just inches from mine. His eyes flicked down to my bottom lip, then back up to my eyes, and he gave me a sideways grin. "Hard to be jealous of a guy who's just trying to get something I've already had."

That same hot breath I'd felt between my thighs brushed across my lips, and I inhaled it, eyes fluttering into a series of blinks. I glanced at his lips, but yanked my gaze away just as soon as I'd let it fall.

Zach sat back again, still grinning. "Whatcha thinking about there, Gemma?"

I flushed, reaching for my beer to take a drink before I remembered it was empty. Zach chuckled, and I glared at him, slamming my empty bottle down just the way he had before leaning back into Ben.

I slipped my arm under his, wrapping my hand around his bicep as the Lions called a timeout on the field. "So, *Ben*," I said, loud enough for Zach to overhear. "Tell me more about yourself."

Ben smiled. "Well, did I tell you I do CrossFit?"

"How fascinating," Zach murmured, and I subtly kicked him, never taking my eyes off Ben.

"You didn't! That explains all these muscles," I said, squeezing his arm. "Tell me about it, I've never done a class."

"Well, so every class is different," Ben started, but then the crowd around us grew louder, and someone tapped me on the shoulder.

"You're on the kiss cam!" the woman said. "Look!"

She pointed to the screen, and sure enough, there Ben and I were — framed by a heart with little lipstick kiss graphics floating around us.

Ben stared at the screen, his eyes wide.

"Kiss her, man!" someone yelled, and Ben turned to me, something of a terrified smile on his face.

I leaned in closer, closing my eyes...

But nothing came.

The crowd groaned in unison, and when I opened my eyes, Ben was still looking at me, but hadn't moved an inch. I glanced at the screen, which had moved on to a different couple.

"I'm sorry," Ben said quickly, taking off his hat and running his hands through his damp blond hair. "I just, I get so shy in situations like that. I froze. I'm sorry."

I swallowed, forcing a smile even though I just got rejected on the jumbotron in front of tens of thousands of people. "It's okay," I assured him, reaching over to squeeze his hand. "Don't stress about it."

The words didn't even have time to roll off my tongue before that damn camera was on us again.

"Kiss her, dude!" a kid yelled from a few seats over from Ben.

Then, a chant broke out in our section.

Kiss her, kiss her, kiss her.

Poor Ben looked at me with eyes as wide as saucers, sweat beading on his forehead. He licked his lips — not because he was turned on, but because he was nervous as hell. And I nodded, encouraging him that it was okay.

But before he could lean in to seal the deal, a hand wrapped around my waist from behind, yanking me in the opposite direction.

I didn't have time to process it all — the hand sliding into my hair, the other arm pulling me flush against his body, the crowd going wild.

No, I didn't realize any of it was happening — not until my hands were fisted in his jersey, my mouth opening more to let his tongue inside, a moan rumbling up my throat at the feel of such a passionate, possessive kiss.

But it wasn't Ben's lips on mine.

It was Zach's.

The crowd cheered even louder when he pulled back, and my eyes fluttered open, hands still wrapped in his jersey as he held me.

Zach brushed my hair away from my face, knuckling my chin. "Yep," he breathed, low enough that only I could hear. "Just as amazing as I remembered."

My heart somersaulted, a flurry of butterflies taking flight in my stomach. I searched his dark eyes, body leaning in for more on its own account.

And then, I realized what I was doing.

With my hands still in his jersey, I tossed Zach back with a scoff. "Oh, my God, Zach!"

He just held his hands up, smile crooked up with that damn dimple showing.

"I'm so sorry, Ben," I said hurriedly, turning back to him with my face red for a completely different reason.

Ben's jaw was tight, his gaze fixed on Zach.

"I'm sorry, I didn't know what was happening. The camera was on and everyone was cheering and—"

"Not cool, man," Ben said to Zach, ignoring me.

"What?" Zach said, leaning back. He stretched his arm over the back of the chairs, leaving one of them around me. "You hesitated. I was just giving the crowd what they wanted."

"Zach!" I whisper-yelled, thumping him across the chest.

"I'm going to get another beer," Ben said, standing.

I stood, too. "I'll come with you."

"No," he said quickly, glancing at Zach again before his blue eyes fixed on mine. "You should stay."

When he left, the rows around us broke out in a mixture of *ooooh's* and laughs. Janet waved at me from her row, pointing at Zach and holding up two thumbs-up signs.

"I like him better," she mouthed.

I groaned, plopping back down in my seat after I peeled Zach's arm from the back of my chair. I kicked back, crossing my arms and watching the field.

"I would say I'm sorry, but..."

"Shut up," I clipped, cutting Zach off.

The ball was snapped, and I watched from what felt like another universe as the Lions intercepted our pass, running it back the other way seventeen yards before they were taken down. I barely registered it, though. Instead, my fingertips floated over my lips — lips that Zach had just kissed like he owned, like they weren't even mine to offer to anyone else.

I closed my eyes, forcing a breath that was meant to calm me but just made my heart beat faster.

You're still in control, Gemma, I tried to tell myself. *It was just a little kiss.*

I glanced at Zach out of the corner of my eye, and my stomach flipped again, hands itching to run through his stupid, messy hair — the way they had one week ago.

Totally in control.

This time, I laughed out loud.

Chapter 8

ZACH

Okay, maybe the kiss was too far.

I was man enough to admit when I was wrong, and while in the moment it seemed like a romantic, hero-like thing to do, I realized after that it was a little over the line. She was here with another guy, and I'd embarrassed them both.

Though, I really felt like it was *him* I'd mostly shamed. If anything, it would have been worse for Gemma if I had just sat back and let her get rejected — for a *second* time. The crowd ate it up, me stealing Ben's kiss.

But Gemma, on the other hand...

She sat beside me with her arms crossed after Ben went up to get more beer, breathing like a dragon as she watched the field. She hadn't reacted to the last few plays, so I wasn't sure she was even watching at all. She was just staring.

And probably thinking of all the ways she could murder me.

To an extent, my plan was working. I'd thrown her when I showed up, and even with her best attempts to ignore me and prove a point that she was here with Ben, I knew I was getting under her skin.

She liked me.

She might not want to admit it, and she clearly didn't want to submit to it. But, I wasn't alone in my feelings for her.

Still, I'd crossed a line, and I wasn't sure where I was anymore. Was I still in the persistent, flirty gray area I'd aimed for? Playing her own game against her, trying to get another date?

Or had I crossed over into Creepersville, not taking her clues to leave her the hell alone?

Sighing, I shifted my weight until I was leaning toward her. Gemma moved to rest on the opposite side of her chair, and I let out another deep sigh.

"Look, I'm sorry."

"Sure you are."

"No," I said, reaching out to squeeze her knee. She glared at that hand like she could set it on fire with her gaze before she finally looked at me. "I'm serious, Gemma. I really am sorry. That crossed a line."

She watched me, eyes flicking back and forth between mine suspiciously. But, she must have seen the sincerity there, because she let out a long breath, shoulders rounding forward.

"Yeah. You really did."

"Look, I realize now that what I did, buying these tickets... well, it might have been a little crazy."

"You think?"

I gave her a pointed look. "But at the time, I just wanted another shot with you."

She tossed her hands up with a dramatic eye roll. "It's like I'm talking to a brick wall. Did you not hear anything I said when I explained what my plan for the season was, or did you just choose to ignore it all?"

"I heard every word, okay?" I shook my head. "I just thought after last week, after the night we had, that maybe you'd change your mind."

Gemma didn't respond to that.

"I can leave," I offered. "If you really want me to. I'll go right now."

"No," Gemma said on a sigh, pinching the bridge of her nose. "No, you bought the tickets, you should stay and enjoy them. Just," she said, holding up one finger. "Don't pull that again. Deal?"

I smiled, because it didn't matter that she was telling me to keep my hands to myself. She wanted me to stay — and *that* was a win.

"Deal."

We sat in silence for a while, Gemma checking behind her a few different times to see if there was any sign of Ben. Each time she turned back around without seeing him, she sighed, tapping her little sneaker on the back of the chair in front of her.

"He'll be back," I assured her.

"Doubtful."

"He will. I mean, the guy may be about as interesting as a clump of dirt, but he's not stupid. And trust me when I say he'd have to be an idiot not to come back."

Gemma pulled her long hair over the shoulder opposite me, running her fingers through it as she glanced at me through her lashes.

And when she looked at me like that, I hoped like hell that guy would never come back.

I wanted her for myself.

"Ladies and gentlemen," the announcer spoke as all the screens filled with the American flag. "Please rise as we honor a local soldier in the salute to service."

I was immediately on my feet, clapping loudly as everyone slowly made their way to stand. The announcer went on about the woman being honored on the field, and with every word, I felt a surge of pride. Her name was Hazel McCoy, and she was a member of the United States Navy who had just returned from her fifth tour.

My chest squeezed a little as I watched her accept an honor from one of the leaders on the field, her husband and two boys standing beside her. When she teared up, waving at the fans — I couldn't help but tear up a little, too.

I felt Gemma's eyes on me when the salute was over, everyone taking their seats again.

"Go ahead," I said, widening my eyes to keep the water brimming inside them from leaking over. "Take whatever crack you want."

"I wasn't going to say a thing."

"Uh-huh."

She smiled, but then her face softened, eyes searching mine. "You're just a big softie under all that sarcasm, aren't you?"

I chuckled. "I'm only a softie when it comes to three things, and the military is one of them." I reached for my beer, something to give me back a little of my manhood, but I remembered once it was in my hand that it was empty. "Any chance your boyfriend there might be bringing back a beer for me, too?"

Gemma cocked a brow, pursing her lips. "What do *you* think?"

"Yeah, no chance." I sighed, but held onto the empty bottle, anyway. "My dad was in the Army for almost thirty years," I said, avoiding her gaze. "He sacrificed a lot for our family, for our country. I don't know. I guess I just know a little better than most what kind of things you have to give up in order to serve, and I respect the hell out of anyone who will do that."

"I think that's sweet," Gemma said, and I didn't miss how she shifted her weight, leaning more toward me than away from me now. "What did he do in the Army?"

"He was in bomb disposal."

Her eyes widened. "Whoa."

"Yeah." I nodded, sharing her sentiment. "Imagine being my mom."

"She must have been so scared."

"Every deployment, she'd freeze when the phone rang. I think in her head, she had to prepare before she answered. Just in case."

Gemma watched me for a long moment. "My grandfather was a veteran. He served in Vietnam, and he was so proud of that. He used to always wear his veteran hat, his jacket, and he was down at the VFW outside his small town every night."

Gemma had this far-off look in her eyes, and I knew it so well. It was the same way I looked at my past, at what could have been.

"Were you close with him?"

She smiled at that. "Very. My parents traveled a lot for work when I was younger. Well," she added. "They still do, actually. He kind of raised me, taught me everything I know."

"Like how to be a giant pain in the ass."

"Especially that."

I smiled, and Gemma leaned in a little closer, watching me.

"Were you in the military, too?" she asked after a moment.

"No. I thought about it, but football took up so much of my time, it became priority number one." I shrugged. "If anything, the military was only an afterthought. Football was everything."

"And what happened to football?"

Now I really need a beer.

I scratched my chin, and then the Bears completed a pass down the field. Gemma stood with the rest of the fans, cheering the receiver on as he ran, her question temporarily forgotten. But when she sat back down again, her eyes were on me. Waiting.

"That's a long story, for another time," I offered. And I couldn't help myself. I leaned over, invading her space.

And just like before, her face went red, her eyes wide when I tucked her hair behind one ear.

"Maybe if you let me take you on another date..."

"Nice try," she teased, batting my hand away. But she was smiling — and that was better than looking at me like she wanted to rip my head off.

I'd take it.

"What are the other two things?"

I tilted my head. "What?"

"The other two things you're a softie about."

"No way, you don't get any more freebies. You'll have to give me another date to find out."

Gemma crossed her arms. "You do realize this is never going to work out in your favor, right? You're playing the wrong game."

"That's fine," I conceded, leaning over her seat again. This time, I locked my eyes on hers, holding her gaze as my hand slid over her knee. "As long as I'm the right winner."

Gemma blinked, mouth opening like she was ready to pop off her own remark, but it died somewhere on her tongue. Her eyes flicked to my mouth and back up again, but then someone cleared their throat behind me.

"Ben!" Gemma stood, making my hand fall from where it had been on her knee. I ran that hand back through my hair and stood, too, so Ben could pass.

He watched me the entire time.

"Thank you," Gemma said when he handed her a beer. He had two for himself. "Ben, I'm so sorry, about what happened. I—"

"It's all good, babe," he said.

Babe? Who did this guy think he was. He'd known Gemma for all of two hours.

Ben wrapped his arm possessively around her, his glossy eyes finding mine. "I know who'll be getting the *real* kisses later."

He cocked a smirk at that, and I tongued my cheek, fists tightening at my sides. I wanted to knock that pretty boy smirk off his perfectly-symmetrical face, but that wouldn't work in my favor. Gemma was pissed at me earlier, but somehow, I'd earned back a little of her trust. She was laughing with me. She wanted to know more about me.

And pretty boy *Ben* could play his best cards. I still knew who'd win.

Gemma watched Ben like a slimy green substance she wasn't sure about — like he could be fun putty or vomit. "Uh, okay. Well, thank you for the beer."

"Anytime, *babe.*" Ben tugged her even closer, and I saw Gemma's top lip visibly curl.

I laughed, holding up my empty bottle. "My turn for a beer run. You two love birds enjoy." I gave Gemma a pointed look, and she fought back a grin, shaking her head in warning.

She might still have been here on a date with him, but I knew who she was thinking about — regardless of *his* arm being the one around her.

There wasn't a single doubt in my mind who would be getting the "real kisses" later.

And it sure as hell wouldn't be Ben.

The Bears lost, and if I wasn't enough of a football fan for that to chap my ass already, I would have been upset just by looking at Gemma when the final whistle blew.

She was heartbroken.

Her shoulders were slumped, hair a little greasy from how much she'd run her hands through it in the final quarter as we weaved our way through the crowd filing out of the stadium. Ben held her hand, and I waited back, letting them be.

She pulled him to a stop in front of the same totem we'd met under last week before the game, and I could have left, could have started making my way toward the parking lot where I'd parked my car — but I waited. I told myself it was because traffic would be hell and there was no sense in hurrying.

But even a blind man could have seen I was waiting to see what Gemma did next.

Ben had gotten a little sloppy in the last part of the game, and as Gemma spoke to him under that totem, his eyes bounced around, body swaying. He said something to her, presumably something funny, since she laughed, and then they hugged, and he started pin-balling himself through the crowd toward the cab line.

Gemma sighed, folding her hands on top of her head as she watched him go. Then, she turned around, and when she spotted me, her eyes narrowed.

You would have thought *I* was the reason the Bears lost for how she stormed through the crowd toward me like a raging bull. I knew her glare was meant to scare me, but it had the opposite effect.

I just wanted to take her home, take that jersey off her, and take my sweet time making her come with my name on her lips.

She was too fucking adorable when she was angry, and my smile was splitting my face by the time she reached me, jabbing her index finger straight into my chest.

"This doesn't mean you win."

"Ouch!" I laughed, rubbing my chest. "Damn, you need a permit for those things. I'm going to start calling you Finger Guns."

"I didn't sleep with him because he's trashed," she said, ignoring me as she explained her actions. "And because he couldn't stop pissing on me after that little stunt you pulled."

"Gross."

"It's a metaphor."

"Whatever you say, no judgment here if you're into golden showers."

She poked me again.

"OUCH."

"You did not win. I could have taken him home and gotten laid if I wanted to."

"Okay," I said, holding up both hands. She was still pointing that finger at me, ready to jab. "I surrender. Can you put that thing away now?"

Gemma glanced at her finger, chuckling as she let that hand fall to her side. "Goodnight, Zach."

She turned, but before she could take a step, I called out, "Take me to the next game."

Gemma paused, glancing at me over her shoulder with a grin before she turned back around. She tucked her hands into her back pockets, watching me for a long moment before she shook her head.

"I told you, that's not part of the plan."

"Your plan sucks."

Her little mouth popped open at that. "*You* suck."

"Ah, so she *does* remember." I licked my lips, stepping toward her with a satisfied grin as I watched every shade of pink and red color her cheeks. I reached forward, tucking one finger into the loop of her jeans. "You know, we never did get to the whole being *railed into next year* thing."

Her skin flamed, mouth pursing as she fought the urge to smile. I trailed my hand up her side, running my fingertips up her arms on a track to frame her face. I wanted her lips on mine again, her little mouth opening to let me in for more.

But before I could make that move, she poked me again.

"Ou-ch-uh," I said on a laugh, enunciating the one syllable in the word and adding two more of my own at the end. I eyed her, rubbing my arm.

"*Goodnight,* Zach," she said again, one brow raised. Then, she held up the finger she'd just poked me with, thumb framing it like it was a gun, and she blew the tip of it as she walked away, tucking it into her pocket like a cowboy in an old western movie.

She strutted off with her shoulders back, chin held high, a little skip in her step like she'd won. But she didn't know — that little move had only added fuel to my fire.

Nothing worth having ever came easy, that was something I learned at a young age. I never expected Gemma to cave fast, to give into me without fighting back. If anything, I loved that she had her plans, her list-filled goals she wanted to stick to.

It was part of what made her unique.

I watched her hips sway until she was out of view, running a hand over the stubble lining my jaw as every bone in my body ached for me to chase after her.

But, I was a patient man, and I'd played football long enough to know you never spent all your energy in the first quarter.

There was still plenty of game to play.

And when the ball was in my hands again, I'd be ready.

Chapter 9

GEMMA

His hand rested on her hip, the same way it had rested on mine that morning when he kissed me goodbye. He was kissing this girl, too — but not because he was leaving.

He stepped into her, pulling her closer, his lips seeking hers. And when they kissed, I felt those lips like they were pressed against my own. I knew those lips. I had memorized the way they felt when they touched my forehead, my cheek, my mouth.

Did she know his kisses the same way I did?

I blinked, and then she was there, in the back of the church where he and I were married. She wore black, just like me, but her tears came easier than mine. She cried for a lover taken too soon by death.

I cried for a lover taken too soon by her.

And when I faced the casket, he was there, staring back at me with tired, gray eyes.

"I'm sorry," he whispered, but my heart felt no relief.

He wasn't sorry he'd cheated. He was sorry I'd found out. He was sorry I had to stay by his side while he withered away, burying his secret along with his body.

When they closed the casket door, I screamed.

I bolted upright on my couch, one hand flying to my head as it pounded in protest at my sudden movement. I squeezed my eyes shut, falling back down on the cushions and kicking the blanket off me.

I was hot, slick with sweat, my chest heaving and heart racing. I didn't know where I was. I didn't know what year I was in. I didn't know what was real, and what was a dream.

Or rather, a nightmare.

I groaned, the sweat cooling on my chest now that I'd abandoned my blanket. Letting my hand flop to the floor, I felt around for my cell phone, peeking at the screen with one eye. I had three missed calls from Belle and a text from Zach.

It was just after six in the evening.

I pressed a hand to my chest, feeling the beat of my heart slow more with every new breath. I'd laid down somewhere around three to take a cat nap, just wanting to recharge after an early day at the office before I dragged Belle out to watch tonight's game with me. It was Monday night football, and an away game for the Bears.

We were playing the Packers — our biggest rivals.

I'd been excited, but tired from the day, so I laid down to rest.

And here it was, three hours later, and I felt like I'd died and come back as a zombie.

Carlo's eyes from my dream were still as vivid as if he were there with me when I sat up on the couch, looking around my empty condo. It was hard to believe it was mine. I still remembered buying it, the papers signed and everything in motion before I'd even driven home with the intention of telling Carlo I knew what he was doing.

I had a plan. I had set everything in motion. I had the proof to show him, the words to say to him, and a place to go once I'd gotten all of that out. I was going to move on. I was going to be okay.

But he spoke first that day, and my plan went up in flames.

Sometimes I couldn't wrap my head around the fact that I lived here — or anywhere — alone. Other times, it seemed impossible to believe that I'd woken up in a little house with him one year ago, thinking everything in my life was fine.

With my cell phone still in my hand, I padded over to the kitchen, pouring a cold glass of water from my fridge. I drained half of it before unlocking my phone, deciding to read Zach's text first.

- **Hey Finger Guns, you free tonight? Could use some back up down at Doc's Bar, what with it being Monday night football and all. Plus, I know you need somewhere to scream at the Packers with like-minded people. -**

I smiled, just like I did every time he texted me. I hated that I smiled, because there were about a million neon signs hanging above Zach's head, warning me to steer clear. He was just the kind of guy I could fall for, the kind I could let in, get close to.

And he was just the kind of guy who could make you swoon and sigh as he told you lies, making you believe he meant the words he said.

Still, I couldn't help but be drawn to the comfort I felt when I was with him. Even when he infuriated me, showing up at that game in the seat next to mine, he still somehow managed to make me feel safe when he was around.

I couldn't remember the last time anyone made me feel that way.

And the last *person* who did proved why I should never trust that feeling.

Carlo had been easy to trust. He had been careful with my heart. He proved time and time again that I had no reason to worry, that I could relax, that I could feel safe with him.

And then, he betrayed me.

That's why you never trust your heart, even when you think it's safe.

- Sorry, the guns are out of commission tonight. Enjoy the game. Go Bears! -

The little dots were already bouncing on the screen, indicating Zach was typing back, but I closed the text and pulled up Belle's missed call. When I hit the green button to call her back, she answered before the first ring even finished.

"What the hell, woman?" She huffed. "You told me to be ready by five, and here I am, all dolled up waiting on you like my period."

"I'm sorry, I took a nap and…" I groaned as another rip of pain zinged through my head. "Let's just say I died a little in the process."

"Oof," she said sympathetically. "That kind of nap, huh? Did you forget what day it was?"

"More like what year."

I rummaged through my purse on the counter for some ibuprofen, knocking two pills back and chasing them with a shot of water.

"Sorry, but I'm bailing on tonight. As crazy as it sounds, I think I could just go back to sleep if I tried."

"Um, you absolutely will *not* do that," Belle said. "I have makeup on. And I re-curled my hair. I'm even wearing your stupid team's colors, for Christ's sake."

"You're wearing orange?" I asked. "Oh, my God. You really do love me."

"Calm down, I'm not that crazy," she said quickly. "But I am wearing navy blue and white, which is close enough."

"I'm sorry, I'll owe you one. I just don't feel like going out right now."

Belle paused. "What happened? Did you have another nightmare?"

I swallowed, and when I didn't respond, there was a heavy sigh on the other end.

"Oh, sweetie..."

"I'm fine," I said hurriedly. I was okay when she sympathized with my nap of the dead, but not with this. "Seriously. It's all good, I just feel a little weird now."

"What happened in it this time?"

I shrugged, refilling my glass of water. "Just reliving the first time I saw him kiss her, and then her being at the church the day of his funeral. Only this time, when I looked at him, he was alive in the casket."

"Jesus, Gemma."

"He said he was sorry," I whispered. "But, it wasn't the kind of apology where you knew the person actually was sorry. It was like... I don't know, like he pitied me."

She was silent for a long moment, and I sipped my water, nausea settling in my stomach to join my headache in kicking my ass.

"Anyway," I said, brushing it off. "It was just a dream. But I woke up with a headache and I'm just not feeling too hot."

"Why don't I come down," she offered. "I'll bring some ice cream, we can watch the game on your couch."

"I kind of want to be alone right now, Belle."

She laughed.

"Oh, no you don't. You're not going to sit in that empty condo and be all up in your sads thinking about your shitty, cheating ex-husband." She paused. "May he rest in peace."

"But—"

"Nope. Get your ass up and put on something presentable. We're going to watch the game."

"Belle," I whined.

"Hey, listen to me." I could almost imagine her leveling her little blue eyes with mine. "I know it sucks sometimes, and it hurts. Honestly, if it were me, I'd be the hottest of hot messes. What I really want to do is come down there, hug you, rock you, pet your hair and make you tell me everything that hurts that you've never talked about. But how does that make you feel when you picture that?"

I grimaced. "Like crawling out of my own skin."

"Well," Belle conceded. "Beer and avoiding it is, then. Meet you downstairs in thirty."

There was no arguing with her at that point, so I let her go with a sigh, glancing at myself in the reflection of my now-black phone screen.

I needed dry shampoo. And concealer. Stat.

- Change of plans. Save me a seat at the bar. -

I shot off the text to Zach, who had sent me four pouty emojis in a row in response to my last text. He responded to my affirmative one with a little purple devil smiley face and then an angel.

I tried to find comfort in Belle's words, in the fact that she was speaking my own love language to me. She knew I didn't want to talk. I didn't want to sit around and mope. No, my personal brand of therapy came in the form of avoidance — and she was willing to support that.

Sometimes I swore my best friend knew me a little *too* well.

I couldn't pull any of my excuses with her, not without her reading right through them. And as much as I did want to lie around and feel sorry for myself, I knew I'd have fun at the bar. I knew I'd want to watch the game. And I knew being around her, and being around Zach, would help me feel better.

Still, something felt off as I applied my mascara, slipping on my Bears hoodie and a fitted pair of ripped jeans before I walked out the door. My head was foggy, my heart still beating too rapidly or not at all — depending on the minute. I just wanted to sit inside in my pajamas, but then again, I also didn't want to be alone.

It was the first little sign that I didn't feel in control.

Maybe it was because no matter how much control I had in my life — what I did each day, who I spent time with, how I coped with Carlo's passing — I couldn't control my brain. When I went to sleep, it had the power to completely mess me up. All it had to do was show me a memory, or his face, or *her* face, and every ounce of control I had was gone.

That dream had thrown me, and now I was spinning in space, trying to find orbit again.

I hoped a beer and the game was the answer.

I think I knew even before I left my house that it wasn't.

ZACH

Eight days had passed since the game, and I hadn't seen Gemma.

Well, *technically,* anyway.

I'd seen her in my dreams, in my memories, in my fantasies as I wiped down the bar or ran the loop by my apartment. I'd seen the look on her face when she saw me in that seat next to her, and I'd relived that moment when I stole that kiss from her — over and over, again and again.

But I hadn't seen her *in person* since the night she strutted away from me after that Bears loss.

It wasn't like I hadn't been *trying* to see her again, since the last game. I'd tried twisting her arm into a coffee date, a movie night, and even just a stroll on the river walk that wasn't too far from her place.

She'd declined every time.

I wasn't surprised, given that she was still hell bent on sticking to her *plan.* But, she was texting me every day, responding to my requests with the same witty banter we'd had since the day we met.

She was playing hard to get, but she'd be lying through her teeth if she told anyone that she didn't want me, too.

At least, that's what I wanted to tell myself.

And me? Well, I couldn't get the girl out of my head.

I wasn't ashamed to admit that, at first, the connection was physical. She was a gorgeous girl — stunning, really. With her dark hair, her emerald, almost neon eyes, and her tight body that somehow curved in all the right places, it was hard not to be instantly attracted to her.

But then, she gave me shit back just as easily as I gave it to her. That was the bait, drawing me in, making me want a closer look. And seeing her at a football game?

That was the hook.

Playing football my entire life, I was no stranger to girls who *said* they were into football. Of course, for most of *those* girls, it meant they were into football *players*. Ask them about a team, or a position, or any fundamental rule? They were clueless.

But not Gemma.

Watch her jumping around and smiling like a goon in that stadium, or holding her breath and lacing her fingers over her head as she watched a high-stakes play, and it was easy to see she had a genuine love for the game. She was invested, a true fan, and she knew what she was talking about.

Still, there was more to her than just her love for football and her adorable sense of humor. Under that smile, under those eyes, she had a story.

And I wanted to read it.

It'd been a long time since a woman had captivated me past a first date. Honestly, because most of the time, women were easy for me to read. I could see right through their fake laughs, their insincere compliments tossed my way with their hands wrapped tight around my bicep. When I was younger, they wanted me for my potential — for the money I'd get if I made it pro. And after that, *especially* after my last actual girlfriend, I learned that I didn't want someone who only wanted me for what I could do for *them*.

Gemma wasn't that kind of girl.

I didn't know nearly as much as I wanted to about her, but I knew she was different. I knew she'd been hurt, and maybe because of that or maybe just because of who she was as a person — she didn't look at the world and ask what it could give her.

She didn't want a damn thing from me or from anyone else.

And maybe that's what made me want more of her.

Too bad she had that book of hers closed tight, under lock and key like it was in the restricted area, not even flirting with the idea of giving me a look past the cover.

But it was Monday, a sacred night during football season, and our city was taking on the Packers in Wisconsin. They were our biggest rivals, and the bar would be packed with Chicagoans yelling at the television screens.

Including Gemma.

I smiled at her text — not the one that she originally sent, that said she wouldn't be coming, but the one she sent ten minutes later that said she'd changed her mind. That smile was glued to my face as Doc and I filled orders at the bar, running back and forth as we took care of our clients as fast as we could. We were busier than hell, and Doc was stressed and grumpy.

But I couldn't stop smiling.

When two of our regulars left the bar when the crowd started pouring in, I'd stolen their barstools and stashed them behind the bar. We were too busy for me to do any kind of seat saving from where I was, but I was hell bent on having Gemma close to me.

And when she walked through the door twenty minutes after kick-off, her hair pulled into a high ponytail and eyes outlined in a smoky charcoal, I had to actively work to keep my jaw from hitting the floor.

Along with every other guy in the bar.

Belle spotted me before Gemma did, and she grinned, skipping over to where I was pushing through the crowd to deliver their barstools. I wiggled my way through some of our regulars, apologizing and telling them their next beers were on me just so they'd back away from the bar. I sat the stools down, grinning as Belle plopped herself down in the first one.

"Wow," she crooned, smoothing her hands over the countertop once her butt was in the seat. "You save these two seats just for us, Mr. Bartender Sir?"

"Just for you." My eyes flicked to Gemma, and I stood on the other side of the bar to see if maybe there was a hug in my future.

There wasn't.

She did let me pull the stool out for her, though, and I gently touched the small of her back as I scooted her in. There was a small smile on her lips, but her eyes seemed distant, and she did little more than that smile to greet me.

I tried not to take it personally, wondering if maybe she was just playing her same hard-to-get games as I made my way back around to the other side of the bar. I slid a coaster in front of Belle first, the next one landing in front of Gemma just as she ran a hand through her pony tail and let it swing back over her shoulder. Her eyes caught mine, and her cheeks tinged a light pink, a bigger smile threatening the corners of her mouth.

She looked at Belle, but I kept my gaze on her.

"It's like knowing the guy who can get us backstage at a concert," Belle said.

"Except way less cool," Doc chimed from behind me. He clapped a hand on my shoulder, extending his other for Belle. "I'm Doc, and I own this place. So if you want to have any kind of connection that counts, it's me you should flirt with."

Belle laughed, her head shooting back. "You know, I thought I liked you, Zach, but I just found my new favorite person."

"Hard to compete with this guy," I said. My eyes were still on Gemma.

Belle shook Doc's hand. "I'm Belle."

"Nice to meet you." Doc reached for Gemma next, and her eyes skated to mine briefly before she smiled at him and slid her tiny hand in his. "You must be the woman this guy can't stop talking about."

She flushed even more, tucking a stray strand of hair behind her ear once she had her hand back. "If by that you mean the woman he won't stop pestering, then yes, I'm the lucky one."

Doc chuckled, squeezing my shoulder. "Looks like you're real close to another date there, son. Keep it up."

I smirked, nodding as Doc walked to the other end of the bar to take another drink order. But my eyes were still on Gemma.

And I was calling bullshit.

"I'm a pest now, huh?"

She nodded, leaning one elbow on the bar. "But, you're the cute kind of pest. Like a family of mice."

Belle laughed, tapping her knuckle on the bar in front of our staring contest. "Okay, before you two battle this out, can you get me a martini, please? Extra dirty." She flicked her long, curled, strawberry-blonde hair over her shoulders. "I already have to suffer through a football game. If I also have to suffer through your middle school flirting, I at least need lubrication."

Gemma laughed, and I broke our eye contact long enough to stir up Belle's drink and slide it in front of her.

She thanked me with a wink, popping an olive between her lips after the first sip.

"And for you?" I asked Gemma.

"Double shot of your best Añejo tequila. Chilled."

I whistled through my teeth, filling her order and garnishing it with a slice of lime. "That kind of night, huh?"

I was just kidding, but when I noticed the way Belle was watching Gemma, I frowned. And it wasn't until then that I really saw it.

She was there, in the bar, her makeup done and her team's logo on her chest. But she wasn't *there* — not really. Her eyes were a bit glazed, distant, and every smile she gave me seemed subdued and far off, like she was medicated or living in some sort of dream.

I realized what I'd seen before, what she'd shown me up until this point — all that toughness and that blasé attitude — it was her mask.

And tonight, she'd let it slip.

Gemma just shrugged, taking the first sip and letting her eyes focus on the television above me. I watched her for a long moment, ignoring Doc's snap telling me he needed me to take more orders down at that end.

I didn't know what it was that was bothering her, what was on her mind, but I had one mission: get the girl out of her head.

"You know, I think you're bullshitting," I said, keeping my eyes fixed on her. "About me being a pest."

"Do you now?"

I nodded. "Uh-huh. After all, you came here. To *my* bar." I pushed back from the bar, throwing her a cocky smirk. "You wouldn't be here if I bothered you."

She gave me a pointed look. "You *asked* me to come here."

"And you came," I reminded her. "Just admit it — you like me. You wanted to see me, too."

Gemma smiled, but she rolled her eyes, taking another sip of her tequila as her gaze fixed on the screen again. "I came here to watch the game — at a bar I came to plenty of times before I knew you worked here, by the way."

I pointed at her. "That's a lie."

"Is not."

"Um, it absolutely is. Because I've worked here for almost twelve years now and I would bet money on the fact that you never set foot inside this bar before the night we met."

Her eyes found mine then, and they narrowed into slits. "You're *that* confident, that you'd bet money on that fact?"

I nodded.

"Why? Doc could have taken my order," she tried. "Or another bartender. It could have been a night you were off work."

"There are no other bartenders, and I don't take nights off."

"Ha! *Now* who's the liar?" She pointed her finger back at me. "You do too take nights off. You did when you went to the first home game with me, and again last Sunday for that game."

"First two nights in twelve years, including when I had the flu."

Technically that was a lie, since I did have Saturdays off and we did have two other temp bartenders on staff, kids who just liked to make some extra cash while they were in college. They were the ones who covered the bar on Saturdays. Still, I knew she was *also* lying. She hadn't been to Doc's before that first night I saw her.

Gemma's eyes softened, questions lining them as she watched me. But she schooled her features in the next second. "That's just not sanitary." She ran a hand back through her ponytail. "And still doesn't mean I've never been in this bar before the night we met."

"You haven't," I said, this time leaning over the bar on both elbows. I leveled my gaze with hers, my focus slipping to her ruby-painted lips briefly before we locked eyes again. "I know, because there's no way in hell I wouldn't have noticed if you had walked through those doors." I shook my head, grinning. "Just like I can't forget you ever since the night you did."

A smile tugged at the corner of her full lips, and Belle visibly swooned from where she was watching us — not the game — on her barstool. But Gemma just watched me, that hint of a smile, her eyes softening a bit before she cleared her throat.

She pulled back, breaking our eye contact and taking a drink from her glass. "You're wrong about me being here for you," she said, hissing through her teeth at the taste of the tequila. Then, she glanced over her shoulder before facing me again with a wild grin. "And I'm going to show you just how wrong you are."

In the next second, she tilted that tequila back and chugged it like it was apple juice instead of a thirty-dollar alcoholic drink. Her eyes watered a little as she sucked the lime, and she didn't offer me another glance before she was walking across the bar in the opposite direction of me.

"Oh, boy," Belle murmured, and both our gazes followed Gemma until she stopped.

Right at a table full of rowdy, drooling guys.

Chapter 10

ZACH

"You know, if you're really that into torturing yourself, I could always loan you my flogger."

Belle sipped on her martini, shoving another olive in her mouth. I'd just given her a bowl of them this time.

"It's meant for sexual pleasure," she continued, waving the little wooden sword she kept sticking the olives with around as she spoke. "But, if you whipped it hard enough, it could do some damage."

I blew out a breath through my nose, digging a shovel into the ice bin and dropping the cubes loudly into a glass. I filled it with Jack Daniels first, pushing the button for Coke on my gun and topping it off before sliding it down to one of the Packers fans at the end of the bar.

When I glanced at Gemma again, just in time to see the guy she'd been hanging on for the past two hours slip his hand into her back pocket, I clenched my jaw.

"She's drunk," I said, bracing both hands on the bar as I blatantly stared at her. She'd been going to Doc to fill her drink orders after I not-so-subtly ignored her requests for more drinks on my end of the bar.

She wasn't so drunk that we needed to cut her off, but she was well into the area where she could make some bad decisions.

And the lap she was currently crawling into had *bad decision* written all over it.

"You're not wrong," Belle said, popping another olive before chasing it with a drink of her martini. Her eyes were on Gemma, too, and she cringed a little at the sight of the meathead tickling her when she was finally in his lap. "She's had a rough day."

My chest tightened at that. "What happened?"

"Not my place to say," Belle answered, swinging back around in her chair. "But, if it makes you feel any better, I think you're right about what you said earlier."

I cocked a brow.

"About her wanting to see you." Belle shrugged, finger skating the rim of her glass. "It's been a long time since that girl has had something to really smile about, and every time you text her? She lights up like a sparkler on the Fourth of July."

I scratched my jaw, tearing my eyes away from Gemma long enough to look at Belle when I asked, "What's her deal with not wanting to date? Who hurt her?"

Belle sucked air through her teeth. "Ah, again — not my story to tell. All I can say is she has a reason, and honestly? I don't blame her. I mean, I'm already president of the Single Forever Club, but even if I wasn't, I wouldn't push her to do something until she was ready." Belle eyed her best friend from across the bar, a shadow of something washing over her face. "Not after what she's been through."

Her words circled in my head as my gaze swept back to Gemma. She had her arm around the guy she was sitting on, and he was drawing circles on her thigh with his thick, meathead fingers. I didn't like him. It didn't matter that I didn't know him. He was looking at Gemma like she was something for him to conquer, like a joke between him and all his buddies there at that table.

And if he didn't get his hands off her soon, I was going to lose my fucking mind.

"You want another drink?" I asked Belle, still staring at Gemma.

"Nah. Better stop here." She paused. "I *would* take another bowl of olives, though."

I eyed her under an arched brow. "We have pizza, you know."

"Hey, don't judge, just fill." She pushed the bowl toward me, and I smirked, shaking my head as I filled it to the top with olives again.

It really was self-mutilation, the way I watched Gemma for the rest of the night. I couldn't even answer if someone were to ask me what the score was, or what had just happened in the previous play. She was the only thing I could focus on, other than filling drink orders — and I did that just to keep myself from jumping over the bar, charging over there and ripping her out of that meathead's arms.

When the game was almost over — the Bears winning by two touchdowns and an extra point — Gemma sauntered back over to Belle and me at the bar. I felt the knot in my chest give way once she was away from that table, and my breaths came a little easier.

Until she spoke.

"Andy and I are going to take off," she said to Belle, eyes glossy and a lazy, drunken smile playing on her lips. The lipstick that had painted them so beautifully before was smudged now, the edges of it bleeding onto her skin.

"Um, you sure that's a good idea?" Belle eyed the guys at the table.

"Mm-hmm," Gemma said with a giggle. "He's going to show me his favorite way to celebrate a Bears win."

Belle's eyes shot to me as a roar of anger and jealousy ripped through me like wildfire.

"What about your *plan*?" I spat, grabbing two beers out of the ice bucket and slamming them on the bar in front of the guys who had just ordered. They exchanged glances, eyes wide, but I ignored them. "Thought you were hell bent on sticking to it."

Gemma blinked, like she was digesting what I'd said. "I am."

"So, this guy can get your time when it's not a home game, when it's not on your terms, but I can't?"

Gemma's defenses went up like a visible wall, and she narrowed her eyes. "It is on *my terms*. You changed the rules, so why can't I?"

I ground my teeth together, planting my hands on the bar as I leaned toward her. "Gemma, please, don't do this."

Her eyes were on her manicured fingernails as she swallowed, swaying a little. I covered that hand with my own, leaning down more until her eyes connected with mine.

"I know you've been hurt."

Her bottom lip quivered, and I squeezed her hand in mine.

"You hide it from everyone — from strangers, from Belle, from *him*," I added, nodding to the asshole waiting for her at the table in the corner. "Probably from your family, too. And I don't know what happened; I don't know who hurt you." I swallowed. "But I can see it. I can see you hurting and I promise you, from experience, running from it won't make it go away."

Gemma's eyes flicked back and forth between mine, like she was trying to see me through a fog.

"This isn't the answer. *He* isn't the answer," I said, pointing a finger right at the meathead. "If you let anyone take you home tonight, let it be me."

Gemma rolled her eyes with a scoff.

"Not so I can touch you in any way other than to help you get into bed. Trust me when I say you'll feel better if you just sleep it off tonight. And if you want to call him again in the morning, when you're *sober*," I added. "Then go for it. Hell, I'll even dial the number for you."

Gemma tongued her cheek, ripping her hand from under mine and crossing her arms over her chest. "You're unbelievable," she said, then she planted her hands right in front of mine, leaning over the bar to meet me in the middle. "I'm fine, thank you, and I don't need your permission or your *blessing* or whatever it is that you think you need to grant me for me to take a guy back to my place. I'm a grown-ass woman, and I'll do what I want." She pointed back to Andy. "He's nice, okay? And he's not complicated. He's perfectly fine with what I want, and what I *don't* want — unlike some people."

"Gemma," I tried.

"Gemma," Belle echoed, pulling her best friend's hand into hers. "Hey, you know I'm all about the one-night stands and I'm queen of no commitments, but I think I agree with Zach here."

Gemma's little mouth popped open, like her friend trying to stop her from going home with a drunk neanderthal was the most offensive thing she'd ever seen. Then, she narrowed her eyes.

"You agree with Zach," she deadpanned. "Of course. Well, you know what? I don't need permission *from either of you*." Gemma pointed her finger at Belle and then waved it over at me. "I'm tired of being told what I want and what I don't. No one is listening to me."

"I hear you," Belle said. "And like Zach said, if you want this in the morning? I'm all about it. But I know what happened earlier," she said, and I watched Belle curiously then.

What had happened earlier?

"And I know how you get when you feel out of control."

"I don't feel out of control," Gemma argued, shaking her head. "I'm *in* control, which is exactly why I'm leaving. Because I *want* to."

She ripped her hand from Belle's, and with that, wavered a bit in her stance.

"And for the record," she said, eyes pinning me again. "You have no *idea* what I'm 'running from'." She held up air quotes sarcastically around the last two words. "Or what I'm not. So stop assuming you know what's best for me." She swiped her purse from where it'd hung on Belle's barstool all night. "Stop acting like you know me at all."

With that, she turned on one heel and stormed across the bar, sliding her hand into Andy's and tugging him toward the door. Meathead tossed a thumbs up behind him to the tune of a laughing, cheering table of his douchebag friends, and I growled, launching a half-empty glass across the back-end of the bar. It shattered when it hit the dish bin, and Doc threw his hands up.

"Damn it, Zach!" He shook his head, ripping the broom from the back and tossing it to me. "Clean that shit up. And stop acting crazy, she's just a girl."

Belle watched me with sad, sympathetic eyes as I caught the broom, fingers wrapping around it so tight my knuckles turned white. I met her gaze, and she looked like she wanted to hug me and like she also wanted to throw a glass, too.

"I'm sorry," she said, sliding off her stool and dropping cash on the bar. "I'm going to go save her from herself."

"Let me come."

Belle shook her head, holding up a hand. "Don't. Okay? She can push me and get mad at me tonight and she'll be over it tomorrow. But..."

"Not so much with me, huh?"

Belle's eyes softened again. "I'm sorry, Zach."

I didn't answer, just nodded as she made her way through the crowd to where Gemma had disappeared. It took every ounce of self-control I had left not to go after her, not to barrel through every person there until I was outside connecting my fist to *Andy's* face.

But what would be the point?

She made it clear tonight how she feels about me.

And it isn't the way I thought she did.

"Sorry, Doc," I said when he passed by.

He gave a sympathetic, tight-lipped smile, clapping me on the shoulder. "It's okay. Just clean it up."

I forced a breath, hating the way my chest ached with the words he'd spoken as I started sweeping.

She's just a girl.

I didn't try to find Belle again, and I didn't look to see if Gemma had already climbed into a cab outside with Andy. I just swept up the shattered glass, wondering how I'd gotten so caught up in a woman who couldn't care less about me, wondering how a night could do such a one-eighty in such a short amount of time.

Maybe Gemma wasn't different at all.

Maybe she was just like everyone else.

And maybe, though it stung my chest like a branding iron, I needed to do just what she wanted me to.

I needed to let her go.

GEMMA

I made a mistake.

I made a huge, *huge* mistake.

Of course, that realization didn't hit me until it was ten minutes past way too late.

It didn't occur to me that I was making bad choices when I sauntered over to that table full of guys, hell bent on proving my point to Zach that I had not gone to that bar for him. At that time, it was just a game — which I'd recently discovered that I apparently loved to play. I just wanted to tease him, to let him know who was in control when it came to whatever it was that was happening between us.

I still had a plan. I still didn't want to be in a relationship. And he was still wasting his time.

However true all of that might have been, I made a mistake walking up to that table of guys. Even if it had been a fun night, cheering on the Bears to a victory over the Packers and throwing back tequila like it was water, I should have realized I was playing with fire.

I'd had a dream about my ex-husband less than an hour before I'd walked into that bar, and I shouldn't have had as much as I had to drink. I shouldn't have drank at all. I should have just stayed home, should have let Belle come up, should have faced something — *anything* — instead of just avoiding.

But that was my modus operandi, and while I'd successfully avoided the mess of my past, I'd somehow found myself in an even bigger, smellier pile of mess in my present.

Andy grabbed my ass as I thumbed through my phone for an Uber, and my heart pounded in my chest, drowning out the tequila.

I don't want him touching me.

I don't want him to come home with me.

I want Zach.

That last thought hit me like a truck, and I shook it off, blaming the alcohol. I was just emotional after blowing up at him. Belle I could apologize to, but he would be a different story.

Maybe I should go apologize to him now...

That thought stunned me, and my thumb hovered over where I needed to tap to officially order us our ride.

"I can't wait to get you home," Andy said, nuzzling into my neck.

I pushed him off, stumbling back toward the bar. "Change of plans."

"Wait, where are you going?"

"I need to talk to someone."

I was almost to the door when Belle bounded out of it, colliding with me as we spun in a tornado of hair and slinging purses.

"Whoa, whoa," she said, catching me by the arms and holding me upright.

Her eyes turned to slits when Andy tried to steal me from her grasp.

"I've got her," she said to him.

"We were just leaving."

"And now, *we're* leaving," Belle said, pointing between the two of us. "As in, me and her, and not you."

Andy scoffed, looking to me for back up.

"She's right," I slurred, shaking my head. "I don't want to leave with you."

"That's not what you said literally five minutes ago," he breathed like a dragon.

"She changed her mind." Belle puffed up her chest, shielding me behind her. "Now, scram."

Andy rolled his eyes, and I swore I heard him mutter something about me being a cock tease as he ripped open the door to the bar and flew back inside. I closed my eyes, but they shot open again once I remembered what mission I'd been on.

"I have to go talk to Zach," I slurred.

"Oh, no, you don't," Belle said, catching me by the waist and spinning me away from the door again. "Look, I ordered us an Uber, we're going home, you're going to bed, and then you can figure the rest out in the morning. Okay?"

"But—"

"You're drunk, Gemma," Belle said. "And, you had a shit night. Sleep it off, and you can call him in the morning with whatever it is you need to say. Deal?"

I could barely register her words, so I just nodded, and she pulled me into her on a long breath. She held me until the moment the car came, and then we piled in, and the ride home was just as blurry as the night had been.

Belle got me inside and tucked into my bed, but as soon as she was gone, I stumbled to my bathroom and fell to my knees on the tile in front of my toilet. The entire room spun as I stared at that porcelain, the water just waiting to catch whatever I needed to throw at it, but nothing came.

I closed my eyes, twisting until my back was against the toilet as I let out a sigh. My feet flopped out in front of me, and I sank down, running my hands back through my hair that had fallen out of my ponytail.

I was a mess.

The tequila swam in my bloodstream as I sat there, and I didn't know how much time passed before I crawled out of the bathroom, locking my front door before I swiped my phone off the kitchen counter. The screen blurred as I typed, fingers moving in slow motion like they were under water as I texted Zach.

- Ha, guess I win, huh? Told you you were wrong about me being at the bar to see you. -

I sent the text with an emoji, one winking and sticking its tongue out. But when nothing came through from Zach in response, I sighed, typing out another.

- I'm sorry. -

I let eleven minutes pass, staring at my screen like I could will him to text me if I held my eyes open long enough. I shouldn't have texted him. If Belle was there, she wouldn't have let me. She was right. I needed to sober up, to apologize to him the way he deserved.

But the tequila was swirling in my stomach and my head, making me want to text him again, and I threw my phone across the room onto my couch before I gave in to temptation.

I needed sleep.

I couldn't solve anything tonight, and truthfully, I didn't know how to make sense of anything, anyway. When I left the bar, I was gloating, satisfied with proving my point. I was angry at Zach. I wanted him to leave me the hell alone.

But when the car had driven me and Belle across town, I couldn't stop thinking about what he'd said.

I don't know what happened, I don't know who hurt you. But I can see it. I can see you hurting and I promise you, from experience, running from it won't make it go away.

It seemed the more I tried to push him away, the more Zach tried to get me to let him in. I just couldn't figure out why.

What's more, I couldn't figure out why part of me wanted to give in.

I knew what happened when I did, when I believed a man who told me he cared about me. I knew the kind of heartbreak that came from being betrayed, from being lied to. And yet, I was still a slave to my emotions.

I liked him.

I shook my head as soon as the thought hit me, digging the heels of my hands into my eyes. "Ugh, you're drunk, Gemma. Go to bed."

Speaking the words out loud seemed to make them true, and I took my own advice, peeling off my clothes and climbing under my sheets again with my head still spinning.

I didn't like Zach. I didn't want to date him or anyone. There was a reason I agreed to Belle's idea, to her plan for using my season tickets — because it was safe. It would be football, and fun, and making new friends without the possibility of having my heart — what was left of it, anyway — shattered again.

And the bonus was having a little human contact, something I'd been missing, and something I could get without falling in love.

Why did he have to be the *one guy* who wasn't okay with banging me and leaving me alone? Any other man would have jumped for joy at the arrangement. But not Zach Bowen.

I sighed, wincing against the headache that was already starting to pound through. Maybe it was residual from the one I'd had earlier, or maybe it was the tequila punishing me before I'd even had the chance to sleep. Regardless, I forced a calming breath and rolled onto my stomach, stretching out and focusing on what I could control.

I can call him in the morning.

I can apologize.

I can explain that I was having a bad day, and that I didn't mean to upset him.

I'd messed up, but I could fix it.

In the morning.

When I was sober.

GEMMA

I did not feel better in the morning.

In fact, I did not feel better in the afternoon or the evening, either. It was the first time I'd called out of work in years.

Luckily, I had a very forgiving, and very understanding boss — one who had witnessed the train wreck that was my life the night before.

"How ya feeling over there, sport?"

I groaned, putting Belle on speaker phone and dropping my phone on the bed before pulling the covers up over my shoulders. "Why are you yelling at me?"

"I'm practically whispering. Are you still feeling that bad?"

"Like I was beaten and thrown in a dumpster."

Belle clicked her tongue. "Well, tequila will do that."

"How is work? I'm sorry I didn't make it in."

"Well, seeing as how it's seven pm, work is over."

My eyes popped open, and I rolled, squinting at the decorative clock hanging on the opposite end of my room. "Oh, my God. It's *seven*?"

"You're still in bed, aren't you?"

I didn't answer, and Belle chuckled.

"Work was fine. You're the best assistant in this world and while I'm willing to admit that I'm insanely happy I don't have to do this without you every day, I am proud to report that I made it through just fine on my own."

I smiled. Belle was one of the most sought-after interior designers in the city, offering everything from consulting and design to full furnishing and decorating. Since I'd never really wanted anything other than to have a family, I'd happily taken her up on her offer to be her assistant once her business started booming.

After all, making plans, lists, keeping things organized? It was like getting paid to do what I loved to do, anyway.

Besides, Carlo was the money maker in our family. He didn't want me to have to worry about working, especially once we started talking about kids.

My stomach twisted at that thought. I had cried so many nights during our marriage, wondering why it was taking so long for us to get pregnant. Now, I didn't know if I was more devastated that I didn't have a piece of him to keep here with me, a child of his to raise, or if it was a blessing in disguise.

"I'm very proud of you," I said through a yawn.

"Wish I could say the same right now, bestie." Belle sighed. "Talk to me. How are you feeling?"

I pushed myself to sit up in bed, groaning as my muscles ached in protest. "Like a kite in a hurricane." I sighed, picking at my nail polish. "I was actually okay with this plan, you know? I had it all figured out. And then my *practice round* turned out to be a big pain in my ass and threw everything out of whack. Now, I don't have control of anything. I mean, the next home game is Sunday. I haven't even found someone to go with."

"Do you even still want to do this anymore?"

I chewed the inside of my lip, considering her question. "I do. I mean, look..." I ran a hand back through my greasy, rat-nest-like hair. "I'm not ready to date, to be in a relationship." I kind of laughed at that. "Clearly. And honestly, I don't *want* to do that again. But you were right..." I sighed. "I miss being touched, being looked at by a man who wants me, spending time with the opposite sex or, honestly, *anyone*. And Zach showed me that *that* part of me I thought was dead is still *very* much alive. So, yes. I do want to keep going to the games, and I do want to stick to our original plan."

"Do you think," Belle asked, pausing a moment before she continued. "Is it possible that maybe it's *Zach* that you want, not just some random guy? Maybe that's why it's hard for you to pick the next one."

I shook my head firmly. "No. I mean, yes, I like Zach. He's fun, he's hot." I chuckled. "He infuriates the hell out of me. But, I really do feel like I'm being true to myself when I say I don't want to go past one night with a guy. I mean, I hope Zach and I can be friends, but... nothing more."

My chest was tight as I said those words, probably due to my drunken confessions to myself last night. But that was the tequila talking. I was attracted to Zach, which was normal, but I didn't want more from him than what we'd already had.

I *couldn't* want more than that.

My sober mind was all too aware of what its drunken counterpart had neglected to take into consideration last night, which was that no matter how safe Zach felt in *this* moment, he wasn't.

No one was.

I could hear Belle moving around in her condo, but no words came. After a long pause, she cleared her throat. "Well, if that's the case, then my theory is you feel out of control because you acted out of character last night. If you want to get the reins back, I think you should call Zach and apologize. Talk to him. Establish a friendship, make it crystal clear you want nothing more, and then you'll feel better and you can move on to the next guy."

"In theory, that all sounds grand," I said. "But, do you think there's any chance in hell he'll want to speak to me, let alone be my friend, after last night?"

Belle sighed. "There's only one way to find out."

We ended the call not too long after that, and I sat in my bed, staring at my cell phone and debating whether I should call Zach or not.

On the one hand, I sort of felt validated in my actions. After all, I'd told him he was wasting his time. I told him I didn't want anything more with him than that one night, and he just wouldn't take no for an answer. So, last night, I proved to him that I was serious. It might not have been the *classiest* way to get my point across, but it worked.

Still, the larger, louder part of me felt like putting my own self in timeout. It didn't matter what I was trying to accomplish, my actions last night had been deplorable — even my own *body* was punishing me for it. I felt like shit because I should have. Just because I didn't want to date Zach didn't mean I didn't like him as a human being.

And wasn't that part of my whole plan, to make friends, too? Why didn't I just explain to him that I liked him, but that I couldn't be more than friends right now? I played the game because it felt like fun, because I wanted to prove a point.

The only thing I'd proven was how much of a jackass I could be.

I could have sat and argued with myself all day, blaming my actions on the dream I'd had of Carlo, or on my past, or whatever else I could think of. But instead, I grabbed the phone, and I dialed Zach's number.

"Hello?"

His voice was gruff, like he'd had just as rough of a night as I'd had.

"Hey," I said, and suddenly, any idea of what I should say was thrown out the window. "Uh... how are you?"

"Just peachy. Did you need something?"

He was being short, and I could tell he was angry. He should have been. *I* would have been.

I inhaled, blowing out my next breath slowly and kicking the covers off my lap. "I'm sorry about last night, Zach."

My heart was in my throat, especially when he didn't respond. But once I opened the flood gates, everything just poured out.

"It's not an excuse, but you're right, I have been hurt. And yesterday was a bad day. I just... I wasn't in the right mindset to be out and drinking, and I had all this stuff on my mind."

There was still silence on the other end, and suddenly I couldn't have the conversation while sitting still. I crawled out of bed, pacing the floor in my bedroom.

"At first, I was just having fun. I was playing your game."

"I wasn't playing a game."

I swallowed. "No, no, I just mean, you know, I was teasing you or whatever. But I took it too far, and then I was all butthurt after some of the stuff you said last night. Again, I just wasn't in the right mindset. But, that doesn't mean I should have done what I did, or said those things, and I just feel like shit and..." I sighed. "I'm sorry, okay? Truly."

There was a long, heavy breath on the other end, and then Zach's dejected voice. "It's fine."

"No, seriously. I really am sorry. Look, I mean it when I say I'm not ready to date you... but it's not just you. It's anyone. And I know that sounds stupid and cliché, but I just... I've done the dating thing, and the love thing, and I don't want to do it anymore."

"It's cool. I get it."

"But just because I can't go on a date with you or be in a relationship, it doesn't mean we can't be friends, right?" I stopped pacing, hope springing to my chest. "I really do have so much fun with you, Zach. I think it'd be awesome to hang out more, watch the games together, get to know each other more. Belle and I can come crash your shifts at the bar," I added with a laugh. "What do you say? Truce?"

Zach laughed, but it wasn't the same kind of laugh as mine. It almost seemed laced with sarcasm, or disbelief.

"Sure, Gemma. We can be friends."

"Do you really mean that, or are you being sarcastic?"

He sighed, and my heart leapt into my throat waiting for his reply. When it didn't come, I kept rambling.

"This plan, I'm sure it seems stupid to you, but it's really important to me. I think that's why I went to such drastic lengths to preserve it. It's the first time I've put myself out there since... since I was hurt, and—"

"It's fine, okay? It's cool. Friends. Got it."

I sighed, smiling. "Okay. Thank you, Zach, for listening. For understanding."

"Uh-huh."

"Are you going to the game Sunday? Will I see you there?"

There was another sigh. "Yeah, I'll be at the game. And don't worry. I got your message loud and clear. I won't give you any trouble."

I swallowed a thick, sticky ball, wondering why my stomach was tying up so tightly when Zach was telling me exactly what I'd convinced myself I wanted to hear.

"Thank you." I paused. "You know, you should bring someone. A friend. We could all hang out, it'd be fun."

"Sure."

"Okay," I said, pacing again. I'd always felt awkward when apologizing, mostly because I hated admitting I was wrong. And the longer I stayed on the phone with Zach, the more the heavy silence between us became too much. "Well, I should get going. But I'll see you Sunday."

"See you Sunday."

As soon as the words were out of his mouth, the line went dead.

Part of me felt sick, like I'd made a mistake, but I was willing to recognize that that was the part of me that still believed in love. She was small, and weak, and beaten and bruised, but she was there. And *that* part of me was sad that I'd blown off such a sexy, funny, amazing guy.

But, the larger part of me, the *new* me, was happy and relieved. Now that Zach and I had established a friendship, now that I knew he would no longer be pulling any tricks out of his hat to try to get another date with me, I could focus on the original plan.

My next breath came easier, the relief of being back in control already hitting me like a shot of heroin. It was my drug — control — and I needed it to survive.

I opened the dating app, swiping through my messages until I found one that looked promising. And once I had a date lined up for the next home game, it was like my hangover was gone altogether.

I was back in control, the plan was back in place, and everything felt right again.

Stripping out of my underwear and t-shirt, I ran a hot bath, sinking into the steaming water and letting it soothe my aching muscles. I knew Zach was still upset, and he had every right to be. But, tonight was a stepping stone for both of us. We'd both move forward, knowing where we stand with the other, and we could finally stop playing all the games.

In fact, I was pretty sure this was the *best* thing that could have happened, the more I thought about it. Now, Zach and I were friends. He was a great guy, and we had so much fun together. Maybe one day, we'd look back on all this and laugh.

I smiled, closing my eyes and sinking deeper into the water.

Everything was back to normal.

ZACH

"What's wrong, sweetie?" Mom asked at dinner Saturday night, her eyes sad as she watched me push another bite of my lasagna around my plate. "You love lasagna. It's your favorite."

"He's probably just sad that I denied his request to work tonight," Doc said.

Mom gasped, like I'd personally offended her. "You wouldn't miss family dinner. Why would you want to work tonight?"

I sighed, dropping my fork to the plate and sinking back into my chair. "I just have a lot on my mind, Mom. I figured working would keep me from sulking."

"That's not how we raised you," Dad chimed in, wiping his mouth with his napkin. He took a sip of his red wine, leveling his gaze with mine across the table. "Suppressing whatever is bothering you is only going to make it more of a mess when it all boils over."

I ran a hand over my head, roughing up my hair and suppressing a groan. I would never be disrespectful to my father, but right now, the last thing I wanted to hear was his preachy shit about how I should embrace my feelings.

That was what got me into this mess in the first place.

"What's going on, son?" he asked after a moment. "Talk to us."

"Oh, oh," Micah said, shoveling a large piece of garlic bread into his mouth and holding up one hand like he was in school. "Let me guess. Football girl broke your heart already, didn't she?"

"Shut up, Micah."

He just laughed. "Oh, man, I nailed it, didn't I? What, she didn't fall for the rose pedals on the bed and the Nicholas Sparks double feature?"

I gritted my teeth together, letting my fist fall hard on the table. "Damn it, Micah, I said don't."

The whole table shook with my action, and Mom reached out to steady her wine glass before her eyes narrowed in on me. "Zachary Abel."

"Sorry, Mom. I'm sorry." I sighed, folding up my napkin and placing it on the table. "I'm okay, I promise, okay, guys? Just not in the mood to be razzed tonight."

"Hey, I'm sorry, bro," Micah said, sincerity in his eyes. "I was just messing around."

"It's okay." I cleared my throat, standing. "I'm going to get some fresh air. Excuse me."

I didn't look at any of them as I ducked out of the dining room, my next breath coming once I was on our back porch. I draped my arms over the railing, watching the sun set over the trees in the distance, the Chicago skyline outlined behind them.

I was pathetic.

It had been five full days since I'd seen Gemma, since the night she'd made her point *crystal* clear at Doc's bar, and yet I was still moping around like a boy who'd lost his dog. I should have been able to let her go by now, to accept that what I wanted wasn't going to happen — but it seemed like my attitude about the whole thing only got worse the more time passed.

At first, I'd just been pissed. There I was, excited as hell to see her that night, to talk to her, to learn more about her, and she'd shown up to my bar and hung all over another guy in front of me. What was worse was that she *knew* what she was doing to me. It was on purpose. It was a game. She even admitted it when she called me the next day.

But, it was after that call that my anger turned to a feeling of helplessness.

She was finally honest with me, telling me she'd been hurt, and asking me to respect the fact that she just wasn't ready to date yet. It had been all fun and games before, buying the season tickets next to her just to rattle her. I thought it was about sticking to her plan, about her OCD personality that needed to check shit off her list.

But it was more than that.

Someone had fucked her over. I didn't know who, or what they did, and I probably never would. All I did know was that she'd asked me to be her friend with desperation in her voice that let me know she meant it when she said that's all she could let me be.

Friends.

I laughed out loud again at that, shaking my head as the last little sliver of sun dipped below the skyline. The thought that I could be just friends with that woman was ludicrous, and yet somehow, I knew I'd take the torture. I knew I'd go to that game tomorrow and sit beside her, and try to be around her in whatever capacity she'd let me — simply because I wanted her that bad.

Fucking *pathetic.*

My phone buzzed in my pocket, snapping me out of my pity party. I didn't recognize the number, so I sent it to voicemail, content to sulk on my own for a while longer. I knew, eventually, I'd have to suck it up and move on. Doc was right — she was just a girl. There were a million others out there.

The problem was there wasn't a single other one like *her.*

That much I knew.

My phone buzzed again, and I huffed, frowning when I saw the same number. I answered this time, resorting to taking my frustration out on whatever poor telemarketer was on the other end.

"Whatever you're selling, I'm not buying. Fuck off."

"Whoa," a soft, familiar voice said. "That's messed up. What if I was like a single mom just trying to sell carpet shampoo and make ends meet, you jerk."

I frowned. "Belle?"

"Indeed. You free to talk for a sec?"

I leaned a hip against the railing. "Uh, yeah. How did you get my number?"

"Well, I'm at the bar right now, but the cute little bartender who's here said you're off on Saturdays. She gave me your number."

I sighed. "So much for protection of employees."

"Oh, shut it, I would have stolen it from Gemma if I had to. Which brings me to why I'm calling."

"Look, she already talked to me, okay?" I pushed off the railing, crossing the porch to sit on the swing Dad built for Mom a few years back. "I got it. Just friends."

"Yeah, well... about that."

Belle paused, and I sat up a little straighter.

"Here's the thing, PITA Boy."

"PITA?"

"Pain In The Ass. That's how Gemma affectionately refers to you."

I chuckled. "Why does that not surprise me."

"Anyway, look, I like you, okay? And I know Gemma does, too. She's too fucked up to admit it, and her favorite thing to do is shove anything resembling an emotion down into a basement full of boxes so she can continue living upstairs and ignore everything lurking in the dark down there." She sighed. "I know what she told you, and I know she *thinks* that's what she wants — but, I also have the good fortune of knowing her better than she knows herself."

"What are you saying?" I asked, leaning forward on the swing and resting my elbows on my knees.

"I'm saying that my dumb ass best friend likes you, and she's scared of you because of it. And, I think we should band together to get her to open her big, beautiful, dumb eyes."

I smirked, and though hope floated through me like a feather in the wind, reality snatched it in a fist, crushing it almost instantly.

"You're sweet, Belle," I said, voice low. "And I appreciate you reaching out to try to make me feel better. But, Gemma made her point very clear on Monday night, and she sealed it with her call on Tuesday. She seemed to know very well what she wants... and what she doesn't. I think we should both respect that."

"You're right. We probably should. She told me she wants to keep going through with the new guy every game thing and I want to just support her in that but..." she sighed. "Well, the thing is, that even if it makes me an intrusive best friend, I don't think I can do that."

I didn't know what to say, so I just waited for her to continue.

"This is classic Gemma. She spiraled on Monday night, and then she felt like shit," Belle said. "In a desperate attempt to gain back control over the situation, she took everything in front of her and looked at it as logically as she could. She packed the emotions away, tucked them in her basement, and focused on making lists, and plans. You're not something she can easily fit into either category, therefore she had to push you into a zone she understood — the friend zone. There, she knows how to handle you. There, she thinks she's in control. But I know her, and I know she likes you — more than she's willing to admit."

"How do you know?"

"Because she can't stop talking about you," Belle answered easily. I couldn't help the way my stomach flipped at that, a smile climbing at the corner of my lips. "Even if it is only to say how much you infuriate her."

I laughed, and suddenly the energy running through me was too much. I stood, pacing the porch. Hope tried to fly again, but I couldn't let go of everything Gemma had said to me on the phone, and I couldn't erase everything I'd seen that night at the bar.

"She doesn't want me around, Belle," I said on a sigh. "She made that perfectly clear. Why would I waste my time with someone who doesn't give a shit about me?"

"Because you want her just as much as she wants you."

"I'm not saying that's not true," I conceded. "But at what point does it go from me being persistent and romantic to me being pathetic and weak? Or worse — to not listening to what she is telling me she wants and respecting that." I shook my head, stopping at the railing again and staring off in the distance. "She took another guy home, right in front of me. And then she called me and asked me to be *friends*. I mean, seriously," I said, almost laughing. "How much more of a sign can she give me?"

"She didn't take him home."

I paused. "What?"

"Andy. When I went outside, she was already on her way back into the bar to talk to you. I told her to wait until she was sober."

My heart stopped in my throat, kicking back to life somewhere in my chest where it was supposed to be.

"She told Andy to get lost," Belle continued. "And I made sure he did what she said. Andy went back inside the bar, Gemma went home with me — and she went to bed alone."

She hadn't taken him home? I searched my memory of that night, wondering how I missed Andy coming back inside the bar. I couldn't remember seeing him again. Then again, I couldn't remember seeing anything other than the red blazing behind my eyelids as I managed my way through the last of my shift.

Belle was quiet as I processed.

"She still called me the next day and told me she wanted to be friends..." I said after a moment, though my heart squeezed in protest under my rib cage, telling me to go after her even though she'd told me to leave it alone. I was torn between listening to her, respecting her wishes, and wanting to believe her best friend *and* my own intuition that said she was interested in me.

What a fucking gray area.

Belle stayed quiet a long time, not answering me, and then there was a long huff on the other end.

"Fine. You're right. You should just give up. I mean, I'm sure you haven't thought about her once since that night, anyway, right?"

My jaw clenched, stomach churning.

"And I'm sure you don't care that she's got another date lined up for tomorrow's game, that she could potentially take *that* guy home with her — even if she didn't do that with Andy."

I gritted my teeth more.

"Yeah, I'm sure you've completely moved on and filed her away in that box of normal, boring, dime-a-dozen girls who got away. I'm sorry I even called, I'm wasting your time."

But Belle didn't hang up, she just paused, waiting for my response because she knew I'd have one.

"You made your point," I managed between clenched teeth, another long exhale leaving my chest. But I still wasn't sold. It didn't matter how much Gemma had been on my mind — she'd asked me to fuck off as politely as she could.

Then again, if she'd meant that, why was her best friend calling me?

I wanted to believe Belle — if for no other reason than because what she was saying was what I wanted to hear. But, I also cared about Gemma, and I didn't want to push her away. I had already settled on being her friend — in whatever capacity I could be.

"Why do you care?" I asked after a moment, picking at the paint chipping off the wood of our porch railing. "You see the way she acts with me, and you were there Monday night. I'm sure you also talked to her the next day, before she even called me."

"Exactly," she said, as if the answer was obvious. "I was there. I see everything you do, but I know her better than you do, too — probably better than anyone. She was sick the next morning when she woke up, Zach. All day, actually. And whether she wants to admit it or not, she likes you. She's just terrified."

I nodded, because I knew that fear all too well. There was only one girl I'd ever dated and told I loved her, and she'd turned her back on me as soon as my promise of going pro was out the window. I knew what betrayal felt like, how long that sting lasted. It was enough to never want to try again.

"I know it seems like I'm being a dick best friend," she continued when I didn't say anything. "I mean, here Gemma is telling us both what she wants. I should listen. I should just... back off. But, I love her," she said on a sigh. "And *that's* why I can't listen to what she says, not when everything she's *not* saying is speaking so much louder. She's told me before to save her from herself, to do for her what she would do for me. And, well... I believe this is one of those scenarios."

"I get that, I really do," I said. "But... instead of trying to read her, to say you know what's best, why not just listen to what she's telling you, what she's telling *me*?"

"Because," she answered with a huff, exasperated. She caught a breath before she continued. "I'm just... I'm tired of watching my best friend hurt and not doing anything to try to fix it. She has done so much for me, Zach... so much."

Her voice faded then, and for some reason, my heart squeezed again — for Belle this time instead of Gemma. I didn't know much about her, but I knew she loved Gemma fiercely.

She was the kind of friend anyone would be lucky to have.

"I like you," she finally said when she'd taken a breath. "You're a good guy. You're a fighter. No one has ever fought for Gemma in her life." She paused. "And she's the kind of girl who deserves to be fought for."

I rolled my lips together, swallowing down a knot of emotion at her words. Maybe it was because I was honored she saw so much in me, or maybe it was because I was sad she saw so much in her best friend that Gemma tried so desperately to hide.

"Alright," I said, nodding. "I'm listening."

"Are you? Because I don't want the half-ass version of Zach Bowen. I need the full on third quarter, four points down, twenty seconds to land a hoop Zach Bowen."

I frowned. "Literally none of that makes sense."

"Whatever. I'm not a sports girl. What I'm asking is, do you still want her?"

My chest tightened, a flash of her smile assaulting me like the answer I already knew I had. "I want her. I want to fight for her."

Belle let out a relieved breath, lowering her voice like she was telling me a secret. "Good. Now that we got all that out of the way, brace yourself for the crazy."

"I'm just *now* supposed to brace for that?"

She laughed. "Well, let's just say that I know my best friend, and while I know she has feelings for you, that doesn't mean this is going to be easy." Belle paused. "We might have to do something a little... *drastic*... to wake her up."

Something told me I was going to regret my next question, but I was already in too deep. It really was like being in the last quarter, down by seven, coach screaming at the entire team in a huddle for us to give everything we had left to clinch the win.

Belle was right. Gemma *was* worth fighting for.

And I was all in.

"What do you have in mind?"

ZACH

I couldn't stop tapping the heel of my foot as we watched the teams warm up the next afternoon.

It was an early game, kick-off at one pm, but even with the earlier start, we couldn't escape the chill of October in Illinois. Gone were the warm days of summer, fall in full effect now, and the gray sky matched my mood and general outlook on the day.

This was a bad idea.

Belle wasn't kidding when she said she wanted to do something drastic to get Gemma's attention. Not only was I here at the game, knowing Gemma would be here soon, too, with her date — but I *also* brought a date.

Belle.

"God, I would pick the first game all season that's been cold," she said, shivering a little as she tucked her hands in the front pocket of her hoodie. It was tight, hugging her slim frame, and her jeans had strategically ripped holes up and down her thighs. She didn't exactly dress to be warm, but then again, she wasn't there to be comfortable.

She was there to provoke her best friend.

"Are you sure this is a good idea?" I asked, foot still bouncing as I watched the field. "I feel like this could really piss her off."

"That's the point." Belle propped her feet up on the back of the chair in front of her. "Look, this is the perfect way to call her on her bullshit. If she really just wants to be your *friend*, then it won't matter to her that you brought another girl."

"Even if it's her best friend?"

"Well, yeah, okay, so it's a little bit of a jab," she admitted. "But she'll be more pissed at me than she will be at you, and once she loses it and goes off on me, I can give her the reality slap."

"This just sounds like everything she would never want us to do." I shook my head. "I don't know, I think we should call it. I don't feel great about the plan."

"Zach Bowen, listen to me," Belle said, her little teeth chattering. "I know this is kind of crazy. I realize we are playing with fire. I am also fully aware that Gemma told us what she wanted and we are blatantly disrespecting that." She paused, sincerity falling over her features. "But... just trust me when I say that I know my best friend. And if what I think is actually happening is true, then this will snap her out of everything. And she'll finally talk to me. And to you."

"And if you're wrong?"

"Well, then, she'll probably slap me and you and hate us both forever and that'll be the end of it all."

"Great."

"But I don't think it'll go like that."

I chuckled. "Of course you don't. Let me ask you this. What if she doesn't give a shit that I'm here, or that you're here with me?"

Belle smiled at that, cocking one brow. "Again, trust me. She'll care."

I wasn't as sure as she was, but regardless, I'd signed on. So, I reached forward for my beer, taking a drink and trying to settle my nerves. If anything, it would still be a fun day. I could watch football, hang out with Belle, and worst-case scenario, Gemma would prove that she really did just want to be my friend by not caring that I was there with someone else. If that were the case, then maybe I could finally move on and put her behind me.

Then again, maybe Belle really did know her as well as she said she did, and maybe she really did want me, too.

That little thread of hope was enough to make me smile. I felt it when Gemma looked at me, when she blushed any time I touched her, but her words and actions at the bar Monday night made me question everything.

She was like a Rubik's Cube in a blind man's hand — impossible to figure out.

And yet I was the blind man determined to try.

Belle leaned over, threading her arm through mine. "Thank you so much for bringing me," she said, brushing a piece of my hair from my face.

I frowned, looking at her like she was crazy. "You told me to."

Belle widened her eyes, still smiling as she spoke through her teeth. "I'm so excited to be here."

It was then that I glanced behind her, just in time to see Gemma stop dead in her tracks on her way through the aisle to her seats.

My heart kicked to a thundering gallop at the sight of her, its rhythm racing in my ears as I tore my gaze away quickly and brought my attention back to Belle. I smiled at her, tapping her nose and pretending like I didn't see Gemma behind her.

"Of course, I'm glad you came," I said.

Belle smirked. "Game time," she whispered. Then, she turned in her seat to face the field, smile growing when she pretended like she'd just noticed Gemma. "Oh! Hey! There you are!"

Belle stood, wrapping Gemma in a hug, though she was stiff in her arms. One hand held a beer, the other a hot dog, and her eyes were wide and zeroed in on me as her best friend held her. I stood, stuffing my hands in the pockets of my jeans as I put on my game face.

"You must be Jordan," Belle said next, releasing Gemma and reaching a hand back to the guy standing behind her. He was tall, lean, with the build of a soccer player or a golfer. He wore a navy blue Bears sweater, an orange and white plaid shirt cuffed underneath it, and khakis.

"Hey," he said, smiling wide. He had the smile of a news anchor. "Yeah, nice to meet you..."

"Belle," she answered for him. "I'm Gemma's best friend. This is Zach," she said, gesturing back to me. "My date."

Jordan leaned past Gemma and Belle both to shake my hand, and the entire time we said our greetings, I watched Gemma out of the corner of my eye.

She was steaming.

Her cheeks were red, and though I could have assumed it was from the brisk chill in the air, I knew it wasn't. She still hadn't said a word, eyes wide and murderous as she flicked her gaze back and forth from me, to Belle, and back again.

And though I schooled my features, keeping my focus on Belle, I couldn't help but check Gemma out in my peripheral. Her jeans were a dark denim, hugging her hips and thighs like they were painted on. She had on a hoodie, just like Belle, but it was a little baggier, covering her curves but giving her the girl-next-door feel that she pulled off so well. Her makeup was flawless, eyes outlined in a smoky charcoal, and her hair was flowing in soft curls over her shoulders.

She was beautiful. Just like always.

"Here, sit," Belle said, pulling me down to sit next to her as she gestured to Gemma's seats. "Oh, yum, a hot dog. I definitely want one of those," she added, looking up at me. "Can we get one of those in a bit?"

"Whatever you want," I answered easily, propping my arm up on the back of the chair behind her.

Gemma watched that arm for a brief second, then she tore her gaze away, plopping down into the seat next to Belle as Jordan took the one on the other side of her.

I half wanted to hide, half wanted to trade Belle spots and sit next to Gemma. I didn't want to play this game. I just wanted to talk to her.

Maybe that's exactly what I should do...

As if she could read my mind, Belle tugged on my arm, pulling me back into her plan.

"This is so fun," she said, bouncing.

"You hate football."

It was the first thing Gemma had said, and as soon as the words left her lips like they were poisonous darts, she cleared her throat, forcing a smile.

"I mean, it's not really your thing, I'm surprised you're here."

"Well, maybe a zebra can change its stripes, after all," Belle said in a sing-song voice. She leaned closer to me, looking up at me through her lashes. "Besides, these seats have a great view."

I smiled, but before I could respond, there was a commotion in Gemma's seat. Belle and I both looked over in time to watch ketchup and cheese drip from Gemma's hand onto the concrete between her legs.

She held her squished hot dog out and away from her clothes, cursing under her breath.

"Here," her date said, handing her a stack of napkins. "You okay?"

"I'm fine," Gemma clipped. She shoved her ruined hot dog under her seat without taking a single bite, using the napkins Jordan had handed her to wipe the ketchup off her hands. "There was a bug."

"Oh," Jordan said, frowning. "Want me to go get you another hot dog?"

She hook her head. "No, no, it's okay."

Gemma forced a breath, tucking the messy napkins under her seat with the hot dog and sitting back up with a new resolve. She glanced at me with a tight smile before leaning into Jordan. "Guys, Jordan here is a *doctor*."

The way she stared at me, I saw it — what Belle said would be there.

She was playing the game.

We'd triggered her, and I was about to find out if that was a good or bad thing.

Belle raised her brows. "Oh, is he now?" She turned her attention to Jordan. "What kind of doctor?"

"Ah, I'm just a pediatrician," he said, rubbing the back of his neck with a blush. "I love kids."

"That's so sweet," Belle said. "Good pick, Gemma."

Gemma seemed validated by Belle's comment, and her smile loosened, taking on a more smug appearance. "Right? *And*, he has a dog."

Jordan whipped out his phone, showing us all a picture of a golden retriever. I had to give it to him, he had the whole perfect date thing down. He was easy to look at, educated, had a great job, and a love for animals. If I was a chick, I'd swoon, too.

But I couldn't help but notice that while Gemma's hand was holding his, her eyes were still on me.

Jordan kept swiping through photos, telling us all about his dog while Belle laughed and Gemma held her chin high like Jordan was her prized pony instead of her date. Once Jordan tucked his phone away again, Belle squeezed Gemma's knee.

"Yep, you picked a winner, Gem."

Jordan smiled, tucking Gemma under one arm. "We both did."

Gemma smiled up at him just as a breeze blew through, blowing a few strands of her hair over her face. Jordan swept them away, tucking them behind her ear, and my throat tightened.

I didn't know how long I could wait to find out if this hair-brained scheme would work if I had to watch him touch her like that all night.

But Belle must have sensed it, my inner freakout, because she played our next move like a genius.

"Brrr," she said, shivering and crossing her arms over her chest. "I will say, we could have picked a warmer day to come."

Gemma smiled. "I don't know, I like the cold. Fall is my favorite season."

Mine, too.

It took everything in me not to say those words out loud, not to drag Gemma out of her seat and into my lap and ask her to tell me everything she loved about the season.

Instead, I glanced at Belle, who was glaring at me with wide eyes like I missed a cue.

I cocked a brow, and she pursed her lips, glancing down at my hoodie.

Oh.

Clearing my throat, I stood, stripping my hoodie off and handing it down to Belle. "Here," I said. "Take my hoodie."

Belle lit up, pressing a hand to her chest as she looked up at me. "Oh, my God. That's so sweet. Thank you, Zach."

I shrugged, sitting back down like it was no big deal, but I could feel Gemma's stare burning a hole into the side of my head.

Belle tugged the hoodie on over hers, and it swallowed her, covering her from her neck to her knees. She burrowed into it, inhaling a deep breath.

"Mmm," she said. "It smells so good. I love your cologne."

I chuckled, pulling the hood over her head playfully as she batted me away and fixed her hair. "Looks good on you."

Belle just smiled, reaching forward for her beer and turning her attention toward the field. She started talking to Gemma, pretending like nothing had happened as she asked her to explain what everything on the scoreboard meant. And even though Gemma answered every single question, her eyes were lasered in on me, jaw tight as she spoke.

We all stood for the anthem and remained standing for the coin toss right after. Our boys won, and we elected to receive first. We were playing the Patriots, champions many years over, and our team needed to bring their A game if they wanted to win today.

They weren't the only ones.

So, as we took our seats again, I put my arm around Belle, and I settled in for the first quarter that I didn't even expect to play. I didn't want to have to do it this way.

If it were up to me, I would have just taken Gemma out to dinner, or to a movie, or to the freaking zoo. I would have made it clear to her that she was the only girl I was interested in, and that she could trust me not to hurt her.

But when her best friend says she knows a better way? Well, who am I to say she's wrong? Belle has known Gemma for years, and judging by her reaction over the last ten minutes, I had a feeling Belle wasn't wrong in her planning.

It wasn't my favorite way to tackle things, but it *was* my last-ditch effort to win over Gemma Mancini, and that meant it was all or nothing.

Game time.

GEMMA

I'm going to kill her.

I'm going to literally wrap my hands around her dainty little neck and shake her until she stops breathing.

I'd tried to talk myself out of murder for the past two quarters. I did everything I could to focus on Jordan — the insanely attractive doctor with the adorable dog who *should* have had all my attention, anyway. But it was useless. I couldn't listen to a word he said or even give myself the chance to get butterflies when he held my hand or brushed the hair out of my face because all my senses were tuned into the two jackasses next to me.

Belle was my best friend. She had been since high school, when we bonded over our mutual hate for algebra. She'd been there when my grandpa died, and I'd been there when her first love broke her heart. She'd helped me stand up again after Carlo, and I'd helped her build an empire in interior design.

So then *why* was she here, at a football game I knew she couldn't give two shits about, hanging all over a guy she knew I liked.

I mean, I didn't *like* him — not like that. But he was a friend, and he *had* gone down on me roughly three weeks ago. No, I hadn't planted a flag on him or claimed dibs, and yes, I'd told her I didn't want to be in a relationship with him, but still... there was some kind of girl code being violated here.

And no matter how I tried to slice it, no matter how rational I attempted to be, the only thing I could think was that I was going to kill my best friend.

"Come on, come on," I whispered under my breath, watching the field as our boys lined up for the next play. I was still overly aware of Belle and Zach, but that didn't stop me from paying attention to the game. It was third down, and we were losing by three. We had less than two minutes before halftime to either tie up the game up or go all the way in for a touchdown.

The ball was snapped, and our quarterback handed it off to the rookie running back. It didn't look good at first, the Patriots defensive line thick, but then, a hole opened up, and our running back jetted through it, high-tailing it twelve yards down the line and securing the first down.

The stadium roared just as the Patriots called a time-out, and I high-fived Jordan, letting out a *whoo* before I snatched my beer from the holder. I tilted it back, bouncing in my excitement.

"Aw, look," Jordan said, pointing to the screen. "Kiss cam."

I followed where he was pointing, and my chest tightened, my next breath barely squeezing through. An older couple blushed and laughed on the screen before leaning in for a sweet kiss, the entire stadium singing a collective *aww* together.

My eyes flicked to Zach, and like a magnet, I pulled his gaze from the screen to me, instead. He swallowed, and I watched the way his Adam's apple bobbed in his throat, eyes bouncing up to look at his mouth next.

I could still feel that mouth on mine — that first night at my place, and perhaps even stronger at that next game, when he stole a kiss that should have belonged to Ben. I was so mad when he kissed me, but was I *really*?

We both knew the answer to that.

I wanted him to kiss me — that first night, that next game, Monday night.

Now.

I wanted him to kiss me. And I hated that I could never hide that from him.

Belle smacked Zach's chest, snapping his attention away from me and back to her. She smiled, pointing up at the screen, and Zach and I both looked back up at it at the same time.

It was them.

Zach's eyes were wide with shock, his mouth gaping open a little as Belle laughed, turning toward him with an adorable, expectant grin. The crowd cheered, and Zach looked off camera, but not at Belle.

I couldn't take my eyes off the screen.

Because I knew he was looking at me.

Instead, I watched like I was somewhere else, like I was in a completely different state or country altogether as Zach ran the pad of his thumb over Belle's cheek, and then he leaned in and kissed the spot his skin had just touched.

There was another chorus of *aww's,* but he did earn some *boo's*, too, since it was just a kiss on the cheek. Still,

Belle lit up like she'd never been kissed before, like she was a little girl with her first crush, and she leaned into him with the camera still on them, wrapping her arms around his waist as he tucked her under his arm.

And that's when the thought hit me.

Maybe he liked her.

I hadn't even considered it, but he had asked her here after all, right? Maybe, when I'd blown him off, he'd moved on. They had hung out all night at the bar on Monday, when I was with Andy and his friends. Maybe they bonded. Maybe they made a connection.

My stomach twisted, and I doubled over with the pain, covering my mouth as the possibility played out in my head. Jordan rubbed my back, asking if I was okay, and I nodded, sitting back up straight just as the guys lined up for the next play.

I didn't breathe the rest of the quarter.

My eyes were on the field. I stood and cheered when appropriate, I groaned when the play didn't go the way it should have, and though I couldn't have told a single soul how it happened, we somehow got the touchdown by the time the whistle blew for halftime.

I cheered as our guys ran into the locker room, high-fiving Jordan and a few others around us, all the while using every cell in my brain just to take my next breath.

"Wow, this is such a great game!" Belle said. We were all still standing, and she hung her hands on her hips, turning her attention up to Zach. "I'm hungry. Let's go get those hot dogs."

"NO."

The word flew out of my mouth on my next exhale, which was still coming painfully from my chest. Every breath was a struggle, my will to keep my cool fading fast.

I cleared my throat. "I mean, let the guys stay here. I'm hungry, too, and since I messed up my first hot dog, I'll go with you."

"Oh, okay," Belle said, oblivious. She smiled, running her hand down Zach's arm. "Want anything?"

"I'll take another beer."

"You got it." She smiled, giving him a wink as she started for the aisleway. I followed, not asking Jordan if he wanted anything and not looking up at Zach when I squeezed past him, either.

My eyes were zeroed in on the back of my best friend's pretty little head as I imagined what it'd look like if I kicked her to the ground.

Belle bounced up the stairs, falling in line behind the other fans filing up to the concession stands. When we made it to the top, she pulled off to the side, smiling and flipping her hair over her shoulder.

"Hmm, now that we're up here, I think I might want pizza. Do you want pizza?"

I wrapped my fist in Zach's hoodie and tugged her into a corner out of the way. "Cut the shit, Belle."

"Hey!" she pouted, swatting my hand away and smoothing the fabric of the hoodie.

"What are you doing?"

Belle blinked. "I'm watching the game, just like you."

"No. I mean what are you doing *here, with him.*"

She smiled, looking back to our seats like she could somehow see him over the crowd. "He asked me to come. We hung out that night at the bar, and I don't know, he's fun. I figured it'd be cool. Plus, you're here. I can hang out with both of you."

I gritted my teeth. "Belle."

"What?" she asked incredulously, pulling her hair over one shoulder and running her fingers through it.

"What does it matter that I came with him, anyway? I thought you didn't want to date him. I thought you wanted to be his *friend*."

"I do," I answered with a huff, blinking more than necessary. "That's not the point."

"What *is* the point?"

"The point is, you're my best friend," I said, stepping into her. "And you're on a date with a guy *I* was on a date with three weeks ago."

Belle smirked, one brow perking up as she crossed her arms and leaned her weight on one hip.

"I thought it wasn't a date."

I tossed my hands up. "Oh, my God. You know what I mean. Stop playing dumb. I—"

"YOU FIRST," Belle said, cutting me off as she poked me hard in the chest.

Her eyes narrowed, lips flattening into a thin line as I rubbed the spot she'd just poked, taking a step back.

She shook her head, like I was blind or crazy or both. "Gemma, I'm not here because I want to date Zach. Although, to be completely honest, if he would have showed interest in me before you, you can guaranfuckingtee I would have jumped all over that."

I blinked, digesting her words as the crowd shifted around us, but she didn't give me much of a chance to catch on before she continued.

"I'm here because you're being stupid. You're letting this guy go when you *know* you like him, you know he's amazing, and all because what? You're afraid of being hurt?" Belle laughed. "Yeah, dating is scary. It's fucking terrifying. But look at how happy Zach makes you when you're *not* dating him. Can you imagine what it could be like if you were?"

I swallowed, pressing my lips together, not a single word coming to mind to refute her point.

"You'll never know what happiness you could have with him if you don't take the risk of being hurt, Gemma."

My shoulders sagged, mind running over what she'd said as my heart squeezed painfully in my chest. But then I crossed my arms, shaking my head at the pot calling the kettle black. "Says the queen of being single," I popped off. "You never date. How can you preach to me when you're the spokesperson for this shit?"

"Yeah, you're right. I never date," she said, her jaw tight. "I never let anyone in. And you know what? I'm *miserable*. I'm lonely, and detached, and I haven't had a real, genuine connection with anyone other than you in years. So yeah, I have some shit to figure out, and I'm working on it." Her bottom lip quivered a bit, but she stood taller, holding her shoulders back. "But don't be fooled into thinking that this is some sort of glamorous life," she continued, gesturing to herself. "Because it isn't."

I softened at that, reaching out to squeeze her hand. At first, she flinched, but she didn't pull away. She squeezed my hand in return, a heavy sigh leaving her chest.

"I know Carlo hurt you, okay? I know," she said softly. "And I know that me showing up here with Zach wasn't the best thing I could do as your friend. I knew I was pushing your buttons — that was the goal. And it was against everything you told me you wanted," she admitted. "But Zach is a good guy. And unlike Carlo, he's here, *fighting* for you. He wants you. And I know you want him. Stop fighting against him and just... try. Trust him. See what happens."

In theory, her advice sounded so pleasant. It sounded like everything I wanted, to go fall into Zach's arms, to let him in, to try.

But my wounds from Carlo were still fresh, not even scabbed over and scarring yet. They throbbed in protest of the thought.

"What if I get hurt again?" I asked her, something stinging the back of my eyes. I knew it couldn't be tears. I hadn't cried since the day of Carlo's funeral, and even then, those tears hadn't felt like mine. "I can't... I don't know if I could ever come back from that again."

Belle ran her thumb over my knuckles. "If he hurts you, then you do exactly what you did last time. You pick yourself up, dust that shit off, and keep walking. You stand a little straighter and you learn." She paused, glancing to the left like she was thinking of something else metaphoric to say. But when she turned back to me, she shrugged. "And I'll castrate him, for good measure."

A laugh shot out of me, just one at first, but then she laughed and I laughed again, and before I knew it, we were both crying from surrendering to a fit of giggles.

"Ugh," I said, wiping at the corner of my eyes. "Damn it, Belle, I wanted to kill you. You know that? Like, I was weighing the risk of going to prison for life."

Belle smiled, wrapping me in a hug. "I know. I'm a great actress, aren't I? Maybe I should change careers."

"Please don't."

She was still smiling as she let me go, holding her hands on my shoulders. "Fine, I won't. And I'm sorry I had to do that, but I had to wake you up somehow, and this was the closest bucket of cold water I could find."

She watched me for a moment, fixing my hair and straightening my sweater before she smacked my ass playfully.

"Now," she said, pulling back to assess me. "Go get your man."

"What about Jordan?"

She grinned. "Oh, I think I can handle him."

I returned her smile, wrapping her in one more hug and whispering a thank you. Then, I was jogging down the steps back to our seats, not knowing what the hell I was going to say once I got there.

Belle was right behind me, and when I plopped down in the seat next to Zach, he frowned, eyes questioning me before they flicked up to look at Belle.

"Hey, Jordan," she called over my head, ignoring Zach. "Can you come help me with something?"

Jordan looked at me, but I didn't return his gaze, keeping my eyes fixed on Zach.

"Uh, sure."

He stood, letting Belle tug him up toward the concession stands as Zach looked back to me.

"Hi," I breathed.

Zach smirked. "Hi?"

Swallowing, I extended a shaking hand toward him. "I'm Gemma Mancini. And I am really, *really* stupid."

He laughed, taking my hand in his. "I'm Zach Bowen. I can also be pretty stupid."

"Looks like we already have something in common."

I smiled, heart pounding out of my chest as I searched for the right words to say. I kept Zach's hand in mine, but dropped it down until it rested in my lap. I held onto him like he was the one thing grounding me, trying to remember everything Belle had just said as my heart screamed at me to reconsider what I was about to do.

"I'm sorry, Zach. For everything." I shook my head, shrugging. "I had this plan, right? Like, I had this thing that I felt like I could do. Take a different guy to every game, don't get attached, have fun without having to risk getting hurt." I paused. "*Again*." Swallowing, I squeezed his hand in mine. "I felt like I was in control. But then *you* happened."

Zach cringed, but smiled through it. "Sorry?"

"You should be," I said on a laugh, but I covered his hand that was still in mine with the other. "Stepping out of that plan, it freaked me out. *You* freaked me out," I admitted. "You still do. And that's why I've fought against the way you make me feel. It wasn't you I was trying to prove a point to on Monday," I whispered. "It was me."

He smiled, touching my chin with the thumb and pointer finger of his free hand. "The way I make you feel, huh?" he asked. "And how's that?"

I blew out a breath. "Like I'm dancing on top of the world and falling off of it into a dark oblivion all at once."

Zach laughed.

"I don't know what I have to give, or how crazy I'll be while I try to figure it out, but..." I shrugged. "I do like you, Zach. And I don't want to be friends." I paused. "I don't want to be *just* friends."

His hand tightened around mine, and he shook his head, watching me like I was the most infuriating, yet adorable creature in the world.

At least, that's where I *hoped* I'd landed.

"I have a wild proposition," he finally said, still holding my hand.

"What's that?"

"I know it's only halftime, but how do you feel about watching the rest of this game back at your place?"

His eyes sparked with heat, a devilish smile curling on his lips as he watched me. That heat spread from my neck to my toes, pooling between my legs as a completely different kind of throbbing took over my body.

"At least no one will yell at us for standing up there, right?" I teased.

He barked out a laugh, and in the next second, I was in his arms, his lips pressed against mine as my entire body melted into him. It was the kind of relief you felt after a fight, or after hearing the good news you've been praying for for weeks. Every worry, every ounce of tension flowed out of me at once, releasing the knots in my muscles in a single breath.

I was still petrified as we stood there, kissing in a crowd full of football fans, but it was a different kind of fear. It was the kind that came with taking a risk instead of avoiding one, and the kind that was as exciting as it was terrifying.

I didn't know what would happen next. I had no guarantee I wouldn't be hurt. And, honestly, I had no idea what I could give, what I could let go of.

But I knew I wanted to try.

Zach pulled back, his eyes searching mine with his hand still in my hair. There were a million words in those coffee eyes of his, a thousand reasons to smile — but there was a bit of fear, too. And it was his fear that somehow brought comfort to me.

He was taking a risk, too.

"Let's go, then," he said after a moment, eyes still fixed on mine.

I wrapped my hand in his, letting him tug me up through the stands in the opposite direction of everyone else. They were all filing back into their seats while I was texting Belle that we were leaving early. She just responded with a winking face emoji, and I smiled, tucking my phone away and saying another silent thank you to my best friend who knew me better than I knew myself.

We climbed into a waiting cab, Zach pulling me into his arms and running his fingers through my hair, both of us settling into a comfortable silence on the way to my condo.

And for the first time all season, I didn't give a damn how the game ended.

Chapter 13

GEMMA

My hands shook just as much as they did the first night with Zach as I twisted the key in my door. The nerves were almost stronger tonight, born less out of anticipation of what would happen and more out of the high of letting go.

I had surrendered to my feelings for him, backing down on a plan I was so hell bent on sticking with. And now, I was no longer in control.

That both excited and terrified me.

I dropped my keys on the little table by the front door once we were inside, kicking off my sneakers and socks and leaving them by the door, too. The city lights filled my condo with a cool glow, and I only turned on one lamp, leaving it mostly dim.

"Wine?" I asked, already halfway to the kitchen as Zach closed the front door behind him.

He watched me, kicking off his own shoes and leaving them next to mine. "Wine sounds great."

"Red okay?"

He nodded, and I pulled down a new bottle I'd purchased that week, uncorking it and filling two glasses. My hands were still shaking, breath shallow.

You're shaking because you want to touch me, because you want me to touch you.

I heard his words in my mind just as clearly as if he'd just said them, and I bit my lip, cheeks flushing as I crossed my living room to hand him his glass.

I did want him to touch me.

I wanted him to touch me so, *so* bad.

"Thank you," he said, tapping his glass to mine once I'd handed it to him.

We both took a drink with our eyes dancing over each other, smiles playing on our lips.

"I turned on the game," he said, nodding to my TV. I hadn't even noticed it was on.

"Perfect," I said, but I didn't even glance at the score. "Better than the music I put on last time."

Zach laughed at that, shaking his head. "Hey, Marvin set the mood, didn't he? You knew what you were doing."

"I knew *nothing* about what I was doing."

Zach's smile softened, his eyes watching mine. "I know. It was adorable."

"As long as you think so."

I let out a long, slow breath, crossing the room to where the floor-to-ceiling windows overlooked the south side of the city. The stadium was glowing in the distance, and I watched it as the crowd roared on my television. It was quiet, the volume low, but I felt that crowd deep in my chest like they were cheering for me.

Kiss him! Kiss him!

My stomach flipped, and I took a sip of my wine instead of turning around to face Zach again. I couldn't stop shaking. I couldn't stop overanalyzing the fact that I didn't have a plan now.

The ball was his. And my defense was weak.

I gripped my glass a little tighter, eyes widening.

Holy shit.

It was like all the adrenaline from the game, from Belle's pep talk, from having Zach's arms around me faded all at once in a dramatic *whoosh*. Suddenly, the nervous energy shifted from excitement to panic.

I'm not in control.

I don't have a plan.

He was in my condo, again, after I swore he never would be after that first night. I told him I liked him. I admitted I had feelings. I left the guy who *was* in my plan at the game without even telling him I was leaving.

And now, we were back at my place.

And I had no idea what to do.

I took another sip of my wine, forcing a breath, but it got caught somewhere in my chest when a warm hand brushed my hip.

"It really is some view you have up here," Zach said, sliding up behind me. One hand still held his wine, the other gently holding my hip as his eyes washed over the city lights.

"Still hard to believe this place is mine, sometimes," I breathed, pulse ticking up a notch with him so close to me. His breath was warm on my neck, his hand firm as he held me, and where I was visibly shaking, he was serene and calm. Zach commanded my attention simply by standing there behind me, tall and confident, and it was then that I realized.

I'd given the control to him.

And somewhere, deep down beneath my anxiety and fear — I liked that.

Zach turned his gaze from the city to me, but I couldn't look at him. I just stared out the window as he lowered his lips to my shoulder, eliciting a shiver as he kissed the tender skin there.

"You're still nervous."

"Even more than last time," I blurted out on a breath.

Zach chuckled, his warmth leaving me long enough for him to abandon his still-full wine glass on the table next to my couch. He slid up behind me again, this time both hands wrapping around my waist, pulling me flush against him as he breathed me in.

"Remember what I told you last time?" he asked, his breath husky and raw as his hands slipped under the fabric of my hoodie. His hands pressed flat against my stomach, lips brushing against the skin of my neck again.

"Mm-hmm," I managed, but I'd already closed my eyes, soaking in the feel of his hands on me.

"This is the best part," he said, repeating his sentiment from that first night. "You're nervous, because you're excited, because I'm new and I make you feel something."

I swallowed as his hands slid up a little more, under the tank top I wore beneath my hoodie, his fingers splaying over my rib cage.

"You want to touch me," he breathed, rolling his hips against my ass. I gasped at the feel of his hard-on, knowing he was already so turned on, so ready.

"Yes," I breathed.

His hands drifted up even more, fingers slipping beneath the wire of my bra. He brushed the bottom of my breasts, gently at first, and then his fingertips rolled over each of my nipples just as he sucked the lobe of my ear between his teeth.

"And you want me to touch you."

"*God,* yes." I panted, back arching of its own accord. I wanted his hands on me, *fully* on me, wanted to press every inch of me against every inch of him.

I almost forgot about my wine, the glass slipping in my hand, and I took a step toward the table where Zach had abandoned his glass. But his hands tightened around my ribs, holding me in place.

"No," he commanded, and his fingers inched their way up, rolling over my nipples once more. I moaned, head falling back against his shoulder. "Hold onto that wine glass," he said, dragging his tongue over the back of my neck. "And don't you spill a fucking drop."

He squeezed my nipples tighter before letting go of them altogether, and I whimpered, body shaking at the loss.

Zach kissed down my neck, over my shoulder, biting down on the muscle as his hands slipped from under my hoodie and dived down to my jeans, instead. I barely got another breath in before the button was unhooked, the zipper yanked down, and his hands hooked in the hem, rolling the denim down over my hips as he pressed against me harder from behind.

"Ever since the night I first touched you, I've been dying to touch you again," he breathed, tugging my jeans down as I wiggled to help him in his efforts. "To taste you again."

I moaned, rubbing my ass against his rigid cock once my jeans were around my knees. He felt so big against my bare skin, thick and hard and ready to demolish me. But he didn't rip my jeans off farther, didn't yank me around or take even a single article of his own clothing off.

Instead, he let me wiggle the rest of the way out of my jeans, all while holding my wine glass as steady as I could. Then, he gathered my hair in one hand, tugging a little as he moved it over one shoulder and whispered into my ear.

"Can I taste you, Gemma?"

"Yes," I breathed, the word reverberating through me. "Please, *please*."

I felt his lips curl against my skin, and Zach pressed one more kiss beneath my ear before his hands ran their way down my back, over my hips, and he held them tight as he lowered himself to the ground behind me.

When he did, his face was directly in line with my ass.

I sucked in a breath, one hand still clutching that damn wine glass as the other hung awkwardly at my side. I didn't know what to do with that empty hand, where to put it, what to touch. I wanted it in his hair, but he was behind me. I wanted to touch him, but he was out of reach.

But when his tongue ran along my left ass cheek, a satisfied growl ripping from his throat before his teeth sank into my flesh, I didn't have to think about what to do with that hand anymore.

I gasped, hand shooting out to slam against the window as a mixture of pain and overwhelming pleasure washed over me.

Zach chuckled, both hands taking a firm grip on my ass. "You love to shake this thing when you strut away from me," he husked, hands massaging my cheeks. "Drives me absolutely insane."

He spanked me, and I yelped, nearly forgetting about the glass again until the red liquid sloshed up the side, threatening to spill.

"Ah, ah," he tsked, rubbing the skin he'd just reddened with his palms. "Don't spill."

I groaned, throwing my head back as he snaked one hand between my thighs. The side of his index finger rubbed against my clit, the lace of my panties giving the perfect amount of friction to bring every nerve to life.

It'd never been like this with Carlo, with anyone. Just like every other aspect of my life, I always honed control in the bedroom. I was the one who went down first. I was the one who climbed on top. I was the one who initiated, who set the pace, who finished first.

But when Zach touched me, he sucked every ounce of control out of me like a god taking my soul. When his hands were on me, I was his — his to own, his to do with what he wanted.

I never knew the kind of pleasure that could come from letting go.

"God*damn*," Zach breathed, a guttural moan leaving his throat as he slipped one fingertip beneath my panties. "You are so fucking wet, Gem."

I didn't have time to moan or husk or agree with his assessment before he slipped that finger inside me, hard, thrusting all the way until he was knuckle deep. I gasped at the feel, hand searching for grip on the glass, but there was no relief. So I tightened my fist around the stem of the wine glass, surrendering to the goosebumps covering my skin.

"Bend," Zach commanded, and he pressed the small of my back down as the other hand hooked at my hip, showing me how he wanted me.

I leaned forward, cheek hitting the glass as I tilted my ass out, legs still straight, back arched.

"Good girl," he said, and he hooked his thumbs in the straps of my thong, pulling it down my thighs all the way to my feet.

I tried to step out of them, to free myself from the lace, but he clamped his hands around my ankles.

"No."

He didn't say anything more, but in the next second, I felt that same lacy fabric tighten around where his hands just were. He tied the straps into a knot, securing my feet in place, and then his hands hooked in my waist, bending me even more.

And then, without warning, without giving me a chance to catch another breath, he buried his face between my thighs.

His tongue swept over my clit, swirling before diving between my lips as I gasped for oxygen. My breath fogged the window, and the hand holding my wine glass weakened to the point that it was almost painful to continue holding on.

"Fuck," Zach breathed, his voice rumbling between my legs. "So sweet."

"Zach, please," I whimpered, but I had no idea what I was begging for. Did I want more? Less? Did I want him to stop or dive in completely?

I didn't know, not until the exact moment he delivered on what I hadn't even realized I was asking. Slowly, he ran the pad of two fingers up my seam, and just as they slipped inside, his tongue ran over the crease where my cheek met my thigh.

And then, he was eating my ass.

My eyes bulged open, like my brain was on autopilot to immediately object. But my body stopped my words from coming before they even had the chance to form.

Holy shit.

His fingers worked relentlessly inside me, curling and pumping, while his tongue swirled the tight, puckered, forbidden hole. He didn't breach it, just applied the perfect amount of pressure to spark a wave of taboo pleasure through me. I moaned, trying to widen my stance, to give him more, but my ankles were shackled.

And in all my squirming and panting, I spilled my wine.

"*Shit*," I cursed, tilting the glass back upright and eyeing the red stain on my carpet.

Zach clicked his tongue, withdrawing his fingers and mouth from me all at once. The loss was instant, my body convulsing, and I cried out in protest.

"You spilled the wine," he said, running his hands up my thighs and spanking my ass again as he stood. "Now, it's my turn."

In the next second, my wine glass was in Zach's hand instead of mine, and he'd spun me, my bare ass pressing against the window as he slammed his mouth hard-on mine. I moaned at the taste of me on his tongue, his hard on rubbing against my clit as he rolled his body into mine. Then, he pulled completely away, leaving me gasping for air and another kiss as he placed the wine glass on the table next to his and turned back to face me with a wicked grin.

"Careful getting out of those," he said, eyeing where my panties were still tied around my ankles. His grin disappeared as he yanked his long-sleeve shirt over his head, and though I wanted to move, to untie my shackles, I couldn't do anything once he was half-naked in front of me.

His chest was broad and tan, a deep line cutting him all the way from the middle of his pecs down to the very last ab that rested right above the hem of his jeans. Every muscle ebbed and flowed as he shifted, tearing his shirt the rest of the way off and letting it drop on the floor at his feet. I followed the movement, scanning every inch of his bare chest and stomach, breath shallow.

My eyes caught on a small patch of hair that started just below his belly button, dipping beneath his jeans, and framed on each side by a dip in his muscles that framed his groin in a perfect V.

Zach really *was* a god.

His eyes raked over me, hands working the button and zipper on his jeans as he watched me. He bit down hard on his bottom lip, tugging his jeans down and letting them drop to the floor, and I swallowed, keeping my gaze trained on his face.

I took his cue, pulling my hoodie and tank top over my head in one, fluid movement. My hair caught in the neck hole, tumbling over my shoulders once I was free, and I unclasped my bra next, letting my breasts spill free.

Zach paused where he was ready to pull his briefs down, shaking his head as his eyes raked over my now-completely naked body. "Jesus fucking Christ," he breathed, his hand rubbing over the bulge straining against his briefs. "Come here."

I bent, carefully pulling the lace of my panties wide so I could step out of the contraption he'd tied me up with. And when I stood again, there wasn't a single piece of clothing left on Zach's body.

He stood there like a king, stroking his impressive length as his eyes set me on fire from across the room. Every roll of his fist over his cock made his hips flex, made my mouth water, and my heart started beating so fast I was afraid I'd pass out if I didn't get in the safety of his arms to hold me upright.

I took the first step, but then he was charging toward me, too. We crashed together in the middle of the room to the tune of another roar of the crowd on the television, and I didn't know what was happening at that game, but I felt like they were all cheering for us.

Zach wrapped his arms around me, pulling me into him like he couldn't get close enough, his tongue slipping inside my mouth like he wanted to brand every part of me.

The way he touched me wasn't timid or nervous, it wasn't hesitant or unsure. He touched me like I'd only been his to touch, like I was born for this, for him — and now that he had me, he knew exactly what to do, from years and years of wanting. Of waiting.

"Purse," I breathed, pointing to the counter behind him. "Condom."

Zach tore his mouth from mine, crossing the room in three steps and dumping my entire purse on the counter.

I laughed. "Oh, no, it's cool. I'll clean that up later."

Zach didn't apologize, just smirked, tearing open a condom and rolling it over his length on his way back to me. He wrapped his hands around my wrists, pulling them over my head as he backed me up into the window again. "Did you hear me apologize?"

His mouth captured mine before I could respond, and as my ass hit the window, he dropped his grip from my wrists, wrapping his hands around my waist, instead. I planted mine on his shoulders, and as he lifted, I pushed, wrapping my legs around him as he leaned me against the glass.

My breath caught as he lined up at my center with just a dip of his hips, and we both paused, foreheads pressed together, oxygen dancing between us.

"Fuck," he breathed, pain etched in the crease of his brows. "I don't want to hurt you, but *God*, I don't know how to take this easy right now."

The tip of him slid between my lips, and just another flex of his hips would have him inside me. We both inhaled stiff breaths, and I swallowed, running my hands back through his hair.

"Let me," I whispered, clearing my throat when the words didn't come out strong. Zach cracked his eyes open, searching mine. "Sit down. Let me."

My voice was still soft, quiet, unsure, and Zach smirked, running the tip of his nose over the bridge of mine before he kissed it. "Let you what?"

I flushed.

"Say it, Gemma," he husked. "Let you *what*?"

I rolled my lips together, hands fisting in his hair as he flexed his hips a little more. The tip of him pushed inside me, and my eyes fluttered shut, both of us moaning in sync.

"Let me ride you."

Zach growled, the cold glass off my back in the next instant as he carried me across the room. He sat on the couch, leaning back and pulling me into him as I situated myself, straddling him, hands pressed against his hard, slick chest.

He kissed me softer, longer, hands resting on my hips as he let me take control. And though I was shaking, I took only one, deep breath before I lined him up at my entrance and slowly, carefully, lowered myself down.

I clamped a hand over my mouth, moaning into the skin and squeezing my eyes shut at the feel of him as Zach let out a long, heated groan. I'd only worked him in a little, and when I pulled up again only to sit right back down, taking him in a little deeper, he cursed.

"You feel..." He shook his head, grappling. "Incredible. Unreal."

I shook, nails digging into his shoulders as I lifted again, this time lowering until he was all the way inside me. For a moment, we just sat like that, breathing, feeling, his throbbing cock stretching me open.

Then, I started to move.

My thighs burned as I rocked, up and down, forward and back, rubbing my clit against his lower abs every time

I touched down. A wave of panic threatened to surge as I realized it was the first time I'd had a man inside me since Carlo, but it receded as soon as it'd come, Zach's hands fastened on my hips bringing me back to the current moment.

I was okay. I was safe. I was in control, and so was Zach.

And as scary as it was, in *that* moment, I trusted him.

My toes tingled as blood started rushing faster toward my center, and Zach pulled my mouth to his, hands tight in my hair as he kissed me hard. I rode him faster, wilder, nails digging, thighs slapping. And when I was close, I broke our kiss, leaning back to balance with my hands on his knees.

He shook his head, eyes taking in the new view of me tilted back. He ran his hands over my stomach, up to frame my breasts as they bounced. And when he rolled his fingers over my nipples, I let my head fall back, a gasping moan slipping from my lips.

"Oh, God, Zach," I breathed, riding him harder.

"Yes," he rasped, tugging each nipple. "Do it. Come for me."

I bounced more, and behind me, the announcer grew louder as the crowd screamed.

He makes the catch! And he's going, going, that's the thirty...

He paused, the crowd still roaring as I rode faster, faster.

The twenty... The ten...

"Oh, fuck," I cried, eyes squeezing shut. Fire burned through me, slow and warm at first before it was an all-out inferno, searing every inch of me as my orgasm caught and took me under.

Touchdown!

"Yes!" I cried, rocking my hips more. Zach reached down to rub my clit, lengthening my orgasm as I shook and throbbed around him. "Yes, yes, God, *yes*."

Zach groaned, and the hand that was working my clit moved to my breast. He squeezed it tight, his other hand on my hip, and he started to move with me, taking control as my orgasm slowed. His hips moved faster, meeting mine from beneath, and then he winced, mouth falling open as his entire body stiffened and shuddered.

Something between a growl and a moan ripped from his throat, his own release pulsing hot and thick inside me. Even through the condom I felt each ripple, and I moaned at the feel of him reaching the same ecstasy I'd just had, of knowing I was the reason he was there.

He thrust inside me once more, this time holding me still, his cock throbbing inside me as he expelled the last of his release. And then, like a whistle had just blown, like the game had been called, we both collapsed into each other, arms wrapping, hands shaking, breaths loud and heavy and exhausted.

We sighed, we smiled, and then Zach rolled until he was lying down with me resting on his chest.

"God*damn*, little girl," he said, whistling.

I just giggled, burying my face in his slick chest as he wrapped me into him tighter.

He laughed a little, too, shaking his head as his breaths settled. His hand wove in to my hair, rubbing the scalp before gently running through the strands. "So much for being nervous," he said, peering down at me.

I flushed, burying my face in his chest more and wrapping my arms around his waist. "I'm *still* nervous," I argued. "And it's already over."

Zach chuckled. "Well, round *one* is over, anyway."

I swallowed, stiffening in his arms, which earned me another haughty laugh.

"Can I at least have like, ten minutes?" I asked. "And maybe some water. And a PB and J."

"Only if you make me one."

"Deal," I said, popping up to peck my lips to his.

But he held me there, wrapping his arms around me tighter and lengthening that kiss until I was melting into him. He kissed my nose once he finally released his grip, smacking my ass when I hopped up from the couch.

"I have grape jelly," I said, stealing his long-sleeve shirt off the floor and pulling it over my head. I flipped my hair out of the neck hole when the shirt was on, pointing at him. "Obviously. And if you like any other kind of jelly on your PB and J, you're wrong."

He scoffed. "Please, like I'd be some sort of monster and ask for strawberry."

Smiling, I skipped past him into the kitchen, pulling out two plates and the ingredients I'd need. But before I could twist open the cap on the peanut butter, Zach was there behind me, wrapping me in his arms.

He rested his chin on my shoulder, squeezing me tighter, and I gave in, dropping the peanut butter and lacing my hands over where his rested on my stomach.

"What are you thinking about?" I asked him, leaning back against him.

"You actually think I can form thoughts right now?"

I smiled. "Well, you came over here and wrapped me up in your arms," I pointed out. "I just didn't know if you were getting all soft on me again."

"Nah, not yet," he said, but then he turned toward me, shifting me in his arms so he could look in my eyes. "I do have one, serious question though."

I swallowed, searching his gaze as my chest tightened. I didn't know what he wanted to ask, but something told me that whatever his question was, I wouldn't be ready to answer it, yet.

"Okay," I said, voice barely a whisper.

Zach's eyes flicked between mine, his thumb brushing the side of my cheek. "I have to know…" He swallowed, like the words were hard for him to say, and I felt my chest tighten more. "Did you orgasm because of me, or because of the touchdown?"

A smile split his face and I blinked, laughing and shoving him off me. He laughed, too, swinging back in to wrap me in his arms as I grabbed the knife for the peanut butter.

"Come on," he begged. "You gotta tell me."

I just shook my head, running a finger through the peanut butter and sucking it off with his eyes on my mouth. Then, I smiled, and tapped his nose with that still-wet finger.

"That's for me to know, and you to forever wonder."

"Oh," he growled, catching my wrist in his hand and pulling me into him. "I think I know a way to find out for sure."

ZACH

We managed to make it through two peanut butter and jelly sandwiches and the rest of the game before I pulled Gemma back into her bedroom for round two. After all, the Bears had pulled out another win. We couldn't *not* celebrate.

And though I would have sworn it wasn't possible, she was somehow even better the second time, like my body hadn't been able to fully process how amazing she felt the first time around. In her bed, I'd taken my time, working slowly between her thighs and savoring every touch, every kiss, every moan.

I couldn't believe I was there.

I couldn't believe she was in my arms.

I couldn't fucking believe Belle's plan had worked.

It'd seemed so absurd, and I hated playing the games — but Belle was right. Gemma had feelings for me, but she was so damn stubborn she didn't want to admit it. Not until she saw me there with Belle, until she saw she had possibly lost me, did she wake up and admit it to herself.

In a way, it was juvenile. But in a way, I didn't care *how* it happened, how she came to her realization, how she changed her mind and stomped down those stairs and over to my seat with determination etched on her adorable face.

All that mattered was instead of kicking me out tonight, she let me stay. She took me to her bed, and she crawled into my arms, and though I knew it scared the shit out of her, she let go of her plan and held onto me, instead.

I could work with that.

She was quiet as we listened to the city still buzzing outside her window, the lights twinkling in through the windows. I played with her hair where it spilled over my chest, feeling the unsteady beats of her heart where it pressed against my waist.

"Family," I finally said, my voice a little gruff.

"Huh?"

I cleared my throat, adjusting my hold on her. "One of the other things I'm a total softie about," I clarified. "Family."

I felt her lips curl into a smile against my chest, and she shifted, rolling until her hands were on my chest, chin resting on top of them as she watched me. "Like *your* family? Or just families in general?"

I thought about it. "You know, before I would have said mine. But I think it's just in general."

"Explain."

I sighed, still playing with her hair as I stared up at her ceiling, searching for the right words. "When I was growing up, my family was everything. It was just me and my parents for the first fourteen years, and they were like..." I laughed, shaking my head. "I don't know, they weren't like parents as much as they were like my best friends. Dad helped me with football, when he wasn't deployed or working at the different bases we'd been stationed at when I was younger, and he really challenged me. But, he also listened when I was going through something. Mom was always on me about school, but she was also the first person I wanted to run to when I had girl problems."

"Girl problems, huh?" Gemma teased. "Bet you were such a little heartbreaker in high school."

"More like I was the one getting my heart *broken*," I argued. "I wanted a girlfriend so bad, but apparently I was too much for girls that age."

"Ah, you were the nice guy. No one wants to date the nice guy."

"So I learned," I grumbled. "Trust me, I learned how to not be so... forward about my feelings. And once I did, I couldn't keep the girls off me. That's how I landed my first real girlfriend, my longest relationship. It was like as soon as I started ignoring her instead of pursuing her, she wanted me."

"Girls are really the most furious creatures."

"Tell me about it," I said, tickling her side. Gemma swatted my hand away, smiling as I continued. "But yeah, she was my first real relationship. We dated all senior year and into my freshman year of college."

It had been over a decade since that relationship ended, and yet still, the scars from that girl remained. That was how powerful love was. It could save you, could help you live for the first time, see the world in a new way — but it could also knock you to the ground, the force so blunt you never forget the way it felt to fall.

Failed love built walls, but it was our choice whether we decided to hide behind them, or sit on top of them, waiting for someone to come along who could knock them down.

I was the latter, but something told me Gemma was the first.

"Anyway," I said after a long pause. "Family was just always really important to me. And once my brother was born, when I was fourteen, it was even more so. I never knew how badly I wanted to be an older brother until I was one."

Gemma smiled, leaning up more. "I think that's sweet. He's so much younger than you."

"He is. He's a great kid, though," I said, throat tightening. "He's had a rough life, but he's always so positive. He inspires me."

"Yeah?" she asked, her finger drawing circles on my chest. "What did he think of your girlfriend, the one you dated for a long time?"

"Smooth segue," I said, smirking.

She blushed. "What? You brought her up."

"Yeah, and also brought the conversation back around to family."

"Well, now I'm bringing the conversation back around to her."

I laughed, but then shrugged, twirling a strand of Gemma's hair around my fingers. "There's not much to say. We were serious, at least, I thought we were. I wanted to marry her." I swallowed. "But, when my football career ended, so did our relationship. Turns out she was more interested in the money I was on track to come into when I went pro than she was in me." I scratched my neck. "But, in my defense, she was a great actress. I thought she loved me."

Admitting that out loud stung, and I grimaced a little at the twinge in my chest. Even as young as I was — a senior in high school, a rookie in college — all my coaches saw the pro potential. That was all Emily, my ex, held onto. It was all she pushed me toward. And when I explained to her that Micah was more important, that I wanted to spend my time with him and not with football?

She was gone.

And my family was everything.

"That's awful," Gemma whispered. "I'm so sorry. But, why did your football career end?" She ran her fingertips over my chest. "Did you... were you hurt or something?"

I grabbed her fingers, lifting them to my lips to press a kiss to the tips of them. "That's another conversation for another time," I told her, not ready to go there yet. "It's your turn."

"My turn?"

"Tell me something."

"Wait," Gemma protested. "You can't just leave me on that. I mean, what happened after? You just what... lost her and football at the same time?"

I nodded. "Yep. That's exactly what happened."

Gemma softened, her entire body melting into mine. "That had to be so hard."

I shrugged again, suddenly aware of how deep I'd taken the conversation without meaning to. I'd just wanted to open up a little about my family, and suddenly I'd stepped into a realm I didn't know how to explore further. "Shit happens," I finally said. "I learned my lesson, haven't really dated much since. Nothing long-term and substantial, anyway."

Gemma nodded, resting her chin on her hands again. "I get that."

"I know you do," I said. "But I still don't know *why*."

She blew out a long breath. "I don't... Zach, I'm not ready to talk about that. Not yet."

My chest squeezed, not because I was hurt she didn't want to share with me, but because I knew that look on her face — the one that comes only from being betrayed in the worst way. I didn't know what happened, but I knew without her saying another word that whatever it was, *whoever* it was — they'd changed her. Permanently.

I knew, because my ex had done the same to me.

"It's okay," I assured her, rubbing her lower back. "How about something easier."

She scrunched her nose, then snapped her fingers. "I'm afraid of heights."

"Lame."

"Hey, don't make fun."

"I'm not," I said. "I'm saying that's a lame thing to share. Although, good to know, we'll have to get you over that eventually."

Gemma laughed. "Don't even try. Trust me, I've wanted to conquer that fear so many times, but every time I attempt to, I chicken out."

"Doesn't mean you *always* will," I pointed out. "If you want to face it, to overcome it, you can. With the right circumstances." I paused. "And the right people supporting you."

She smiled, leaning her cheek on my chest as she watched me.

"But for now," I continued. "I want something more. Come on." I poked her side. "Give me the goods. I just confessed my first heartbreak to you."

She sighed, rolling off my chest to lie next to me as her eyes found the ceiling. "Okay," she said, drawing the word out. "You know how you said you're big into family?"

I nodded.

"Well, I don't really know what a family is supposed to feel like," she said. "Not really, anyway. My parents always traveled, and I was an only child. I spent most of my time with my grandpa, who was amazing, but... I don't know. He felt more like a teacher than a family member sometimes."

She paused, and I let the quiet stretch between us. My heart ached for her, for what it must have felt like to grow up without the same family atmosphere I'd had. I knew there were plenty of kids who weren't as fortunate, but to hear it first-hand was tough.

"Why were your parents always gone?"

Gemma shifted. "So, my mom and dad are kind of like the modern-day Romeo and Juliet. Their families hated each other, all the odds were against them, but they somehow made their love work. They bought a house, had me, all the American dream things. And then, they wrote a book about it. And it was a bestseller in the first two weeks."

"Whoa."

"I know. They wrote another one about a year later, and the more they wrote, the more people wanted. They covered everything in their books — putting love first, trusting each other, communicating." She laughed, shaking her head. "Parenting — although, that was a joke to me. They could teach it, but didn't really know how to put their own teachings into practice."

I swallowed. "But you had your grandpa?"

"I did. And like I said, he was amazing... he had a great balance between being my guardian, my friend, and my teacher."

"That's the second time you've referred to him that way — as a teacher," I said. "What makes you think of him that way?"

Gemma smiled then. "Oh, he was always finding ways to make every day a lesson. He's the one who got me really into football, actually. And honestly, I'd also say he's responsible for my incessant need to plan and set goals and check off lists until I reach them."

"Driven man, I presume?"

"Very. And he made sure I was the same." Gemma closed her eyes then. "I miss him. Every day."

I pulled her into me, running my hand over her arm as I held her. She tucked into my chest, and her legs weaved with mine under the sheets.

"Can I ask you something?" I asked.

"Oh, God, what now?"

I laughed. "How freaked out are you about ditching your plan tonight? About me being here?"

She blew out a breath at that. "Honestly? I don't know if it's really hit me yet."

"Any regrets?"

Gemma leaned up, and her eyes searched mine before she lowered her lips to mine. We both inhaled at the touch, and even though I'd just had her twice, my entire body woke up again, thrumming with the need to touch her more.

"Not yet," she answered when she broke the kiss. "But we're still early in the game."

"Please, no more games," I said on a laugh, and she chuckled, too. "But seriously, I want to make you feel comfortable. And hey, next week is an away game, so we're not *technically* breaking your rules, right?" I pointed out. "You can hang out with me the next couple of weeks, and if you change your mind, there's always time to line up a date for the next home game."

"Oh, is that so?" she asked, smirking. "You'd just let me set up another date like that?"

My jaw clenched. "Uh-huh."

"Bullshit." Gemma laughed.

"No, I mean it," I said. "If you still wanted to take another guy to the next home game, then I'd respectfully bow out. But," I said, tapping her nose. "You have to give me these next couple of weeks to try to make it so that doesn't happen."

"Deal," she said, and then she crawled on top of me, legs straddling each side. "But, I'll tell you this..." Gemma leaned down, pressing her lips to mine and leaving them there as she whispered. "You're already doing a pretty great job, because I'm not thinking of anyone else right now."

"You haven't thought about anyone else since the night you met me," I challenged, gripping her hips and rolling mine into her. "You just didn't want to admit it."

"I don't know," she said, rolling her body and nipping at my bottom lip. "There was Ben, you know. He was *so* interesting... you might have some real competition there."

I growled, rolling until she was under me, wrists pinned to the pillows as she laughed. "Stop talking about other guys before I lose my damn mind again."

"Make me," she challenged, one brow arching.

And so I did.

Chapter 14

GEMMA

I hadn't even been awake more than fifteen minutes the next morning before Belle was bursting in through my front door.

"Okay, bitch," she announced, slipping her spare key back into her purse before she tossed it on my counter. She eyed the contents of *my* purse — which were still scattered all over the granite — before bringing her attention back to where I stood at the coffee pot. "First of all, you're not allowed to ignore my texts. I don't care how much fun you're having. Secondly," she added, sniffing. "It still smells like sex in here. Coffee can't cover that, honey. So, spill. I want all the deets."

I laughed, shaking my head as I leaned one hip against the counter. "Good morning to you, too."

"Yeah, yeah, good morning," she said, waving me off. "Let's skip the pleasantries and get right to the pleasure. Tell me things. How was the dick. Did he eat your pussy like it was a cupcake again?" She leaned her elbows on the counter then, framing her face in her hands. "Oh, my God, please tell me you're walking funny today."

I covered my mouth to keep from laughing, letting her continue.

"I hope he wasn't small. If we went through all that yesterday and he ended up having a micropenis, I might actually cry."

I was still standing there with one hand over my mouth, smiling beneath it. Belle cocked a brow, letting her hands flop out toward me in a *why aren't you speaking* gesture.

"Well?" she asked. "Did he fuck you silent or what? Tell me things!" But then, her eyes skirted to where the coffee pot was filling beside me, and she frowned. "Wait, why are there three mugs..." Her eyes widened, and she lowered her voice to a whisper as she pointed down at the counter. "Is he still here?"

And as if he was cued from stage right, Zach sauntered into the living room behind where Belle sat at my kitchen bar. He cleared his throat, and Belle sat rigid, eyes wide as he rounded the bar and slipped into the kitchen with me.

Wearing his clothes from the night before.

"Morning, Belle," he said with a smirk, leaning in to kiss my cheek before he grabbed the coffee pot.

"Morning," she squeaked out, and she started mouthing something to me as soon as his back was turned, but I couldn't make any of it out.

"Thanks for the go-go juice," he said once his to-go mug was full, holding it up to me. Then, he wrapped his free arm around my waist, pulling me into him. His eyes washed over me. "You know, it's really not fair that you look this amazing in the morning."

I flushed, leaning up on my tiptoes to kiss him.

"I'll call you later?" he asked.

"You better."

He smiled, tapping my nose before heading toward the door. He stopped to gather his wallet and keys off the table. "Oh, and, by the way," he said, turning toward Belle as he took a sip of his coffee. "I ate her pussy like it was a four-course meal this time."

A laugh shot out of me, and my face warmed as I buried it in my hands. Through the slits in my fingers, I saw Belle blush a little, too, knowing he'd heard everything she'd said. But she didn't let embarrassment show for long. Instead, she stood, crossing the room and high-fiving Zach before opening the door for him.

"Atta boy. Now, get out so I can get the dirty details."

Zach chuckled, lifting his coffee to me before he disappeared into the hallway. Once the door was shut again, Belle bounded back into the kitchen.

"HE STAYED THE NIGHT."

I nodded, pouring us both our first cups of coffee. I added a little creamer to mine and a little sugar to hers, sliding one mug across the counter to her as I cupped the other in my hands. "He stayed the night."

"And you're not freaking out."

I sighed. "Surprisingly, no... at least, not yet." I took a pulse check. "I think the freakout part is coming, though."

"Well, we will handle that later. But, for now, you're smiling! And blushing. And, and..." Belle squeaked again, clapping her hands together. "Okay. I want all the details. Now. Start from the beginning. Andddd go!"

Belle followed me around the apartment as I got dressed and ready for work, and I told her all about the night before. She wouldn't let me skip a single detail, as was par for the course with my best friend, and by the time we were locking up my condo to start the trek to work, she was fanning herself and I was ready to skip our morning meeting and go to Zach's for a morning romp, instead.

"Wow," Belle breathed, shaking her head once we were in the elevator on the way down. "I'm impressed. I can't believe he licked your asshole."

"Belle," I whisper-shouted.

"What? No one's in here," she said, just as an older woman stepped onto the elevator with us. We both smiled at her, but Belle didn't skip a beat before turning back to me again. "Did you like it?"

"Can we not right now, please?"

Belle smirked. "Oh, you liked it." She shook her head. "Who would have thought. My best friend, an ass girl."

"Belle!" I smacked her as the older woman glanced over her shoulder at us with a concerned look.

"I'm happy for you," she said through her laughter, and then she schooled her features. "No, seriously. I really am. He's a good guy. So, does this mean you guys are like... official?"

I shrugged. "I don't know. We didn't really talk about it."

"Well, are you exclusive?"

I thought about it, running over the conversations we'd had the night before. "Yeah. I'd say so."

"So, then you're boyfriend and girlfriend."

"We didn't really get that far."

Belle rolled her eyes as we stepped off the elevator, pushing through the lobby doors onto the streets of downtown Chicago. "Ugh, dating today sucks. You never know what you are and what you aren't. But, let me just be the first to tell you that you've got yourself a man, Gemma Mancini. And I like him."

I smiled. "I like him, too."

And I did. I liked him *a lot*. I couldn't fight off the smile that seemed to be a permanent fixture on my face since I woke up. It'd been the most perfect night, and letting go of the control I'd had with my plan before was proving to not be as much scary as it was exhilarating.

Zach made me feel safe, he made me feel comfortable. It was like he knew all my biggest fears and how to handle them before I'd even told him.

I should have been scared of that. I should have been worried about how much I wanted to trust him, to let him in. But I couldn't find it in myself that morning to care.

Still, Belle brought up a good point — we hadn't discussed what happens next. I didn't know what we were, what we weren't, and my grappling self was ready to start being weird if I didn't get some firm rules and boundaries established. I made a mental note to talk to Zach about it more later.

"But for real, don't ignore my texts again." Belle pointed at me. "What if I really needed you?"

"Oh, yeah, more like you really needed to be *nosy*," I said, pulling my phone from my purse. "Honestly, I haven't even looked at this thing since we left the game. It's been in my purse all night." When I looked over the screen, I saw the missed texts from Belle and a few from the guy I'd blown off the night before, but they weren't what caught my attention. "Whoa."

"I know. I got a little needy," Belle said, holding one hand up. "But, in my defense, I was half being nosy and half wondering if you were still alive."

"No, no it's not that," I said, pulling up the notification that had made me pause. "Carlo's mom called me."

"Sofia?"

I nodded. "Yeah. At midnight."

"That's weird."

"It is," I said, stomach somersaulting at the sight of her name on my phone. It wasn't especially out of the ordinary to hear from Sofia, but our communication had died down considerably after Carlo's funeral. It seemed once all the papers were dealt with, the will done, the body laid in the ground... there wasn't much more for us to talk about.

Her son, my husband, was gone.

He was the only thread that tied us together.

"Are you going to call her back?"

I shook my head, tucking the phone back in my purse. "I will, later. I'm sure it's nothing. Maybe she was just feeling sad last night."

"Maybe," Belle said, and she reached over, squeezing my forearm. "Hey, don't let this steal your joy today, okay? You're allowed to be happy." She smirked, looping her arm through mine. "*Especially* after getting your ass eaten."

"Oh, my God, Belle." I snorted. "No couth."

"No shame, either." She flicked her hair over her shoulder.

"Why don't you tell me about *Jordan*," I said, directing the conversation back at her. "Did he go home with you?"

Belle smirked. "Come on. A lady never climaxes twice and tells."

"I knew it!" I laughed. "Hey, at least the hot doctor with the adorable dog didn't go to waste."

"Oh, trust me. There was no waste. By the time he left last night, I'd used up every drop of energy he had to offer."

I snorted, rolling my eyes. I couldn't even find it in me to be surprised, though. This was my best friend at work.

"Now," she said, looping her arm in mine. "Tell me about Zach's cock again."

"Should I just draw it?"

She blanched. "Could you?"

I smacked her off me, both of us laughing as she admitted that was too much and turned the conversation to our morning meeting, instead. She was pitching an office design to one of the advertising firms downtown, and I pulled out her sketches as we rounded the corner toward our office building. But even as we talked about desks and frames and natural lighting, I still couldn't stop smiling — I couldn't stop thinking about *him*.

I didn't know what came next. I didn't know if I was moving too fast, if I was asking for trouble by abandoning my safe plan and trusting Zach not to hurt me. And even though Carlo's mother calling me had thrown me, Belle was right — I *did* deserve to be happy, even if just for one morning.

I'd call her back later. And maybe I'd wake up tomorrow and realize everything I'd done was stupid. Maybe by the next home game, I'd go right back to being in control like Zach said, taking someone new to the game and falling right back in line. Maybe Zach and I were temporary, and we'd just have some fun for a couple weeks and then go our separate ways.

But maybe it didn't matter what happened next.

Maybe all that mattered was that right now, in this moment, in this blissful morning, I was happy.

And I hadn't been that way in a long, long time.

ZACH

I was high.

I'd never done a single drug in my entire life other than alcohol, yet still, I knew I had to be on some sort of high as I floated around Doc's bar, filling orders and humming along to the music blaring through the speakers. The Monday night football game would start in a half hour, and we were slammed again, but it didn't matter how busy we were or how grumpy Doc was because last night? I'd had Gemma Mancini in my arms.

That was its own special brand of drug right there.

"Would you stop being so... *happy*?" Doc grumped, frowning at me as he slid two beers in front of a couple of our regulars. "You're scaring the patrons."

"Tease me all you want, Doc, but you won't get me down today." I passed behind him, clearing the empty glasses from the bar and taking a new order from a group of girls who had just sat down.

"You at least going to tell me what has you all Cheshire Cat smiley over there?"

At that, my smile doubled, and I worked on filling the order I'd just taken as Doc slid up beside me. I shrugged. "My plan worked."

"Your plan?"

I met his eyes. "I slept over at Gemma's last night."

Doc's brows shot up. "Really?"

"Mm-hmm," I said, grinning.

"So, she finally got tired of your annoying ass sitting in those seats next to her and gave in, huh?"

I laughed. "Something like that."

"Well, I'll be damned." Doc crossed his arms, leaning against the bar as he watched me make a few flavored martinis. "For the record, I still think that was a hair-brained idea."

"But it worked."

Doc shook his head. "So it did." He watched me for a moment, his smile leveling out. "Are you sure she's the kind of girl you want to get involved with?"

I slid the martinis over to the girls who ordered, taking a card to start a tab. "What's that supposed to mean?"

"Well, last time I saw this girl, she was hell bent on making you jealous or pissed off or both," he said.

"She was scared," I explained. "She liked me, too, and didn't know how to deal."

Doc cleared his throat. "Okay, Romeo. As long as you're sure. Just be careful, okay?" He squeezed my shoulder. "I met you the last time you had your heart broken, and I don't want that sad kid hanging around my bar again."

Someone called for me down at the end of the bar, but I held up one finger, chest tightening at Doc's words. "She's not Emily."

"I know," he said quickly. He watched me for a moment, concern etched in his features, but then he shook his head. "You know what, this is just me being an old, grumpy man. Forget I said anything."

I smiled. "You really are a grumpy old man, but I appreciate you looking out for me."

"Meh," he huffed. "By the way, we still need to talk..."

"I know, I know," I said, brushing past him toward the other end of the bar. "But, you can't fire me today, Doc. Today is a good day." I pointed back at him, turning on my heels and doing a sort of moon walk toward the guys wanting to order.

"I'm not firing you."

"Not today, you aren't."

Doc laughed, waving me off. "God, you're so... *smiley.* I hate it."

I popped the tops off a few bottles of Bud Light, lining them up in front of the guys before I walked back over to Doc. "I'm just kidding, Doc. What do you want to talk about?"

He picked up the rag he'd abandoned on the bar, folding it over his shoulder before he turned his gaze back to me. His eyes bounced between mine, and he opened his mouth to say something, but then just shook his head, clapping me on the shoulder again. "Nah, don't worry about it tonight. We're busy. We'll talk about it next week, when you're back to being grumpy like me."

"You sure?" I asked, sensing the shift in him. "We can run to the back real quick, still have time before the game."

"I'm sure," he said. His old, tired eyes crinkled a little as he smiled. "And all jokes aside, I like seeing you like this. I don't know about her yet, but at least she's making you happy. You deserve that."

I grinned. "Thanks, Doc. You old softie."

He batted me away. "Don't push your luck. I'm going to go back and change the speakers from the music to the TV." He paused, watching me a moment more before he started walking toward the back. "You should invite the girl over for a family dinner. I want to get to know her more."

"Maybe I will," I said, pulling my photo from my pocket and swiping to Gemma's contact. "But for now, I've got another date in mind." I shook my head as I typed out the text. "We'll see if she's still talking to me after this one."

"You can't just take her out to dinner and a movie, can you?"

"Come on, you know that's not my style," I said with a scoff. Once Gemma texted back confirming I could see her after work on Wednesday, I smiled. "Go big or go home. Always."

Doc shook his head, disappearing into the back office. "Good luck, kid."

I tucked my phone away, floating back onto the cloud I'd been on since I left Gemma's that morning. We'd been texting all day, and now that I had another date lined up, I felt like I was floating even higher.

I didn't know how long I had her, how long she'd stay put without letting her past talk her out of whatever she was feeling. But I knew I wanted to peel back her layers, I wanted more, I wanted to know who hurt her and how to make that pain go away. But first, I had to gain her trust, and the first step in doing that was helping her face her fears.

Starting with heights.

Chapter 15

GEMMA

"**I** can't do this."

I watched in horror as the family who had waited in line ahead of us for the Tilt experience laughed and squealed in joy as they were leaned out over the city of Chicago. Tilt was a relatively new addition to the 360 Observation Deck, and approximately number four on my list of Things I Will Absolutely Never Do, Ever — right behind get a tattoo, eat oysters, and go hunting.

It was a death trap.

Here you are, in this perfectly stable building — although, up too high for my liking, if I'm being honest — and instead of taking in the beautiful view of the city from the normally safe vertical viewing window, you opt to instead be tilted out not once, not twice, but *three* times until you're at a thirty-degree angle looking practically straight down.

No, thank you.

"You *can* do it," Zach argued, massaging my shoulders like I was the quarterback about to go into the second half of a losing game. "It'll be all of two minutes, and then it'll be over."

"Exactly. Why did we even pay for this again? If you wanted to scare the shit out of me, you could have just jumped out at me from behind a wall... for free."

He chuckled, taking my weight into him as I watched the family be tilted forward even more. They shrieked happily as I said a Catholic prayer under my breath.

I wasn't even Catholic.

"I'm not trying to scare you. I'm trying to help you face a fear. You said you wanted to, right?"

I nodded. "No."

"You're going to feel like such a badass after this," Zach promised on another light laugh.

"Or," I argued, holding up one finger. "I'm going to feel like throwing up and kicking you square in the groin region."

Zach winced. "Please don't do that."

As much as I was terrified of what was about to happen, it was nice, standing there in Zach's arms. It'd only been a couple of days since the game, but in a way, this felt like our first *real* date — he asked me to come, came to my apartment to get me, we walked together, ate dinner beforehand.

And, I wasn't trying to make him think I didn't want him. That was a nice change, too.

I opened my mouth to retort to his comment, the ease of our banter comforting me marginally, but it was too late. The family ahead of us was already being tilted back up to standing, so any smart-ass comments I had died in my sticky throat at the realization that we were next.

"Oh, God, Zach," I panicked. "I really don't think I can do this."

"Hey," he said, turning me to face him while the family dismounted. "Look at me. We are perfectly safe. Nothing is going to happen other than you getting an amazing view of the city you love, okay? And I'll be right beside you the whole time."

I whimpered.

"Do you really want to walk away?" he asked, eyes searching mine. "If you really think you can't do this, I'll leave with you. We just have to turn around and weave back through the line. We can bail."

"Okay, let's go."

Zach sighed, his shoulders deflating a little, but he smiled in understanding. "Okay."

But as he grabbed my hand in his, turning to the family behind us to let them know we needed to squeeze by, a tinge of guilt and something else settled low in my stomach. Perhaps, determination?

Damn competitive side.

Or maybe it was that Zach had planned this date for us, had listened to me tell him one of my fears and now here he was trying to help me face it.

And I was being a wuss.

"Wait," I said, bouncing a little as I ran my hands through my hair. "Gah, okay, I can do this. I can do this."

A smile split his face and he smacked my ass. "Atta girl!"

I'm not sure if I blacked out or if it really did only take a few seconds before we were standing on the little platform, hands braced on metal handles on either side of our respective windows as we looked out over the city. The windows were floor to ceiling, just like the ones in my apartment, except we were seventy-four floors higher and the windows were three times as large.

I swallowed.

"Holy shit," I breathed, scanning the city as the sun set over it. It was really a breathtakingly beautiful sight...

If only I didn't feel like my heart was coming out of my butt.

"Holy shit, holy shit, holy shit," I said again, over and over, breathing so hard I thought my chest was going to explode.

Zach folded his hand over mine from where he stood to my right, holding me tighter to the railing. Someone tried to get me to turn around for a photo, but I couldn't.

They snapped a photo of me freaking out from behind.

"Breathe, Gemma. Look at me," Zach said.

"I can't."

"Look at me."

Sighing, I did as he said, and when I did, my heart flitted in my chest.

God, he was handsome.

The orange and blue glow from the city sunset highlighted the strong features of his face while casting the rest in shadows, and he smiled, that little dimple popping on his cheek as he squeezed where his hand laid over mine.

"I'm right here," he said, eyebrows lifting. "Okay? Take one deep breath for me, and then we're doing this."

I nodded, and took a breath, but it was tiny and labored. Zach kept his eyes on mine, taking deep breath after deep breath and waiting until mine matched his. Once we'd gotten in a solid, long inhale and exhale, he smiled again.

"Here we go."

I turned back toward the window just in time for the first tilt.

And then I screamed holy murder.

None of the words that flew out of my mouth even made sense, and they were punctuated with F bombs instead of exclamation points. Zach squeezed my hand tighter, laughing, and somehow, by the time we were tilted again, I was laughing, too.

Tears sprung at the corners of my eyes, but not from fear. I couldn't catch a breath, but not because I was scared. No, all the anxiety had turned to joy, all the screams to laughter. And as I scanned the buildings, the lights, the river — everything that made Chicago the city I loved — I didn't find a single regret for stepping out onto that ledge.

In fact, I wanted to stay there longer.

"This is incredible!" I screamed, laughing even harder as they tilted us one last time.

"I told you!" Zach squeezed my hand.

"Stop trying to make this moment about you, Zach Bowen."

He laughed at that, and before I could even take it all in, we were already being tilted back to standing, the experience over.

As soon as we were upright, I leapt into Zach's arms, and he caught me, spinning as the attendants ushered us out of the way so the next group could step up. They said something about picking up photos in the gift shop, but we barely heard it over our excitement, both of us talking over one another.

"I did it! Zach, oh my God, did you see that?"

"I knew you could." He laughed, shaking his head as I pulled back, my legs still wrapped around his waist. "And how do you feel right now?"

"Like I could run a marathon," I breathed, eyes wide. "Or like I just took heroin."

Another laugh shot out of Zach as he lowered my feet to the ground, and he tilted my chin up with his knuckle, lowering his lips to mine.

"I am so proud of you," he said, and when his lips pressed into mine once more, I inhaled him as deep as I could — his scent, the feel of his hands on me, the sound he made as he deepened the kiss.

I wanted to bottle it all up and keep a stash of it in my purse, just in case I ever wanted a shot.

I was still jittery, hands shaking like I'd had too much coffee as we made our way back across town to my condo. It was only a half-hour walk, and though October had spread the full fall spirit in Chicago, it was still warm enough to walk without being uncomfortable. If anything, I liked the walk more with the brisk breeze sweeping between the buildings, chilling my nose and hands.

"I still can't believe we did that," I said, looping my arm through Zach's. "Thank you. And also, I'm sorry, because you might have just turned a scaredy cat into an adrenaline junkie."

Zach chuckled. "As long as you take me along for the ride."

"No promises."

"I can't believe you've never been up there before," he said. "I mean, I know it's a little touristy, but you've been in Chicago your whole life. How have you never gone?"

I shrugged, taking a deep breath as we stopped to wait for a traffic light. "I don't know. I mean, like I said, my parents were always gone, and my grandpa, he was more of a country kind of guy. He used to have me stay with him out at his little farm house outside of the city rather than coming into the suburbs to watch me at my parents' house." I smiled, the memories resurfacing. "You wanna talk about a man who loved to help me get over fears. He once locked me in the little barn with all the chickens to prove they wouldn't attack me when I went to feed them."

"Sounds like my kind of guy."

"Oh, you would have loved him," I said as we started walking again, and my stomach twisted. "Honestly, I think he would have loved you, too."

Zach pulled his arm from where I held it, draping it over my shoulder and pulling me closer to him, instead. "You think so?"

"I do."

"Why's that?"

I leaned into him more. "Because you're persistent, and you don't take life too seriously. He was the same way."

"I'm honored that you would even put us in the same category," he said. "Seems like he meant a lot to you."

"He really did."

We fell silent, Zach rubbing my shoulder as we walked, both of us taking in the city around us. And maybe it was that energy, the buzz of the lights, of another evening being lived by everyone around us, or maybe it was the high still surging through me from Tilt. Whatever it was, something shifted in that moment, with me tucked under Zach's arms, and my next words slipped from my mouth before I could even consider stopping them.

"I was married."

Zach didn't miss a step, but his arm stiffened where it held me against him, and I glanced at his throat as his Adam's apple bobbed once, hard and strong. My eyes drifted back to the sidewalk, watching my sneakers as I tried to figure out what to say next.

"We were college sweethearts, got married not too long after I graduated," I said, not sure what to say about Carlo now.

Had he passed before I found out he was unfaithful, I would have had nothing but amazing things to say about him. I would have bragged about how strong he was, how handsome, how funny. I would have celebrated his accomplishments in the technology industry, told Zach about the apps Carlo helped make. Maybe I would have told him that Carlo liked simple things, like reading the newspaper on Sunday even though he worked in technology, or like holding the doors open for others.

But I wondered now how much I actually knew about the man I was married to.

"I loved him," I said, because at least that was still true.

I knew I should say more, but I was suddenly all too aware of the bomb I'd just dropped. Silence weighed on us, the wind cooler now, harsher as it nipped at our noses.

Zach cleared his throat, and it was as if that brought him back to the moment, like he'd had to step out of his own body to process what I'd said and now he was back again.

"What happened?" he asked.

I pressed my eyes closed hard before letting them flutter open again, my heart dipping into my stomach. "He died."

This time, Zach did stop, pulling me to a halt with him when we were just a few blocks from my apartment. His mouth hung open, eyes shielded under bent brows as they searched mine.

"Gemma..."

"It's okay," I said quickly, tearing my gaze from his. I shoved my hair behind my ears and folded my arms over my chest. "Really. It's been almost a year now."

"I..." Zach paused, shaking his head as another thick swallow grazed his throat. "I just, I don't even know what to say. *I'm sorry* sounds so weak and... nowhere near accurate for how I feel right now."

"*I'm sorry* works fine, Zach. That's a normal reaction."

He shook his head more vigorously, stepping into me as his fingers hooked through the loops on my jeans. "It's not enough. I wish I had the right words." A long exhale left his lips. "Gemma, I hate that you had to endure that. I can't even imagine what that was like, and I'm just sorry that you had to experience it."

"It's okay, really," I said again, and I tugged him forward. "Can we just, can we keep walking? I'm cold, I want to get inside."

"Of course," he said, pulling me into his side.

I wanted to say more, but I think we both knew in that moment that I was spent. All the adrenaline, the rush from before, it had passed through me like a ghost or a high-speed train, and now I was weak and tired, and more vulnerable than I'd ever been.

I wasn't ready to tell him more. For now, this was all I could give.

"Thank you," he whispered into my hair as we walked, pressing a kiss to my head. His arm was tight around my shoulder, and it seemed his breaths were as pained as mine. "For telling me that."

I nodded. "Thank you for making me feel like I could."

When we made it back to my place, Zach rode the elevator upstairs and walked me to my door, but didn't ask to come inside. In a way, I wanted him to, wanted to lose myself in him physically so I could get out of my head. But I was also exhausted, and more than anything, I just wanted my bed.

"Thank you again for tonight," I said, shaking off the weight of what I'd told him and forcing a smile. "It was... terrifying." I chuckled. "But amazing, too."

Zach smirked. "I'm honored you spent the night with me."

"You know, I'd love to see you in your element sometime," I said. Zach just quirked a brow, so I explained further. "Football. I'd love to watch you play."

"Ah," he said, one hand reaching for the back of his neck. I noticed the way his smile fell, his cheeks blushing. "Well, kind of hard to watch me since I don't play anymore, but maybe we could play catch or something. Before the away game next Sunday?"

"I'd like that," I said. "A little birthday present for me."

At that, Zach frowned. "Um, what?"

"Sunday is my birthday."

"Sunday is your birthday and you're just telling me *now*?"

I laughed. "It's not a big deal."

"You're turning thirty."

"Don't make a big deal of this."

"But, you're turning *thirty*."

"Zach," I warned, and I pulled out a finger gun, threatening to poke him. "I want hot dogs, football, and beer. Not necessarily in that order, but all three are required. Past that, I don't want anything else. No cake, no frills, no balloons or crazy signs. I just want to watch the games and enjoy a normal Sunday."

Zach's face scrunched up like it pained him to agree to anything I'd just said, and I raised one brow, advancing my finger like I was going to poke him.

"Fine," he conceded, letting out a big breath. "But I'm getting you a gift."

"No."

"It's non-negotiable," he said, and before I could argue more, his hands slipped into my hair, framing my face as he pulled me in for a kiss. His lips warmed against mine, a sigh leaving both of us as we melted into each other, and he dragged his hands down my shoulders, my arms, my hips, his palms smoothing over my back before he dropped them lower and gripped my ass firmly.

I wasn't tired anymore.

But he just gripped hard, another longing sigh on his lips before he pulled back, smacked my butt, and winked. Then, he started walking backward toward the elevator with a devilish grin.

"See you soon, birthday girl."

I stood there, gaping.

"That's just *mean*, Zach Bowen."

"Payback is a bitch, isn't it? At least you don't have to watch me leave with another girl."

I gritted my teeth, but couldn't fight back the smile. "Okay, fine. That's fair. But this isn't over."

The elevator dinged, and Zach smiled even wider as he slipped one foot inside. But he paused, hanging half-in, half-out of the box as his eyes found mine.

"Thank God for that."

Chapter 16

ZACH

Make a wish, birthday girl.

I watched Gemma laugh over the top of the two candles, one in the shape of a three and the other, a zero. Of course, she'd asked for no cake, so instead, the candles sat smushed between a hot dog and the outer buns. It was the strangest thing I'd ever seen.

And it was absolutely perfect.

When she said she didn't want any fanfare for her thirtieth birthday, it'd taken everything in me to actually listen. I wanted to throw her a big party, or take her out for an expensive night on the town. I wanted to spoil her.

But, she looked happier than I'd ever seen her, surrounded by a few friends from her office, Belle, and the other usual Sunday patrons at Doc's bar. The Bears had won their one o'clock game against the Minnesota Vikings, and Gemma had celebrated with a round of shots for the entire bar.

She was tipsy, and smiling, and adorable.

Still, as she blew out the candles, laughing and immediately taking a bite of the hot dog once Belle pulled the extinguished candles away, I couldn't help but stare a little longer. I couldn't help but think of all I'd come to learn about her in the past week, and all I still had no idea about.

Gemma wasn't who I thought she was when I first met her.

I thought I had her figured out. It was the classic "girl who's been hurt and is afraid of love" scenario. I'd seen it in a hundred romantic comedies, and I was ready to step in and play my part as the hero, ready to peel back her layers slowly, to gain her trust and her heart — should we make it that far.

But she'd dropped a bomb on me Wednesday night.

I'd literally laughed out loud at myself on my way home that night, thinking of how over-confident I'd been. I should have known that Gemma was far from the norm, far from any other woman I'd ever met before, and therefore, the story of her past would be the same.

She had been married.

Those words had slipped from her mouth as easily as someone saying they were hungry or tired or that they'd had a long day at work. And after, she didn't say much else. I supposed there wasn't really much to say after she told me her husband had passed away, but now, I saw her in a new light.

I saw a completely different woman.

She wasn't just strong, independent, fiery, and fun. She was a survivor. She had been through something that not many could emerge on the other side of.

I wasn't sure *I* could have, if it'd been me in her shoes.

And still, there was more to the story. There was more to her late husband than she'd told me. I didn't have an explanation for how I knew that other than I watched her as she talked, as we walked those city streets, and I felt it. I felt her holding back, being careful with her words, revealing only what she wanted to in that moment.

It wasn't much, but it was more than she'd shared with me before. And I found out later in the week that it was more than she'd shared with anyone, other than Belle, since he'd passed.

She didn't talk about him to anyone.

And maybe that's how I knew there was more to say.

"Hey, you," Gemma said, sliding her hands around my waist. She leaned up on her tiptoes to kiss me, a lazy smile on her face when she pulled back. "I'm a wee bit tipsy."

I laughed. "As you should be, birthday girl." I wiped a bit of ketchup from the corner of her mouth. "I still can't believe you like hot dogs with *ketchup* on them."

"And cheese."

"So disgusting."

"Hey," she pouted, poking out her lip in a way that made me want to cuddle her and take her to the bedroom all at once. "It's good, okay? Just because I don't like stupid Italian sausages or Polish sausages or whatever."

"It's fine that you like hot dogs, but you could at least like *Chicago*-style hot dogs. Ketchup isn't allowed."

"Says the one who wasn't even born *or* raised in Chicago," she pointed out.

"Exactly. And even *I* know the proper way to eat a Chicago dog. I mean, I'm not judging you," I said, voice fading. "But you're wrong. Just so you know."

She stuck her tongue out.

"You know," Gemma said after a moment, pointing her finger right at my nose. "You promised me we'd play football today, and it's almost sunset and you have not fulfilled said promise."

She hiccuped, and her eyes widened, like that damn hiccup had snuck up on her and she had no idea what the hell it was.

I laughed. "Yeah, well, I'm not sure you could catch a football right now if you wanted to."

"I could, too," she argued. "Did you bring one?"

"I always have one in my car."

"Well, go get it, then."

And that was all she said to me before she strutted her ass out of the bar. I turned, finding Doc watching me from behind the bar, and he shook his head on a laugh. "That one's yours, huh?"

"I'm calling all the dibs."

Doc chuckled. "I'll hold it down in here. Go find her before she wanders off alone."

I jogged out after her, stopping by my car out back before finding her in the little lot of grass between Doc's bar and a local clothing boutique. She stood staring at graffiti art that covered the brick siding of Doc's, her hands tucked into the back pocket of her jeans. And as I got closer, I noticed her shivering.

"It's freezing out here," I told her. She turned, smiling when she saw the football. "You need your jacket and scarf."

"I'm fine. We'll warm up. Here," she said, clapping her hands together. "Hit me. I'm open."

I cringed, worried about her ability to catch. So I wound up, and as gently as I could, tossed her the ball.

She caught it easily, and immediately scoffed.

"What the hell was that?" She shook her head, lining her fingers up with the white laces. "I know you were a receiver and not a QB, but that was terrible."

She pulled the ball back behind her, and then threw with all her might, the ball soaring across the little field in a perfect spiral. I snapped my hands up just in time to catch it before it hit me square in the chest, and I fought to keep my jaw from dropping.

"Now," she said, holding her hands up. "*Really* throw it. I promise, you're not going to break me."

I just stood there, gaping, blinking more than necessary before I finally blurted out, "Marry me."

She laughed, hiccuping again. "Throw the damn ball, Bowen."

I did, and this time I threw it the same way I would to my brother or dad or any of my guy friends. Gemma caught it easily, tucking it into her side and charging at me like she was running down the field toward the red zone.

I smirked, blocking her advance and picking her up in my arms to twirl her around. She kept the ball safe, though, and when I let her back down to the ground, she jogged across the lot, turning once she was farther away than before.

She threw it again, and I caught it easily, tossing it back to her with a little more gusto than before. For a while, we just fell into the rhythm of catching and throwing, and the more my arm warmed up, the more every inch of me itched to play.

This was the most I'd touched a football in years.

It wasn't that I didn't have opportunities to go play. I'd been asked to be in countless community leagues, and my coach from college had asked me to come out and help with their training camp three years in a row before he gave up. But the truth was, as much as it brought me joy to play, it also broke my fucking heart.

Because I'd wanted it so bad — to play all through college, take my team to the championship game, win a ring, go pro.

But I'd wanted my brother to have everything he needed, more.

And I wanted to spend as much time as I could with him — especially since I didn't know how much time we actually had.

"Alright, let's run a drill or something," Gemma said, tossing the ball up as she backed farther away from me. "Show me your moves."

"Don't hurt yourself now, birthday girl."

Gemma narrowed her eyes, catching the ball and gripping it hard in her tiny hands. "Go long."

She wound up, taking a few steps back as I jogged lazily out a ways. But when she threw it, I realized I hadn't gone nearly far enough.

"Shit," I murmured, sprinting to get under the ball. I was still short though, so I jumped, sailing in the air with one hand outstretched toward the pigskin. The leather fell into that hand, and I jerked it quickly into my side, rolling to the ground to complete the catch.

"TOUCHDOWN!"

Gemma screamed, jumping up and down before sprinting over to me. I was on my way to standing, but she tackled me back to the ground, laughing as we rolled in the dead grass, the ground cold beneath us.

The ball was still tucked into my side, but I let it fall, pulling Gemma into me, instead. She was still laughing as she leaned up on one elbow, the other hand resting on my chest as her hair fell over her shoulder. There were little pieces of grass stuck in it, and I smiled, plucking them free as she watched me.

"You still love it, don't you?" she asked, catching her breath. "You miss it."

I nodded. "I do."

"Why did you stop playing, Zach?"

I exhaled long and hard, eyes floating up to the overcast sky above. It was a perfect fall evening, cold and gray, exactly what I loved October to be. "I just realized that there were other, more important things in my life that needed my full attention."

Gemma frowned. "Well, that's not vague or anything."

"It's just hard to explain," I said, pulling another blade of brown grass from her hair. "I will, one day. I'll tell you. But not today, okay? It's your birthday. Let's talk about happy things."

"Like what?"

"Oh, I don't know," I said, eyes rolling up to the sky again before I brought them back to hers. "Tell me about your job."

"My job?"

I nodded. "Yeah. I know you work for Belle, and we kind of talked a little about what you do, but I want to know more. You don't talk about it much."

Gemma laid her cheek on my chest. "There's not much to say. When we graduated college, she started her interior design firm, and she was a mess." She chuckled. "She's insanely talented when it comes to making someone's home or office or event space gorgeous, but when it comes to balancing finances or sorting paperwork? Girl is helpless."

"So, in steps you, the Planning Queen."

"Exactly."

I smiled. "So was that your dream, to work for your best friend?"

She shrugged. "Honestly, I don't know what my dream was. I don't know that I ever had one. I love working for Belle, because she's my best friend and I want to be a part of her journey. Plus, being her assistant, I get to do everything that comes naturally to my OCD brain, anyway." She paused, eyes focused somewhere in the distance. "But, I don't know. When I met Carlo, I just kind of fell in line behind him."

My throat closed a little at the sound of his name. She hadn't mentioned it before, and for some reason, giving her late husband a name made him more real.

"All through college, I did whatever he wanted to, even majored in business because he told me it would be the most beneficial," she continued. "He was older than me, and already had a strong foot in the technology business when I graduated. He was making startup apps and selling them to the highest bidder, kind of like flipping houses." Gemma shrugged. "And when I graduated, we got married, and I stepped into my role as his wife, and helped Belle build her business. I think I've always been an assistant, in more ways than one."

I ran my hand through her hair, now grass-free. "I bet Belle loves having you."

Gemma smiled at that. "She does. She's so thankful, and she treats me so well. Pays me more than she should. But..." She shook her head. "This is going to sound weird, but ever since Carlo passed away, I'm starting to realize that I just *did* all this stuff without really asking myself what I wanted. Like, we were a unit, we did everything together. I don't really know what I want or who I am without him."

I frowned, pushing to sit up and bringing her with me. I wrapped my arms around her, kissing her hair. "I don't really know what I want, either," I said. "I haven't really paused to ask myself, not since I gave up football. I mean, I love working at Doc's. He's like Belle in a way, pays me more than he should, probably more than he can afford, and he's like a dad to me. But... I don't know. Is it what I want for the rest of my life?"

"Exactly," Gemma said on a sigh. "That's the question, isn't it?"

"Maybe we can figure it out together," I offered, leaning back to search her eyes with my own. "But, I'm in no rush. Life isn't all about where you work, anyway."

"Right?" Gemma tossed her hands up. "Everyone always starts off with that, like at parties and stuff. They want to know where you work, what you do for a living. But isn't it about so much more than that?"

"It is," I said. "It's about what you do when you're *not* working, how you spend your free time in life. Where do you go to recharge, to find peace?"

Gemma leaned into me. "And where is that place for you?"

"Your bed."

She swatted my arm.

"I don't know, there are a lot of places. My parents' house, the gym..." My voice faded, and I ran my fingers through her hair, tucking the strands behind one ear. "And, in all seriousness, places like this. With people like you."

Gemma smiled, leaning into my hand still framing her face. She watched me for a long moment before closing the distance between us and sealing her lips with mine.

I wrapped my arms around her waist, pulling her into me, and we both inhaled that kiss like it was a fresh breath after being submerged under water. Her little hands fisted in my sweater, and she shivered, goosebumps racing all the way up to her neck.

"Let's get back inside," I whispered against her lips.

"Wait," she said, swallowing. Her eyes watched my lips, crawling slowly up until they met my gaze. "What if we... left."

"You want to leave your own birthday party?"

Gemma shrugged. "Game's over, candles have been blown out. They'll survive the rest of the night without me."

A smile tugged my lips to one side. "And where is it that you'd like to go?"

She dragged her finger down my arm, gaze following it as she bit her lip. When her eyes found mine again, she watched me through her lashes, a slight tinge of pink on her cheeks. "Take me to your place?"

She licked the lip that had just been pinned between her teeth, and heat sparked low in my stomach, rolling through me as desire eclipsed everything else. I wanted those wet lips on me. I wanted Gemma in my bed, in the suit she was supposed to wear on this day.

So, I stood, tugging her to her feet before I pulled her in for one long, hot, intentional kiss.

And I gave the birthday girl what she wished for.

"Welcome to the palace," I said, holding the door to my apartment open for Gemma. She rolled her eyes, stepping through and staying near the door as I locked up behind us, hanging my keys on the hook near the entrance.

Gemma tucked her hand in her back pockets, looking around with a small smile. My apartment was modest compared to hers — a small studio on the south side of town. The kitchen and living area were basically one room, with the bedroom and bathroom being separated only by a thin wall. It had a modern feel, brick and concrete and high-hanging wire lighting, but it was clean and minimal. I didn't need much.

"This is so nice," she said, and she started walking around, eyeing what little décor I had — old football photos, pictures of me and the family, some old bar signs from Doc's. "It's... *cool*. Modern."

"You sound surprised," I said, feigning offense as I sat the two boxes I'd carried up on the kitchen bar. They were her birthday presents, but I told her she couldn't open them until we were alone. "What, I don't seem cool to you?"

"About as cool as Carlton from *Fresh Prince*."

I laughed. "I can actually do that dance."

"That doesn't surprise me even a little bit."

"It's very entertaining after a few beers. It's even better when my pants are off."

"I'll take your word for it," she said with a giggle. "But seriously, this space fits you." Her eyes hovered over the photo of me, Mom, Dad, Micah and Doc that we'd taken at Christmas a few years ago before she turned to face me. "I really like it."

I rubbed the scruff on my jaw. "Thanks. You want a drink?"

"No," she said, immediately shaking her head. "I've had plenty. I do, however, want to open these."

She propped her ass on one of my barstools with a wide grin, tapping the top of one of the boxes I'd wrapped up for her.

"What happened to not wanting me to get you a gift, huh?"

"Well," she said, dragging the word out matter-of-factly. "You didn't listen. And now that I know you got me something, I wanna know what it is."

"Funny how fast that story changed."

She crossed her arms. "Don't act like you're not dying for me to open them."

I couldn't argue that, so I just smiled, pushing the first one — the larger one — toward her. "Well, put us both out of our misery then."

She lit up when the box was in front of her, clapping with an excited squeal before her hands were flying over the box, tearing back the brown parchment paper I'd wrapped it in. When the paper was gone, she eyed the Blue Moon logo on the box before lifting a questioning brow.

"I work at a bar," I reminded her. "I'm not paying for boxes when I have a shit ton lying around."

"I mean, I wouldn't have been mad at beer," she said, and when she cracked the box open, her brows shot up. "Okay, now I would *prefer* the beer."

I covered my mouth to hide my smile as she pulled the first item out, a little orange and blue scrap of fabric that she held between her fingers like it was a dead bug she had to dispose of.

"You're kidding," she said, face flat. "A *cheerleader* uniform."

"You love football," I defended.

"Yeah, I love *football*. In what world does that mean I also love cheerleading?"

"You cheer for the Bears, and you're a chick." I shrugged. "It's kind of like you're already one. I just thought you could dress the part." I paused. "Mainly, for me."

She scoffed, mouth popping open, but she couldn't fight back her smile as she threw the little skirt at me. "Pig."

"I even got it in the Bears colors for you!"

"I'm not wearing that," she said, pointing to the skirt laying on the kitchen island where it'd bounced off me now. She didn't even pull the top of the outfit from the box.

A laugh shot out of me, and I circled the island, taking the seat next to her and yanking her barstool until our legs threaded together.

"I can't believe you don't like your gift." I pouted.

"That wasn't a gift for me," she said, crossing her arms. "That was a gift for *you*. And I'm sorry to say that, even on *your* birthday, I'm not wearing that."

I chuckled again, but then I grabbed the smaller box, wrapped in the same paper, and slid it toward her. "Fine. Let's see if I did better with this one."

She eyed the gift like it was a Jack in the Box and she was cranking the handle. "If that's a football-shaped dildo or something, I'm leaving."

"It's not," I said through another laugh. Then, I cocked a brow. "How exactly would a football-shaped dildo work, anyway?"

"There would be lots of lube required."

I laughed again, but my throat tightened when she grabbed the box, tearing into it just as fast as the first one, although this time with a slightly less excited and slightly more terrified expression on her face. I was equally freaking out, but I hid it with a tight smile, my heart ticking up without Gemma being any the wiser.

The first gift had been a gag, a joke, but this one was real.

And I desperately wanted her to like it.

When the paper was gone, she shoved it out of the way, eyes widening when she popped the lid on the box to see what was inside.

"Zach," she breathed, her hands disappearing into the box before she pulled out the first item. It was a custom-made, chrome fountain pen, with an elegant G inscribed at the head. The chrome was a navy blue, the inscription silver, and she rolled the pen in her hand like it was a diamond necklace.

"It's beautiful."

"There's more."

She still held the pen, but reached inside the box again, this time pulling out the small stack of notebooks. There were three of them, all different sizes, with high-quality paper and leather binding. They were inscribed, too, each labeled with all capital letters.

LISTS.

PLANS.

RANDOM SHIT.

She laughed when she read the last one, shaking her head as she took it all in. "You got me stationery."

"I did." I let out a breath, hoping the idea wasn't stupid instead of romantic, which was what I'd been going for. "One for your lists, one for your plans, and one for whatever you want it to be. And I saw you had a few of those kind of pens around, I figured they were your favorite."

"They are," she said, still staring at the gift. "I hate typing. I love the feel of pen and paper, of having a physical document to hold."

I swallowed. "Well, there you go. I just... I felt like when you first told me about this part of you, you were ashamed, or embarrassed. But, just know you shouldn't be. Because it's part of what makes you the most unique and amazing woman I've ever met."

She looked up at me with a smile then. "Don't get all heavy on me now."

I hooked a hand behind my neck, nodding to the notebook labeled *LISTS.* "I started that one for you, by the way."

"You did, huh?" she asked, and she was still grinning as she flipped open the leather binding. I watched her eyes dance over the letters on that first page, and she closed her eyes, shaking her head.

"What?" I asked innocently.

"*Sex Positions I Want to Try with Zach Bowen?*"

"I thought it was a perfect list to start with."

She looked back down at the page. "Number one: doggy-style."

I waggled my brows. "Classic."

"You even illustrated with stick figures," she mused. "Thank goodness, because I had no idea what doggy style was."

"I like to be thorough."

Gemma laughed, closing the binding and sliding off her barstool. She slipped into my arms, wrapping her own around my neck. "Thank you. Seriously, I love it." She shifted her weight to one side, fingers playing with the neck of my sweater. "Honestly, this is the most thoughtful gift I've been given in a very long time."

My throat was tight again, but I swallowed the knot down. "Well, I'm glad you like it."

We stood there a moment, her eyes on mine, my hands resting on her hips, and then she cleared her throat. "Can I use your restroom real quick?"

"Of course, it's right back there," I said, pointing back into my bedroom. "I'll put on some music."

Gemma gathered up her presents while I tapped through my phone for a playlist.

"No Marvin," she said, kissing my cheek as she passed on her way to the bathroom. I didn't even look up, but I smirked, remembering how adorable she was that first night.

I settled on a playlist with acoustic rock, walking over to my Bluetooth speaker by the TV and powering it on before I hit play. The first slow, steady melody filled my apartment, and I took a seat on the couch, kicking my feet up on the coffee table.

Gemma was taking a while, and I wondered if she'd maybe gotten sick. She didn't seem anything past tipsy, but she had mixed liquor with beer at the bar. I played on my phone, checking social media and the game scores and trying to give her space. But after about ten minutes, I called out for her.

"You okay in there?" I asked, swiping through the ESPN highlights on my app.

"I don't know, why don't you tell me?"

Her voice didn't come from the bathroom, and I jerked my head up, confused. I hadn't heard the bathroom door open or the toilet flush or the water run. When my eyes adjusted, though, I realized it didn't matter.

Nothing else in the entire fucking world mattered.

Because Gemma Mancini was standing in my living room in a tiny, tight cheerleading outfit.

I dropped my phone onto the coffee table, jaw scraping the floor as I shamelessly devoured every inch of Gemma with my eyes. The burnt orange and navy blue fabric hugged her curves, the space between the top and the mini skirt exposing her tight, tan stomach, and her legs stretched on for miles under the frills. She'd tied her hair into pigtails, and they swung over her shoulders as she did a little turn.

Her ass peeked out from under the skirt when she did.

She wasn't wearing any panties underneath it.

I groaned, biting my fist as I stood.

"How does it look?" she asked, batting her lashes with a knowing grin once she'd given me the full view.

"Like I'm not going to last long tonight."

Gemma chuckled, but the smile fell quickly as she sauntered over to where I stood at the couch. She leaned in close, her lips nearly touching mine, but she paused with just a centimeter of space left between us.

"As long as you make me come first," she whispered, then she pressed one hand into my chest, backing me away from the couch.

I couldn't do anything but gape as she spun, shimmying in the skirt with her eyes watching me from over her shoulder. Then, her knees hit the couch cushions, her hands balancing on the back, and she arched her back, the bottom of her juicy ass peeking out from under the skirt. Her pigtails swung as she looked back at me again, and this time, she had her lip pinned between her teeth.

"Time to check that first item off the list."

A groan ached out of me, and I'm pretty sure I broke some kind of record for how quickly I stripped out of my sweater, jeans, and briefs. Gemma just smiled, watching me the entire time with her perfect little ass propped up in the air, waiting.

"You know this was just a joke," I said, sliding up behind her. My hands automatically went to her ass, and I flipped the cheerleading skirt up to get a better view. "The list and this outfit. I never thought you'd actually wear it."

"Well, you know I love to prove you wrong."

"It is your favorite pastime," I murmured, but I was done joking once I hooked my hands in the bend of her hips, brushing the soft rounds of her cheeks against my throbbing cock.

We both inhaled a breath, Gemma's eyes rolling backward at the touch.

"We shouldn't start with this position," I warned, running my index and middle finger down between her cheeks. I groaned again when I felt how wet she was at her center, and I slipped the tips of both fingers in at once, warming her up. "Flip over, let me go down on you, let me get you close."

"Do you not feel that?" she husked, arching her back and pushing her pussy down onto my fingers so I filled her more. "I've wanted you all day, Zach. I'm close already."

"Fuck," I growled as she lowered down more, sucking my fingers inside her without me even moving an inch. She lifted her hips and brought them down again, fucking my fingers as her head dropped back, pigtails falling over her shoulders.

"Please, Zach," she begged, her voice between a whisper and a plea. "Fuck me."

Her entire body convulsed when I pulled my fingers out, and in the next second I yanked my jeans from the floor, flipping open my wallet and pulling out the condom I'd stashed in there earlier. I tore open the packaging and rolled it on, and then I was behind her again, erection pressed against her ass.

"Not as shy with that uniform on," I mused, running my head between her cheeks.

We both moaned when my tip lined up with her entrance, and Gemma arched her back more, allowing me entry. Just the tip of me penetrated her first, a gasp escaping between her lips at the feel of me stretching her open. When I flexed my hips, I filled her slowly, and every inch seemed to go on for miles until I was all the way inside her, balls deep, hitting her in a way I couldn't when she rode me last week.

My hands gripped her hips, and when I withdrew, filling her again as slowly as I could manage, Gemma let out a loud, passionate cry.

"It's so deep," she breathed, and I paused, not wanting to hurt her. But she reached back, grabbing my thigh and pulling me toward her for more.

I started slow, picking up the pace the wetter she got, the more she stretched. Every thrust of my hips sent the bottom of that skirt bouncing, the flaps of it hitting my hands that wrapped around her small frame under the hem. It was criminal, the way her ass looked peeking out from the bottom of that fabric, and I had to look away and up at the ceiling to stop myself from coming too fast.

"You feel so fucking good," I rasped, slowing my pace. Between how loud she was moaning, the outfit, and the position, I was going to come any second if I didn't rein it in.

But Gemma was hell bent on making it nearly impossible for me. She widened her legs, knees stretching out as one hand slipped from where she held the back of the couch to between her thighs, instead. I couldn't see what was happening under that skirt, but judging by the way her pussy throbbed, gripping me like a fucking firm handshake, I had a pretty good idea.

"Are you playing with your pussy, baby?"

"Yes," she breathed, moaning and arching her back more.

"Are you going to come for me?"

"*God*, yes," she moaned again, and she picked up speed, her hand working fast and merciless between her legs.

I thrust my hips quicker to match her pace, bending forward and slipping one hand beneath the fabric of her cheerleading top. Her nipples were hard and peaked, and I rolled the right one between my fingers, plucking it with just enough force to have her gasping for her next breath.

That was all it took.

She squeezed around me, body shaking as she came, her hand still working her clit under that skirt. I slowed my thrusts, pushing deeper to help her ride that orgasm as long as she could. And just hearing the way she moaned, my name rolling off her lips like I'd delivered her, it was enough to get me there with her.

I always thought coming together was a fictional phenomenon, something they romanticized in movies and books. It'd always been my job to get the woman there first, and that was my only focus. I couldn't even *think* about my own release until she'd already come.

But with Gemma in that fucking skirt, I couldn't wait a single second longer.

As soon as I knew she was climaxing, I reached up, grabbing both of her pigtails and tugging back with a firm grip. Her moans grew louder when I had that hair wrapped around my fists, and I pounded into her harder, my own release pulsing out after just three hard pumps.

"Fuck," I groaned, dragging out the word like it was a song. Gemma cried out even louder, and I pulled her into me, holding still inside her as I came, cock throbbing, her pussy still so tight it almost hurt.

It was fast. It was porn-like and cheesy and like every high school boy's fantasy.

And it was the best fucking sex I'd ever had.

I withdrew slowly and carefully, untwisting Gemma's hair from around my hands before I plopped down on the couch next to her, panting, the condom still on.

"Holy shit," I breathed, and Gemma laughed, crawling into my lap and straddling me. She kissed up and down my neck in quick little pecks before she found my lips, and I held her there, deepening the kiss until our breaths were synced.

"I have to check this off," she said, wiggling out of my grip.

I was too weak to hold her there, though I tried. "Right now?"

"Right now." She opened her birthday box again, pulling out the notebook labeled *LISTS* and scrawling a slow, purposeful checkmark next to what I'd written with her new pen.

I swore she lit up in a way I'd never seen before, checking off that damn list like it was her life's purpose.

And I loved watching her little ass shake under that skirt while she did it.

"I was never into cheerleaders, but I think you just changed my mind," I said, still catching my breath as she climbed back into my lap.

"Right," she deadpanned. "I'm sure you played football your entire life and never once cared about the cheerleaders on the sideline."

"I mean, I'm not saying I didn't *see* them there."

"Uh-huh." Gemma smirked, cuddling into me. "That was fun," she said after a moment. "*Today* was fun."

"I'm glad you let me be a part of it, birthday girl," I said, voice low as I kissed her forehead.

We were quiet for a moment, me playing with her hair as she drew circles on my shoulder with her fingertips. She laid her head on my chest, a long exhale leaving hers.

"I really like you, Zach Bowen," she whispered.

I smiled, not too proud to admit my chest tightened at her words.

"You mean you don't want to get back on the app and find another date for the next game?"

"Absolutely not."

I chuckled, resting my chin on her head as a thought passed through me. "What if I told you I have a guy in mind for you to take."

She pulled back, brows bending together. "What? Why on Earth would you want me to go to the game with someone else?"

"I'll be there, too," I clarified. "And it's not a date. More like... a third wheel."

"I'm confused."

I smiled, reaching up and tugging on the bands that held her hair up until it all spilled down over her shoulders. "Just trust me. It'll be fun."

"Why do I feel like I'm getting set up here."

"I swear, it's not a date. I just have someone I really want you to meet."

At that, her eyes softened, and she leaned into me again. "Okay," she conceded. "Who is it?"

I swallowed, pulling her closer. It would be the first time I'd ever introduced a woman to him since high school, since before his diagnosis.

Since *her*.

And though my nerves were already sparking, I quieted them the longer I held her, because I knew I wouldn't regret it. I knew without a doubt I wanted him to meet her.

I wanted everyone I loved to meet her.

"You'll see."

Chapter 17

GEMMA

The first drop of ice cold rain hit my nose as I hustled inside the stadium the following Sunday, flowing with the other Bears fans as we made our way to our seats. Not that the stadium would do much to offer relief from the rain, since it was an open dome, but we hustled inside because rain, snow, or sleet — we were Bears fans.

And it was Football Sunday.

My phone buzzed once I was through security, and I dug it out of the pocket of my jacket, assuming it would be Zach. He and whoever his mystery guest was were already sitting in our section, waiting for me, and I was running behind. Traffic had been crazy, and I'd gotten a late start out the door. He was probably telling me I was going to miss kick-off if I didn't get my butt down to our seat.

But it wasn't his handsome face that filled my screen when I finally tugged my phone free.

It was my ex-mother-in-law's.

I swallowed at the old photo of us, taken on a family cruise to the Bahamas a few years ago. Sofia held her oversized floppy hat with one hand, the other squeezing my shoulder from where her arm was wrapped around me. We were both a little sunburned, both laughing.

Carlo had taken the photo.

My thumb hovered over the green button that would answer the call before I slid it over to the red one, instead, sending her to voicemail. Then, I quickly typed out a text.

- Walking into Soldier Field for the game, can't talk right now. Call you later? -

I didn't wait to see what her response was before I tucked my phone away again, quickening my pace to our seats.

I felt a little bad, declining, especially since I hadn't taken the time to call her back from the first time I'd missed a call from her two weeks ago. It had been half because I wasn't sure what to say to her after months of silence, after knowing there was nothing and no one who tied us together anymore.

The other half had been because I was too busy having fun with Zach.

I yanked on my Bears beanie, covering my ears with the soft wool and shoving my hands in the pockets of my jacket. I couldn't help but smile thinking of him, knowing I'd see him in just a few short minutes when I made it to our seats, that I'd be in his arms again. I hadn't seen him yet this weekend, not since our lazy movie night Thursday night, and I was anxious to be near him.

I was also nervous to meet whoever it was he'd brought with him.

He'd sold his other ticket, but asked me to save mine so he could bring his mystery guest. I'd pestered him about who it was all week, guessing everything from a college best friend to a gay lover, but he hadn't budged. Whoever it was, he was important to Zach.

And so, he was important to me.

A chill ran through me when I made it to the section where our seats were, the cool wind whipping down and icing my nose. It was starting to drizzle now, and I peered up at the sky before keeping my head down on the jog to our seats. I had to laugh a little at the juxtaposition of this game next to the last home game — the one where I'd shown up with Jordan, and Zach had shown up with Belle.

So much had changed.

It was hard to wrap my head around everything that had happened since then — facing my fear of heights with him, dinner dates and movie nights, my birthday. I'd crossed over into my next thirty years, leaving the first thirty behind, and I already knew the next would be so different. I hadn't expected to start my new year with another man, with someone who wasn't Carlo, but there Zach was.

He'd made everything perfect.

On top of giving me exactly the low-key birthday I wanted at Doc's bar, he'd opened up to me, and he'd made it easy for me to do the same. And his gift? It was absolutely perfect. It was everything I wanted that I didn't even know to ask for. The pen, the notebooks... they were personally crafted with me in mind.

It was the most romantic gift I'd ever received.

Minus the cheerleading uniform.

Although, I ended up not entirely hating that, either.

And so, I was too busy floating on clouds to think of calling my ex-mother-in-law back. I was too busy soaking in the feeling of euphoria Zach gave me to even think about getting back out into the cold air, of wrapping myself in the itchy towel of reality.

I just wanted to stay submerged a little while longer, until my hands and feet were pruney and I was tired of the heat.

If ever such a day were to come.

Until then, I would sink down into the water farther, letting it heal my aching muscles and soothe my tender heart.

And that heart doubled its pace as soon as I saw the back of Zach's head.

I smiled, hopping down the stairs two at a time on my way to our seats. I shimmied past the usual ticket holders in our row, greeting them as I squeezed by, and I slid up next to Zach just as the announcer called for the singing of the national anthem.

"Hi," I said, throwing my arms around his neck as soon as he turned to face me. He caught me with an *umph* and a smile against my lips as I kissed him, his hands meeting at the small of my back.

Zach was bundled up in a thick, rain-repellent jacket, a beanie covering his own ears and jeans covering his legs down to his sneakers. He felt a little thicker as he held me to him, and it made me want to ditch the game altogether and go cuddle inside by a fire, watching the rain outside instead of being in it.

Of course, I'd never say that out loud. Because, football.

"Well, happy Sunday to you, too," he said when I pulled back, his dimple popping on his cheek as his eyes drank me in.

"Happy Sunday. Such lovely weather we're having, isn't it?" I joked, peeking back up at the miserably gray sky. It was still drizzling, but I had a feeling the rain would come harder and colder any moment.

I was smiling when I looked at him again, but it slipped when my eyes skirted to the boy standing beside him, my heart stopping in my chest before it started back with a hard kick.

Oh, my God...

It was like stepping back in time, like I'd hopped a DeLorean with a time dial set back to Zach's high school years to see what he looked like then. Except, instead of the dark hair, dark eyes, and scruff-lined jaw, it was sandy blond hair, golden eyes, and a face as smooth as mine that stared back at me. But the resemblance was unmistakable — the boyish grin, the same little dimple on the same cheek, the same broad build and nearly the same height.

I'd seen that boy in a photo in Zach's apartment.

It was his little brother.

The anthem started playing before Zach had the chance to introduce us, and a knot formed in my stomach for reasons I couldn't place as we all turned our attention to the flag. It was just meeting someone in his family — which, in a way, I sort of had already done with Doc. And it was just a football game, it wasn't like we were going to sit down and talk for hours over a dinner.

But Zach had admitted to me that family was important to him, that his little brother was a huge part of his world. And now he was here, to meet me.

For some reason, I was instantly nervous at what that might mean to Zach.

At what it might mean for us.

"Gemma," Zach said when the anthem was done, leaning back a little so his brother could see me. "This is my little brother, Micah."

The grin on Zach's mini me's face doubled as his hand reached for mine, and as soon as he held it, he let out a long whistle, kissing my ice-cold hand with a playful grin.

"Damn," he said, shaking his head as he took me in. "My brother said you were smokin' hot, but honestly, I didn't believe him. He doesn't exactly have the best taste in... well, anything."

Zach rolled his eyes, nudging his little brother hard in the ribs as he dropped my hand. But I chuckled.

I tucked my hands back in the pockets of my coat. "Thanks... I think?"

"Oh, it's definitely a compliment." Micah looked up at his brother. "Bold strategy bringing me here, bro. Might just steal your girl by the time this game is over."

"In your dreams," Zach answered, throwing one arm around Micah's neck. He rubbed his head with the opposite fist, fluffing up his hair before Micah finally shoved him off.

My stomach flipped at the way he'd called me Zach's girl.

Was I his girl?

I mean, we were clearly only seeing each other, and we'd turned our back on the games we'd played that first month we'd known each other. But, was I his?

Was he *mine*?

Why my brain picked that exact moment to remind me that we'd never talked about it was beyond me. But it was like standing behind a curtain that had slipped, and I saw everything outside. I tried righting the curtain, but I couldn't. Now that I'd thought about it, now that my brain had latched on, I couldn't let it go.

I hadn't been thinking about it. But, we never set any guidelines, we never decided what we are and what we aren't. Now, I'm here meeting his younger brother — someone important to him.

And that little asshole part of my brain that needed control, that needed boundaries and explicit direction, took over everything.

"Are you okay?" Zach asked, leaning closer and lowering his voice to where Micah couldn't hear. The Jets had won the coin toss and had just received the first kick, anyway, so his attention was on the field. "With this, I mean. With me bringing Micah?"

I blinked, shaking off the daze Micah had somehow stunned me into. "Yes, of course. I'm excited to meet him. I'm honored," I said, voice lower. "I know how important he is to you."

Zach smiled at that, his hand leaving his own pocket to dive into mine. He laced our fingers together, eyes shining. "He is. And so are you."

I smiled, heart swelling at his words at the same time my brain picked up weapons and body armor. They were on two different pages, as they had been since I'd learned of Carlo's infidelity.

"Wait," Micah said from Zach's other side, his eyes narrowing as he scanned the field. "Where are the cheerleaders? Are they inside or something because of the rain?"

"There are no cheerleaders," Zach answered.

"WHAT?!"

I laughed at Micah's outrage, leaning more into Zach to harbor his body heat. The rain was picking up, and it was getting colder with each new drop. "Come on," I chided. "Every Bears fan knows we don't have cheerleaders. We have the band, instead," I said, nodding to the section where our band was, waiting to fire up the "Bear Down" song whenever we scored.

"Man, we got gipped," Micah said, flopping down into his seat and crossing his arms.

The rest of the section was sitting, too, the ball down at the other end of the field as the Jets tried to score, so Zach and I took our seats.

"Just wait until we score," I said, trying to bring him comfort. "This stadium roaring out the lyrics to 'Bear Down' is way more entertaining than some skirts on the field."

"Psh," Micah said, one brow climbing into his hair line. "Speak for yourself. I'm sixteen years old. There's nothing more entertaining to me right now than some skirts flying up and showing a little booty."

"I mean, I'm thirty and I feel the same," Zach chimed in, raising his hand not intertwined with mine.

Micah high-fived that hand before they both sat back, satisfied grins on their faces. I just shook my head.

"It's a *football* game," I argued. "That's what you should be excited for."

"Oh, and I am," Micah said. He kicked his feet up on the seat in front of him with a casual shrug. "I'm stoked to watch the Bears whoop up on some Jets' ass. I just *also* would like to get a peek at some other ass. Preferably that of a hot blonde."

My mouth popped open at his language, but Zach just laughed out loud, nudging his little brother.

"What, got something against brunettes now, little bro?"

"No way. I just know no other brunette could compete with the chick sitting beside you right now, and you know I hate losing. Gotta keep my eyes open for a hot blonde if I want a chance here."

Micah grinned at me then, and it was a grin so close to Zach's that my mouth just fell open wider. They were like teacher and student, except I wasn't sure who had taught who, and I felt like I was back at that first game with Zach and his cheesy lines.

And that's how the rest of the game went.

Zach and Micah were like two cocky peas in a modest pod, and I had front row tickets to the show. They bantered back and forth, laughing and ragging on each other between plays as we watched the Bears take a comfortable lead over the Jets. By half-time, all the nerves I'd had were completely gone, replaced instead by so much laughter my sides were aching from the strain.

"I'm going to go get us a couple beers and some food," Zach announced at half-time, popping up out of his seat. "Hot dog, ketchup and cheese?" he asked me.

"Ew," Micah said, pressing a hand to his chest like he was personally offended. "What the hell is that?"

"Don't even ask," Zach said. "Trust me when I say you don't want to know."

"Hey, both of you just leave my food choices alone," I said. "Until you've tried it, you can't knock it."

Micah's lip curled up, his nose scrunching at the thought of me consuming that hot dog as Zach turned to him. But when he asked what Micah wanted, Micah's eyes leveled with mine, and he nodded.

"You know what, you're right," he said. "I can't knock it until I've tried it. So, I'll have the same."

Zach's brows shot up and I smiled, crossing my arms in victory.

"You want a hot dog with cheese," Zach deadpanned. "And *ketchup*."

Micah cringed a little, but nodded. "Yep."

Zach shook his head, throwing his hands up. "Whatever. It's your dinner. Be right back."

He leaned down to kiss my forehead as he passed, and then it was just me and Micah.

A comfortable silence fell between us as we watched the halftime entertainment, which happened to be two scrimmages being played by Pop Warner players on either half of the field. The rain had stopped, mercifully, but the temperature had dropped another seven degrees. I was thankful for my heavy coat and long socks under my jeans, and I huddled into myself more, missing Zach's warmth.

I always loved the little halftime shows they had, and Micah seemed to be enjoying watching the young players scrap it out on the field, too. It was hard not to think of all their possibilities. One day, they'd be grown, and maybe playing on this very field again in a different uniform.

We both laughed as one of the little receivers on our end scored and did a celebration dance that looked like the Floss dance from the YouTuber known as The Backpack Kid, the crowd going wild as he did. Micah was still chuckling as he propped his arm up on the back of Zach's chair between us, eyes staying on the field as he finally spoke.

"So, you and my brother, huh?"

I smiled, but kept my eyes on the field, too. "Is this when the interrogation starts?"

At that, Micah leaned across Zach's chair a bit, crossing one ankle over his knee and balancing his chin on his hand. "What exactly are your intentions with my brother?" he asked in a mock Dad tone.

"That was actually pretty good. I'd be scared if I was Zach's prom date."

"If you would have seen his prom date, you would have been more scared *of* her than for her."

I laughed. "That bad, huh?"

Micah shook his head, a shiver running over him as he recalled her. "Don't get me wrong, she was hot, but man, she was a bitch."

"That's some mouth you've got on you."

He shrugged. "I like to curse. I stopped apologizing for it and started embracing it at the age of fourteen. Something I learned maybe well before I was supposed to is that trying to be what other people think you should be is a waste of time. Life is too short to be or do or say anything other than exactly what you want. And in the end, no one's judgment matters, because it's *your* life you're living." Micah's shoulders lifted again. "Not theirs."

Something about his words hit me square in the gut, like a punch I didn't see coming. The words he said were something even *I* was still trying to believe — that I should live my own life, stop apologizing, do whatever made me happy. For most of my friends, that revelation came around thirty or maybe a few years after.

But this kid was sixteen, and he somehow already understood it.

"I can respect that," I said, turning toward him.

I still couldn't get over how much he looked like his brother, how much their features favored each other. Maybe it was because I didn't have a brother or sister to look like, to share those characteristics with. It was such a fascinating thing to me.

"So, was this prom date the same girl he dated in college?"

"For the brief time he was there? Yeah."

"How do you even remember her?" I asked. "You couldn't have been more than what... five, then?"

"Four," he corrected, and something passed over his eyes then, like a shadow or a ghost. "And I remember a lot from when I was younger."

"She sucked that bad, huh?" I asked with a chuckle.

"Something like that." Micah watched me for a moment, all humor gone from his eyes now. "But seriously, what are your intentions with Zach?"

I smiled again, but it faltered when Micah's expression stayed level. "Wait, are you serious?"

"Kind of." He shrugged. "Look, I know we joke around a lot, Zach and I, it's kind of in our blood. But if I'm being honest, my brother is about as tough as a bunny rabbit. He's a romantic at heart, always has been, and I just... I haven't seen him like this with anyone in a really, really long time."

I swallowed, wrapping my arms around my middle and tucking me feet up onto my chair. "Really?"

Micah nodded. "Really. I think he knew when he met you that you were different. You grabbed his attention like no girl I've seen him talk about before. And now that you two are dating, or whatever it is you're doing," he said with a wave of his hand. "I don't know, I'm just worried. I don't know much about you, but I know everything about my brother. And I can tell you right now that he cares about you. A lot."

I swallowed, anxiety creeping in again. "We just started dating," I pointed out. "It's not that serious."

"I know," Micah said, but he shrugged again. "Doesn't mean it couldn't become that way."

My heart squeezed at that, once again warring with my brain. Part of me was still floating, maybe even higher than before knowing that Zach wasn't like this with every woman he met. But the other half of me was dropping a leg down, trying to reach the ground again and come back to Earth. It wanted to feel that dirt and grass, to get back to center, to remember why floating is dangerous.

Zach could feel this way now, but it didn't mean he had to feel this way forever.

I knew that, but it wasn't something I could say to his little brother. He was too young, perhaps too inexperienced to understand how love could change, how it could fade over time. I didn't want to be the one to break that to him, so I just nodded and smiled, letting the conversation die.

"I'm just saying, I know you're the chick, and it's his job to protect you and all that," Micah said. "But, he's been hurt, too. Just remember that."

I didn't have a chance to respond before Zach appeared behind me, squeezing between my knees and the seat as he sat back down between me and Micah. Micah gave me one last small smile before he took one of the hot dogs from Zach, and I took the other.

Zach made fun of Micah while he ate the hot dog with a grimace of pain on his face, and I ate mine in silence, digesting it along with everything Micah had said.

All this time, I'd been so focused on me, on not getting *my* heart broken again.

I hadn't even considered that I could do the same to Zach.

The past two weeks had been blissful, living inside a world where we didn't ask questions, didn't think of consequences. The game we'd been playing was over, and we'd let ourselves just have fun, just enjoy being together.

But how long could that last?

If we didn't talk about what we wanted, about what each of us expected, one of us was guaranteed to get hurt. That was just easy science. Micah asked me what my intentions were with Zach as a joke, but the truth was, he'd lifted a curtain I didn't even know I was hiding behind and revealed the truth.

I didn't know what I wanted.

I didn't know what my intentions were with Zach, not completely, anyway. I knew I liked him. I knew I cared for him. I knew he made me feel safe and comfortable, that he was pushing me, that he gave me the space to open up to him in a way I never thought I could open up to any man ever again.

But after the last home game, all we'd agreed to was to see what happened. We were just having fun. We were just *being* together.

And it didn't occur to me until that game how stupid we were being.

We needed to talk. We needed to have a conversation about what came next, about what all of this meant. He was introducing me to important people in his life, and I was letting him inside my past — showing him my bruised, bleeding heart and letting him hold it in his hands.

I didn't ask Zach what his intentions were after the last home game, and I never asked myself what mine was, either.

The question now was, how long could I stay on my little cloud before I had to return to solid ground and figure it out?

The next day at work was a shit show.

My anxiety had been triggered at the game, and when I was back in my condo alone, it drove itself right into high gear, keeping me up all night. I'd been late waking up, which meant I hadn't had coffee ready for Belle *or* myself — not that Belle minded, but *I* did. I was her assistant, and she relied on me to have things ready. Coffee might have seemed trivial and not like a big deal to her, but it mattered to me.

And that's how the entire day went.

I couldn't find folders that I knew I'd organized and filed away correctly. I couldn't find words to convey what I wanted in our morning meeting. I couldn't get our scheduling system to work so I could set up consultations for the week.

I couldn't do anything except think about Zach, about us, and about everything I'd jumped into with him without thinking it through.

"Do you have the file for the Marlow account?" Belle asked, breezing into my office after lunch. Her hair was pulled back in a clip, and she tapped away on her phone from the doorway of my office.

I didn't *need* an office — a simple desk and filing area would have done. I tried to tell Belle that when we first secured the prime location in one of the hottest buildings on the river walk. But, Belle was Belle — she got what she wanted. And she wanted me to have an office.

"Um, yes. I have it. I have it," I repeated, spinning in my chair and looking at the cabinets behind me. The sunlight streamed in through the office windows, filling the room, and my eyes bounced to a couple holding hands and walking alongside one of the riverside restaurants.

Belle cleared her throat. "So... can I get it, then?"

I shook my head, snapping myself out of my daze. "Yes. Yeah. Um... Hang on, I know I have it."

I started filtering through the files, but for some reason, I couldn't even think about where I would have put it. Everything was in its place — alphabetically, by category — depending on if they were residential, commercial, or something in-between. But the Marlow file wasn't where it was supposed to be, and I panicked, heart picking up speed as my fingers flipped through the files again.

"It's here," I said, more to myself than to Belle.

"Well, it's okay. We have the files digitally. I'll just look it up in the system."

"You can't," I ground out, slamming the cabinet door shut. "Because the system is down, and I've been on the phone all morning with IT trying to get them to figure it out, but they're moving about as fast as the last ten minutes of a work day."

I huffed, flipping through more files as Belle crossed the room and sat on the corner of my desk. She tucked her phone away, crossing her arms over her chest as she watched me. "Hey. Talk to me. What's going on?"

"Nothing," I spat, chest tight. "I just need to find these files and everything is just going wrong today and..." I shook my head. "It's fine. I'll find it and bring it to you."

"Gemma."

"I'm fine."

"Right. And I'm a football fan."

I groaned, flopping back in my chair and slinking down until my butt was hanging off the bottom cushion. My hair fell in my face, and Belle smirked from where she watched me.

"What's going on?"

I wiggled my way back up to sit, letting out a long exhale. "You know how I went to the game with Zach yesterday, and he brought his brother?"

"Yes. You said you had a great time, that his little brother was refreshing and fun."

"And all that's true," I said. "But... it's serious, right? Meeting his family? And Micah was saying some stuff about Zach, about how he's been hurt and I need to be careful. And I just realized that we never set up any kind of rules when we started this whole..." I waved my hands. "Thing."

"And so you're freaking out."

"Basically."

Belle smiled, sliding herself around the desk until she was right beside me. "Okay, look. It's going to be okay. Honestly, I'm surprised it took you this long to freak out."

"We've just been having so much fun," I said, exasperated. "I didn't have time to think about what it all meant."

"And now you do, and this is classic Gemma, okay? This is your anxiety and your need for control sparking and saying that you need to grab the reins again."

"Maybe I should break up with him. Just save us both the hurt that will come later."

Belle laughed, snatching my phone from my hands before I could slide to unlock it. "Oh, no you don't. This is what I mean. When you feel out of control, you resort to the crazy. Just... pause for a second. Take a breath."

I stared at her.

"Inhale, you bitch."

At that, I laughed, but then I did as she said, and when I let the breath go, the grip around my chest loosened a bit.

"Now, call Zach, and tell him how you're feeling. Say that it's been a couple of weeks now, and you just would like to set up some boundaries and define what you guys are a little more. He will understand and he will definitely talk to you about it. And then, you'll feel better, and you can get a little control back." She looked around my office, uncharacteristically messy from my haphazard morning. "And maybe a little cleanliness, too, because this is just so not you."

I chuckled, holding out my hand as a long sigh left my lips. Belle plopped my phone in my palm, tapping my cheek with her knuckle before she stood. "Okay, I'm going to go make a few calls before I do this consultation at one."

"Wait!" I said, standing and filtering through a stack of files on the corner of my desk. I handed her the Marlow one, remembering I was entering information from it into our system before it crashed. "The Marlow file."

Belle held it in one hand and smacked it against her other, smiling at me with a wink. "There's my girl."

"Thank you, Belle."

"Always. Come talk to me after the call."

She left my office, and I sat back down with my heart beating hard and fast in my ears. I dialed Zach's number before I could change my mind, and when he answered, I couldn't even find it in me to start with small talk.

"Hey there, beautiful," he greeted.

"Zach, we need to talk. We never *talked*. We never said what we were, and what we weren't, and what we both expect out of this... whatever *this* is. And now I'm meeting your brother, and you've been hurt and I've been hurt and I love hanging out with you but like when does it start to get hard and messy? And when do you start telling your friends how annoying I am and how you don't know how to tell me that you don't want to do this anymore? And since we aren't like, official, or whatever, do you even have to tell me? Can you just ghost me? And how do we decide when things happen, like when we meet certain people or open up about certain things. Like, are we moving too fast, is this all too soon? I just—"

"Whoa, whoa, whoa," Zach said, and I took my first breath, cringing and dropping my face into my free hand. "Hey, it's okay. Slow down. We can figure this out."

"I'm a mess today, Zach. I just... I don't know what happened but my anxiety is out of control."

There was shuffling on the other end of the phone, and I realized it was late enough in the day now that Zach would be at the bar, getting ready for the Monday night football crowd. "It's okay," he said, voice softer now that the background noise was muted. "Look, you're right. We never did talk about any of that. So, let's talk about it."

"Really?" I sat up, heart squeezing.

He chuckled. "Yeah, really. Look, in my eyes, you're my girlfriend. I'm not seeing anyone else, and I don't want you seeing anyone else. I care about you. I'm not just dating you to hook up or be entertained. I'm dating you because I potentially see a future with you."

My stomach was somewhere in my throat instead of where it should have been anatomically, and I tried to swallow past it without success. "Okay. Yeah. I agree with that." I sighed. "But, I don't want to move too fast. Okay? I just... I need some guidelines here. Some rules."

Zach laughed. "You and your rules. Okay. Tell me what would make you feel comfortable."

"No promises we can't keep."

"That's fair. What else?"

I thought about it, realizing that I hadn't actually taken the time to figure out what guidelines I needed. "I don't know," I confessed, pulling my hair over one shoulder. "I guess I don't really need guidelines, but..."

"You're scared."

I sighed. "Ugh, it's like a repeat of the first night we hooked up."

Zach laughed again. "Look, it's okay to be scared. I am, too. We've both been hurt, and we both are still getting to know each other. We're trying to figure out what works, and if the other person is safe. But... can I tell you something?"

I nodded before realizing he couldn't see me. "Yes."

"I like you, Gemma. A lot. I care about you, I want you to succeed, I want to hang out with you all the time. I want to introduce you to everyone I love because I want *them* to know how amazing you are, too. I want to watch football with you and take you to fancy dinners and make memories I'll never forget, even if this doesn't work out in the end."

My chest squeezed at that.

"So, what if we just start with that?" he proposed. "What if we start with the fact that we're dating, we're exclusive, and neither of us are going to make any promises we can't keep. Okay? We'll go slow, take it easy, and just... enjoy each other."

I smiled. "I like that."

"It's like when you go camping," Zach continued. "Did you ever camp when you were younger?"

"A few times, with my grandpa."

"Well, my dad would always say that we needed to leave our camp site in the same or better condition than what we found it in. I think dating is kind of like that, too. No matter what, I want us both to walk away from this in better condition than we walked into it — *if* we have to walk away at all." He paused. "But, if I'm being honest... I hope that isn't the case."

I covered my smile with one hand, shaking my head as I took a deep breath. It was exactly what I needed to hear. It was everything I didn't realize I wanted to know.

"You saying you might want to set up permanent camp?"

Zach chuckled, letting out a breath of his own. "I mean, maybe. We'll see how long I can squat without getting arrested."

I laughed a little, and relief washed through me like a tidal wave. "Thank you. I know it was a little out of nowhere and a little crazy but..."

"It's not crazy," he corrected. "And you don't have to thank me. Any time you feel like that, you just call me, okay? Anytime. I'm always here to talk. Always."

Always.

I liked the way that word sounded.

Even if I didn't trust it yet.

Chapter 18

ZACH

"You look like that cartoon character," Mrs. Rudder said, swirling the merlot in her glass before taking a sip of it Friday night. She waved her other hand in the air as she tried to recall. "Oh, what's his name. The love-drunk skunk."

"Pepe Le Pew," Doc chimed from the back.

Mrs. Rudder snapped her fingers. "That's the one!" She shook her head, big, dangly pearl earrings swinging with the motion. "You might as well have hearts popping out of your eyeballs, and be floating on a pink cloud of whatever it is this girl has you drunk on."

I smiled, popping the cash register open with the push of a button. I counted out the change for the group down at the end of the bar and shut the drawer again. "You sound jealous, Mrs. Rudder."

"Jealous!" she scoffed, taking a larger sip of her wine as I handed the group their change, thanking them for coming in. "Ha. More like grossed out. I liked you better when you were kind of grumpy."

"Like Doc?"

He humphed from the back, and Mrs. Rudder and I shared a smile.

"Well, it is part of the appeal of this place," she said.

"I can't argue that."

I also couldn't argue her point about me being like a cartoon. With how happy I'd been lately, I felt like one — bebopping along, smiling at every stranger I passed, handing out drinks on me to the patrons.

Doc had especially hated that one.

But, I couldn't help it. Gemma had me under a spell, one I didn't want to come out of.

The game on Sunday had been even better than I'd expected. Gemma fit into mine and Micah's banter like she'd always been there, and when we left, Micah couldn't stop talking about how great Gemma was. He was hard to impress, even though he liked to joke like he was attracted to anything that had boobs. I knew more than anyone else that he was a hard sell, and after just one night with her, Gemma had earned his approval.

It was a huge nod in her favor for me.

And even though I hadn't seen her much since, other than one dinner date this week, I couldn't stop thinking about her. She'd called me in a vulnerable state the day after the game, and we'd finally talked about the purple elephant in the room.

We were official. Boyfriend and girlfriend. Exclusively dating.

She was *mine*, and I was hers.

We texted every day and called each other every night. She told me about the big residential client she and Belle had just landed and I filled her in on the musings at the bar. We started and ended every day with each other, and we had plans with each other all weekend long.

The most important of which being that, tomorrow night she was meeting the rest of my family.

I hadn't brought a woman to family dinner since... well, ever. They hadn't really started to be a thing until after I'd quit football, and my ex had quit me. My mom was over-the-moon excited, probably planning a four-course meal that was way too over the top, but I couldn't help but feel the excitement, too.

I was falling for her.

More and more, with every passing day that we spent together, I saw how she could fit into my life. I'd known she was fun since the night I met her. I'd known she was witty, beautiful, and that she could hold her own when we went tit for tat. I knew she loved football and could rock the hell out of a Bears jersey.

But over the last few weeks, I'd also come to know that she was afraid of heights. I'd learned that those little lists and plans she loved to make not only made her happy, but also helped make her best friend successful. I'd learned that she loved to cook, that she was actually pretty damn great at it, and that her OCD came out when she folded her laundry.

I'd tried to help her, and learned very quickly that I would never properly understand her particular way to fold her underwear.

Or to fold *any* underwear. Period.

I'd discovered the way her eyes shine when she watched an emotional movie, seen the gentle curves of her face when the morning light stretched through her windows. I'd heard her stories about how she'd never had a pet as a kid, but how she wanted one so desperately — when she was ready. I'd seen her hand five-dollar bills to not just one, but multiple homeless men and women on the streets of Chicago as we passed them, never once giving them a judgmental look or leaning away from them like they scared her.

I was far from knowing everything I wanted to know about her, but I knew enough to know that I wanted more, that I was just getting started, and that I didn't give a damn if I looked like a love-drunk skunk from my childhood cartoons.

Because for the first time in a long time, I was happy — *truly* happy — and she was the reason why.

"Alright, Mrs. Rudder," Doc said, emerging from the back to do a sweep of the bar. "Finish up that glass and then I think we're going to call it a night."

"But it's so early," she pouted.

"It's almost one," he pointed out. "And we've been dead as a doorknob all night. I only kept the place open for you."

He wasn't wrong. We were usually steady on a Friday night, not quite as busy as we were on Saturdays or Sundays, but steady. Tonight, however, we'd had the same miserable, freezing rain that had pelted us at the home game on Sunday. Everyone was staying in, spending their night watching movies or reading or whatever they could do to not be out in the rain.

"Fine, you grump," Mrs. Rudder said, and then she threw back the last of her merlot like it was a shot and not a cheap pour of red wine.

Doc smiled, taking her empty glass. "I thought you liked 'em better grumpy."

She didn't respond, just waved him off as Doc and I shared a knowing look. I stepped outside to hail her a cab from the nearby hotel, helping her into her coat on her way out the door.

"See you soon," I told her as she stepped inside.

"Yeah. Don't be so happy next time."

I smiled. "No promises."

Once she was gone, I made my way back inside, locking the door behind me and turning off our neon signs that lit the dark windows facing the street. I hummed along with the music on our stereo, starting in on the last end-of-shift items on our list. I'd already done a lot of them, with us being slow, but it'd be at least another half hour before I could get out of there.

Doc had disappeared back into his office, but he came back out not too long after Mrs. Rudder left, and he leaned a hip against the counter, watching me.

"You really are like that damn skunk."

I chuckled. "I know. I'm almost annoyed with myself."

"She's got you wrapped up, huh?"

I blew out a breath, counting up my till for the night. "More than I'll admit to you, old man."

Doc chuckled at that, but he was silent, still watching me from the edge of the bar.

"She's coming to family dinner tomorrow night," I said, and I paused what I was working on at the register to watch that fact settle over him.

Doc's eyes widened a fraction, and he crossed his arm, shifting his weight to the other hip. "Wow. Meeting Mom and Dad now, huh?"

I nodded, and my hand reached for the back of my neck on autopilot. "Is this too soon? Do you think I'll scare her off?"

"With your family? Maybe," he said on a smile. "But if she survived Micah, I imagine she'll do just fine."

"As long as you're on your best behavior," I volleyed. "No pulling up those old videos from New Year's the first year we knew each other. She doesn't need to know how easily you can drink me under the table."

Doc smirked, his head popping back a little as a silent laugh touched his eyes. But he just cleared his throat, eyes on the bottles lining the back of the bar.

"Ah, actually, I won't be there tomorrow night."

I scoffed, plucking the pour spouts from the bottles we'd used that night and tossing them in the tub of hot, soapy water. "Sure, you won't be at family dinner," I joked, screwing the lids back on the open bottles and shelving them. "What, you got a hot date with your little island princess? Going to jump on a last-minute flight?"

"I wish," he murmured. "But, I do have some business to attend to."

I was still chuckling, but when my eyes met Doc's, he didn't have even a hint of humor in his.

I paused, holding the necks of two bottles of whiskey in each hand. "Wait, you're really not coming?"

Doc was quiet, his eyes sad as he watched me shelve the bottles I'd been holding. And something about the air shifted, like I'd been walking in a dark alley and just realized someone was walking behind me.

"Doc," I said, cocking a brow at his silence. I didn't move for any of the other bottles, just stood there at the other end of the bar, watching my old friend. "What's going on?"

He let out a long sigh, closing his eyes for a moment before he opened them again, and his gray eyes found mine. "I'm leaving."

My chest tightened, but I leaned a hip against the bar, propping one hand on the wood. "What do you mean?" I asked. "Like, you're going on vacation? You're taking a trip?"

"I mean I'm leaving. I'm moving." He swallowed. "To St. Croix."

I blinked, heart beating three loud times in my chest before I threw my head back on a laugh.

Doc still stood there, silent, committed to the joke.

"Ha-ha," I said, pointing at him when the laugh had subsided. "Very funny. I'm sure you're just *moving to St. Croix*," I joked, shaking my head. "Let me guess, for Rita, right? You guys are just going to get hitched and live in paradise."

"Damn it, Zach," Doc said, his voice booming as he smacked the bar and stood straight.

That motion zapped any and all traces of laughter from me.

"This isn't a joke. I've been trying to talk to you about this for months, but I didn't know how. And then you were happy, with Gemma, and everything has been busy around here, but, I can't wait any longer." He swallowed, his chest heaving as his breaths came heavier. "I'm leaving. Soon. As in, before the new year." His eyes fell from mine to the floor. "Sorry, I didn't mean to snap. But... just, don't make a joke out of my love for Rita, okay? I know we poke fun at each other, but I see her the same way you see Gemma — and we've been in love for years, not months."

I didn't know what to say. I just watched him, blinking.

"Anyway, we're tired of living apart from each other. I've always wanted to retire somewhere tropical, and I've been saving for a long time, and..." He sighed, running a hand over his head. "That doesn't really matter. But, what *does* matter, and what I've been wanting to discuss with you is that when I go... I'm leaving you the bar." He paused. "If you want it, that is."

The tightness in my chest had turned into an all-out vise grip, a giant fist squeezing so hard I felt the edges of my ribcage pressing in on my lungs.

I forced a breath, blinking until my vision cleared. "I... I don't understand."

"You love this bar," Doc said. "You love it just as much as I do, and I know you would take care of it. I want to leave it to you." He pushed off the edge of the bar and walked toward me, one hand finding my shoulder. He waited until I lifted my gaze to his. "But *only* if this is what you want. If this bar makes you happy, if it's where you see yourself in this life, then I will happily give it to you. I don't need the money from selling it. I've been saving for this for my entire life, and the bar has never been a factor in my decision."

He swallowed, his hand squeezing my shoulder.

"But, if there's even a chance in hell that you want to do something else — anything else — coach, fly a plane, run a hotel, whatever, then I want to sell this bar and help you get started on that dream."

I shook my head, blinking my eyes again and again, but somehow my vision was still blurred. "No, no you can't do that. You can't sell this bar. You can't give *me* the money from selling this bar."

"I can," he said, voice firm. "And I will, if that's what you want."

I was still shaking my head, and Doc sighed, walking me around the edge of the bar until I sat down on one of the barstools. He sat with me, and for a moment, we just existed in silence.

"I know this is a lot," he said. "But, I want this. Okay? I've been in Chicago my whole life, and I'm over the winters." He laughed, his eyes growing brighter. "I want to open a little beachside bar that tourists can come to, or that locals can find a home in. I want to fall asleep on the beach and spend my afternoons reading in a hammock. I want to kiss the woman I've loved from afar any time I goddamn want to. I want to fish," he said, throwing his hands up. "For fish I can actually *eat*, unlike these contaminated lake fish I've been catching in Lake Michigan my whole life."

I chuckled, but my chest was still tight, throat thick.

"And I want to give this bar to you," he said, his voice lower, eyes connecting with mine. "*If* it's what you want. And if it's not, then I want to sell it and help you get whatever it is that you do want."

"But—"

"No, this is non-negotiable," he said, brows furrowed. "I'm serious. You're like a son to me, Zach."

His voice cracked, eyes washing over with a gloss of tears, and I had to look up at the ceiling to hold my own tears at bay.

"You brought a light into my life when you walked into it, even though you were a giant pain in my ass."

I laughed, and Doc did, too, his hand finding my shoulder again with a squeeze.

"You turned this bar around. You gave it life again, gave *me* life again — purpose. And you have sacrificed everything for me, for your family." He nodded at me like a proud dad, his eyes still glossy. "It's time for us to give back to you. It's time for you to start living *your* life, Zach."

I didn't know what to say after that, and Doc didn't want me to talk — not tonight. He made me promise to go home and think about it, to give it some serious consideration over the next couple of weeks and then give him my decision. Then, he sent me home early, saying he'd take care of the last items on our closing list.

I walked back to my car without shielding myself from the rain. I felt numb, and maybe part of me hoped the freezing rain would somehow wake me up, that it would somehow give me the answers to all the questions I had — some I hadn't even found words to ask yet.

Doc was leaving. The man who was like a second father to me, who had taken me in when he couldn't afford to, who had given me a place to work, a way to help my family — he was leaving.

My best friend was leaving.

And the bar was either mine, or it was going to be gone — sold to the highest bidder.

The decision was mine to make.

I sat in my car with my wet hands gripping the wheel for ten full minutes, trying to make sense of it all. And then, with nothing more than a blink and a sniff, I pulled my phone from my pocket and dialed her number, throwing my car into drive.

"Zach?" she asked, voice low and croaky. It was almost two in the morning now. "It's late. Are you okay?"

"Come over."

There was shuffling on the other end as I turned, pulling out of the parking lot and into the street.

"Now?" she asked. "Zach, it's almost two. I was sleeping. I... I'm not dressed, I don't have any makeup on—"

"Please."

The word cracked out of me, louder than I expected, with a desperation I didn't realize I felt until it was hanging there between us.

I forced a breath, closing my eyes before opening them wide and blinking away the fog. "Please, Gemma. I need you. Please. *Please* come over. I... I can come get you. I'm driving now. I'm by my house but I can come your way and get you and—"

"Okay," she said, her voice softer as she cut me off, and I could already hear her shuffling around. I imagined her jumping out of bed, pulling on her sweatpants. "Okay, I'll be there as soon as I can. Let me get myself together. Just go home. I'll meet you there."

"Hurry, Gemma. Please. I mean, be safe, but—" I could hear the shaking in my voice, but I couldn't stop it.

"Zach, are you okay?" Gemma asked. But I couldn't answer. "Is everything okay?"

I swallowed, the silence stretching.

"Yes," I finally said, but my eyes blurred again. "No. Not really. I don't know."

There was a short pause. "Okay," Gemma whispered. "Okay, I'll be right there."

Gemma was barely through my front door before I yanked her into my arms, and I buried my head in the crook of her neck, inhaling her sweet scent as I wrapped her up tight. I couldn't get close enough, couldn't have enough of her skin on mine.

She dropped her purse on the ground at the door, folding her arms over me and holding me just as tight. She didn't say a word, didn't ask what was wrong, didn't demand an explanation. In that moment, she felt me — and she didn't push for more than what I could give her.

My chest was still tight, heart thumping so loud in my ribcage I was sure Gemma could hear it, but now that she was here, my breaths came a little easier. I pulled back, and when she lifted her eyes to mine, those emerald irises peering up at me through her lashes, I did the only thing I could in that moment.

I kissed her.

The moment our lips met, I inhaled a breath like it was my first shot of clean oxygen since Doc had given me his news. I kissed her slow, gentle at first, and with my next breath, that oxygen met a spark, and that same fire I'd felt every time I touched Gemma came to life again.

I needed her. I needed to feel her, to have her skin against mine, to have my tongue on hers, to have her eyes on me. There were no words that needed to be shared — not yet, not in that moment. Instead, I walked her to my bed, carefully lowering her into the still-messy sheets from that morning.

Her hair splayed on my pillow, and she pulled me down into her, hands sliding into my hair as I nestled between her legs. She kissed me harder, tugging at my shirt until I leaned back and pulled it off. She leaned up on her elbows, helping me strip out of the sweats I'd put on, and I did the same with hers, peeling them off one leg and then the other.

She didn't wear anything underneath them.

There was no foreplay, no playful banter or sexy costumes. I didn't stop to take her sweater off. She didn't ask me to tell her what had happened. It was animalistic, my need for Gemma in that moment, and I barely had a condom on before I was inside her.

She whimpered at the feel, spreading her legs to allow more access as I buried my face in her neck again. My hands gripped where her thighs met her hips, and I flexed into her, filling her slowly as I rocked back and forth.

My breaths turned from anxiety to passion, from an aching fire to one that burned me in the way I loved to be burned — the way only Gemma could. She wrapped her legs around my waist, her arms around my neck, kissing me and holding my gaze as I worked between her legs.

Time was lost.

There was no music, no words, no laughter. It was just the symphony of the city, still buzzing outside my window as I rolled us to one side. It was just her gentle sigh, my hungered groan as I spooned her from behind, hips thrusting, one hand snaking between her legs to rub her clit as the other gently tugged at her nipple under her sweater.

Every moan eased the pain. Every sigh took away the uncertainty. Every time I filled her, and she tightened around me, I breathed a little easier, a little more of the worry subsiding.

It felt like hours passed as we rolled in those sheets, her climbing on top of me to ride me slow before she laid on her stomach, letting me take her from behind. She climaxed first, quietly, with only her quickened breaths and hands fisting in the sheets letting me know she was coming at all.

And I was next, in the same quiet fashion, biting the soft muscle at the back of her neck as I found my release.

I didn't move to discard the condom, just rolled us again until I was spooning her, our skin slick and chests heaving as we came down. I kissed her neck, her shoulders, her hair, holding her tighter, wishing I could somehow pull her closer, eliminate all space between us.

She came.

I told her I needed her, and at two in the morning, she answered. She came over. She was there for me when I needed her most, and she didn't even ask why.

My heart squeezed for a completely different reason than it had felt tight all night, and I held her closer, shaking my head. I couldn't believe she was real.

I couldn't believe she was mine.

"Doc is leaving," I whispered after a moment, the words croaking out of me like they were the first ones I'd spoken in years.

Gemma stiffened in my arms at first, but then she snuggled in closer, wiggling her hips to wedge us more together.

"He's leaving, and he wants to leave the bar to me. Or sell it, and give me the money to do whatever I want — if I don't want the bar." I sighed, and Gemma listened, fingers drawing lazy circles on my arms where I held her. "I don't know what to do, Gemma. I don't want him to leave."

"I know," she whispered. "You don't have to figure out anything tonight, okay?"

Gemma rolled in my arms, and her eyes found mine in the dim lighting of my apartment. She swept her hand over my face, tucking it behind my neck, her thumb brushing my jaw.

"I'm here," she said. "I'm right here."

I nodded, pulling her into my chest and somehow finding a way to hold her tighter than before. My chest ached again, but this time it was with thankfulness, with a gratefulness I hadn't known I could feel.

I didn't know what I would do. I didn't know how I would survive without Doc in my life, let alone without him there at that bar every night I went to work. I didn't know if I'd keep the bar, if I could run it on my own, if I could bear the thought of losing it or what I would do if he did sell it, what the money would go toward.

I didn't know what I wanted.

But, she was right, I didn't have to figure it out tonight.

Tonight, I would hold Gemma, and listen to her breathing. I'd feel her heartbeat against my skin, and I'd find comfort in the fact that no matter what I chose to do, she was here.

She came.

She listened.

She understood.

She was *here*, with me, in one of the darkest nights I'd known since I found out Micah had cancer when I was only eighteen years old.

I hadn't had anyone then, but I had Gemma now.

And that was what I held onto as I drifted off to sleep.

Chapter 19

GEMMA

My family never had dinner together.

My parents traveled more so than not, and when they were home, they were always working, making plans for their next speaking tour. Since their inspirational speeches about their relationship and how they "made it" were heavily influenced by religion, they also spent more dinners with the Bible than they did with me.

We were a family of fast food, or easy food, and eating in the living room with the television on for me and the computers in reach for them.

Carlo was always just as busy. Being the head of a tech company that was always hungry for more, he didn't know how to leave work at work. But, I was used to it. I'd grown up with it. So, him working at the dinner table never fazed me. I would just text Belle or work on my own lists and projects — whether for Belle's business or just around the house — leaving him be.

The only exception to my "working dinners" lifestyle was when I'd stay with my grandpa when I was younger.

We'd always have dinner together.

Most of the time, it was something he'd hunted himself. When his age started to affect his body more, we turned to easier things, like microwave dinners, but we always had them together.

We'd sit at his little folding table, playing cards and chatting while we ate.

I liked those dinners the best.

But regardless, my family dinners were *never* like Zach's.

It'd been a night of nonstop laughter, with Micah and Zach bantering back and forth and Mrs. Bowen chiming in with the occasional warning or thump on the head. Mr. Bowen was mostly quiet, but his eyes were warm, and when it was his turn to talk, I learned quickly that he loved to exaggerate what actually happened — especially when it came to a fishing or golfing story.

At one point, I sat back and looked around at all of them smiling, seeing how strong their bond was and feeling somewhat like a distant witness. It was something I'd always wanted, something I'd envisioned having one day with Carlo and our kids.

My stomach had dipped at that, and I'd shaken him from my memory. Instead, I let myself focus on Zach.

He'd invited me home for dinner, something I knew had to be important to him. He'd already told me what his family meant to him, and the way they all hugged me when I got here tonight, the way his father kept looking at me across the table with a curious smile, I had a feeling I was the first woman to ever get the invitation.

I let myself mull over it all, the past few weeks running through my mind in little flashes as I stood on Zach's back porch and watched the sun dip lazily over the horizon. The gold rays caught the grass and trees in a slant, casting beautiful, haunting shadows across the yard.

It was quieter out here, the way it had been at the house I shared with Carlo.

I missed it a little bit.

"We're going to have pie," Mrs. Bowen said, sliding up beside where I stood, my elbows resting on the white, metal railing. I'd been so lost in my thoughts, I hadn't even heard her come outside. "If you've got any room in that tiny belly of yours."

I smiled, patting said tummy. "Oh, if you only knew how many hot dogs I have hidden in here."

Mrs. Bowen let out a sharp laugh. "Yes, my son told me you were a hot dog girl. Which, normally, I wouldn't have a problem with. Except..."

"He told you I like ketchup on them."

She grimaced, letting her head hang with a sigh. "I'd hoped it wasn't true."

I chuckled, and she offered me a small smile as she propped her elbows up on the railing next to mine. We both watched the sun sink a little lower, and I couldn't shake the feeling I'd had all night. It wasn't one of anxiety, or nervousness, or worry.

It was one of comfort.

Being there, in that house, with Zach and his family — it felt like I belonged. It felt like I could be there again, someday in the future, or maybe even next week. It felt like I always had a place there if I wanted it.

"You know, Zach told me something else about you," Mrs. Bowen said, her eyes still cast across the yard. "He told me you were there for him last night. When he found out about Doc."

My stomach twisted into a tight knot at the mention of last night.

Zach had called me, frantic, at almost two in the morning. He wouldn't tell me what was wrong, but he asked me to come over, and I got out of that bed faster than I ever had before. I rushed to him, worry laced in every bone of my body, and when he'd opened that door, he'd crushed me in a grip so tight I thought I'd suffocate.

But I didn't. I just held him tight, too.

He'd needed me, and I let him take what I could give. It was an urgent passion, one without words or any trace of playfulness. And when we were done, he held me and told me that Doc was leaving, and that he had to make a choice of either keeping the bar or selling it.

"Did you know?" I asked her. "That Doc was leaving."

She let out a long sigh and nodded. "Yes. He asked us not to tell Zach. He wanted to be the one to do it. I think..." She paused. "I think he felt a little like he was abandoning him, even though this move is something Doc has wanted for a long time. That man is just as much of a parent to Zach as Daniel and I are."

I nodded. "Zach loves him. He's worried about what to do, what the right decision is."

"He'll figure it out, though," Mrs. Bowen said, and I couldn't help but watch as the same smile that always found Zach's face spread across hers in that moment. Zach definitely favored his father, but he had her in him, too.

"He will," I agreed.

Her smile dropped a little, and she turned to face me, worrying her lip like she wasn't sure about what she wanted to say next.

"He's been through a lot," she said softly. "More than anyone at his age should ever have to go through. I know he probably doesn't talk about it much, because that's not the type of man he is, but he's sacrificed a lot. For Doc, for his brother, for this entire family."

I frowned, shifting so I was facing her, too. "He's told me how important family is to him."

Mrs. Bowen nodded. "Sometimes, I think Zach forgets that he's allowed to live life for *himself,* too. He's always so quick to put others first. But... maybe this is his chance. Whether he keeps the bar or sells it to do something else, I hope he'll make the choice that *he* wants to make."

My stomach twisted in the same way it had when Micah had talked about Zach at the game. Both he and his mother knew more than I did, knew how soft Zach was when he wasn't making jokes or taking care of business.

And now, after last night, I was starting to see that side of him, too.

"Hey, you two quit gossiping and get in here," Zach said, peeking out of the sliding glass door.

Mrs. Bowen smiled, squeezing my arm before turning toward the door.

"It was nice talking to you, Mrs. Bowen," I said, following behind her.

"Oh, please," she said. "It's Pamela. And it was a pleasure talking to you, too, my dear." At that, she turned to her son, pinching his cheek with a grin before she turned back to me. "Take care of my boy for me, will ya?"

Zach smiled first at her, and then his eyes found mine, a hint of mischief in those dark irises.

I shrugged. "Eh, we'll see."

They both laughed at that, and Pamela patted Zach's chest once before dipping inside. Zach pressed through the door and out onto the porch with me, sweeping me into his arms and pressing his lips to mine.

I felt the last of the sun sink away behind me as I melted into his arms, hearing the voices of his brother and mom loud in my head. Zach was already falling, and I knew there was no sense in denying that I was, too.

I wanted him.

But I was absolutely petrified to fall any further than I already had.

My heart rate ticked up with my realization, and as if he could sense it, Zach kissed me harder, pulling me into him with a reverent sigh. When he pulled back, he swept my hair from my face and shook his head, eyes searching mine.

"I love when you do that," he whispered.

"Do what?"

"Exist."

He smiled, shaking his head again before he pulled me in for another kiss. And this time, I felt that kiss in my bones, like the mark he'd been making was only skin deep, and now he was branding me for good.

And right then, in that moment, I decided I wasn't going to let fear rule me anymore.

My anxiety stemmed from not being in control, and it was true — I couldn't control what would happen next. I wanted an insurance policy, but that wasn't the way life worked. Zach could wake up tomorrow and decide he didn't want me anymore. Or, worse — he could decide two years from now that he wants someone else more than me.

But as he took my hand and led me inside his home, as we sat there with his family, eating pie and playing cards and laughing as the evening turned to night, I had an overwhelming feeling that he wouldn't.

It was something I hadn't felt in so long, something that filled my body with dread and warning just as much as hope and relief.

It was trust.

I trusted Zach. I trusted him to care for me, to let me care for him, to let me in on the hard days and to be there for all of mine.

I wasn't supposed to ever fall in love again. I wasn't ever supposed to let someone inside my damaged, charred, cold and empty heart.

But he'd somehow found a way.

I'd made that list when Carlo passed to keep myself safe, but here I was, just shy of a year later, feeling that rule bend like putty in my hand. Maybe, I wanted to trust Zach because I knew I could. Maybe not every man was like Carlo. Maybe, just maybe, it wouldn't be stupid to let go, to let love in a little.

Maybe Zach was a man of his word.

Looking around at his family, at the people who mattered most to him, knowing he'd invited me to be a part of that world, I knew there was only one way to find out.

So, I took a breath, grabbed his hand in mine, and mentally trashed my old list.

I was going to trust Zach.

Even though it was scary as hell, even though I knew I could end up on the cold, hard floor again, I still chose to try again.

We continued laughing our way through the night with his family, and by the end of it, we were all hugging and making plans, including them asking me to join them for Thanksgiving dinner later that month. And when the evening had ended, as we climbed into Zach's car to head back to the city, a loud clap of thunder sounded off in the distance.

I should have known then that a storm was coming.

But I didn't.

Not until the very moment she showed up at my door.

GEMMA

"**Y**ou guys are so cute, it's grossing me out," Belle said around a mouthful of ice cream. She sucked her spoon dry and pointed it at where I was texting Zach back with a smitten grin. "Like that. Stop that. Stop that weird smiling right now."

"I can't help it," I said, finishing my text and tucking my phone beside me on the couch. I let out a sigh. "We've seen each other every day since we had dinner with his parents Saturday. Tonight is the first night we haven't hung out. He misses me."

Belle's face was flat. "You saw him this morning when he was leaving your place. And also, you see him *again* tomorrow night for Thursday night football."

I chewed my lip with a shrug. "Okay, we're maybe a little gross."

Belle chuffed, dipping her spoon back in for a new scoop. We had the television on, but neither of us had been watching it, spending the evening catching up, instead. Work had been crazy, and I'd been spending so much time with Zach. We needed a girls night.

"So," I said, changing the subject. "Did you ever hear back from Jordan after that game?"

Belle scoffed. "You mean, the guy *you* brought and then ditched so I politely offered him a place to hang out after the last quarter?" She batted her lashes, pressing a hand flat to her chest. "I was simply showing some hospitality."

"I'm sure he was *very* thankful for that."

"Oh, he might have even gotten down on his knees to thank me a time or two."

Belle winked, and I threw my head back on a laugh. But before I could respond, there was a timid knock at the door.

I paused, Belle and I both looking at each other like we weren't sure we actually heard anything. "Is someone at your door?"

"They would call me to let me know someone was here," I said, trying to make sense of it.

The knock came again, and I hopped off the couch, making my way toward the door.

"Unless it's someone on your guest list," Belle pointed out.

"Yeah, but the only people I have on there are my family and..." I peeked through the peephole, heart stopping in my chest when I saw the small figure standing outside. "*Shit.*"

"Who is it?" Belle whisper-yelled from the couch.

I let out a long sigh, closing my eyes and holding the door handle as I tried to brace myself.

"Gemma, who is it?" Belle asked again, this time louder.

But I didn't answer. I just opened the door, greeting my former mother-in-law with a soft smile. "Sofia... hi."

Sofia was a small woman. So small, in fact, that I'd often wondered how she could have given birth to the giant baby who one day became my hulk of a husband. Her hair was short and dark, and it framed her sharp jaw bones, calling attention to her thin, sad lips. Though she was small, she was fierce — an Italian woman with grit and attitude. But today, she had neither.

Today, she only had a box, one she held in her hands like a bomb set to explode any moment.

"I'm sorry to just show up," she said, her voice timid. "I've tried calling a few times... I know you must be busy."

Guilt knotted my stomach, and I let out a sigh, running one hand through my hair as I searched for the right apology.

"It's okay," she said before I could answer. "It really is. I know things are still... well, I know we're all just adjusting however we know how to."

Sofia shook her head, as if she wanted to say more but realized there was no point.

"I brought this for you," she said, holding the box toward me. "I know we went through all of Carlo's stuff at your old house, and I realize you probably want to be done with it and moving on but... this was the last of his things from the hospital."

"That's the one they tried to give me at the hospital," I said, staring at the all-white cardboard. "I told them to donate what they could and trash the rest."

"I know, I know you did," Sofia said, her eyes falling to the box in her hands. "But emotions were high then. And when you left the room, the nurse gave me the box, instead. I've held onto it, and I guess I didn't want to face what was inside it because... well, because it's the last of him."

Her lip quivered, and she shook off the emotion, clearing her throat.

"But, I didn't go through it. I just opened it and I saw some of what's in there but... there's a letter, Gemma. One with your name on it. And I didn't read it or move anything or go past that I just... I thought maybe..."

Sofia was grappling, and she paused to take a long breath, like what she wanted to say didn't really matter.

"Well, I think he wanted you to have that letter, and I think maybe it's been enough time now." Her eyes shot open. "I didn't read anything. I've just had it sitting around, I was waiting for the right time and I just... I don't know, I feel like now is right."

She was still holding that box toward me, but now *I* was the one looking at it like it was a bomb.

I don't want it. Please, just take it. Throw it away. I don't want it.

"Thank you," I said instead, taking the box from her hands. It was like a shoe box, but all white, no labels or indication of what might lie inside. All I knew *now*, thanks to Sofia, was that there was a letter inside.

A letter for me.

I didn't want to read a letter from my late husband.

But, it didn't matter. I could throw the whole box away without even looking inside it if I wanted to. Right now, I just needed to take what my ex-mother-in-law was offering, and give her whatever peace she needed in delivering it.

Sofia nodded, smiling a little now that the box had changed hands. "If there's anything you want to talk about after you open it... just call me. Okay?"

I nodded. "Okay. I hope..." I swallowed, the words dying in my throat. I hadn't been good at keeping up with her — with anyone related to Carlo. When he died, I wanted to erase him — all of him.

"It's okay," Sofia said, reaching out to squeeze my forearm. "We're all okay. And you're okay. It's all good. We love you."

Tears sprung in my eyes, but I swallowed, holding them at bay. "I love you, too."

With that, Sofia squeezed my arm once more before turning and making her way toward the elevators. I closed the door, pressing my back to it and staring at the box in my hands.

"Holy shit," Belle said, and in seconds, she was already on her feet, standing next to me and staring at the box, too. "What are you going to do?"

I swallowed. "Open it."

Belle nodded, a strange silence falling between us, like Carlo himself was inside that box and now we had no idea what to say with him around. "Do you want me to stay?"

I shook my head. "No," I whispered. "I think this is something I should do alone."

I still stood there with my hands locked on that box as Belle hugged me as best she could, telling me she was just a call away and she could be right back down here. She told me she loved me, that I was strong, that whatever was in that box did not define me.

She said all the right words a best friend should say.

And then, she left, and I was alone with a ghost I thought I'd shaken.

Even with the television still on, my condo felt eerily quiet in that moment. I walked numbly to my kitchen island, sliding the box on top of the granite and staring at it for what felt like an entire hour. I didn't open it at first. Instead, I poured a glass of wine and sipped on it while I stared at the white cardboard.

When the last drop of wine was gone from my glass, I sighed, and I said it out loud even though I was the only one in the room.

"Just get it over with, Gemma."

With that final push, I popped the lid off the box, tossing it to the side as I stared at the newly unveiled contents.

The first thing I noticed was his wedding ring.

I picked it up out of the pile of things, pushing aside the watch and wallet that surrounded it. I held that gold band in my palm, rolling it over and touching the metal with my fingertips.

I hadn't even realized he'd taken it off.

I'd always assumed that the nurses or the mortician had removed it before the funeral. I knew about grave robbers, knew he wouldn't be buried with it. But I hadn't even asked about it.

I hadn't cared.

I wondered now when he had taken it off, or if the nurses had done it. He'd gotten so small toward the end. Maybe it fell off.

Maybe he took it off when the other woman came to visit him.

I placed it to the side.

It was sad, to see the last of what was once a man consolidated like that in a tiny little box. There was his wallet, with a little cash, old cards that had already been cancelled, a couple of photos — one of us, one of his family. There was a watch, a pair of socks we'd brought from home because his feet were always cold in the hospital, a few books he'd requested, and a stack of papers regarding something at the tech company. None of it made sense to me, except that it didn't surprise me he'd worked up until he died.

That was just the man he was.

I filtered through the box, finding little things here and there, nothing of significance. I couldn't figure out why Sofia had thought I would need to go through it, need to see any of it all. Perhaps the wedding ring?

But when I made it to the bottom of the box, there was a stack of envelopes. And on the very top the one Sofia had referred to. It had my name written in his shaky, messy handwriting.

Gem.

I picked it up, feeling the harsh, cold paper in my hand as I ran my fingers over the ink. I'd always wanted Carlo to write me letters. I'd asked him to when we were younger, in college, thinking it would be romantic. But he never wanted to. Then, again, for our anniversaries, I tried hinting to him by writing *him* long letters each year. Still, he never wrote one in return.

Until now.

It felt like I was watching from above, like I was outside of my body as I opened up that envelope and unfolded the paper inside of it.

Then, I took a breath, and I read.

> *My Beautiful Gem,*
> *There are no words I can say to comfort you in this time. If you are reading this letter, it means I've passed away, that I have left this physical Earth and you behind to live in it. And for that, I am truly sorry.*
> *But what I want you to know more than anything is that I love you.*
> *I have loved you since the very first moment I saw you, and my love for you*

has only grown over time. I'm so sorry I had to leave you before we could build our life together, the one we always pictured. There are no words to make this easier, to take away your pain or ease the thoughts I've had haunting me at night as I lie in this bed, waiting to pass. I've never been good with words. That was always your thing. But I wanted to write this letter to you and tell you that you are the love of my life, and I will wait for you in Heaven. Take care of yourself, and take your time.
I love you.
Carlo

I didn't realize I was crying until the first tear fell from my wet cheek, splashing onto the paper and splotching the ink over where he'd said he loved me. And as soon as that first tear fell, I lost it. My face twisted, one hand covering my stomach where it sank and tugged at my heart from the inside. I dropped the letter to the counter and covered my mouth with my other hand, squeezing my eyes shut and sobbing harder than I ever had in my life.

It was like holding my husband in my hands, reading that letter. *My* husband. The one I thought I knew. The one I believed.

The sobs that racked through me in the next minutes were brutal. They ripped me from the inside out, leaving me breathless, and at one point, I fell down to the floor, sitting on the cold tile with my knees hugged into my chest.

I couldn't place why it was I was crying. Maybe it was because I missed him. Maybe it was because I loved him, still. Maybe it was because I hated him, too.

I couldn't be sure, not even when I finally stood again, still sniffling, eyes puffy as I folded my note away and tucked it back inside the envelope. I pulled out the rest of the envelopes next, seeing that he'd written to his mom, his dad, even my parents. Sofia must really have stopped once she saw my name, because the letter addressed to her was still sealed shut.

I put them all to the side, knowing I'd need to deliver those, next.

But my hand paused at the last envelope in the stack.

It was written to someone I didn't know. To a name that wasn't familiar.

Brielle.

Everything slowed — my heart, my breath, my hands as they reached for that bottom envelope. It wasn't addressed to me. I knew I shouldn't read it.

But I opened it, anyway.

> *My Beautiful Brielle,*
> *There are no words I can say to comfort you in this time. If you are reading this letter, it means I've passed away, that I have left this physical Earth and you behind to live in it. And for that, I am truly sorry.*
> *But what I want you to know more than anything is that I love you.*
> *I have loved you since the very first moment I saw you, and my love for you has only grown over time. I'm so sorry I had to leave you before we could build our life together, the one we always pictured. There are no words to make this easier, to —*

I screamed.

I couldn't read another word. Then again, I didn't have to, because they were the same words I'd just read. They were the same words he'd written to me.

I screamed again, louder, the sound ripping through my throat like the last call of a dying animal. I grabbed the note in my hands, ready to rip it to shreds, but I stopped, crumpling it up and shoving it inside the box along with mine and everything else that had been inside it.

Then, I whipped around, and I heaved it across the room.

It hit my coffee table, the contents flying out and littering my floor, and I screamed again.

But that scream turned into a wail.

That wail turned into a cry.

And before I knew it, I was back on the ground again. And this time, I couldn't find the strength to get back up.

How could I have ever have forgotten this pain?

How could I ever have been so stupid to think it was worth it to risk this again, to let someone in, to trust them when no one could be trusted?

Carlo was my everything. He was my light, my life, my best friend. And he betrayed me.

Zach would, too.

He may not want to. He may promise me he never will. He may even believe himself when he says it. But the truth is that no matter what he says, no matter what he believes, it can all change.

Love is a slick, curvy, dangerous road, and no one is in control. It doesn't matter what you drive, how carefully you maneuver, who you trust to sit beside you or take the wheel when you're tired.

The only way to stay safe is to stay off the road altogether.

I wouldn't forget that again.

ZACH

It was a sucker punch.

I had no idea it was coming, no idea I even needed to put gloves on as I got ready for work Thursday night.

I was bouncing around, jamming to music and thinking about how much I couldn't wait to see Gemma. It didn't matter that I'd just seen her Wednesday morning, climbing out of her bed with the sun — I already needed more.

That's how it had been since the moment I met her — I always needed more. I needed another game, another night, another chance. Once I got it, I needed to know more about her, needed inside her heart, needed her to find a home inside mine.

The last few weeks had been a blur and a slow dance all at once. My family loved her, Doc loved her, and when she was there on one of the nights I needed her most... I thought maybe I did, too.

It was too soon for that, I knew it before I even let myself think the words. But just because it was too soon to say them didn't mean I couldn't feel what I felt.

I couldn't wait to see her again, and she was coming to the bar that night. To top it off, if the Bears got another W, we'd put ourselves in great shape for the playoff race.

It was going to be a good night.

That's what I was thinking.

I wasn't aware that across town, that same girl I couldn't wait to see was not the same girl I left in bed Wednesday morning.

Doc and I were in a rhythm, the bar already packed for the Bears away game as we did our best to keep up with orders. Since he dropped his news on me, we hadn't discussed next steps. I knew I had a choice to make, but I didn't know how long I had to make it. So, although we were working like normal, there was a different air around us — a different vibe.

He was leaving, and I hadn't accepted it yet.

"Can you grab those girls down at the end of the bar?" Doc hollered at me as he scooted past, balancing the necks of several beers in his hands.

"I'm on it," I said, eyes skirting up to one of the TV screens. It was five minutes into the first quarter, and Gemma still hadn't shown.

I tried to shake it off, knowing she'd be there eventually. Maybe she got caught in traffic, or maybe she got held up at work. But there was a sinking feeling in my gut that told me something was off.

The chaos continued, Doc and I rushing back and forth, pausing only to take a drink of water or cheer with the crowd when the Bears made a play. When the first quarter ended and Gemma still wasn't there, I pulled out my phone to text her.

And it was that exact moment that she walked in.

She looked like hell. The fact that I could even think that meant something, too, because I'd seen her late at night and early in the morning without a stitch of makeup on her face and she was always beautiful. But tonight, even with a full face of makeup, her eyes were swollen and tired, her mouth set in a flat line, her arms crossed over her middle like she was holding herself together with that grasp.

Something was wrong.

Doc saw her when I did, and he shot me a worried glance at the sight of her. I just nodded, letting him know I needed a minute, and I delivered two beers to the guys I'd been taking care of all night on my way around the bar.

As soon as I reached her, I pulled her into me. "There you are," I breathed into her hair, kissing her forehead when I pulled back. "I was worried. Are you... is everything okay?"

She hadn't softened in my embrace, and now that we were apart again, she seemed to only curl into herself more. Her eyes wouldn't meet mine. She was only a few inches away, and yet it felt like there were miles and miles between us.

"We need to talk."

I swallowed.

"Can we go outside?"

Everything in me wanted to say no. *No, we can't go outside and we can't talk because whatever it is that you want to talk about can't be good — not with your eyes looking at the floor instead of me.*

"Okay," I said instead.

I laid my hand across the small of her back, eyes meeting Doc's just briefly before I ushered her outside. It was windy, the bite of the cold stinging my cheeks as soon as we were outside. My sweater did little to fight against it, and I knew even bundled in her coat and boots, Gemma had to be freezing, too.

"It's cold out here," I offered, voice just a whisper. It was quieter outside, the noise from the bar muffled.

Gemma just kept walking, taking me around the corner to the same little lot we'd played catch in on her birthday.

"I'm okay. Do you want to go grab a coat?"

I shook my head, pulling her to a stop as soon as we were in the lot. The buildings on all three sides blocked the wind, and though it was still cold, I couldn't think of anything other than what it was that was plaguing Gemma.

"What's going on?" I asked her, framing her shoulders in my hands. "Are you okay?"

Her arms were still crossed, and she tightened them over herself, eyes glossing as she looked out toward the street. She still couldn't look at me.

"I can't do this anymore, Zach," she breathed, and I felt my heart crack with the words, splintering like a tree struck by lightning.

I swallowed. "I don't understand."

"I have a date for next week's game," she said, sniffing, her lashes in rapid movement to try to keep the tears in her eyes from falling. "I'm going back to my original plan."

I blinked once, digesting what she'd said. My hands still held her as I blinked again, trying to figure it out, but I came up empty.

I dropped my hands.

I took a step away from her.

And then, she finally looked at me.

"This is a joke," I said, searching her emerald eyes. They were so dark that night, so tired, still glossed over with tears she wouldn't let fall. "You're not fucking serious. After everything... why the hell would you take someone else to the game. What does that mean?" I took a step toward her, filling the space I'd just left between us. "What about us?"

She squeezed her eyes shut at that, tears finally spilling down over the apples of her cheeks.

"Gemma," I said, reaching for her. "Whatever is going on, whatever made you feel this way, we can figure it out. Together."

"No," she whispered, and when my hands touched her, she jerked away. "No!"

I held my hands up, and she watched me with wild eyes, like an abused dog backed into a corner.

"Don't you get it?" she said. "What we've been doing, pretending everything is fine. It's not fine. *I'm* not fine, Zach. Everything feels amazing right now. We're spending all our time together. You're letting me in, I'm letting you in. I'm trusting you, you're trusting me. But you know what?" Gemma stepped into my space then. "It will all change. All of it. This, what we feel," she said, gesturing between us. "It's temporary. And it'll go away. And no matter what you say now, what you believe now, one day it'll change and you'll lie to me and break my heart and I'll be on the floor again and I can't—"

Her voice broke, and she covered her mouth with one hand, shaking her head. And I saw it in her eyes, the ghost of her husband, haunting her still.

She lost her husband, the one she'd thought she'd spend forever with.

Of course, she was hurting. Of course, she wasn't okay.

But I could help her. I could love her through it — through anything.

"Gemma, I'm not going anywhere," I said.

"You can't promise that!" she screamed. "Remember? We said. We made that a rule. *No promises.*"

"Gemma—"

"I've heard those words before," she said, cutting me off. "I've seen those same eyes, believed a man when he said I was the only one for him."

Her words ripped from her throat like the roaring flames of a dragon, but they only confused me.

"He said the same things. He believed them, too, which is why *I* did. I mean, you could have hired an escort to try to sway him, Zach, and he would have shoved her aside and looked for me. You could have promised him the hottest woman on the planet, and he'd still have said he wanted *me*." She rolled her lips together, two more tears slipping from her eyes as she let out something close to a laugh. "But it changed. It alway does. And I'm not doing it again. I *can't* do it again."

"Gemma, I don't understand." I reached for her, but she backed away again.

"He cheated on me!" she screamed.

The words echoed off the brick walls around us, circling us again and again until they finally faded, but I'd hear them forever.

Gemma's eyes watered again, and she couldn't fight the tears off now, they came so fast. She shook her head, running her hands back through her hair as she turned away from me.

"He was having an affair. And the same day I was going to tell him that I knew, the same day I put down a deposit on the place I live in now, the day I was going to tell him I was done and we were getting a divorce?" She turned then, pinning me with her stare. "Was the same day he told me he was dying of cancer."

I opened my mouth, but I didn't know why. I didn't have a single word to say.

Gemma nodded, her eyes reading mine. "Yeah. So I stayed, and I held my tongue, and held my husband's hand as I watched him wither away in just four short weeks. And when he died, *she* was there — in the back pew, crying more than me, mourning the man she loved who was married to a woman she never considered was being hurt in the process." She paused. "*Brielle*. I know her name now. And somehow, that makes her even more real."

Her face twisted at that, and she leaned against the brick wall again, shoulders slumped.

Her eyes were distant when she spoke again. "Yes, she was there, at his funeral," Gemma repeated. "But it was me who buried him. And I buried his secret right along with him. I never told him I knew. I never told anyone, other than Belle."

"Jesus, Gemma," I breathed. My hands ached so bad to hold her, to pull her into me, but I kept them fisted at my sides. "I'm sorry. I didn't know."

"Exactly," she spat back. "You didn't know, because I didn't tell you. Because I don't trust you. I thought I did, but I was lying to myself, and to you. I don't trust *anyone*," she emphasized, shaking her head. "Not anymore."

My heart broke in that moment, but not for me. For her. For this beautiful, amazing, intelligent, strong and resilient woman who had gone through something no one in this life ever should have to.

She thought she was scaring me away. She thought I'd run.

I only wanted to hold her tighter.

"Come here," I said. I held my arms open as she shook her head. "Just for a minute. Please, Gemma, come here."

She was still crying, shaking her head like everything was pointless as she closed the distance between us. I took her in my arms, wrapped her in the biggest hug I could manage, and we both let out a long, tired breath.

For a moment, I just held her, wondering what to say. When I finally spoke, it was soft, words whispered into her hair.

"You're scared," I said. "I get it. Trust me, I do. I mean, dating... love... it isn't a game that you just play your part and everything works out. Unfortunately, you have to have the right person on the other side of the board, too. What he did to you, it's... awful, Gemma. It's absolutely horrifying and I'm so sorry you had to go through it alone."

"I don't want your pity."

"No, I know you don't," I said, still holding her. "I'm just saying that..." *What was I saying?* It seemed I couldn't figure it out, couldn't find the right words. "I'm just saying that, yeah, love hurts. But life without it?" I shook my head. "It isn't worth living."

Those words hung between us, suspended in space, and I waited for her to grasp them. I tried to find something more. What I'd said wasn't all I wanted to say, it wasn't everything she needed to hear. But, I needed time. I needed her to let me hold her. I needed her to just... *trust* me, to give me time to prove her wrong.

And so, I held her, and I waited for her to use what little words I had as something to hold onto, something to believe in.

But she just laughed, and shoved me away.

"Unbelievable," she murmured when she was out of my hold. Her eyes met mine, fire burning around the irises. "He *cheated* on me, Zach. Before he died, he cheated on me, and I had to bury that secret. I will never know why. I will never know how long. Not that any of that matters, because all that *does* matter is that he was the perfect husband, he said all the right things and treated me the way any woman would beg to be treated, and even still... he betrayed me."

I wanted her back in my arms, wanted her to feel my heartbeat when I told her I would never do the same. But she kept stepping away, farther and farther, putting more distance between us.

"You feel these things now, but some day, you'll wake up, and you just won't anymore," she said. "And I can't do it. I can't stick around and wait for that break."

I shook my head, following her as she tried to walk away. "You think you're the only one who has been through shit, Gemma?" I asked, heart thundering in my chest. "You think you're the only one who's been hurt? Micah was diagnosed with cancer, too. Did you know that?"

Gemma stopped, turning enough to meet my eyes.

I nodded. "Yeah. When he was *four*. And I was eighteen. I was in my freshman year of college, on a paid scholarship to play football. I was living my *dream*. And suddenly, I had a choice to make. Could I have stayed and played football, left it to my parents to figure out what to do about my brother?" I nodded. "Of course, I could have. That's what they said I *should* have done. But you know what I actually did? I quit. I made a choice to put my family first, above my dreams, above anything else because *they* are what matters most to me. And yes, I lost the girl I thought was my everything then, when she decided football was what she really loved — not me. But you know what? I'd still go back and make the same choice, again and again. Because I love my family, and they matter most to me. They needed my help — financially, emotionally — and I was there for them. So you can say what you want about Carlo, but you don't know me enough to say that you know how I will or won't act in the future. My family?" I said, beating on my chest. "My wife? She will be my *everything*. I'm a man of my word, Gemma." I paused, standing taller. "That's one thing you can't take away from me."

Gemma blinked, watching me like I was a completely new person. "I..."

"Didn't know?" I shook my head. "Yeah, well, unlike how you so delicately put it before, I *would* have told you. One day. When we got to that point. And I believe you would have told me about Carlo, too. That's how love works. You learn more about each other, you trust, you give and you take in equal measure and yes, you take a fucking risk," I said, exhausted now.

Gemma just watched me, and I took another step, closing in, holding my arms open.

"My brother wasn't promised another year, Gemma, and he's here. He's living his life without a single ounce of fear, even though he was told he wouldn't see the age of five. If he can do that, then you and I? We can do anything. But we can't take another *single* second for granted. We are going to make each other happy, Gemma. And sure, sometimes, we're going to hurt each other, too. We're going to mess up. That's how this works."

She didn't move as I made my way toward her, and a crisp whip of wind swept between us as soon as I reached for her, pulling both of her hands into mine. I lifted them, pressing my lips to her knuckles and holding them there as my eyes found hers.

"You have to take a risk, yes. I won't lie to you. You have to face a fear." I smiled. "But, just like I held your hand at Tilt, I'll hold your hand now. If you'll let me."

Her eyes watered again, her hands squeezing mine in return. I felt it, her want to lean into me, to fall into me.

But she didn't.

"Gemma," I said again, eyes still on hers. "Trust me."

She swallowed, closing her eyes as more tears were set free with the motion, each of them racing down to join the others that had fallen.

She squeezed my hands, and then she pulled hers away.

"I can't."

The words were just a whisper, a truth spoken so softly I wanted to believe it was a lie. But Gemma turned, leaving me to watch her go, powerless to keep her or convince her that what we had was enough — that it could be what she's always wanted, if she only gave it the chance.

All I could do was stay.

All I could do was let her go.

Chapter 21

GEMMA

Everything was fine.

That's what I told myself as I bruised my knees, bent on the kitchen floor scrubbing the bottom of my oven. The fumes from the cleaner somehow brought me comfort, and I sang along to the music blasting from my speaker. It was Sunday, and I'd spent all day at Soldier Field. We got another win. We were well on our way to the playoffs.

Everything was fine.

The week had somehow flown by and dragged on all at once, but I was staying busy. I threw myself into work when I was there, and after, I cleaned, did yoga, tried out some new recipes I'd been wanting to take a stab at. I'd gone through some old keepsake boxes, ones I had put away in my back closet. I'd even picked up the old ukulele I used to play by the bonfires in college. I didn't remember much, but it was a challenge to try.

Everything was *fine*.

It was an early game, noon kickoff, so I was home with plenty of time to finish my to-do list for the weekend. The sun had just finished its sink behind the buildings downtown when suddenly, my music was cut off, and I turned, finding Belle standing by the speaker with wide eyes as she took in my condo.

She looked at the windows — the ones I'd cleaned from top to bottom. Then, she scanned the new frames and canvases I'd hung above the couch. Her eyes continued their survey, taking in the spotless kitchen, the shampooed floor, the ukulele propped in the corner by the edge of the couch, the three pans of brownies I'd baked — I was planning on bringing those into the office.

And then, her eyes found me, still bent on my knees on the kitchen floor by my oven. I wiped my brow with the back of my yellow rubber-gloved hand, and smiled. "Hey, Belle."

Her face crumpled. "Oh, honey. This is bad. This is really, *really* bad."

I sighed, turning back to the oven, Brillo pad already scrubbing before I answered. "I'm fine."

"Clearly."

"I am," I defended. "Look at this place. It's spotless. And I've been doing yoga, and meditating, and I baked some goodies for the office, and I went to the game today and we won and we're probably going to the playoffs and everything is just…" I inhaled a breath, unsure of why my chest suddenly stung, why my eyes were blurring with tears. "Fine. Everything is fine."

Belle rounded the kitchen island, sinking down until she was on the floor with me. She watched me scrub for a moment, and the more she stared, the more I felt like a bug under a microscope.

And the damn spot I was trying to get wouldn't come up. What even *was* it? Baked pizza cheese? Something from the tenant before me?

I scrubbed at it harder and harder, my arms aching, hair falling in my face. But it wouldn't come up. Nothing would make it budge. I growled, throwing the Brillo pad and plopping down on my butt as my chest heaved, and I stared at that spot, my eyes blurring.

"It won't come off," I said, voice breaking as I gestured to the dark, mysterious smudge on my otherwise spotless oven. "I can't get it off."

Tears blurred my vision, and I tried to open my eyes wide so they wouldn't fall, but they built up until they fell over my cheeks, anyway.

Belle sighed, opening her arms from where she sat beside the oven. "Come here."

I crawled into her embrace, and my best friend hugged me close to her like my mother never did. She rocked me a little, soothing me with a gentle *shhhh* as I cried, and I hated that I was crying, I hated that I was being weak.

I hated that *nothing* was fine.

"Talk to me," Belle said, still rocking me, her fingers running through my hair that had fallen from my messy pony tail. "And don't spit bullshit and fake *I'm okay* crap. Tell me the real stuff."

I let out a long breath, pulling back until I was out of her grasp. I peeled off my gloves, and Belle grabbed one of my hands in hers a I used the other one to swipe away the tears from my face. I stared at the shiny, spotless tile Belle and I both sat on, trying to find the right words to say.

"He didn't come to the game," I started, sniffing, not knowing why that mattered. "I went, and I went alone, I didn't even bring anyone. And I told him to leave me alone, I told him I was done, but I don't know..."

"There was still a part of you that thought he might show up," Belle finished for me.

I nodded.

"You miss him."

I nodded again, this time crumpling a little. "I don't know why I feel like this," I admitted. "I'm the one who called it off. It's for the best, I know it is, but I can't eat, I can't sleep, I can't wake up to even one day where it doesn't feel like there's a giant brick on my chest. He hasn't texted me, which is what I wanted, right? But then I look at my phone every time it buzzes hoping to see his name." I shook my head. "It's sick. I'm sick."

Belle chuckled, smoothing her hand over mine. "No, you've just got it bad."

"What? The flu?"

She scrunched her nose. "More like you've been bitten by the love bug."

I groaned, leaning into her. "That's what I was trying to *avoid*."

"We don't exactly get a say in it, baby girl," she said, rubbing my back. "Hate to be the one to break that to you. What exactly did you say to him, that last night you guys were together?"

I sighed. "I basically told him that I didn't trust him, I didn't trust anyone, and even if he was saying he wanted to be with me now, even if he believed it, one day he would wake up and feel differently and I couldn't do it again."

"He's not Carlo, Gemma..." Belle whispered.

I pushed back, looking into her soft gray-blue eyes. "He doesn't have to be. Carlo was desperately in love with me, Belle. You saw us together. You saw the way he treated me, the way he loved me, and then he just... he just..."

"He changed his mind."

I didn't answer. I didn't have to.

"What spawned all this? I thought you had thrown all this out, I thought you were going to give it a chance and try with Zach?" Belle shook her head. "You saw him with me at the game and almost punched me in the throat. You like him. Things were going great. What changed?"

I sniffed, standing without another word and crossing my living room to where the box of Carlo's things was shoved behind my couch. I picked up the letters — both mine and Brielle's — and handed them to Belle, sinking back down onto the tile next to her.

She stared at the names for a moment, casting me a curious glance before she opened mine first. She read it silently while I picked at my nail polish, and as soon as she folded it away and opened Brielle's, it only took three seconds for her to curse and toss the paper across the kitchen.

"That motherfucker."

She stared at the letters across the room like she could set them on fire with her gaze alone. Then, her eyes found me again, her brows bent together.

"This is what was in the box Sofia brought by?"

I nodded.

"God, Gemma... I am so, so sorry. That's awful. I'm just sorry you had to see that."

"He wrote the same thing to her that he wrote to me," I whispered, eyes pooling with tears again. "Neither one of us mattered to him. It was all just a game — up until the very day he passed."

Belle was quiet for a moment, and I swore I could feel that silence like a cold, wet blanket sitting on top of both of us.

"Do you think he just... did he write them before knowing how bad he really was? Did he intend to give me mine in private, and give her hers? I mean..." I shook my head. "I was never meant to see that letter, the one to Brielle. But I did. And now..."

My voice faded, and my best friend just sat there on the floor with me, still quiet, still processing. When she finally spoke again, she did so with her eyes fixed on me, but I just stared at the tile.

"Okay, I know that must have hurt. I know it must have triggered everything you were trying to forget, every awful fear you were trying to overcome by trusting Zach. But babe... Zach is different. You know that."

"Do I?" I challenged. "I thought I knew Carlo, but I was wrong. I never suspected..." I shook my head. "Seeing those letters, it brought back all the hurt. It reminded me of everything I felt, and once I remembered, I couldn't for the life of me figure out how I could have ever forgotten that pain."

Belle frowned.

"I can't trust Zach," I told her. "I can't trust him, or love him, or *be* loved because I just feel like I'm being stupid. I feel like one of the dogs in Pavlov's test that never learned its lesson, that's just waiting to be put down from being too dumb to be useful." I shook my head, picking at my polish again. "Carlo ruined it, he ruined *me*. I want to love, and can't at the same time."

"Do you really think Zach would cheat on you? Do you think he can see anyone *but* you?"

"It's not about that," I said, shaking my head. "It's just... everything. Love is dangerous. Falling for someone, trusting them to take care of your heart, to keep loving you even when times get hard... I mean, you know." I gestured to my best friend. "You're the same way. You're smart. You don't love and you stay safe."

"I also stay lonely. And let me tell you something," she said, making sure I was looking at her before she finished her thought. "The way I live? It's not glorious. It's not free of hurt or pain or any of the shit you go through with love. And at least when you're in love, you have someone else to go through it all with."

My shoulders fell. "I just don't want to get hurt."

"Right," she said. "Because you're totally not hurting right now."

I didn't respond, but her words hit me subtly, softly, but with a punch — like a needle prick to the heart.

"Look, I'm not telling you what to do, Gemma," Belle said. "But I will tell you this. The way Zach looks at you? The way he saw the best in you, before you'd even shown it to him? The way he fought for you, *still* fights for you, the way he opens up to you and lets you see the things that scare *him* most?" She shook her head. "That is rare. It is so, *so* rare, babe. And I'm not going to say what's the right decision, but I will say that if I were you, if it were me in your shoes?" Belle smiled, taking my hand in hers. "Girl, I would chase that boy. And if I caught him again, if he let me have another shot, I'd never let him go."

"And if he leaves me in a year, or two? If he cheats on me? If he..."

"*If-if-if*," she mimicked. "If he leaves, or you leave, if one of you changes your mind and this whole thing goes down in flames? Well, at least you tried. And at least you got to feel the kind of love most people dream about. At least, for even a few short steps in this life, you got to have someone walking beside you — someone holding your hand and caring whether or not you're okay." She swallowed. "That alone is worth the risk."

I closed my eyes, setting free a new wave of tears as the brick on my chest lifted, my lungs trembling for air, heart beating faster.

I wanted him.

I knew he could hurt me. I knew I could hurt *him*. I knew it could all go up in a catastrophic dumpster fire in the end. But I couldn't let go — not yet.

I didn't want to exist in a world where we didn't at least try.

"Oh, God," I said, covering my lips with one, shaking hand. "This is what always happens. I felt out of control, so I just... flipped out. I let my emotions rule everything. I should have talked to you first. I should have talked to *him*." I shook my head. "What do I do? How do I... I said so many awful things. He opened up to me, and asked me to stay, and I just..."

"Hey," Belle said, lowering her gaze to mine. "He doesn't owe you anything, okay? He may not want to try again. But, you won't know that until *you* try." She shrugged. "This is it. You have to make your move, and then, you have to wait and hope he makes one back."

Make my move.

I ran over her words in my head, still sitting on that cold tile floor as visions of Zach's smile, of his dark, loving eyes surrounded me.

Belle was right.

It was now or never, and there was no guarantee that anything would work. He didn't owe me a second chance, but I would beg him for one, anyway.

It was time to make my move.

I hoped I'd make the right one.

ZACH

"Ugh, gag me," Micah said Saturday evening, crossing his arms over where he sat next to me in his bed.

"Shhh." I waved him off, my eyes on the small television screen propped on the dresser at the foot of his bed. We were near the end of *Silver Linings Playbook*, and Bradley Cooper hugged Robert De Niro, heeding his advice about the girl who'd just left the room — the girl who loved him, the girl he loved in return.

Jennifer Lawrence.

"I'm sorry, but this is just crap," Micah continued. "What? He's just going to suddenly drop this obsession he's had this whole time for his wife, or ex-wife, or whatever she is, and go for this other girl instead?"

"Shhh!" I said again, this time smacking his arm. "This is the best part. Shut up."

Micah groaned, but I ignored him, watching as Bradley chased Jennifer through the streets. She screamed at him to leave her alone, and then one of my all-time favorite love professions took place, and I recited it with Bradley, word for word.

That earned me another hard eye roll from Micah.

When the words were out, Jennifer was back in Bradley's arms, kissing him and sealing the truth in every word he'd just said. I let out a long sigh, chest aching, tears stinging the corners of my eyes, though I didn't let them fall.

"You're such a loser."

I pegged Micah with a pillow. "What happened to being here for me with brotherly support?"

"I didn't realize it would be such a chick fest."

"Are you serious?" I asked, pausing the movie. "With all the emotion, the real shit in that movie, you think it's all *chick stuff*? This is real. This is life. And whether you're male or female, you should be able to appreciate this."

Micah shrugged. "I mean, the football stuff was cool. I liked his family. But, come on," he said, gesturing to the screen where I'd paused Bradley and Jennifer in a full-on spinning kiss scene. "She's crazy. *He's* absolutely insane. In what world does this ever work?"

"But *that's* just it," I said, thumping his chest. "They're both a little crazy, both a little messed up. But they're choosing to be messed up together."

Micah blinked.

There was a chuckle from behind me, and Dad came in, sitting on the edge of the bed. He glanced at the screen before his eyes found mine. "I don't think your brother is old enough to appreciate the sentiment in that yet, son."

"Or, I have the wrong reproductive organ between my legs," Micah volleyed.

Dad reached over and smacked his leg.

"There's nothing wrong with being in touch with your feelings, Micah," he said. "Your comment is sexist. Man or woman, you should know how to listen to your emotions and deal with them."

Micah cowered, and I knew the shadow that passed over him. I'd had my ass handed to me by my father plenty of times. When you're battling the rest of the world telling you how to be a man, and telling you that feeling is somehow woman-like, and that being woman-like is somehow inferior? Dad was probably the only one who could ever break through that noise — for both myself and for Micah.

And he always did.

"Most would shut down in a situation like this," Dad continued. "They'd pretend they're fine and keep moving. Your brother is taking the time to sort through some really difficult thoughts and feelings, and he's going to be stronger on the other side of it."

"Or dead," I argued. "Jury's still out."

Dad's eyes softened, and I smiled to ease his worry, trying my best to pretend I was joking. It'd been two weeks since Gemma and I ended things, and still, I was a complete wreck. My appetite was nonexistent, my sleep was the same, and work was about the only place where I felt even a little okay. Even there, I had the decision to make about the bar looming over me, and my time was running out.

Doc wanted to leave after the new year. And that meant I had to decide soon if he'd be selling the bar before he left, or transferring everything over to me.

It was hard to think about that — about anything — because Gemma took up every inch of space in my mind. She was the first thing I thought of when I opened my eyes, and she haunted me every second of the day until I finally faded off into a fitful sleep. And even then, she was there, in my dreams, waiting to fuck me up more.

I was a mess.

I couldn't blame my brother for being sick and tired of trying to help me through it. My parents were a little more understanding, a little more patient, but I was annoying *myself* — I couldn't imagine how my sixteen-year-old brother felt.

"Dinner's almost ready," Mom said, propping her hip against the door frame. She smiled when she took in the sight of all three of us on the bed. "Aw, my boys. Reminds me of when you guys were younger."

"You just miss my hair," Dad said, running a hand over the spot where he was balding on top.

Mom smiled, crossing the room and bending to kiss that bare skin. "You're even sexier without it, my love."

"Ew," Micah groaned, but I smiled.

I wanted that. I wanted it so bad. And I thought I could have had it.

With Gemma.

Maybe I read into it too much, maybe I had always been more invested than she was. I knew she wanted to take things slow, and we had, but she'd opened up to me, too. She'd let me in, wanted me around her every day, wanted to share her past with me and ask me to share mine with her.

Of course, she'd left out one of the most important parts of her past.

I couldn't blame her for not trusting me — not trusting *anyone* — after what her ex-husband left her with. It was a kind of grief I could only imagine, one I could never fully understand.

But I wanted to.

I wanted to hold her hand and love her through it all. I wanted to be a part of her healing, let her know she didn't have to go at it alone.

But, I couldn't choose me for her.

I had to let her go.

I just didn't know how to.

Dad clapped my knee. "Come on. Let's eat, boys." But before he could move up off the bed, the doorbell rang.

We all stared at each other. Doc had already told us he couldn't make it tonight, he was meeting with a real estate agent to discuss his future plans in paradise. Who would be stopping by at dinner time?

"It might be the neighbors," Mom said, already heading to the door. "Might need someone to watch the kids for a bit."

She disappeared, and Micah made another joke about the "stupid kiss" happening on the still-paused screen. I argued with him on the poignant undertones in the movie while Dad watched and smiled from the side.

All of us stopped talking when Mom came back in the room.

Because she wasn't alone.

I thought the image of Gemma haunting my dreams for the past two weeks was bad, but seeing her in real life, standing in my little brother's bedroom with my mother by her side? It was like I was a bird being struck down mid-flight, slamming to the cold, hard ground and losing my breath in the process.

She was beautiful.

Even with her eyes puffy and red, dark circles framing the bottom of them, and even with her little shoulders slumped, her hair in a messy bun on her head. She held something in her hand, and whatever it was, she gripped onto it like it was the only thing holding her in that room with me.

For what felt like an eternity, we just stared. I wished I could read her mind. I wished she could read mine.

I wished I knew what I felt in that moment.

I wanted to jump up, pull her into my arms, kiss her. But, I also wanted to tell her to get the hell out of my house. It was strange, the way those thoughts warred with each other, because I couldn't figure out which one I leaned toward more.

Gemma finally cleared her throat, eyes bouncing around the room as she realized she had my entire family's attention. "I'm so sorry to bother you during dinner time," she said, her voice raspy and soft. "I just... I came here to give you something."

I was still pinned under the covers — Micah on one side of me, Dad on the other — and all I could do was sit and stare as Gemma cautiously crossed the room. She handed me the bent-up-piece of card stock in her hand, immediately stepping back once it was in mine, instead.

It was her other ticket to tomorrow's game.

"I don't really have all the words I need to say right now," she said, eyes on where my hands held the ticket. "I know that I've hurt you... that I've hurt both of us. I know that there are things I said that I can't take back, and possibly things you'll never be able to forget." Gemma caught my eyes then, brows bending. "And honestly, I'm not sure what I have to offer right now. I'm not sure where we would go from here. But... all I'm asking for right now is for you to take that seat next to me at tomorrow's game."

I watched her a moment longer, tearing my eyes from hers to look at the ticket again as my heart thundered in my chest.

"Please don't say anything right now," she continued. "Take your time, take the night to think about it. And if you don't show tomorrow... I completely understand. I do."

All words were stuck somewhere between my brain and my mouth. I couldn't form a single one. I couldn't thank her for coming by, or find it in me to jump up from the bed and pull her into me. I just stared at that ticket, processing what she'd said, wondering what the hell made her come.

"I'll let you all get to your dinner," she said quietly, backing up until she was by Mom again. "Pamela, I'm so sorry I came by without notice. Thank you for letting me in."

"You're always welcome, my dear," she said, and I felt my mom's eyes on me, though mine were still on the ticket. When I didn't move, when no one else said a word, Mom spoke again. "I'll walk you out."

I wasn't sure how long they were gone, how long I stared at the *section 124* text on that ticket before I realized

Gemma had left the room. My eyes shot open wider, and I looked at Micah, then at Dad, and then I scrambled out of the covers.

"She's already gone, son," Dad said, placing a firm hand on my arm before I could wrangle my way out of the bed. "She's gone."

My chest heaved, eyes wild as I searched the doorway and then looked back down at the ticket. I still couldn't speak. I couldn't think. I couldn't do anything but stare, and blink, and stare some more.

Mom came back into the room a few moments later, leaning against the same spot in the doorway. Her sympathetic eyes found mine, and she tried a small smile, but it was weak.

"She brought a pie, too," Mom said. "For dessert. I put it in the fridge."

I nodded, but still didn't say a word.

Everyone was silent for a while, and then Dad cleared his throat. "So... are you going to go?"

The ticket felt like an anvil in my hand, and I twisted it in my fingers, feeling the perforated edges. I stared at it so long that the words went fuzzy, the logo blurred, and finally, I dropped it on the plaid comforter of Micah's bed.

"No," I answered, shoving the ticket farther away as if to hammer it home.

"NO?!" Dad and Micah said in unison.

I shook my head, the word reverberating inside it. "What's the point?" My heart cracked with that question, knowing I couldn't just sweep in like Bradley Cooper, chase my Jennifer Lawrence and have faith in it all. "Two weeks ago, she told me she didn't trust me. That didn't change in the days we've been apart. So, if that's missing, if she doesn't trust me, what is there to build on? It's all a game to her."

Micah opened his mouth to speak, but Dad held up a hand, and he popped it closed again. I waited for him to speak, but he didn't — not yet. He just let me process.

"She's been hurt," I said, voice cracking. "And I understand, because I have, too. Not in the same way, but we've all been through things." I kicked the covers the rest of the way off from where I'd started untangling myself before. "The difference between us, though, is that she doesn't have it in her to open up again. And she's right," I admitted. "I can't make any promises. Love is fucking scary. One day, I could wake up and we could be miserable together. She could wake up to the same conclusion, too."

At that, Dad laughed. "Well, yeah, that's what love is all about. It's fucking terrifying."

I gaped at my father, who I was pretty sure hadn't cursed in all the years I'd been alive.

"What?" He shrugged. "It's a great word for emphasis, and that sentence needed it. Look, love is like... it's like hanging off this cliff, right? This ledge. And the only thing preventing you from falling and painting the bottom of the canyon with your intestines is this other person holding your hand. And they can drop you," he said, holding up his hand as if to demonstrate. "They always have that choice. But it's you *trusting* them that they won't. It's them trusting the same in you. And maybe she doesn't have all of that trust yet... but, she's trying to. Her coming here was her way of saying that she *wants* to trust you."

"I disagree." Micah leaned forward until he could meet my eyes. "All jokes aside, bro... I think her coming here, putting her pride aside like that?" He shook his head. "I think that was her way of saying she *does* trust you — but maybe she was just scared to admit that. I mean, it's like Dad said, she's willing to hang off that cliff if you are." He screwed up his face then. "Or wait, would she be holding you? Or vice versa?"

Dad chuckled. "It's a metaphor, son."

"I know, but I don't understand which is which and who — oh, forget it. You know what I mean." He thumped me on the chest.

I stared at the ticket, now half-covered by the comforter as my heart started to tick up a notch.

"Everything that feels as amazing as love does?" Dad said, shaking his head. "It comes with risk, Zach. So yeah, if you're not willing to take some risks, to hang off the ledge with that girl, then don't go. But if you are, and if she is — which, judging by her being brave enough to come here and ask you to join her at the game, she is — then, who knows." He clapped my shoulder and squeezed it hard. "Just might be something amazing, something worth fighting for. But you won't know if you don't trust it. You won't know if you don't try."

"Jesus," Micah said, shaking his head as he picked up the ticket. "Now even *I* want to chase after the girl."

Dad and I both chuckled at that, and Mom wiped away a tear that had fallen down her cheek, her eyes soft and sweet as she looked at my dad first and then me. My heart squeezed at the sight of her crying.

"Mom?" I asked. "Are you okay?"

She nodded, wiping away more tears at my question. "I'm sorry. It's just... she's such an amazing woman, and you, my son, are the most incredible man. You deserve to be happy, and so does she." She shrugged. "I want you to both find that happiness together. But, it's not up to me. Or your dad, or your brother."

She paused, taking a big breath as she stood straighter, her mascara stained on her cheeks now.

"The choice is yours," she said, her eyes finding my dad again, although she spoke right to me. "Hold on, or let her fall."

With that, Mom crossed the room and leaned over my father to kiss my forehead. She told Micah to go wash up for dinner, and he handed me the ticket before hopping out of the bed.

"Guess it's your turn to be the crazy guy chasing the crazy girl," he said.

Mom chuckled, and with my dad's hand in hers, they left the room next.

Then, it was just me — me and the stupid ticket.

And a choice that I knew I'd already made.

Chapter 22

GEMMA

The stadium was packed.

It was our second-to-last home game before the regular season was over, and we were playing our biggest rivals — the Green Bay Packers. We'd beat them on their own turf earlier in the season — the same night I'd gone home with Andy thinking I was proving something to Zach.

It seemed a little ironic now, considering that we were playing the same team on the day I'd asked Zach to give me another chance.

But today was a bigger deal. If we beat them today, we were guaranteed a playoff spot.

I bounced in my seat waiting for kickoff, trying my best to keep warm. It was absolutely bone-achingly cold, with the promise of snow being just about all the sports newscasters could talk about. I was bundled in a jacket twice my size, gloves, a snow cap that covered my ears, and a face guard with the Bears logo on it. My feet were bundled up in two pairs of thick socks and my best boots, and I wore long Johns under my jeans.

Still, I couldn't stop trembling.

But maybe part of that was more fear-induced.

Belle had finally talked sense into me last week. She knew me better than I knew myself, it seemed, and once she'd opened my eyes to what I was walking away from, I'd wanted to smack myself for being so stupid.

It'd taken me a few days to get myself together, to figure out what I wanted to say and how. I debated calling him, texting him, but every thought in me kept coming back to how we met — to how it all started.

It was just supposed to be a game.

It was just supposed to be me, stepping out and "dating" a little, finding some human connection. It was just supposed to be him, helping me break into it all, serving as a "practice round."

Now, it was hard to even remember what it was like, back when I saw Zach as a nuisance, as someone I needed to avoid, as my trial run. I was so scared of him... and part of me still was. But, the difference now was that I was ready to face that fear with him. I was ready to try, to risk everything — because even though I said I didn't, I trusted him.

I just hoped he trusted me, too.

When I knocked on his door last night, I wasn't sure he'd let me in. Thankfully, it was Pamela who got to decide if I could enter or not. It'd been all I could take, seeing him in that bed with his family, watching *Silver Linings Playbook*, his eyes underlined with the same dark circles as mine. He looked as miserable as I felt, and it took everything in me not to ask his family to leave, not to crawl into that bed with him and have him hold me as I cried and begged him to take me back.

But that wasn't what I wanted.

I didn't want to just show up and beg for a second chance. I wanted him to want this, too. I wanted him to take his time, take the night to think on it, to think on *us*.

If he showed up, I'd know.

And if he didn't...

"And so, we meet again," Janet said, scooting close to me as she rubbed her hands together. Roy took the seat next to her, a small nod his only gesture of acknowledgement.

I smiled, but confusion soared through me. "You guys are sitting here today?"

"Your friend gave these tickets back to us, said he couldn't come to any more of the games this season," Janet answered, her brows pulling together. "I thought he would have told you."

A chill swept over me, but not from the wind. Of course, he'd sell his tickets. He didn't show up at the last game. Why would he want to ever come to a game and sit next to me?

But *when* did he give them back? Was he going to use the one I sent him... or was this it?

"Oh," I said, smiling again. "Yeah, of course. He told me. I just didn't realize he gave the tickets back to you guys. This is perfect, though! I need someone to boo with when the Packers score."

Janet chuckled. "Well, you know I'll cheer and boo right along with you." She nodded back to Roy. "Don't count on much from this one, though. It's down to the wire for playoffs, you'll be lucky if you see him blink the entire game."

I laughed, casting a glance at Roy before my eyes met Janet's again. Her gaze was soft, and she gave me a knowing smile, reaching over to squeeze the puffy arm of my jacket with her mitten-covered hand.

"Hey," she said, voice low. "I don't know what's going on, but whatever it is, it's going to be okay. One step at a time, that's what my mom always told me." She shrugged.

"Even when it was hard to hear, it always seemed to ring true."

I swallowed, the saying reminding me of advice my grandfather would have given. Janet didn't even know about me and Zach, or about my past, but she knew in that moment that I needed to hear her words.

And I never could have thanked her enough.

The game started, and Zach still wasn't there. I kept casually scanning the crowd behind us between plays, hoping I'd see him jogging down the stairs — but I never did. When the first quarter ended, the Packers were up seven to zero, and my stomach was a mess of knots for both my team and myself.

The energy in the stadium was palpable as the second quarter started, our defense getting the crowd on their feet every time we were trying to fight off another score. Our offense picked up the pace, and when halftime rolled around, we'd tied up the game. Seven to seven.

Zach still hadn't shown.

"Do you want anything from the stands?" Janet asked. "I'm going to get us a couple of hot chocolates."

I shook my head. "No, I'm okay. Thank you, though."

My gaze was fixed on the field, where the halftime entertainment was, though I wasn't actually watching any of it at all. Janet just gave me another small smile, squeezing my shoulder before she made her way up the benches.

He could still come.

I held onto what little hope I had left as the halftime clock ticked down, but I couldn't move from the spot where I sat. Even when the next quarter started, the crowd jumping to their feet around me, I still sat and stared.

The third quarter passed in a blur, both teams fighting for their chance in the playoffs. Whoever won had a sure place. Whoever lost still had a chance at wild card.

Everything was on the line for these teams, and I could relate in the biggest way.

I checked my phone, wondering if Zach had texted. But there was nothing. I tried to cheer, tried to focus on the game, but I couldn't stop wondering if he was coming. I wondered what he was thinking, and that had me coming up blank. He hadn't said a word the entire time I was at his house. He'd just stared at me, and then the ticket, and I hadn't a clue what was going through his head.

Maybe he didn't believe me.

Maybe he did, but it didn't matter — because now *he* couldn't trust *me*.

Maybe he laughed when I was gone, throwing that ticket in the trash.

Had I ruined it all?

Had I blown my chance?

Just as the time started ticking on the fourth quarter, the first few flakes of snow fell from the gray sky overhead. The stadium roared to life, the jumbotron showing fans catching flakes on their tongues and in their hands as the energy from the game somehow picked up even more.

This was it. One more quarter. One last chance to win the game.

I checked my phone again, one last time, with my heart in my throat as I did so. But there was nothing but a text from Belle.

- Well? Did he show? -

My heart cracked, and I sniffed, eyes watering from the cold. At least, that's what I told myself. I couldn't text her back, even though the answer was clear. I wasn't ready to accept it yet.

He isn't coming.

My chest squeezed so hard I thought I'd pass out from lack of oxygen, and I leaned back against my chair, not sitting down but not able to hold all my weight on my feet any longer.

There was one quarter left. We were so close to securing our spot in the playoffs.

No one noticed the sad, lonely girl who'd lost a game she never intended to play.

I couldn't feel the excitement from the crowd roaring. I couldn't find the urge to high-five anyone as our receiver made another catch, or to jump up and down with everyone else as they belted out the lyrics to "Bear Down." I couldn't even feel the snow as it landed on my cheeks.

Tomorrow, I might be okay. But today, I was far from it.

I stood there in a daze, the crowd a distant buzz as I ran over all the *what ifs* and *could haves, should haves* in my mind. I should have said more last night when I brought that ticket to him. I should have apologized sooner, should have explained to Zach why I freaked out the way I did. I should have let Belle be there when I opened the letters, maybe she could have talked sense into me *before* I ruined everything.

It was too late now, but it didn't stop me from playing it all over and over again, like a game tape where the end was alway the same, no matter how many times I watched it.

A snowflake fell on my lashes, and I blinked it away, taking a deep breath and looking up to the sky as if I'd find answers written in the gray clouds above.

It's okay, Gemma. It's okay. Just breathe.

"Oh, my God," Janet said, brows pulling inward as she stared at something farther up in the stands behind me. "What in the world?"

I squinted, trying to see through the snow and the sea of people. I imagined it was someone dancing, or maybe a fight breaking out. But the more I wiggled around, peering through the open space between fans, the more I realized no one was booing or cheering.

They were laughing.

And when the source of their laughter got close enough for me to see why, my heart stopped beating altogether. My eyes shot open wide, glove-covered hands flying over my mouth.

I only saw him for little specs of time at first — just when the crowd would move the right way, and I could get a glimpse of his dark eyes through the people weaving left and right. He wasn't smiling, though everyone around him was — pointing and nudging each other as he passed. A few people tried to stop him, tried to take selfies with him, but he just looked around them, through them, searching for something. Or someone.

It was Zach. He was here.

And he was dressed up like a hot dog.

I almost smiled as I watched him, his eyes frantically searching as he fielded off rowdy fans trying to dance with him or high-five him as he passed. He was holding a piece of cardboard in his hands, and he was shivering, his arms and legs exposed under the hot dog costume.

Somehow, he made his way through, and when he got to our row, everyone had to stand up and hug the backs of their chairs to let him pass. He still hit them all on the way through, murmuring *excuse me's* as I watched him and tried not to laugh.

When there were just a few seats between us, our eyes met, and everything else faded — the crowd, the game, the bitter cold.

He watched me, his eyes softening, a small smile finding his lips as he seemed to catch his first breath. He kept making his way toward me, and I met him in front of the seat that should have been his. My heart was racing, beating against my chest like it wanted to break free and run toward him.

He was here.

He was *here*.

I didn't know what that meant. I didn't know whether it was safe to inhale my next breath of hope, to believe that he was here for me, that this somehow meant we would be okay. So, when there was no one else between us, I waited, crossing my arms over my middle.

Zach's eyes searched mine as he swallowed, and then, he shook his head, a small laugh escaping from his lips. He looked down at the cardboard in his hands, and then he grimaced, turning it around so I could read the black ink scrawled across the other side.

WIEN-ER-LOSE, YOU'RE THE ONE I WANT BESIDE ME IN THE GAME OF LIFE.

Janet and Roy roared with laughter at the sign, and the rest of the section that could see it joined in, too. I smiled, but cocked my head to the side, unsure of what exactly I was supposed to gather from that sign. I bit my lip, looking up at where Zach watched me before I read it again.

Zach let out a mix between a laugh and a sigh, shaking his head as he let the sign drop. Then, he stepped closer, shortening the distance between us.

"Romance movies."

It was the first thing he said — the first thing he'd said to me in the last two weeks, since I told him I couldn't trust him, that we couldn't be together.

I frowned, trying to understand. "Um..."

"The third thing I'm a big softie about," he explained. "Romance movies. And books. And just romance in general, I suppose." He shrugged. "Micah makes fun of me for it all the time, and honestly, I wish I could change it. I wish I wasn't such a sucker for grand gestures and romantic comedies where somehow everything works out in the end. But damnit, I can't help myself. And now, when I had the chance to make my own grand gesture, I failed miserably."

I bit back a smile, covering my mouth with one hand as Zach's chest deflated.

"It's fourth quarter. I missed the whole game and let you sit here, shivering in the freaking snow, for Christ's sake, because I was running around town trying to find a damn hot dog suit. Do you know how hard it is to find one now that Halloween has passed?" Zach blew out a breath. "It's impossible. And then I borrowed this piece of cardboard and a marker from one of the homeless men outside the stadium. I gave him a hundred bucks for this, Gemma. A hundred bucks! And you know what, he deserved it, but I don't know if I even deserve for you to listen to anything I say next because I really messed this all up."

I swallowed, that smile I'd been biting back making its way to the surface as I listened to Zach ramble, the entire crowd around us invested in what he was saying.

"I mean, seriously," he said, gesturing to his costume. "I thought I could make the romance heroes proud by dressing up as a *hot dog*?" Zach shook his head. "Matthew McConaughey is rolling in his grave right now."

"Pretty sure he's still alive."

"Well, he's rolling in his lush, 2500 thread count Egyptian silk sheets, then."

A soft laugh slipped from my lips, but tears were pooling in my eyes as Zach took another step toward me. There were still people in the background trying to lean in and take pictures with Zach and his costume, and a few people yelled for us to sit down or move out of the way of the next play. But he ignored them all.

His sole focus was on me.

"I'm sorry I didn't make it here sooner," he said, brows pulling inward. "I'm sorry you had to sit in the cold, alone, and I'm sorry that this stupid hot dog suit is the best thing I could think of. But the truth is?" He shook his head. "I haven't been able to think about anything but you, Gemma. Not since the very night we met."

A few people swooned at that, me included, and Zach inhaled a deep breath as snow started to gather on his costume.

"And I'm sorry I didn't say anything when you came over last night. Honestly? I didn't know what to say. I didn't know how I felt. The biggest part of me wanted to tell you to stop talking, pull you into my arms, kiss you senseless and just forget about everything else." Zach smiled at that. "But, there was still a part of me that was scared, a part of me that knew neither of us could ever forget about our pasts, a part of me that heard you telling me you didn't trust me just a couple of short weeks ago."

My stomach dropped, heart picking up speed again. "But I—"

"Wait," he said, holding up one hand. "Just... let me finish."

He stepped closer, taking my glove-covered hands in his.

"Look, I don't *want* you to forget about your past. I don't want you to run from it, either. I know you've been hurt, and I know you're not completely healed from it yet — and you may never be. Our past has a funny way of becoming part of who we are in the future, and I think that's the way it's meant to be. Without the scars, without the pain, we wouldn't be able to appreciate the times when everything is magical — the days when life is absolute bliss. And trust me when I say that every day I've spent with you has been just that — magic."

I squeezed his hands.

"We don't have to solve it all over night. I know we're going to both have to face some fears, and we're going to have to trust each other. And *God*, isn't that the most terrifying thing?"

I laughed, sniffing back tears. "So scary."

"Like *Nightmare on Elm Street* scary."

"I mean, I think those movies are more gory than anything."

"Just roll with me here, Gemma."

I chuckled.

"So, yeah, it's going to be scary, trusting each other and not being able to make promises as to what happens next," he continued, a slow smile spreading on his face. "But I like you, Gemma. I like that you like ketchup and cheese on your hot dog."

I laughed, and Zach did, too, stepping closer as he pulled my hands to rest on his chest. His found my waist, and he held me there, his eyes flicking between mine.

"I like that you get so riled up during football games that we almost get kicked out of them. And I like the way you scrunch your nose when you disagree with me, and the way you make jeans and a tank top look sexier than any black dress." He paused, scanning my attire. "Hell, you even make a giant, puffy jacket look amazing."

The tears I'd been fighting back slipped out silently, falling over my cheeks, but Zach brushed them both away, his hands sliding in to frame my face.

"I like fighting with you," he said, shaking his head. "And I like it even more when we get to make up after. Honestly, I don't know where this all goes, whether we make it to forever or just to next month, but I know I want to try. I know the same thing is true for me now that was true after that very first game."

"And what's that?"

He smiled, pressing his forehead to mine. "I can't walk away from you. Not yet. Maybe not ever."

I sighed, breathing in his words like oxygen, giving my heart something new to beat for.

"When you showed up at that second game," I said, voice soft, just a whisper between us. "I said you'd never win. I said you were playing the wrong game." I shook my head. "But it was *me* who was wrong. This was never a game. It was always real. And that's why you couldn't walk away... it's why I couldn't either. Why I still can't."

I pulled back, locking my eyes onto his as I raised up onto my toes.

"Wien-Er-Lose," I said, laughing as Zach choked out a laugh, too. "I want you, too. I lied when I said I didn't trust you. And I lied when I told myself I would be fine without you."

Zach raised both brows, his hands sneaking into the pockets of my coat. "So... are you saying you're in for another practice round?"

I laughed, shaking my head and looping my arms around his shoulders. "No," I answered. "This time, I want the real thing. No more practice. Let's play for keeps."

Zach smiled, lowering his lips to mine and pausing right when they touched. "I always was."

And then, he kissed me.

The crowd roared around us, and I wasn't sure if it was because of a play on the field or because of us. All I knew was that kiss sealed a promise neither one of us could speak out loud, because neither one of us could vow to keep it. We knew the risk we were taking, we knew the leap we were making, but we were holding each other's hands and doing it anyway.

He could leave. I could leave. We could both end up heartbroken, sitting on the floor of our souls and trying to piece together our lives again.

But, we could also find forever.

We could take the next steps together — toward a year, five, or maybe, forever.

And *that* was a game worth playing.

Zach tried to wrap me in his embrace more, but his costume got in the way, and I laughed, breaking our kiss and pushing back to take it all in. My hands ran over the puffy buns before settling on the red, air-filled hot dog that surrounded his body.

"I'm touching your wiener," I said, waggling my brows.

Zach groaned, running his hand under my jacket to squeeze my ass. "Does that mean I get to touch your buns later, just to make things fair?"

"Hmmm..." I ran my hands up over his shoulders again, letting my wrists hang behind his neck. "Well, guess it depends on what happens during this game. We might have some celebrating to do."

I leaned in to kiss him again as a playful growl left his throat, but before I could deepen the kiss, Janet tapped me on the shoulder.

"You two are on the jumbotron again!" she said.

Zach and I looked up at the screen, and sure enough, there we were — in all our hot dog glory. We both laughed as the crowd started cheering, and Zach pulled me into him, dipping me in a dramatic fashion as everyone cheered louder. When the screen changed back to the players on the field, Zach lifted my arm in his like he'd just won me in a championship fight, and our whole section roared one more time.

"Alright," he said, pulling me down until we were both sitting and out of everyone's way. "Now that this hot dog has his girl back, let's see if we can land this W."

I threw my hands up. "Let's do it!" Then, with less than five minutes of playing time left, I stood again, starting the *Bear Down* fight song.

Zach joined in first, then Janet and Roy, and before long, the entire stadium was singing together.

The snow fell harder, but we all stayed and cheered on our Bears in spite of the cold biting at our noses. You could see the quarterback's breath as he called out each play, and every time a player took a hit, he took it hard, with the cold working against them in every way.

But still, they played.

Still, they fought.

This was what I loved about football — not just the sport, but the players, the fandom. Nothing stopped us. It didn't matter what the score was, or how impossible the odds were. Until that last whistle blew, we would be there, on our feet, fighting for the win.

I grabbed Zach's hand, squeezing it as our eyes met. And that's when I realized that it was the same for us. We were in it together, no matter what was to come, and we would fight for the win. For each other.

Until the last whistle blew.

We won.

The Bears clenched their spot in the playoff to the tune of the Packers missing a field goal in the last few seconds of the game, sealing our win and our guaranteed spot. It'd been a night for the record books — both with the snow and the score — and for me, personally, it'd been a night I'd never forget.

"Playoff-bound," Zach murmured into my ear as we made our way out of Soldier Field. His arm was around me, and he pulled me to a stop every few feet to take photos with fans holding out their phones. We were like local celebrities, Hot Dog and His Girl.

"How do you suggest we start the celebrations?" he asked after we'd completed a giant group selfie with a family of seven.

"Oh, I don't know..." I said, pulling him to a stop off to the side. The crowd still weaved around us, cheering, music blasting from every direction as the celebrations continued. But in that moment, I only saw Zach, and I leaned up to kiss his lips. "Maybe we should consult that list you started."

Zach swept his tongue over mine, holding me as much as he could with the giant hot dog suit restricting his arms. "I only added one thing to that list, and we already checked that off."

"*You* only added one thing..."

His brows rose with recognition. "Are you saying... are there more items on the list now?"

I nodded, biting my lip.

"Things we haven't done yet?"

I nodded again.

"Like..."

I kissed him again, this time slowing the pace, pulling his bottom lip between my teeth in a sensual bite that we both felt reverberate through us.

"Guess you'll have to take me home to find out."

Zach growled, kissing me hard before he dipped, hands finding my back and the crook of my knees. He lifted me, cradling me in his arms as he wobbled through the still-celebrating crowd. I handed out high-fives as we passed fans on our way to the cab line, the energy finally finding me — because the Bears weren't the only ones victorious that night.

The game was finally over.

The score was finally set.

In the end, we both lost a little, but we both walked away wearing those scars with pride. We ended that game with our heads held high, and with my hand in his as the cab took us across town and back to my place.

"I told you I'd be the right winner in the end," he said, pressing a kiss to my neck.

"I think we both won."

"A tie?" Zach huffed. "Ugh, I hate ties. The worst possible way to end a game." His eyes softened as he pulled me into his side, and he smiled, tapping my nose before he kissed the same spot. "But, in this case, I think I'm okay with it."

Me, too, Zach Bowen.

Me, too.

Epilogue

GEMMA

ten months later

"Hit me! I'm open!" Micah called out, running with one arm outstretched across the part of the lot we'd claimed as our own.

His shaggy hair blew back in the cool September breeze, and Zach wound up, throwing a perfect spiral that Micah caught easily before running past his father.

I smiled, watching Zach sprint across the lot and pretend-tackle Micah to the grass. They rolled a few times before Zach retrieved the ball that Micah had fumbled, running it back this way with his little brother hot on his trail. Their dad just watched with a grin of his own, shaking his head.

It was a cool, gray day in September, and it was a welcome reprieve from the steaming summer we'd had. Not that I minded getting out of the condo and exploring the city with Zach all summer long, but fall was always my favorite season, and I welcomed it with arms wide open.

"I can't believe I let you talk me into another football game," Belle said from where she sat in the shade under our tent. She scooped a chip into the guac on her plate, popping it in her mouth with a loud crunch. "I thought I got out of this once I suckered you into that whole scheme last year."

"Come on," I said, leaning a hip against the table that had our food spread on it. "It's the home opener, Belle. And now that Zach and I have tickets together, we want to start traditions." I stole a chip from her plate and pointed it at her. "You, missy, are part of those traditions. Whether you want to be or not."

"I mean, like you said, it was your idea to get us together in the first place," Zach chimed in, panting and wiping the sweat from his forehead as he leaned in and kissed my cheek. "Besides, maybe you'll find love of your own here at Soldier Field."

Belle scoffed at that, standing long enough to pile more snacks on her plate before she plopped down again. "Fat chance of that, PITA boy. I've got a strict three-night policy, and most guys don't even make it that far."

"What about Doctor Jordan?" I asked with a smirk. "Seems like he's surpassed that three night rule pretty easily."

"We have an understanding," Belle piped back, avoiding my eyes. When I just kept watching her, she shooed me away. "Alright, you, that's enough. Don't give me that look."

"I'm not giving you any kind of look," I said, hands up in surrender.

"Mm-hmm." Belle kicked back in her chair, chomping on a chip as Pamela swept under the tent with another plate full of hot dogs.

"Alright, that's all of them," she said with a wide grin. "Now, come on, boys," she said to Zach, Micah, and Daniel. "And ladies," she said to us next. "Dig in before all this gets cold."

She didn't have to tell any of us twice. It took less than ten minutes for each one of us to have a plate piled high with either a burger, a hot dog, or — in Zach's case — both. There were about twenty sides too many spread out on the table, but somehow, we managed to dig into every container between the six of us. We chowed down, talking over the music blasting from Micah's speaker and sharing stories with other Bears fans that passed by on their way into the stadium.

Belle and Pamela were locked into a conversation about the back room Pamela was redoing in the house, and my gaze drifted to Zach, who sat across the tent next to his younger brother. His mouth was full as he argued about one of the baseball teams fighting for the playoffs, and I just smiled, thinking about how far we'd come in the past year.

It was hard to believe that this time one year ago, we'd only just met. It was almost a year to the day since we'd had our *practice round*, a game that would have more of an impact on my life than I ever could have known. It had all started as something that was never supposed to go past one night, a plan in place so I could avoid getting my heart broken again.

I laughed out loud thinking about it.

It hadn't been an easy year, though it'd been filled with beautiful memories. We'd shared the holiday season together last year, growing closer, sharing more about our pasts and making traditions of our own. The winter had been hard, the year anniversary of Carlo's passing hitting me harder than I expected. But, Zach had been there for me, and he even went to Carlo's grave with me so I could say some things out loud that I never said to him when he was alive.

Being there with Zach, his hand in mine as I cried and spilled truths I didn't even know I'd been holding onto was one of the most therapeutic moments of my life.

And from that moment on, everything seemed to fall into place for us.

Zach had his own tough decisions to make over the holiday season, and I'd held *his* hand through that — although, if I was being honest, I was so happy with the choice he'd finally made.

Doc's Bar was still alive and well — and Zach was the new owner.

Once the paperwork was finished, Doc had flown to St. Croix, and he hadn't been back since. Still, he called all the time to check in on us, and we kept his spirit alive in the bar with all the same décor the patrons had come to know and love. But, with my help on the back end of everything, Zach had been able to make some improvements with the extra cash we'd saved during tax season — making the bar his own, too.

And we were busier than ever.

I'd even started helping out as a bartender on some nights of the week — especially throughout the summer when the Cubs were on fire. But we had a pact — every Saturday night, we took off work to go to family dinner. And, now that fall was back, every Sunday was ours for football.

The rest of the staff could handle the weekends.

"Ew," Belle said, smacking my arm and dragging my attention away from Zach. "Quit staring at him like you're taking his clothes off without any of us being any the wiser. His mother's right here."

I chuckled. "Don't tell me not to ogle my man." Zach looked at me then, and he grinned, casting me a wink before turning back to his conversation. "I mean, have you seen him? You know you'd ogle, too, if he was yours."

Belle made a gag sound, but she smiled, leaning into me with a sigh.

"You two make a pretty good team, you know that?" she asked.

I found his eyes from across the tent again, and I sighed the same as her. "We really do."

An hour before kick-off, we started packing up our tailgating supplies and filing into the stadium. Zach and I had the same season tickets from last year, but we'd purchased four extra in the same row for the home opener, wanting to celebrate the first game of the season with our closest family and friends. We were all jazzed up as we made our way inside, stopping to get beers and sodas before making our way down to our section.

When we made it to our row and started squeezing past the few people at the end, I smiled at the familiar faces in the seats next to ours.

"Oh, we hoped you guys would be back!" Janet said, standing with glossy eyes and wrapping me in a hug as soon as I was close enough. "It wouldn't be the same without Hot Dog and His Girl."

Zach and I both laughed at that as Zach leaned past me to hug Janet next.

"We'll never live that down," he said, waving at Ron once Janet had taken her seat again.

Ron just nodded our way, but there was a hint of a smile on that old man's face.

"Internet sensation that was," Janet said. "My sister down in Utah even saw it on TV. She said it was the cutest thing she'd seen all year."

"Should have seen him trying to get out of it later that night," I said. "*That* was the cutest thing."

Janet blushed, laughing as she nudged me with a wink. "Oh, I bet it was."

We all took our seats, chatting as we waited for the game to get started, and shortly before kick-off, Zach's phone lit up with Doc's face on the screen.

"Well, if it isn't the island man," Zach said, holding the phone up so both his and my face could fit in the screen.

Doc grinned from the other side, a tropical paradise spread out in the background behind him. I couldn't hear the ocean with the crowd around us, but I knew the sound from our other calls, and Rita was there at his side, too, her dark skin shining in the sun.

"How's the weather there, champ?" Doc teased.

"Cool, breezy, and fall-ish. Don't you miss it?"

"Not even a little bit," Doc answered, putting one arm around Rita and tucking her into his side. She waved at me from where she snuggled into him, and though she never spoke much, it didn't take more than a look at the two of them together to see how happy they were in love.

"Doesn't feel the same without you here for the season, Doc," I said.

"Ah, maybe the Bears will actually win it all this year. We got so close last season."

"Gah, why you gotta bring up sore subjects?" Zach said. I frowned, too, remembering how we'd lost the second game in the playoff race, losing our chance at the big game.

"Hey, we'll get 'em this year," I chimed in.

"That's the spirit, sweetheart." Doc lifted his sunglasses, eyes glistening a little. "Well, I know it's almost kick-off there, I just... I just wanted to see you guys on the big day."

"Big day?" I asked.

Doc shrugged, putting his sunglasses back in place. "You know, the home opener. First game of the season, first time starting all your traditions." He paused. "First time at a game together where you're not causing headaches for yourselves or the ones who love you."

"Hear, hear," Belle piped from the side, tilting her beer into camera view.

Doc chuckled.

"Anyway, I'll let you guys go. We'll be watching from paradise."

"Are there even any TVs there?" Zach teased, but Doc just smiled wider.

"No screens, no shoes, no problem."

I leaned into Zach's side, waving goodbye at Doc before Zach ended the call. He tucked the phone into his back pocket before wrapping me up in his arms as best he could with the arm rest between us. His lips pressed against my forehead, and he sighed.

"Hard to believe we're here again, isn't it?" he said.

"A lot has changed."

"It has. But some things are still the same," he argued. "Like how amazing you look in that Bears tank top. That's the same one you wore on our first date, you know?"

"Oh, is it?" I faked surprise, looking down at the logo stretched across my chest. "I didn't realize."

"Sure you didn't." Zach tickled my side. "Little tease, just wait till I get you home."

I laughed, pushing him off me as the anthem started, and we all stood to pay honor to our country. After that, the game kicked off, and we settled in for the first quarter.

I was glad we'd invited our family there for the first game, especially when we scored. It was more fun celebrating with a group of people you knew than a bunch of strangers — not that I didn't still share high-fives with everyone around us, too. But, being there with Zach, with the family we'd made together? It was everything I'd ever wanted in my football season.

He was everything I'd ever wanted in my life.

It was hard to believe how much he'd changed me, opened me, shown me how to trust and how to face my fears. He'd made me feel more loved than I ever had in my entire life in just one short year, and I hoped there would be many more to come.

"Hey, excuse me, miss?"

Janet tapped me on the shoulder, pointing to where one of the interns with the Bears was trying to get my attention from the aisle.

"Would you and your boyfriend like to come onto the field during the quarter break for a game?"

I smiled, turning to Zach with wide eyes. "Oh! Babe, can we? Are you down?"

He looked skeptical, nose scrunching up as he glanced at the kid and then back at me.

"Pleaseeee," I begged, batting my lashes.

He sighed. "Well, like I can say no to that."

"Yay!"

I jumped up, grabbing his hand and tugging him with me as we squeezed past Janet, Roy, and the rest of the row to get to the aisle. We followed the kid with the clipboard and headset up to the lower levels of our section, and the security guards opened the lower field gates for him once they saw him, letting us through.

And then, we were on the field.

"Oh, my God!" I whispered, tugging on Zach's jersey sleeve. "We're on the field. This is so cool! Oh, look! We're so close to the players!"

I pointed at the different players I knew, and Zach entertained me the whole time, though he seemed like he was about to crawl out of his own skin. You would think after him having the entire stadium's attention on him last year when he was dressed up as a hot dog, that he'd be calm in situations like this. But, Zach got nervous, too — and it always seemed to come out in the strangest times.

I squeezed his hand. "This will be fun."

He swallowed. "Yeah."

Smiling, I held his hand tighter as the whistle blew on the first quarter and the intern hustled us into place for the game we were going to play. The girl known for running their social media and break entertainment games came up beside us with a camera ready to go, explaining that we were going to try to get three balls into target holes that were set up at varying distances — the final one being the farthest.

"So, which one of you is going to throw?"

Zach immediately pointed at me, and I laughed. "Guess it's me."

"You'll have sixty seconds to get them all. You ready?"

I nodded as she handed me the ball, and on her signal, I fired away.

I nailed the first target easily, running over to the second target with adrenaline surging through me. I missed the first two throws on that one, but hit the third, and the crowd roared when I started running toward the third and last target.

It was a far throw, and I was having trouble getting the ball to fall in the right way to sail through the tiny hole in the target. It bounced off the right, the left, the right again before the crowd started counting down.

Ten... nine... eight...

My heart was beating so wildly, I could hear every erratic thump of it in my ears as I fired another ball. It missed again, and with the crowd screaming *two*, I wound up and fired my last one.

And I made it.

"YES!" I screamed, shoving my fists in the air as I looked up at the crowd. They were all cheering, the announcer going on about how I'd won a $500 Visa gift card. But I didn't care about the prize. I'd thrown that ball like a champ, and *that* was what I was excited about.

I turned, ready to jump into Zach's arms, but when I spun around, he wasn't standing behind me.

He was kneeling.

And suddenly, everything faded away. The roar of the crowd was dull and muted, the breeze nonexistent, the adrenaline rushing through me stopping altogether like my entire body had forgotten how to function at the sight of the man I loved bent on one knee.

He looked up at me with reverent eyes, and all the nerves he'd had before were gone. I wondered then if they were even real, or if he'd been putting on a show to get the scenario to play out just how he wanted. Because there, bent below me, he looked taller than I'd ever seen him in my life.

"Gemma Mancini," he said, and someone in a Bears t-shirt bent a microphone down so everyone could hear what he said next. "I know you've done this before. There was a time when another man promised you forever, promised you he would be faithful to you, and that love story didn't end up the way you thought it would."

My heart pinched, and I swallowed, chest aching.

"I can't go back in time and meet you first. I can't take away the pain he or anyone else has caused you. But, I don't want to. Because everything that's happened to you, everything you've endured and survived has made you the incredible woman I know and love today."

Though the crowd was still distant to me, I heard the universal *awww* at his words, and my eyes blurred as I stared down at him.

"Gemma, I don't want your past, though I'm thankful for it. But, I want your future."

He opened a box, one he'd been holding in his hands, and the crowd fired up again, but I couldn't even look at the ring inside it. I couldn't look anywhere but right into Zach's eyes.

"If you'll let me, I promise to cherish you for every single day that I get to take a breath in this life. I promise to hold your hand as we face fears together, and hold your heart with the same respect and care that I would hold my own mother's." He swallowed, his own eyes glossing over. "No one has ever meant more to me in my entire life than you do, Gemma. And I don't just want this game, or the next game, or the game after that. I want *all* the games. And all the seasons. From now until forever, whether we win or we lose." He paused. "But, we *better* win this one. Because it's the Packers and that's just a sin if we don't."

The crowd roared at that, the band doing a little diddy that made us both laugh. And before Zach could say another word, I fell to my knees in front of him, hands sliding to frame his face.

"So, what do you say?" he asked. "Spend the rest of your life with the internet-famous Hot Dog guy?"

The crowd laughed and cheered, encouraging me to say yes — as if there were any other answer. But words were stuck in my throat, because all I could do was nod and cry and kiss him to the roar of more than sixty-thousand fans. Zach stood, pulling me with him and wrapping me in his arms as he spun me around. They ushered us off the field with our lips still locked together, and I knew we'd held up the game longer than we were supposed to, but I didn't care.

"Oh, my God, Zach," I finally spoke when we were on the sidelines, shaking my head as tears filled my eyes. "I can't believe this. I can't believe you asked."

"And I can't believe you said yes," he said, kissing me again before he pulled back and offered me the ring that had been inside the box.

I held out my left hand, and he slid the gorgeous, tear-drop-shaped diamond set on a rose-gold band onto my ring finger. The sight of it made me cry harder, and Zach wrapped me up again, kissing away the tears.

"You and me," he whispered for just me to hear. "We're going to make it."

"I never had a doubt."

"Liar," he teased.

I laughed, pulling back and shaking my head. "No, I mean it. I think somehow, I always knew. Even when I fought it. Maybe I knew it then the most."

"Well, I don't care how long it took," he said. "I would have waited forever."

"Now who's the liar."

He grinned. "Okay, so maybe I'm not the most patient man. But, I would have waited, if you needed more time."

"I don't need another second," I said, lifting up on my toes to thread my arms around his neck. "I'd marry you now."

Zach smiled, kissing my nose. "Well, we're not exactly dressed for the occasion, so I say we wait a while longer. But hey, if you want to get hitched on a football field?"

He put his hands up as if he had no other choice. "I'm not going to say I'm *not* into that."

I kissed him again, and this time, I held that kiss like it was the final seal on my promise to give him my forever.

Through all the games, through all the heartache, I think I knew I always would.

And like Zach had said, it didn't matter if the Bears won or lost this game, or the next game, or the game after that. As long as Zach was there beside me watching each one, for this year and next year and all the years to come, the score didn't matter at all.

Because if I was in his arms, I was always winning.

And it was the sweetest victory of them all.

Acknowledgements

I swear, it gets harder and harder with every book to write this part. As difficult as it is to brainstorm, plot, dream up, write, and edit the story you just read, thanking everyone I want to is infinitely more trying. But, I guess I will start with you — the reader. If you're still reading this now, even into the acknowledgements, then I just want to be sure to thank you first before you move on to your next read. There are millions of books out there, and I am so honored you chose to pick up mine to read. I truly hope you enjoyed Gemma and Zach's story, and that you'll sift through my backlist to see if anything else tickles your fancy. Thank you for reading indie, and thank you for reading romance, and thank you for reading. Period. I couldn't do this without you!

Staci Hart — you might as well have a permanent spot in the back of all of my books, because you've become such an important part of my writing process, I'm not sure I could do this without you. Thank you for always pushing me on the hard days, for holding my hand and petting my hair when I needed it, and more than anything, for your critical feedback in the end that helped take this from a B book to an A. You are such an inspiration to me, always, and I love how you push me to be a better writer every single day. I love you more than tacos, babe. Always.

Brittainy C. Cherry — thank you for your morning texts and late night voice notes that always came with a positive vibe I needed. You are a constant light in my life, and with everything that happened in my personal life while writing this book, I needed you more than ever. Thank you for helping me balance my own heart and soul with those of my characters, and for always reminding me that I am enough. I love you.

Momma — You always get a shout out in my books, because you're the one who helped raise me with a writer's heart and a dreamer's soul. Thank you for always pushing me to chase my dreams, even when they seemed impossible, and for always being there to remind me to take life one step at a time. When I'm hurting and struggling the most, it's always your voice I hear. I love you.

Sasha Whittington — thank you for letting me yak at you all day long while we romped around Austin and I was plotting out the premise of this book. Thank you for also listening anytime I hit a snag or got excited about a scene. You helped me work out a lot of kinks in this one, and also inspired the fierce, amazing best friend that is Belle. Without your actual advice and role in my life, I couldn't have ever dreamed her up. I love you.

Karla Sorensen and Kathryn Andrews — both of you ladies were instrumental in the feedback on this one, and you helped me right a lot of wrongs. You also always checked in with me when I was struggling in my heart and you knew I had to write, anyway, and I can't tell you how much your friendships mean to me. I love you both so much I don't even have the right words. Please don't ever leave me. Ever.

Tina Lynne — I don't even have words for you, baby girl. I really don't. To say that you have become an extension of me is an understatement. I honestly feel like my entire life and career has changed since you agreed to join my team, and without you assisting me and organizing my life, I would be utterly and completely lost. Thank you for reading this one, too, and making me cry with your glowing feedback. You mean more to me than I could ever say. I love you.

Okay this should literally be in bold, so I'm going to write it that way: **I could not have done this without my incredible team of beta readers.** I've already mentioned three of them — Staci, Karla, Kathryn, and Tina — who were absolutely instrumental in making *The Wrong Game* what it became in the end. But, I also have to give a huge shout out to the other amazing beta readers who gave their time, effort, and thought to these characters and this story so we could make it better. Thank you so much Kellee Fabre, Monique Boone, Sarah Green, Danielle Lagasse, Ashlei Davison, Trish QUEEN MINTNESS, and Kristen Novo. I can never thank you all enough for continually being there for me, on tight deadlines, and always giving your critical feedback with a few ass slaps and hair pets, too. I love you all.

Elaine York, you should get a freaking MEDAL for this one. I mean, seriously. Not only did I miss my deadline once... twice... three times... and then AGAIN, but I also gave you a ridiculously short amount of time to put your final polishes on this bad boy before release. But, God bless you, you were there for me. You worked with me when I needed you most to make this magic happen, and I can never thank you enough. My team wouldn't be complete without you.

I would also like to thank Flavia Viotti, my incredible agent, for having the same hustle and drive that I do. I appreciate our relationship more than I can say, and I know we're just getting started. The future is bright. ;)

To the magical Lauren Perry of Periwinkle Photography, thank you for taking my vision for these characters and the Chicago setting and bringing it to life so perfectly. This is my favorite cover to date, and it wouldn't have happened without you! I also have to thank your beautiful models, Jori and Thomas, for capturing the essence of Gemma and Zach so well and being so darn cute. You guys are the best!

Angie McKeon — your friendship and support is something I cherish so much, and I can't thank you enough for always jumping on board for my releases to help spread the word. More than that, you were there for me this year as I navigated dating, and heartbreak, in a way I never have before. Your love is something I am so lucky and thankful to have, and I hope you feel the same.

To my amazing team at Social Butterfly PR: Nina Grinstead, Chanpreet Singh, Hilary Suppes, and the rest of the team behind the scenes — THANK YOU. Your hard work on promo never goes unnoticed, and I know for a fact I couldn't do any of this without your help.

To Sam, my Chicago Bears season ticket holder friend who was kind enough to answer all of my questions — thank you! You were so sweet, and didn't owe me a thing since you didn't even know me at all. Your insight was absolutely crucial and helped make this book what it is. I appreciate you so much. Go Bears!

I am all over social, but there's one place that really feels like my "safe place" in the online world, and that's my Facebook reader group — Kandiland. To all the babes in that group, THANK YOU. Thank you for being there for the late night live video chats, for the exclusive teasers, for the random weirdness. Thank you for getting excited, for telling me you guys can't wait for what's next, and for always supporting me — even when I'm not smiling, and I'm actually facing a dark time in my life. You always make me feel safe and welcome, and I couldn't keep moving forward on the hard days without knowing I have this amazing team behind me. I love you all.

To Pocket, who would probably kill me in my sleep if I didn't give her a shout out. Thank you for sitting on my laptop to force me to stop writing when it was super late at night and you knew my eyes needed a break. Thank you for meowing aggressively at four o'clock in the morning when you knew I had to wake up in a couple of hours to edit. And thanks for always being there for me when I needed a cat nap between scenes. You're the best fur baby a girl could ever have.

And, lastly, to #MysteryMan. You probably won't even read this, but thank you for an incredible year of love. Though our story was just for a season and not for a lifetime, you showed me a love I thought I only wrote about in my books, a love that I never thought I'd find in my days on this Earth. I'm so thankful for the time we got to walk together, the laughter we shared, the love we made, and the memories I will keep with me forever. I am a better woman from having been loved by you, and I will truly never forget you. Take care of yourself, Cucumber. And if the nights ever get dark, just know there's someone in this world who will always love you.

More from Kandi Steiner

The What He Doesn't Know Duet
#1 What He Doesn't Know
#2 What He Always Knew
Charlie's marriage is dying. She's perfectly content to go down in the flames, until her first love shows back up and reminds her the other way love can burn.

On the Way to You
It was only supposed to be a road trip, but when Cooper discovers the journal of the boy driving the getaway car, everything changes. An emotional, angsty road trip romance.

A Love Letter to Whiskey
An angsty, emotional romance between two lovers fighting the curse of bad timing.

Weightless
Young Natalie finds self-love and romance with her personal trainer, along with a slew of secrets that tie them together in ways she never thought possible.

Revelry
Recently divorced, Wren searches for clarity in a summer cabin outside of Seattle, where she makes an unforgettable connection with the broody, small town recluse next door.

Black Number Four (http://amzn.to/2fSsQE1)
A college, Greek-life romance of a hot young poker star and the boy sent to take her down.

The Palm South University Serial (http://amzn. to/2vQcj7G)
Written like your favorite drama television show, PSU has been called "a mix of Greek meets Gossip Girl with a dash of Friends." Follow seven college students as they maneuver the heartbreaks and triumphs of love, life, and friendship.

Rush (book 1)
Anchor (book 2)
Pledge (book 3)
Legacy (book 4)

Tag Chaser
She made a bet that she could stop chasing military men, which seemed easy — until her knight in shining armor and latest client at work showed up in Army ACUs.

Song Chaser
Tanner and Kellee are perfect for each other. They frequent the same bars, love the same music, and have the same desire to rip each other's clothes off. Only problem? Tanner is still in love with his best friend.

About the Author

Kandi Steiner is a bestselling author and whiskey connoisseur living in Tampa, FL. Best known for writing "emotional rollercoaster" stories, she loves bringing flawed characters to life and writing about real, raw romance — in all its forms. No two Kandi Steiner books are the same, and if you're a lover of angsty, emotional, and inspirational reads, she's your gal.

An alumna of the University of Central Florida, Kandi graduated with a double major in Creative Writing and Advertising/PR with a minor in Women's Studies. She started writing back in the 4th grade after reading the first Harry Potter installment. In 6th grade, she wrote and edited her own newspaper and distributed to her classmates. Eventually, the principal caught on and the newspaper was quickly halted, though Kandi tried fighting for her "freedom of press." She took particular interest in writing romance after college, as she has always been a die hard hopeless romantic, and likes to highlight all the challenges of love as well as the triumphs.

When Kandi isn't writing, you can find her reading books of all kinds, talking with her extremely vocal cat, and spending time with her friends and family. She enjoys live music, traveling, anything heavy in carbs, beach days, movie marathons, craft beer and sweet wine — not necessarily in that order.

CONNECT WITH KANDI:

NEWSLETTER: bit.ly/NewsletterKS
FACEBOOK: facebook.com/kandisteiner
FACEBOOK READER GROUP (Kandiland):
facebook.com/groups/kandischasers
INSTAGRAM: Instagram.com/kandisteiner
TWITTER: twitter.com/kandisteiner
PINTEREST: pinterest.com/kandicoffman
WEBSITE: www.kandisteiner.com

Kandi Steiner may be coming to a city near you!
Check out her "events" tab to see all the signings
she's attending in the near future:

www.kandisteiner.com/events